My Revolutions

HARI KUNZRU

D0652707

PENGUIN BOOKS

PENGUIN BOOKS

Published by the Penguin Group
Penguin Books Ltd, 80 Strand, London WC2R ORL, England
Penguin Group (USA), Inc., 375 Hudson Street, New York, New York 10014, USA
Penguin Group (Canada), 90 Eglinton Avenue East, Suite 700, Toronto, Ontario, Canada M4P 2Y3
(a division of Pearson Penguin Canada Inc.)
Penguin Ireland, 25 St Stephen's Green, Dublin 2, Ireland (a division of Penguin Books Ltd)
Penguin Group (Australia), 250 Camberwell Road, Camberwell, Victoria 3124, Australia
(a division of Pearson Australia Group Pty Ltd)
Penguin Books India Pvt Ltd, 11 Community Centre, Panchsheel Park, New Delhi – 110 017, India
Penguin Group (NZ), 67 Apollo Drive, Rosedale, North Shore 0632, New Zealand
(a division of Pearson New Zealand Ltd)
Penguin Books (South Africa) (Pty) Ltd, 24 Sturdee Avenue, Rosebank, Johannesburg 2196, South Africa

Penguin Books Ltd, Registered Offices: 80 Strand, London WC2R ORL, England

www.penguin.com

First published by Hamish Hamilton 2007
Published in Penguin Books 2008
1

Copyright © Hari Kunzru, 2007
All rights reserved

The moral right of the author has been asserted

Typeset by Palimpsest Book Production Limited, Grangemouth, Stirlingshire
Printed in England by Clays Ltd, St Ives plc

ISBN: 978-0-141-02020-4

www.greenpenguin.co.uk

Penguin Books is committed to a sustainable future
for our business, our readers and our planet.
The book in your hands is made from paper
certified by the Forest Stewardship Council.

I used to have fiery intensity,
and a flowing sweetness.

The waters were illusion.
The flames, made of snow.

Was I dreaming then?
Am I awake now?

Rumi

The question of what would have happened if . . . is
ambiguous, pacifistic, moralistic.

RAF, *The Concept of the Urban Guerrilla*

to all at 34

Outside in the garden, workmen from the marquee company are bolting together an aluminium frame on the lawn. They shout to each other and make jokes, theatrically throwing bolts and brackets across the blossom-strewn patch of grass under the tree. It's an old tree, taller than the house, and in autumn the fruit smashes when it falls to the ground. We should, I suppose, have had it cut down. The men seem happy. Maybe it's because they work in an atmosphere of constant pre-party excitement. Perhaps celebration gets inside them. The secret of the good life: putting up tents.

Other people are out there too. Caterers, a delivery driver; all preparing for the big do. Miranda has gone out for something or other, ribbon or flowers or place cards. For once, she said, she wanted *me* to be the centre of attention. She knew I wouldn't approve, but everyone deserved the chance to wish me a happy fiftieth. Everyone, I thought. Everyone? They're her friends really, but I knew how kindly it was meant. And I found myself looking forward to my party. For a long time, more than half my life if you want to look at it that way, I've avoided large gatherings. It's become instinctive, part of my personality. However, during the last few years I've started to lower my guard, a little. Which 'karma-wise' (as Miranda would say, meaninglessly) seems to have been a mistake.

I look away from the window. The study has been transmuted by Miles's visit. It's as if, by coming here, he's put the room in brackets. The oak desk silted with spreadsheets and reports, the shelves of books. Even the chipped grey filing cabinet has taken on a provisional, insubstantial look. The party preparations going on outside, which are, I have no doubt, at the very centre of

Miranda's consciousness, feel to me as if they're taking place on TV, a scene from one of those early-evening dramas where well-heeled suburbanites experience a little formulaic frisson in their lives; romance or a murder-mystery.

The workmen are laying out a white awning beside the metal frame. I sit very still, not wanting to disturb the atmosphere of the room, the pattern of the life I've led in it. Miranda will be back soon. What will I say to her? What can I say?

Voices in the hall. Not Miranda or Sam, not yet. I open the study door and meet two young guys, all gum and hair gel, carrying musical equipment. They ask where it should go and I hear myself give them directions, modulating through a series of cheery cadences. *Mine Host* the birthday boy, his mask still more or less intact under pressure.

I have to be clear. It's already over. All this – the house, my family, this ridiculous party – no longer exists. But accepting that doesn't mean I know what to do next, and even if I choose to do nothing, events will carry on unfolding, and very soon now, days or even hours, my life here will be over. In the sitting room there's a photo of Miranda, which I took on a cold weekend walk at the Norfolk coast. She's standing with her back to the camera, looking out to sea. The light is coming straight at the lens, and she's little more than a silhouette: big boots, narrow shoulders wrapped in an ethnic something-or-other, hair streaming in the wind. Somehow that's the image which comes to me: frail, romantic Miranda, rather than the arranger of breakfast meetings, the recipient of local chamber-of-commerce awards, the Miranda of the last few years. Soon a wave is going to break over her: police, maybe the media. How will she cope? I wish I could feel optimistic, but Miranda isn't a person who deals well with the world's unpredictability. She's always fought hard against randomness, with all the weapons in the stationer's: a little arsenal of agendas and diaries and wall-planners dotted with coloured stars. Poor Miranda, no amount of Post-its will ward off what's about to happen to you. You're utterly unprepared.

The stairs creak as I climb up to the bedroom. I have to duck my head to go through the door. I've never found the low ceilings and narrow corridors of country cottages quaint, at least not straightforwardly. They're scaled to the small stature of poorly nourished people; an architecture of hardship and deprivation. Of course I've never said this to Miranda. Irregular walls and creaking floorboards please her. I think she'd like to forget she was born into an industrial society. I can't, at least not in the same way. That kind of mystification has never seemed right to me. It's so incoherent, for one thing. A country life, but with plumbing and telecoms and antibiotics. A rich person's fantasy.

But this is our house, or rather Miranda's house, the house she allowed me to share and always wanted me to love as she did. I realize I'm standing with my fists clenched, glaring at the William Morris wallpaper, the patchwork cushions on the armchair. Above our bed, hanging from the oak beam, is a dream-catcher. I tug at it, breaking the string. I've wanted to do that for so long. Such an absurd, out-of-place thing. Our house is filled with these objects – tribal, spiritual, hand-crafted little knick-knacks that are supposed to edge us nearer to Miranda's wish-fulfilment future of agrarian harmony. There are corn dollies and old glass bottles and prints of medicinal herbs with quotations from Culpeper printed underneath in calligraphic lettering. 'Only from lucre of money they cheat you, and tell you it is a kind of tear, or some such like thing, that drops from Poppies when they weep.' That's outside the bathroom. Culpeper is *natural*, and *natural* is the flag Miranda waves at the world, the banner standing for righteousness and truth.

Why am I doing this, breaking her things? None of it's her fault. She's worked hard to make the life she wanted. She's tried to be a good person. And she has loved me. I know what will be the most terrible thing – the look on her face, the gradual opening of the abyss. Everything she has known or believed about me, her lover, her partner for sixteen years, the man who has been a stepfather to her daughter, is untrue. Or if not untrue – for I've tried not to tell unnecessary lies – then partial, incomplete.

3

Listen to me. *Partial, incomplete.* I'm even lying to myself. It could hardly be worse; she doesn't even know my real name.

My bowels are loose. I lock myself into the bathroom, among the lavender bunches and embroidered hand-towels and the rows of Bountessence products in their little recyclable bottles. Bountessence is the highest expression of Miranda's romance with nature. Bountessence *is* Miranda, though in public it's the two of us, because I still cling to some undefined administrative role and occasionally squire the boss to events and dinners in the West Sussex area. I'm a sort of Denis to her Margaret. Michael Frame and Miranda Martin of Bountessence Natural Beautycare.

It's peculiar. Those words make no sense to me. I can't connect myself with them, or with the couple they represent. They're just sounds. Ever since I became Michael Frame, all those years ago, I've existed in a kind of mental crouch. When I was a child I used to have night terrors, not quite dreams, more semi-conscious imaginings that took on narrative form, like scenes from films. In one recurrent situation I was wedged under the floorboards, holding my breath and waiting for the German soldiers to stop searching the attic where I was hiding. I could hear the clatter of their boots, a guttural voice barking orders. I used to lie rigid under the covers, the blood pounding in my head, my entire consciousness occupied by the effort of not making a noise. I think when I went underground those night terrors colonized my waking life. Remaining undetected has consumed all my energy, has hollowed out my sense of self. Nothing that has taken place in the meantime has ever quite felt real.

Except that tomorrow Mike Frame will be fifty, five weeks after me. This life, this Michael Frame life, has been it. This is what I have had.

I flush the toilet and wash my hands at the basin, trying not to look in the mirror. What will happen to Miranda? Will she have to move away? She's put so much into this house. If she's very lucky they might leave her alone. Maybe it won't make any difference to the world at large, what I did. Maybe it will end with the

4

two of us. And maybe she'll find a way to feel we did have a connection. Although there were things she didn't know, there were also things she did, which were important and real. I could say that to her. I could say, *Maybe one day you'll come to understand and find consolation.* But would I believe it? Not really. And would she? I don't know. Because I don't know if it's true about understanding and consolation. And I'm not certain we had anything at all.

Miranda will be back soon. She has allowed Sam to drive her to the shops in her nineteenth-birthday present, a second-hand Fiesta. An act of faith on Miranda's part: she's a nervous passenger and Sam only passed her test a few weeks ago.

Sam's room is just as she left it at the start of term; the neat row of shoes in front of the cupboard, the pile of outgrown soft toys on the bed. An orderly and rather conventional room. Only the backpack and the Discman dumped on the bed signal that, despite the argument we had last week, she's come down from university for Mike's officially-becoming-ancient party. I can't imagine what this will do to her, the media circus, the betrayal of trust. There's a chance she might just shrug it off. She's a practical girl, and startlingly worldly for a nineteen-year-old, at least as I would have judged a nineteen-year-old of my generation. Certainly Sam isn't your idealistic type of law student, interested in righting injustice or fighting for the little man. She says she wants to 'do corporate' because that's where the money is. And, I think, because she knows it scandalizes her mother and me. Little Sam and her embarrassing hippie parents; by now 'Soma' will be off her passport too. She hasn't allowed us to call her that for years.

Fuck. I can't do it, I can't face you, Sam. There's no way.

Working quickly, I open cupboards and pull out a sports bag, start stuffing in socks, underwear, a couple of shirts. I need to move fast, before they get back from the shops. My passport is in the study, in a box file. At least, that's where I think it is. I check and find it isn't and for the first time since Miles left I lose control. When you panic you forget to breathe and your heart-rate rises. I know this; I tell it to myself; but things start to speed up and soon

I'm sweeping papers on to the floor, pulling out drawers and sobbing with rage and frustration. Outside there's the sound of a car and I freeze, but it isn't them, just one of the marquee riggers. At last I spot the passport on a bookshelf. *Frame. Michael David. British citizen. 10 April/Avril 48.* 'British citizen' is the only part that is true.

Five minutes later I'm in Miranda's big silver BMW, approaching the junction with the ring road. I head out of town and along the coast towards Newhaven, obsessively checking the rear-view mirror to see if I'm being followed. A blue Sierra preoccupies me, then disappears at a set of traffic-lights. I'm so busy staring at it that I narrowly avoid rear-ending the car in front as it slows for a turn.

What am I worried about? By now Sam and Miranda will have got back home. Before long they'll realize I've gone. So what's left to salvage? At the port I pull into the ferry terminal and park between cars packed with luggage and fighting children, all waiting to be transported across the Channel for the holidays. I only really admit to myself where I'm heading as I queue for a ticket.

Last year I made this journey with Miranda. She was exhausted. Over time the business, which once involved filling little bottles on the kitchen table, has grown, slowly but steadily, into a substantial operation. It now consumes all of her energies. Bountessence sells beauty products – face cream and shampoo and conditioner and massage oil and so on – through a network of telesales agents, mostly women, some working at home and others in an office above a tanning salon in the town centre. When I met her, Miranda was making the stuff herself, boiling witchy cauldrons on the hob at her flat. Now 'her ladies', as she insists on calling them, sell factory-made 'natural botanicals' on commission to customers whose names appear on a list she rents from a marketing agency in London. A surprising number of people don't seem to mind being phoned by strangers to talk about moisturizer, and lately Miranda has begun to glimpse a grand and lucrative future.

I insisted on the holiday. I wanted to slow things down. She'd just secured funding for further expansion and was looking at space in an industrial park. There was talk of online sales and meetings with a brand consultant, whatever one of those is. When she came home from signing the contract with her new investors (a pair of ambitious local solicitors) I expected her to be elated. Instead she sat and sipped pennyroyal tea in the garden, fidgety and withdrawn.

Unlike me, Miranda has the knack of living in the world. Almost effortlessly she seems to find herself on the crest of whatever preoccupation is currently sweeping the lunch table or the Sunday supplements. I've come to think of it as a gift. It isn't something she works at; Miranda certainly isn't a modish person, at least not consciously. In the last few years everyone around us has become very excited by money and, sure enough, her talent has led her to it, like an ant following a pheromone trail. There used to be a contradiction between money and Miranda, a short circuit. Like me, she belongs to a generation whose selfishness was tempered by a more-than-passing interest in renunciation. We had the notion that in some variously defined way, simplicity was glamorous, hip. So although she's now a thrusting entrepreneur of the type celebrated in the glossy magazines she buys with increasing frequency, Miranda remains conflicted about consumerism. I diagnosed her silent tea-drinking as a symptom of guilt, the unease of a woman who'd once spoken about alternative lifestyles with the emphasis on 'alternative' rather than 'lifestyles'.

Or maybe she was just tired. Either way, I could tell she wasn't sure that expansion was what she wanted – and I had my own private reasons to worry. I was being stretched thin by Miranda's ambitions. It was increasingly hard for me to keep a channel open to something important, something I don't really have a name for any longer. An ideal, maybe, though I'm not comfortable with the word. A vision of the future? Perhaps just to a person, someone I never was but once hoped to become.

It was clear we both needed space to breathe, so I rented a holiday apartment in the Languedoc and in my best stern-but-loving tone ordered my common-law wife (a charmless and apparently legally null phrase that winds Miranda up whenever I use it) to take ten days off. She complained bitterly. Didn't I understand it was a crucial moment for the company? I was insane if I thought she could just pack up and leave, we weren't kids any more, and so on and so forth. I held firm, tried various arguments, told her she had to think about her life holistically – meaning, in Miranda-code, that her work was getting in the way of her relationship with me. That got her attention, to an extent.

In the end I think she was only persuaded because of the car. To my horror, the woman who had for the first five years of our cohabitation driven a Deux Chevaux with an *Atomkraft Nein Danke* sticker on the back bumper had arrived home one evening in a brand new silver BMW, which she called a 'Beamer' in an affected Cockney accent and justified to me by saying the car gave her 'credibility' and made 'a statement' to her suppliers. I've always been grateful to Miranda for pulling me out of a hole and, heaven knows I've reason to be wary about setting myself up in judgement on anyone, but the car crossed a line. A strong stomach and a streak of low cunning were required to sell the holiday to her as a chance to take the thing on a road trip. Depressingly my ploy worked. Her eyes sparkling with advertising imagery of alloy on scenic country roads, she agreed.

So we drove through France and for a few days, as I'd hoped, Bountessence receded from our lives. We were just ourselves again, two people who had the capability to make each other happy. We avoided the motorways and made our way south on Routes Nationales, Miranda overtaking lorries on long straight roads lined with cypress trees, me humming along to a tape of Charles Trenet *chansons*, wishing I understood more of the words to the one about being happy and in love on Nationale 7. We stopped overnight at a hotel in a forgettable small town where we ate Coquilles Saint-Jacques and slept in a room papered with an alarming pink rose pattern, which had migrated like a fungus to cover not just the walls but the ceiling and the panels of the wardrobe and the bathroom door. We had sex in the soft, lumpy bed, giggling like children

8

as the iron frame creaked and the headboard banged against the wall. Our neighbour retaliated by turning on the TV and we fell asleep to the muffled sound of gunfire. In the morning we woke up and dragged our cases out of the rose room and back into the car, silent and hung-over. I put on the Charles Trenet and Miranda switched it off again. Eventually we arrived.

The place I'd booked was described as an ancient stone house on the outskirts of a tranquil village near Béziers. It turned out to be a cramped little maisonette, with the rough white textured plaster, dubious wiring and mismatched crockery of holiday apartments all over Europe. Miranda went out to buy flowers, and I opened the shutters and was hit by clean white southern light. We decided to be happy.

Our idyll lasted four days – days of waking up to the noise of the village street under our balcony, of chopping tomatoes, speaking bad French in shops, driving to the river, sopping honey on to fresh bread and drinking little bottles of beer that accumulated in a green gang by the side of the loudly humming fridge. We visited markets, Miranda pointing whimsically at produce she packed into a wicker basket as I picked through a phrasebook, vainly searching for the names of fish and vegetables. I followed her around contentedly, enjoying the way her thin cotton dress silhouetted her legs.

Miranda liked to take a siesta. She wanted, she said, to live to a Mediterranean rhythm, at least for a couple of weeks. I'd brought a fat book with me, a thriller I couldn't get into, and as she snoozed in the heat of the afternoon, I lay beside her on the bed with it balanced on my chest, my eyes skating off the print as I cycled through a familiar sequence of thoughts. How circumscribed my life was, how regulated. How – I hesitated to use the word *trapped*, even to myself, but then again I was with Miranda Martin, who'd been one of those little girls who get to the age of ten with every detail of their wedding day prearranged in their heads, who retained the ability to make a plan and then slot the world into it, like a peg into a board. That was certainly how it had been with us. She had a vacancy; I was interviewed; I got the job. As usual when my mind worked in this fashion, I resolved nothing, just ran through my list of complaints like a man turning the wheel on some rusty piece of agricultural machinery.

On the fourth afternoon I finally fell asleep beside her, and woke up refreshed, comforted. I suggested we spend the afternoon at a village I'd been reading about in the *Green Guide*. Sainte-Anne-de-la-Garrigue was an hour's drive away. It was a place with a bloody history, the site of a siege during the Albigensian crusade, after which its Cathar defenders had been burned at the stake. The Michelin people gave it two stars.

We packed hats and bottled water and turned the air-conditioning up high to dispel the awful heat in the car. Though it was late afternoon when we crossed it, the sun was still beating down like a drummer on the narrow stone bridge over the river. We drove on through a paper-flat world of white limestone, yellow-green scrub and cloudless blue sky as the road picked its way up the side of a gorge, passing through a pinewood to emerge into gorse and thistle and a series of hairpin bends whose vertiginous drops were punctuated on the worst corners by white-painted rocks and battered metal barriers.

As we passed over the col I caught sight of Sainte-Anne, a spiral of red-roofed stone houses knotted tightly round a jutting white rock. When we got closer I saw that on top of the rock was a stark broken rectangle, the stump of a tower, which the guidebook informed me was 'of uncertain age'. We parked outside a church in a little square, completely without shade. The village appeared deserted; the heat had driven everyone inside. The only place that seemed to be open was a café, the generically named Bar des Sports. We sat down at a table under an umbrella and drank little round-bellied bottles of Orangina, trying to work up the energy for sightseeing.

'It's pretty,' said Miranda, a note of approval in her voice.

'You sound like a teacher giving out marks.'

She frowned. I'd meant it as a joke. Sainte-Anne-de-la-Garrigue was undeniably pretty. There was a little *mairie* and a war memorial, and behind the church a narrow cobbled street that wound upwards in the direction of the tower.

'That was where they executed the heretics after the siege,' I told her. 'Over there. Right in front of the church door.'

'Mike?'

'Yes?'

'Put the guidebook away.'

'But that's the whole point of this place.'

'What is?'

'What happened here.'

'Why should I care what happened here? Nothing has happened to me here. It's just a pretty little village on a very hot day.'

'But –'

'Mike, I want to feel peaceful, not think about people being burned at the stake.'

So we sat in silence. Miranda took a picture of me and I smiled distractedly. There was something occulted about Sainte-Anne, something I wanted to decipher. The mid-afternoon quiet had a physical quality, an apparent potential for form and weight.

'Do you want to climb up to the tower?' I asked.

'Not yet. Give it ten minutes. Let's have another drink.'

We ordered mineral water, and I sat and listened to the tiny fizz in my glass as it mingled with other tiny sounds: insects, a transistor radio muttering in the back room of the bar. I watched an old man cross in front of the church, leaning heavily on a walking-stick. He was dressed in some kind of long robe; I wondered if he was the curé. Then something peculiar happened. I could put it down to the heat, I suppose. Perhaps I fell asleep for a few seconds, enough time for the old man to round the corner and a second person to appear in the same spot. However it happened, I suddenly realized the person I'd taken for an old man was actually a woman. There was no robe, no stick, nothing even to suggest them. The transition was seamless: one minute one figure, the next another. This woman was tall, wearing pedal-pushers and a sleeveless cotton top that revealed a pair of wiry, muscular shoulders. Shadowing her face was a big straw hat. She carried a string bag filled with fruit: oranges, peaches, a green-skinned melon. Though she was a long distance away, I sensed something familiar about her. Maybe it was her walk, an unhurried but somehow purposeful amble, one brown arm swinging the bag, the other raised occasionally towards her hidden face. Smoking a cigarette. Who used to walk that way? Who used to walk along smoking, swinging a bag?

The woman didn't look like a villager. A tourist? I thought not; at least, not a day-tripper. She looked too purposeful. From such a distance it was impossible to say how old she was. She turned the corner into the street that led up to the tower.

'Come on,' I said to Miranda. 'Drink up. Time for some exercise.'

She looked at me sulkily. 'Right now?'

'Why not? I'm bored. I want to move.' I tried to put something jaunty into my tone, to disguise the sudden need I had to get up, to walk after the woman and see her face.

'But I haven't finished my drink.'

I grinned a big fake grin. 'All right, see you up there.'

'Christ, Mike, can't you wait two minutes?'

'Of course. Take your time.'

I was gripped by a powerful anxiety. What would I miss if I lost sight of the woman in the straw hat? I tried to wait patiently for Miranda, then gave up. Opening my wallet, I tucked a banknote under the ashtray, scraped my chair back from the table and stood. Miranda sipped her drink with deliberate slowness. I turned round and started walking. I was half-way across the square before she caught up with me.

'You obviously didn't want your change,' she said sarcastically. I didn't reply.

The street that led up to the tower was steep and narrow. As we reached the church I could just see the woman up ahead, turning a corner. I walked fast, not looking behind to see if Miranda was keeping up, passing rows of identical little doorways and shuttered windows with terracotta flowerpots on the sills. I reached the corner just in time to see the woman stop and fit a key into one of the doors. As she went inside, she half turned towards me. I suppressed an impulse to break into a run. She was still too far away to be sure, but I thought – It was ridiculous what I thought. Increasing my pace I approached the point where she had disappeared. Sweat was pouring off my forehead. My shirt was plastered to my back. When I judged I was outside the right door I stopped, feeling dizzy and slightly sick. The house looked newer than some of the others, but patches of its cement facing had peeled away, giving it a forlorn, down-at-heel aspect. My dizziness worsened. I couldn't be certain, could I? I leaned forward, propping my hands on my knees.

Miranda bustled up, flushed and annoyed. 'What on earth's got into you? Are you all right?'

'I don't feel well.'

'Sit down. Sit on the step. Why did you charge off like that?'

I flopped down on the doorstep and lowered my head between my legs.

'You shouldn't do these things,' Miranda admonished gently. 'You're no spring chicken. And in this heat –'

'Yes, all right. Don't go on.'

'Well, excuse me.'

It couldn't have been her. That's all I could think. It couldn't have been. But there was something about the way she held herself. Familiar and yet unfamiliar. I thought of my own body, letting me down after a short climb uphill. How had twenty-five years changed the way I walked, the way I swung my arms? Weakly, I allowed Miranda to help me back down to the car, where she made me drink gulps of warm plastic-bottled water. Then she drove me home.

After that, nothing was easy. In the evening, Miranda pottered about in the kitchen and I lay in the darkened bedroom, frozen into a kind of rigid panic. The next morning I felt physically better, but I couldn't reconnect mentally with the way I'd been before we drove to Sainte-Anne. Could it really have been Anna? We went to the market and I found myself nervously scanning the crowd.

Two days went by. I was sullen, unable to settle or to enjoy anything. I'd lose myself in thought and realize Miranda had asked me a question. Several times I caught her staring at me, her jaw tight, her eyes narrowed. Our holiday was almost over and the atmosphere between us was so poisonous that, regardless of what else happened, I began to wonder whether we'd still be together when we got home. When we finally had a proper argument, I felt weirdly relieved. One minute we were preparing a tense salad in the kitchen, getting in each other's way. The next we were standing in opposite corners of the tiny room, shouting. The content was irrelevant – I can't even remember now what sparked it off; underneath she was telling me I was impossible and selfish and cold, and I was telling her she was controlling and stupid and shallow. I grabbed the car keys from the table and stamped downstairs. I had the excuse I needed.

The weather was cooler than before. A light wind blew dust over the road, hazing the air and moving flecks of cirrus cloud across the sky. I took the hairpins on the way up to Sainte-Anne-de-la-Garrigue at speed, pulling the wheel hard and sending little showers of white gravel spitting on to the crash barriers. Roaring into the village I brought the car to a halt in front of the church. Outside the Bar des Sports a group of old men were playing cards. As I got out, they stopped their game to glare at the foreigner whose loud car had disrupted the afternoon's peace.

As I walked up the steep hill towards the tower, all I knew was that I needed to see the woman's face; after that I hoped the rest would become clear. I'd arrived soon after lunch, earlier than before. If she had a routine, and if I waited long enough, maybe I'd see her. I was wearing dark glasses and a floppy cricket hat with a wide brim, the kind of hat that identifies its wearer as English, beyond any shadow of cultural doubt. It was supposed to be a disguise. The glasses obscured my eyes and the hat hid what was left of my hair, which when Anna had last seen me had been long and wavy.

I realized I'd begun to take seriously the possibility that it was her. I wasn't sure whether the chill I felt was fear or excitement.

Outside the cement-faced house, a pair of old women sat on high-backed chairs. Despite the heat they wore headscarves and pinafores and thick black stockings. A lean tabby cat rubbed round their feet, mewing. As I approached they put down their sewing and inspected me balefully. I said a gruff *'Bonjour'* and walked past, trying as I did to peer through the open door into the house. The thinner of the two, whose jaw worked in a constant nervous motion, squeezed her neighbour's wrist and said something. The neighbour made a dismissive gesture. A little further up the hill, I stopped. I was confused. Maybe I had the wrong house. With two pairs of eyes boring suspiciously into my back, I didn't want to loiter around to check. The street showed no other sign of life, just a long row of closed doors and shuttered windows.

I walked back to the old women and said a second *bonjour* into the silence. *'La femme – la femme qui habite ici?'* I asked, gesturing at the house.

'Une femme?' asked the thin one, her chin quivering accusingly.

I made 'tall' signs with my hand. *'Ici.'* I pointed to the house. *'L'Anglaise.'*

The thin one spoke rapidly to her friend. They both shook their heads.

'La Suédoise?' suggested the friend.

'Suédoise?' I asked eagerly. *'Elle est suédoise?'*

They nodded warily, pursing their lips at my insistence. The thin one pointed to the next-door house.

'Elle habite là?' I asked. They adopted the closed expressions of respectable women who know there is a limit to the amount of information one should give a foreigner in the street. Realizing they weren't going to reply, I thanked them and walked on.

So I'd been imagining things. The woman was Swedish, some teacher or accountant or civil servant with a holiday home in the village, and somehow from out of the depths of my stress I'd conjured Anna Addison. Relieved but inexplicably disappointed, I headed on up the hill. The street gave out into a narrow path, bordered by a mat of dry undergrowth that made me think about snakes. Feeling like a tourist again, I stood for a few minutes, catching my breath and looking down over the roofs of Sainte-Anne. Beyond them the valley dropped away towards the glittering snail-trail of the river. I toiled on up to the tower, which was completely featureless, four blank masonry walls with no sign of an arrow slit, let alone a door. It was hard to see what it might have been used for. Around its base was a path, which I followed, trailing a hand against the warm stone. As I completed my circuit I thought I heard a man's voice, but when I turned round to look, no one was there. It was time to go home.

I was completely unprepared to meet her. As I made my way down she appeared in front of me on the path, very suddenly, as if she'd risen out of the ground. She was wearing a sleeveless blue dress and the same straw sun-hat as before. It was crammed down low on her head, the way Anna always wore hats. When we lived at Lansdowne Road I used to tease her by asking if she was expecting a high wind. 'Pardon,' she said, and stepped round me, striding on up the hill. Her voice was pitched higher than I remembered. My legs felt weak. I could hear the crunch of her footsteps; all I'd have to do was call her name.

And what then?

God, her face. Anna's face. The high cheekbones, the full mouth; a mouth now nested in lines but *the same mouth*. There was always something primitive about Anna's face. In certain moods she could fix it into a carved wooden mask, a thing to be worshipped, feared. Did I even see her eyes? Anna's eyes were green. When things were good between us, I couldn't bear to meet them for too long in case I gave myself away, blurted out all the promises I was trying so guiltily to extract from her. But she hadn't looked up. And I hadn't been recognized – her pace didn't falter as she passed by.

Anna Addison. Who'd been killed in the conference room of the German embassy in Copenhagen in 1975.

* * *

Nothing is permanent. Everything is subject to change.

I walked back down the hill past the two old women, who gave me the evil eye as I went by. Under my feet the cobbles felt distant, almost spongy, like a street in a dream. Then I began to run, and once again it was 1968 and I was pressed against the trunk of a tree outside the American embassy in Grosvenor Square.

Annica is the Buddhist term. The cosmic state of flux.

I was trying to link arms with the guy next to me, whose long hair was matted with blood. The tree provided some shelter because the mounted police couldn't ride under the branches. As long as I was there, I was relatively safe. All around me there was an incredible rushing noise, which I knew was composed of shouting and screaming and firecrackers and stamping hoofs, but sounded to me like a great wind, like history.

I was twenty years old. I thought about history a lot.

Up close, coming towards you, police horses are bigger than you could imagine. Facing the metal-shod hoofs, the jangling harnesses, wild eyes and flaring nostrils, you know how it must have felt to be a serf in a medieval battle. The wall of flour-spattered blue tunics in front of the embassy parted and the horses charged into us, kicking up clods of turf, their riders standing up in the stirrups to add force to their baton blows. There was no pretence in that charge. It was about unleashing as much violence as possible. People were thrashing about on the ground. I saw a girl trapped beneath a horse, desperately trying to cover her head with her hands. The horse reared up, almost unseating its rider, a red-faced sergeant with a toothbrush moustache. People were shouting at him, one or two of the braver ones edging forward to try to pull the girl out. Red-face thought they were attacking him and twisted round in his saddle, flailing left and right with his stick. Finally the horse shied away and the girl was left unconscious on the ground, a tiny broken thing in a suede jacket with a young man on his knees beside it, trying to gather it up.

Protesters were running in all directions. Pressed against the tree-trunk I was only a few feet away from the police line, which had re-formed on the far side of the ironwork fence that marked the western boundary of the square. From time to time they'd reach over it and grab someone; we'd cling on from behind, clutching at ankles or belts in little comic tugs-of-war. To do this we'd have to emerge from the shelter of the tree. I was hanging on to some guy's leg, looking over my shoulder to check I wasn't about to be trampled or coshed, when I spotted her running forward, a thin girl in blue jeans and a torn army jacket, her long brown hair tied back from her face with a scarf. There was something both reckless and self-possessed about her, about her loping run, the clean overarm action she used to throw the stone; as I watched it arc through the sky, I felt both aroused and ashamed, aroused by the casual beauty of her act and ashamed of myself, for so far that afternoon all I'd done was push and shove and jog around confusedly, trying not to get arrested. She had the clarity I lacked. It had become a fight, so she was fighting back. The stone fell somewhere behind the line of black vans drawn up in front of the embassy steps. When I looked round again, she'd disappeared.

Later, when I met Anna, I told her I'd seen her before, at Grosvenor Square. I told her the way she carried herself had 'profoundly affected me'; that was the phrase I used. It sounded pompous even as it came out of my mouth and I wished I'd found a better one. We were at the house in Lansdowne Road. I can remember sitting on the floor in front of the fireplace, leaning against the ratty old couch. She held her hand in front of her mouth as she laughed. I laughed too, just from the pleasure of being next to her. I'm no longer sure why I thought she was lying when she told me it wasn't her: she had no reason to lie. She said she'd been on the march, but a girlfriend had felt faint and she'd taken her home. She'd never made it to the embassy. The strange thing is that, although I dropped the subject, I was so certain I'd seen her that it became part of my personal mythology, an unexamined truth that in later years took on a dubious aura of prefiguration, confirming to me that though they'd felt disordered at the time, even terrifyingly random, the events of my life with Anna were in some sense necessary, that the future had been pulling me towards itself, reeling me in.

* * *

I don't remember much about how I got back from Sainte-Anne-de-la-Garrigue. At the apartment, Miranda greeted me with a curt nod and a silence that persisted through the remaining days of our holiday, cloaking our final packing and washing-up, the return of the keys, the long drive to the coast. She didn't ask where I'd been and I didn't tell her; we travelled, as it were, in two separate capsules, as lonely a journey as I've ever taken.

As soon as we got home she threw herself into Bountessence, driving up to London and returning with loan documents, ad-agency artwork, sheaves of financial projections, bags and boxes from department stores containing elements of a new 'business' wardrobe of tailored suits and high-heeled shoes. She walked around the house talking ostentatiously into her phone and whenever I asked how things were going she'd reply with a torrent of jargon, as if to underscore how far beyond my sphere of competence she'd moved. I was being warned: I might just find myself surplus to requirements.

Sam's departure for university gave us a short respite. She'd spent the early part of the summer waitressing at one of the pizza joints in the town centre, then bought herself a bucket-shop flight to – of all places – South Africa, a country I was still unused to thinking of as a tourist destination. She returned soon after we did, happy and sunburned, to fill the house with loud music and stories about her adventures, which seemed mainly to have involved her and her schoolfriend Ally climbing up or jumping off or into things with the clean-cut boys whose pictures now took pride of place in the collage of snapshots above her desk. I tried not to speculate about whether she'd lost her virginity to one of these variously grinning white teenagers, the one in the striped rugby shirt, the one with the shark's-tooth necklace and the sunglasses pushed up like an Alice band into his streaky blond hair. None of my business if she had, of course. As Sam occasionally reminded me, usually just before slamming her bedroom door, I wasn't her real dad. She was the product of Miranda's month-long fling with a musician, a drummer in an Australian band who'd gone home at the end of their tour not knowing about her pregnancy. I'd been around since Sam was two years old, and though I loved her very much I was annoyed to find myself so clumsily possessive. I felt ambushed, tripped up by fatherhood, a ridiculous and slightly creepy cartoon of a stepdad.

With Miranda so busy – increasingly her trips to London seemed to involve overnight stays – I was the one who oversaw Sam's preparations for university, helped her decide which of her clothes to take, which textbooks she absolutely had to buy before she got there. We made piles and lists, and when Miranda was around, the three of us colluded in putting a happy face on things. Miranda and I drove Sam to Bristol, carried her bags into the hall of residence and sat through an interminable restaurant lunch watching her sigh and fidget, visibly wishing we'd vanish and let her get on with her new life. Afterwards we watched her run away from us up a flight of concrete stairs; sitting in the car, Miranda leaned her head on the wheel and burst into tears.

'Now what?' she asked. I knew what she meant. It wasn't just that her little girl had grown up. It was us. We were going to have to face one another.

In old cartoons, the Hanna Barbera shorts I used to watch as a child, Wile E. Coyote would frequently run off a cliff. When this happened, he'd stop moving forward, his legs windmilling in the air, but it was only when he looked down that gravity started to work and he fell. Until then he was magically suspended, held aloft by his conviction that there was still ground beneath his feet. This was how I dealt with seeing Anna again. By pretending I hadn't. I repressed the memory thoroughly and completely, and when it struggled to the surface I pushed it back down, telling myself that with my relationship to Miranda crumbling, the last thing I should have on my mind was the reappearance of someone from my political days. But it wasn't just someone. It was Anna. Dead Anna. In those first weeks, the point I kept making to myself, neurotically, repetitively, was that, though I'd seen her, she hadn't seen me: if I could just forget what had happened, the meeting would be an event without consequences, a mirage.

It meant she'd survived Copenhagen, of course, which seemed impossible. The news reports had been unequivocal. They'd published photos, disgusting prurient photos of her corpse, the arms spread wide, a bloodstained suit jacket hiding her charred face and torso. Somehow a living Anna made less sense than a dead one. In her beliefs, her political choices, she belonged to a past almost geological in its remoteness from the present. Even back then, death had always been on her horizon; that was what I'd understood, eventually. You can't hate the world's imperfection so fiercely, so absolutely, without getting drawn towards death. Beyond a certain point it becomes the only possibility.

So, instead of thinking about Anna, I tried to mend things with Miranda, ignoring her pointed questions about how I was passing the days while she was out at work. I kept the house clean and the fridge full; I tiptoed round her as she worked on her business plan, and when Bountessence moved into its new premises I attended the opening drinks party and held a glass of *cava* and tried to pretend, as I applauded the speeches, that I didn't feel as if I were spinning out of control.

For a while it worked. Our conversations became less strained. We found things we could do together without getting on each other's nerves, watching whole seasons of American drama on DVD as we ate ice cream on the couch, the very model of the modern consuming couple. We started sleeping with each other again. The sex was good, better than it had been for years, but I cringed from the scratch of her newly manicured nails on my back, which felt to me like a cat clawing at a door, begging to be let in.

Then came the evening when Miranda invited her backers and their wives for dinner. The two lawyers exuded the bland machismo of small-town worthies everywhere. They talked about skiing and their wine cellars and how there was money to be made from the Internet. I'd cooked, which they evidently found amusing; as I served the food there were barbed comments about housework and pinnies. The women seemed to find me exotic and slightly unsavoury. Where had I learned to make Oriental food? Thai, I corrected. I told them I'd lived in Thailand for a while, during the seventies.

'Mike was in a monastery,' interjected Miranda, trying to make me sound interesting. I wished she hadn't: from the fake smiles round the table, I could tell I was now seen as a crackpot, some sort of religious cultist. 'I was never a monk,' I clarified. 'I just worked there.' I tried to make it sound like a tourist destination, as innocuous as a spa or a yoga retreat. There was nothing I wanted less than to discuss Wat Tham Nok with those people. Miranda herself had only the vaguest idea about the place. It had always been a sore point that I'd never wanted to go back to Asia with her. She liked the idea of being shown the 'real Thailand', by which she meant kite festivals and sticky rice and girls making wai, rather than back-room shooting-galleries in Patpong. And there we were again, up against yet another barrier to truth, another thing I'd elided in the authorized version of my life-story: the way I'd actually lost my lost years.

When the cheek-kissing and coat-finding and insincere expressions of concern about driving over the limit were finally dispensed with, we closed the front door and wandered round in silence, clearing the table and stacking plates and glasses by the sink.

'I'll do this, Mike,' offered Miranda.

'It's fine.'

'Really –'

'Really, it's fine. Pass me a cloth.'

She flicked down the bin lid and sighed. 'I'm sorry I put you through that. It's just –'

'Business. I know. You don't have to apologize. I understand.'

'I do appreciate it, Mike. You were great.'

'Don't overdo it. I just cooked a meal.'

'Putting up with them, I mean. I had to have them over. It was beginning to feel awkward.'

'Why didn't you invite them before?'

'Well, I knew you –'

'I what?'

'Not you. Them. I knew how they'd be with you, the patronizing way they'd treat you.'

'So you were protecting me.'

She kissed me. 'I'm not saying you need protecting. They're major investors. I need them to like – to respect me. You were a saint to put up with them.'

'Ah, I see, it's about status. So, what do you reckon? Are they driving home talking about what a great couple we are, or about why a successful entrepreneur like you is married to some fucking socks-and-sandals religious freak?'

'Mike, don't be like this. Caroline and Judith really loved your food.'

'You think so?'

'Look, I know they aren't very – cultured. I could have died when they said Oriental like that. Like it was a pizza flavour.'

'Miranda, as long as it's about Bountessence, fine. I understand. You do what you have to do to make money. See whoever you need to see. Be however you like with them. Just keep them away from me. I don't want to know them and I don't want to have to pretend to like them.'

'They're not so bad, Mike.'

'They're smug, Philistine, reactionary, self-satisfied morons.'

'I don't think that's fair. They're conservative. Old-fashioned.'

'Old-fashioned? They're fucking Neanderthals. You could almost see those two golf-club Fascists asking themselves if I was queer.'

'I wish you wouldn't swear.'

'Oh, really?'

'I can see why you're irritated, but you have to understand. In their circle they don't meet a lot of men who – who don't work.'

'Now it comes out. Work! Of course. It's been on your mind for months. Well, the way I heard it, I work with you. We work together, isn't that right? A partnership?'

'Of course it is, Mike. But things are changing. You have to see that.'

'I think I'm beginning to.'

'Bountessence has to be – it has to be put on a more professional footing. And you've got to admit you don't have the business background.'

'I don't want the fucking business background.'

'Exactly. And, besides, I'm not sure it would be appropriate for either of us. Going forward, I mean.'

'Going forward?' I made sarcastic little quote marks with my fingers, which she ignored, doggedly carrying on with her speech.

'To work together, I mean. Things are strained enough as they are. I'm not sure I could – What I'm saying is I think you need something. Something of your own. A project.'

'So what do you reckon I should do, darling? Take up crochet?'

'God, you're impossible! I just meant – well, there's nothing to stop you getting a part-time job, is there?'

I walked out of the room before I said anything I'd really regret. And once I'd calmed down, two or three days later, I realized she was right. Anything was better than festering away in the house, obsessing about Anna Addison. Miranda didn't want me around Bountessence and I didn't want to be there either. There was, as she put it, nothing to stop me. So I followed the path of educated misfits through the ages and got a job in a bookshop.

Pelham Antiquarian Books is a refuge of slackness in the economically efficient high-street hell of our little market town. Specializing in nothing in particular it has, over the years, turned into a dusty cavern of yellowing paperbacks, a place where books go to die. It's run (slowly, into the ground) by Godfrey Kerr, an elderly alcoholic who doesn't seem to give a toss whether he makes any money or not, as long as no one disturbs him before eleven or asks if he has anything by Jeffrey Archer.

I'd known God slightly for years, reached the stage where he'd grunt at me and perhaps raise his coffee cup when I came through the door. I'd always liked going into Pelham's, with its moth-eaten rugs and rickety shelves, its odour of cat-piss and intellectual decay. As the old town-centre tradesmen have gone out of business, butchers and ironmongers and family-run tea rooms edged out by branches of Starbucks and Pizza Hut, it's one of the last places you can pass the time without feeling you're in some sort of wipe-clean playpen for the consuming classes. When I spotted God's discreet card in the window, advertising for an assistant, I knew it would be the perfect bolt-hole.

Soon I was the one drinking coffee behind the counter and playing with Stearns, the elderly ginger cat. I went in even when I wasn't needed, when God wasn't too busy drinking himself to death in his 'parlour' to come downstairs and open the shop. I spent a lot of time rummaging in the cardboard boxes stacked chest-high in the basement, pulling out buried treasures to read in the broken-down armchair in the back room. I hadn't the faintest idea why God thought he needed an assistant. There wasn't any work to do. The atmosphere of genteel derangement reminded me of one of the places I'd worked when I first came back from Asia, the shop where I'd met Miranda. Avalon sold various kinds of new-age junk, crystal healing kits and dream diaries and cheap silver jewellery. It was run by a witchy woman called Olla, a refugee from Kristiana, whose life was plagued by omens and portents; several times a month she received supernatural word that it was temporarily dangerous for her to sell scented candles and tarot packs to the people of the town and disappeared, leaving me in charge. Miranda was a regular customer, buying books on herb-alism, packets of pot-pourri, greetings cards. I was suspicious, unused to being back and still half in hiding as I gingerly built up the paper-trail around Michael Frame. I'd moved to Chichester almost at random, because of a picture postcard I came across at the monastery, which had made me feel homesick. So English, that segmented blue-and-green selection of views. *Cathedral Close. The High Street*. It turned out to be a stuffy little town, good to bury myself in. It was only when I started chatting to Miranda that I realized how lonely I was.

Olla and Avalon disappeared years ago, so long that when I first tried, I found it hard even to remember Olla's name.

After twenty years without a cigarette I'd started smoking again. Stress, I suppose, though in part it was an infantile reaction to Miranda's new order, which now encompassed a personal trainer called Lee, who took her running in the park and hung around our kitchen talking about her body-mass index. No fags in the shop was one of God's few rules, so every time I wanted one I had to go for a walk. I was smoking under the Market Cross, remembering the phone calls from Olla where she'd whisper instructions into the receiver, telling me to light a sprig of St John's Wort and not answer the door to any red-haired men, when I realized the well-dressed tourist who'd been walking up and down photographing the cathedral had turned in my direction and was doing a sort of theatrical double take. I was wrapped up warmly against the November weather, in a thick coat with a hat pulled down low over my head. There was nothing to distinguish me from a hundred other middle-aged shoppers, which made it all the more disturbing that this man was now starting to walk towards me, smiling a familiar quizzical half-smile.

'Chris,' he said, in the tone of a man in the throes of pleasure. 'Chris Carver.'

I felt sick. Ever since France, I'd been waiting for this. I didn't know what shape it would take, didn't know who it would be, but I knew there would be someone. I should have guessed. It was always Miles who signalled the changes.

'I'm sorry,' I said. 'I think you've mistaken me for someone else.'

'I don't believe so.'

'My name's Michael. You've made a mistake.'

'Come off it, Chris. I know we've all changed, but not that much.'

He'd grown into himself, somehow. His hair, which had been fine and blond, was shaved close to his narrow skull. His glasses, which I remember as thick, black-framed things like old-fashioned TV sets, had slimmed down into tiny steel-rimmed rectangles. He was wearing an expensive-looking car-coat over a suit in a brash Rupert Bear check. As he examined me he shot his cuffs, showing off the cufflinks, two little enamel portraits of Elvis Presley. Evidently Miles Bridgeman was still the dedicated follower of fashion. It seemed unlikely that this man, with his aura of well-heeled cocaine abuse and lunches at West End clubs, just happened to be wandering around in Chichester at two on a Wednesday afternoon. Whatever lay behind this encounter, it wasn't chance.

'Please, Miles,' I said, as gently as I could. 'At least call me Mike. That's my name now. Mike.'

All things are transitory. All things must pass. Attachments, whether to material possessions, to people, to places or a name, are futile. Despite your clinging, these things will fade away.

I first met Miles in the cells after Grosvenor Square, the same day I saw the girl I still believe was Anna. I'd begun that morning, listening to speeches in Trafalgar Square, as a fairly typical second-year student at the London School of Economics, which is to say I'd spent the previous eighteen months in an overheated coffee-bar argument about the best way to destroy the class system, combat state oppression and end the War. For us there was only one war. Even though we weren't fighting there (one promise our so-called-socialist government hadn't broken), Vietnam defined us. It was Vietnam that drew us together and made us a movement. I was sometimes a little vague about who I included in the word 'us', but that Sunday it seemed clear. There were tens of thousands there, the famous and the unknown, gathered together in the name of peace and internationalism. We were the People. It was our day.

The speakers harangued us in relays from a platform in front of the National Gallery, approaching the mike against a backdrop of fluttering North Vietnamese flags. Someone let off a smoke bomb and an orange haze drifted across the fountains, licking at the feet of the lions guarding the base of Nelson's Column. The smoke was a reminder of why we were there, of the horror being played out in jungles and rice paddies on the other side of the world. The speakers linked this to other things: Aden, devaluation. They told us Britain was on its knees. They told us the system was tottering.

My name then was Chris Carver. I'd grown up in Ruislip, in the commuter belt of west London. I'd done well at grammar school, so well that even my father, a man whose emotions got lost at the bottom of the North Atlantic on some wartime winter convoy, had evinced a little pride in my LSE place. In stale sixties Britain, university meant upward mobility. My family were proud members of what is still termed, with the disgusting precision of English snobbery, the *lower middle class*. When he heard the news over the breakfast table, Dad, who owned a shop selling electrical goods, had cracked a smile behind his copy of the *Express*, not because he cared about knowledge or particularly respected those who possessed the education he lacked. Quite the contrary: he always made his feelings very clear about eggheads, spewers of hot air. It wasn't even about money, not really. He smiled because his son was on the rise, edging a little closer to the high-walled place occupied by the governors, the top people. And, of course, because my ability to pass exams reflected well on him. 'Blood,' he'd said, gesturing at me complacently with a marmalade smeared slice of toast, 'will out.'

Standing in the crowd that morning with my fist in the air, there was one thing I was certain of: I'd had enough of my father's world, enough of the idea that life was a scramble to the top over the heads of those poorer, slower or weaker than yourself. I hadn't spoken to either of my parents since the previous Christmas, when I'd announced over the lunch-table that I was a Communist. My mother, numbed by pills and her own lack of expectation, had been incredulous. To her it was simply nonsensical, as if I'd just told her I was a Negro or a circus clown. Communism was for Glasgow dockers and bearded Jews. People like us didn't just *turn* that way. But my father understood. He knew I was telling him to get fucked.

For my dad, disrespect was always a threat, not just to himself but to the wider world, the nation, whatever it was he thought he'd fought a war for. Where would I be if he hadn't known how to obey an order in 1940? That was his trump card. His war, my warlessness. I think he'd have found it easier if I'd told him I was homosexual; then at least he could have submitted me to the appropriate authorities – the psychiatrist or the vicar. Something could have been done.

Even now I hate remembering the gloomy little Oedipal scene that played out in our front room, the four of us, Mum and Dad, me and my older brother Brian, wearing paper crowns from cheap Christmas crackers, the kind that left slight stains of colour on your forehead when you took them off. I talked into the silence, trying everything I could think of to get a response, a sign of life. I told my parents the ruling class were scum, fattened by nine hundred years of greed and oppression. A cough. The clink of cutlery on the second-best china. Warmongering bastards, burning the skin off little children. Dad segmenting a boiled potato. 'Christopher,' he said eventually, 'if this is typical of what they're teaching you –' I knew the second part and repeated it along with him – 'then I don't know why I'm paying my taxes.' My mother asked if I wanted more gravy. I pushed my chair back and left the house.

So Trafalgar Square was part of a new life, a project of self-invention. I'd come on the march with my friends, who were all members of something called the Vietnam Action Group, one of a dozen different councils and committees that existed at my university, all dedicated with varying degrees of clarity to the proposition that ending America's war in Vietnam was our special duty. My own anger about the war rendered everything else disgusting. Every small pleasure was bleached out by the knowledge that elsewhere such horror existed.

My friends loved to argue. They loved to talk, and though I had a shelf of Marcuse and Marx and knew the jargon as well as they did, their talk had begun to seem ineffectual, masturbatory. In meetings and teach-ins I was the first to stand up and call for action. I was hopeful – this was how young I was – that I might just be the one, that it might be given to me, Chris Carver, to smash up the old world and build something new.

Beside us in the crowd that morning, a boy with a scrap of bedsheet tied round his head knelt down and doused an American flag in lighter fluid. He hunched over, shielding it with his parka as he tried to light a match. I knelt down beside him and flicked open my Zippo. The flag caught and we smiled at each other. He raised it up on its pole, shook it a few times. Around us, several people cheered. Comrade Bob, a pol. sci. postgrad and orthodox CP member who'd only reluctantly deviated from his position that the march was recklessly adventurist, tugged urgently on my sleeve. There was movement nearby, angry voices. A little knot of blue helmets was clearing a path towards us. I wanted to stay and confront them, but my friends were already moving away. Reluctantly I went along, craning my neck to get a glimpse of the boy with the headband. Some kind of scuffle was breaking out; the charred flag wobbled wildly on its stick. People booed and hissed.

As we pushed through the crowd, the others chattered excitedly, patting me on the back and puffing up their chests like real revolutionaries. Alan in his new Carnaby Street floral shirt, Bob trying to relight his pipe. An American news reporter thrust a microphone at Ginger Ken, asking him sarcastically why we were there. Ken fingered his glasses and talked at a whirring camera about the Tet offensive and Imperialism and the need to stand together in solidarity with the people of the third world. The reporter, a small wiry man with a prominent nose and a flat-topped scrub of sandy hair, suggested that 'all this', meaning the march, was 'just a substitute for sorting out your problems closer to home'. Ken, blindsided, couldn't think of anything to say and the newsman pressed home his advantage: 'Isn't it easier to criticize America than to do something about injustice here?'

I interrupted, trying to explain that it was all connected, that the differences between the Viet Cong and poor blacks in Mississippi and factory workers in Bradford were artificial, but the reporter had his footage of Ken failing to answer and signalled for the cameraman to cut. I was outraged: I felt we'd been duped. Evidently I wasn't the only one to feel angry. As Flat-top turned away, rivulets of spit ran down the back of his jacket.

When the march moved off, we found ourselves near the front, behind a phalanx of German SDSers who were wearing helmets and jogging along in formation, much to the amusement of the ragbag of freaks around them. My friends were sniggering too, but I was impressed by the Germans' organization, their seriousness. Most people were treating the march like a bit of fun, a day out: a guy in a cloak and a cardboard wizard's hat capered around, casting spells on LBJ; some street-theatre types were carrying a coffin. But there was an edge to the atmosphere. A group of Scots, marching under red-and-black anarchist banners, cat-called and shouted insults at the police lining the route. Fucking pigs! Fucking Fascists! One or two people were wearing helmets, or had covered their faces with scarves. We made our way down Oxford Street, watched by Mr and Mrs Average: centre parting, matching bag and hat. You could tell one or two of them thought it was VE Day or something, so we called out to them to join us. Yes, you, sir, you at the back! We're having a revolution. Why, right now, of course. Come and join in!

As the march approached the American embassy it came to a halt. Word filtered back that the police were blocking the entrance to Grosvenor Square. Comrade Bob announced that in his opinion things were about to turn ugly and he, for one, was not about to get arrested to further the political careers of the gang of opportunist Trots who'd called this tomfoolery. I told him he could do what he liked. Of all the VAG people, only Alan came along with me as I pushed my way forward. 'I wish I had a mouth-guard,' he said. I looked blankly at him. 'You know,' he explained, rolling his shoulders like a rugby forward, 'scrum down.' I had the disconcerting sense that Alan, with his horsy face and public-school good cheer, was just pitching in. Whatever was up, he'd want to be part of it. It could be going over the top on the Western Front or pushing corpses into a pit, just as long as there was a team element.

Soon we became part of the crush, staggering from side to side, pressed forward by the crowd and back by the police. A double line of helmets was just visible over the heads of the people in front of us. Behind the cops, press photographers were holding their cameras up high, trying to get shots of us looking threatening. Around me some people were laughing; others were angry or beginning to panic. A thin girl in a plastic mac was twisting around, beating her hands against the back of the man in front of her. 'I can't breathe,' she sobbed. 'I can't bloody breathe.' Another girl told her not to worry, showed her how to make some room with her arms. I was heartened by that. We were helping each other. We were the People and this was our day.

Something came sailing over my head, exploding in a puff of white. A flour bomb. Then another one. I heard whistles and the sound of screaming, and felt a sudden violent lurch backwards. For the first time, I saw truncheons raised over the line of helmets, coming down once, twice. A chant cascaded forward from the mass of the crowd. 'Hands Off Vietnam! Hands Off Vietnam!' and quickly we were all shouting, enjoying the power of the words, punching the air and throwing peace signs at the enemy. Horsemen had appeared behind the foot soldiers, shying from side to side. Under the roar of the chant you could hear the percussive sound of hoofs on the paving-stones.

There was a convulsion and I lost sight of Alan. Then I was right at the front, facing the first line of police constables, who were straining to keep their arms linked. Behind them, one or two of their superiors were getting nervous, jabbing with their truncheons, screaming at us to move back. Their jabs became blows, but there was nowhere for us to go. Order was beginning to break down. Suddenly a boy was ejected from the friendly cocoon of the crowd, somehow squeezing through the forest of legs and arms to emerge behind the police line. He couldn't have been older than seventeen, with tousled hair and a big cardigan that looked like his mum had knitted it. I watched him turn left and right, realizing he was completely on his own. He tried half-heartedly to run, but he didn't stand a chance; a second's grace and then they were on to him, four of them pulling him down and carrying him bodily away. To my left someone else broke through, a guy in a crash helmet who didn't even make it to his feet before he was buried under a pile of uniforms, all trying to get a fist or a boot in. Someone tore his helmet off. Underneath he had a beard and a mop of curly black hair. He writhed around, yelling and kicking. A constable grabbed a fistful of hair and a sergeant, not bothering to hide it from the cameras, punched him hard in the face. He went limp and they dragged him off.

Frightened, I pushed myself back, only to find myself shoved forward again, barrelling into a policeman who tripped, breaking his hold on the man next to him. Flailing around, I tried to stay on my feet. All about me police and protesters were grabbing at one other for balance, like couples performing a violent jig. A great surge from the belly of the crowd had broken the police line, forcing the front few rows into the open space of the square. I just about kept my footing, wheeling round in panic to see if I was about to get coshed. Around me, others were doing the same thing. For a moment, disoriented, we hung back; then we were running into the square, in ones and twos and then all together, the whole ragtag London mob, students and street hippies and East End mods and striking builders and Piccadilly junkies spilling like an overflowing council bin into the big green open space, superciliously surveyed by the elegant town-houses of Mayfair.

The embassy was – and is – an imposing modernist bunker, with a short flight of steps leading up to the main entrance. A line of

Black Marias had been drawn up outside. I sprinted towards it as fast as I could. Coppers were running here and there, some trying vainly to push people back, others engaging in weird comical chases with individuals unlucky enough to have caught their eye. I zig-zagged, looking out for horses. My heart was pounding. Were we about to storm the building? Earlier there had been talk of armed guards, snipers on the roof, but I was sure we wouldn't stop. If somebody got killed, it would be their fault, not ours. This was it, our Winter Palace. This was 1917. I swerved away from a couple of policemen, but they weren't interested in me. One had lost his hat. The other was covered with flour. They were desperate to get back to their mates, who were hastily hopping over the ornamental iron fence in front of the embassy.

Faced with this second police line, our charge ran out of steam. People were still pouring into the square, but we'd stopped short at the fence, milling around, shouting and waving banners. The atmosphere had changed. We'd seen what would happen if we got caught, so there was both a new apprehensiveness and a new anger bubbling in the crowd. A constant rain of missiles was flying over my head. Not just flour, but marbles, bottles, clods of earth, broken banners, bits of fence. Someone had let off a smoke bomb. I could see a policeman lying on the ground, unconscious. I picked up a placard so I had something to defend myself with.

Then they charged us with the horses and the scene turned medieval. As I watched the battle from my spot under the tree, I realized this was as far as we were going to get. We were a tempo-rary crowd, a mass of disparate people. When threatened, there was nothing to hold us together; we had neither the guts nor the organization. And perhaps not the imagination either. How many of us would know what to do if we got inside the embassy building? How many would freeze, then run back down the stairs into the world we knew?

From beneath the tree, I watched the police make little sorties, hauling people back with them. Everything seemed to be happening at a distance, on a screen. Suddenly I found myself thrown forward on to the churned-up grass, my palms squishing into cold wet mud. Snapping back into close-up, I rolled my shoulders and windmilled my arms, trying to shake the grip that had tightened on my jacket, only to find a second pair of hands lifting me up by the waistband of my jeans so my feet lost contact with the ground. Someone took hold of my legs. Someone else grabbed a handful of my hair. Lolloping along as fast as they could, the policemen frogmarched me towards the fence and threw me over. Before I could pick myself up my arms were twisted behind my back and someone punched me hard in the stomach. At that point I started to lash out, from fear as much as anything. A new group of hands lifted me up, landing a few more workmanlike blows as I tried to get away. There was little real malice in it; I think by this time they were too tired to be properly nasty. My face was mashed against some copper's blue serge tunic; I could hear his laboured breathing as he helped cart me along, smell his reek of sweat and fag-smoke. 'Get out of it, you little cunt,' he muttered. I was thrown face first into the back of a van, where I sprawled on the ridged metal floor, winded and gasping for breath. I found myself wondering if the stone-throwing girl had seen my arrest, had seen me fighting back, like her.

The van was packed with prisoners, five men and a woman, each handcuffed to an escort. A middle-aged man in work overalls nodded warily at me. The others, younger, looked at the floor or held their heads in their hands. On the way to the station, the policemen made small-talk. Their eyes gradually settled on the woman prisoner, whose blouse had lost its buttons and was sagging open, revealing a section of white breast cupped in a lacy beige bra. After a while she gave up trying to cover herself and stared dejectedly at her feet, pretending not to hear the dirty jokes being made at her expense.

Finally the van stopped and we stepped out into the pandemonium of Bow Street police station. The corridors were full of arguing, scuffling people; police and prisoners, lawyers, newspaper reporters. We joined the crowd, jostling and pushing, the uncontrolled energy of the demo still surging on through the solid old building. As I lined up outside the charge-room I spotted someone from the LSE, a friend who'd been involved in the occupations. He raised his fist in a salute. I called out and waved. It felt good to see a familiar face, a reminder that I was there for a reason, part of something larger than myself.

I waited for almost an hour, as the prisoners in front were taken down to the cells and what seemed like hundreds of new arrivals piled in behind. In the charge-room an angry sergeant stood on a chair and shouted over the din, as another man took down details in a ledger. 'I didn't do anything,' I told him when it was my turn. 'I was exercising my right to peaceful protest.'

'Put a sock in it,' he said.

A few minutes later I was shown into a cell. The first hour of my captivity was spent uncomfortably, as I tried to delay the moment when I'd have to use the stinking, lidless toilet in front of five strangers. We sat, three to a bench, staring at one another in silence. Finally I couldn't wait any longer and shuffled over to the porcelain bowl, where I produced a shameful stench.

Gradually, I began to slide into a state of trance-like despair. In my back pocket I found a penny piece, which I used to scratch 'Victory to the NLF' in the plaster of the wall behind my head. The slogan took its place in a palimpsest of names, dates and obscene drawings. I felt hungry, but the stink from the toilet was so strong that when a constable brought in dinner, I couldn't eat. I'd been staring at a discoloured patch on the ceiling for what seemed like days when I heard the sound of raised voices in the corridor and the rattle of keys. A man was pushed into the cell. As soon as the door slammed behind him, he pressed himself against it, shouting through the spyhole in a noticeably well-bred voice, 'Let me out of here, you fucking pigs! Let me out! One day we're going to raze this fucking place to the ground, you Gestapo fuckers, you fucking Nazi cunts!' He kept this going for several minutes, pausing occasionally to cough and spit on the floor. From the corridor a bored voice told him to shut up.

After a while the man stopped shouting and slumped down on the bench beside me, forcing the others to shuffle up to make room. I leaned back and scrutinized him. He was dressed unremarkably in jeans and a brown corduroy jacket, but his expensive Chelsea boots caught my eye. I knew what they'd cost because I'd seen them the previous week in a shop on Newburgh Street. I'd wanted a pair but didn't have the money. How clean they were! My own shoes were scuffed and spattered with mud. The boots annoyed me. He annoyed me. 'You seem to have come out of it OK,' I observed sarcastically.

He stared at me, running his hands through his wavy blond hair. He had an equine face, drilled below the forehead by small eyes walled off from the outside world behind thick black glasses. Below the glasses hung a long nose and a pair of lips, full and fleshy and rather pink, which drew the gaze involuntarily to the inside of his mouth. It was as if he was only now registering my presence in the cell.

'What do you mean by that?' he asked, folding his arms.

'You're looking very fresh. They obviously didn't knock you about too badly.'

'I'm not feeling well, so I couldn't put up much of a fight. And, anyway, I was trying to save my equipment, not that it did much good. The bastards took it all anyway.'

'Equipment?'

'Camera equipment.'

'Are you a journalist?'

He cocked his head to one side and examined me. 'They certainly gave you a going-over,' he said, showing his teeth in a sort of half-smile. To my surprise, he reached forward and touched my bruised cheek with his fingers. I recoiled. He sat back. Again came that same half-smile. There was something illicit about it; an under-the-counter expression, suggestive of brown-paper wrappers, specialized tastes.

'Blast my throat,' he said, rubbing his neck with one hand and sticking the other out for me to shake. Reluctantly, I took it.

'Miles Bridgeman.'

'Chris.'

'Chris what?'

As soon as I told him my surname I felt like checking to see if my wallet was still there. As I was to discover, Miles always jumped on things. He was never content until he'd pinned them down, all the specifics, the whys and wherefores. I used to forgive him for it; in an odd way, his clumsy avidity felt like the most straightforward thing about him, the part closest to honesty.

Years later, under the Market Cross, it was still there. The same question, the same poorly concealed intensity.

'Mike what?'

'Frame. Michael Frame. As I'm sure you know already.'

Miles sat down beside me, tugging fussily at his trouser legs and smoothing his coat under his bottom. His movements were stiff. He seemed to be having trouble turning to his left side. 'Bad back,' he said, answering my unspoken question. 'I have to use this bloody awful chair at the office. Designer must have worked for the fucking Stasi.' The afternoon shoppers wandered past, averting their eyes from the *Big Issue* seller on the corner. I thought uneasily about all the people who might walk by and see us. Miles told me about his chiropractor. Miracle worker, reasonable rates. So how had it turned out for me? I must have looked puzzled. 'Life,' he explained, gesturing at Chichester. 'All this. I have to say – it's not what I'd have guessed.'

'No, I suppose not.'

'You know, it's amazing to see you. I always wondered what had happened to you. I assumed you'd gone abroad – and then – well, I don't know what I'd assumed, but I never thought I'd see you again. Certainly not – well, not in such *ordinary* circumstances. But here you are. You haven't changed, by the way.'

'Bollocks, Miles. All bollocks, from start to finish.'

'No, I mean it. You look just the same. You're looking fit.'

'I take vitamin supplements.'

For all his pampered sheen, Miles didn't look so well himself. The skin on his face had a coarse, slightly flushed look. Around his nose there was a little web of broken capillaries. He shook his head, as if in wonderment. 'There's so much to say. I barely know where to begin. How many years is it? I last saw you in – when did we last see each other?'

He knew perfectly well. The houseboat in Chelsea. The conversation in which I'd told him all the specifics, the whys and wherefores.

I felt like one of those Japanese soldiers they used to find holding out on remote Pacific islands, still fighting the Second World War decades after it had ended. At last, here was Miles Bridgeman, come to receive my surrender. I felt an overwhelming need to confide, to place myself in his hands. Perhaps his appearance meant my problems were over and no one cared any more. But that seemed too optimistic. I'd seen Anna and now Miles; there had to be a connection. Whatever Miles wanted, my well-being was unlikely to be a factor in his calculations. Once upon a time, I'd have immediately checked any thought of my own needs with the stern reminder that there was something greater than the personal – but that was when I thought I knew what it was. I had enough presence of mind, though, not to make it easy for him just because I felt sentimental. Just because he'd called me by my real name.

'Why are you here, Miles?'

'Pure chance. It seems almost spooky.'

Unless he was prepared to be honest, I wasn't going to put up with any facile chumminess. And I knew he could keep it up, his flow of nostalgic bullshit. Miles could always talk.

I remembered, in the cells at Bow Street, how he'd crossed his legs and begun to speak lucidly and with surprising passion about his work as a revolutionary film-maker, how he took advertising reels and old information films and cut them together with his own footage of the alienated lives of cleaners and shop-workers and the purposeful lives of political activists and young people moving out of the cities to create a new existence in the countryside. He wanted to illustrate the existential poverty of the System. He wanted to propagandize for internationalism, for a free and progressive style of life. He'd been to America, and to Sweden. Things were very free in Sweden. 'Cinema is a weapon,' he said, 'for changing consciousness.'

I was uncomfortable with the topic of consciousness, which was a problem, since in those days it came up a lot. It lay in that grey area between the personal and the political where I found a lot of things got jumbled up with one another. I'd smoked a little dope, but that was as far as I'd got with drugs. I'd never meditated. And as for political consciousness, I tended to rely on a small storehouse of slogans. *All liberation depends on the consciousness of servitude.* That was one of mine. Before Miles arrived in the cell, I'd been trying to steel myself by thinking politically. I'd told myself my anxiety over getting arrested was just a symptom of class privilege: other young men, born in Biafra or Vietnam, didn't have the luxury of worrying about their safety, let alone their career prospects or whatever I thought I might be risking. I felt threatened by Miles, by his six-guinea shoes and his interesting-sounding life. The other prisoners were listening in and I didn't want to be exposed as a scared suburban kid. So I went on the attack. 'Oh, yeah?' I sneered. 'So how come the police took your camera? Not much of a weapon, at the end of the day.'

'What, precisely, would be a suitable weapon?'

'Well, what would you rather have in your hand next time they come to arrest you? A camera or a gun? It's going to take more than *montage* to start the revolution.'

'Interesting. Are you perhaps a member of a group?' He put an odd sarcastic emphasis on the word.

'I'm co-chair of the VAG – the Vietnam Action Group. It's a student organization.'

'I see.' He appeared to think for a moment, then asked in a low voice whether I'd known about the plan to storm the embassy.

I shrugged and told him there had been talk. I told him the rumour about snipers, that if anyone had tried to get through the door they'd have been shot.

'We could have done it, you know,' he said. 'In my opinion, we could have taken the place.'

'You think?'

'Well, you didn't back down, did you?'

'No, I suppose not. But most people did. There didn't seem to be the energy to do it. The will.'

'I thought a lot of people wanted to go for it. I'm sure you and your friends, for example, in the Vietnam – what was it?'

'Action Group. No, not them. They're not particularly serious.'

'But you are.'

'Of course. It looks like there's a chance for change and I think we ought to take it.'

'Ah, yes. Change.'

Everyone in the cell was listening to me now. I felt I had the upper hand. 'No one else is going to do it, if we don't. No one else is going to build the revolution. I think we owe it to the future.'

'But what kind of future will it be?' he asked, leaning across again and gripping my arm. 'What exactly? That's the question.'

'Free,' I said, suddenly uneasy.

'Yes, I know. But what would it look like?'

'What do you mean?'

'Picture it in your head. What's different? How does it work? How do they do things? What do you see?'

I saw myself walking down the street smiling. I saw a sunny day. Everything I saw looked like an advertisement.

'People,' I lied. 'People together.'

Miles looked deflated. 'I think I've got TB,' he said, rubbing his chest. 'It's hard to tell.'

I was angry with myself. Was that really all I could imagine? Not even to have a picture of freedom. How abject. How bleak. 'So what do *you* think is in the future?' I asked. 'What do you see?'

Miles considered the question for a moment. 'Action. It's where everyone's at now. Either shit or get off the pot.'

'And what about us?'

He laughed and made a vague expansive gesture with his arms.

I saw he was extremely thin: underneath his jacket his shirt hung off his body in folds.

'Oh, I think they'll let us out one day.'

'Don't patronize me. That's not what I meant.'

He stared at me with what appeared to be pity, then stood up and went to the door, banging it with his fist. 'I want to see my solicitor!' he shouted. 'Do you hear, pig? Get me my fucking solicitor.' Then he turned and said something that at the time seemed snide and hectoring, but which later I realized I agreed with.

'It's not about how you feel, you know. How you feel isn't the point.'

The door was opened by the sallow custody sergeant. 'You,' he said to Miles. 'Come with me.' Miles brushed his jacket with his hands. 'Catch you at the revolution, I expect.'

Under the Market Cross, Miles bathed me in a warm stream of nostalgia. So much water under the bridge! Old comrades, painful memories, oughtn't we to head for the pub? I knew I had to get away from him. I couldn't think straight. 'I don't drink,' I told him, standing up. 'Nice to see you, Miles, but I've got to go.'

He looked aghast. 'You're kidding. Twenty-five years, you can't just walk off. We were friends. I've pieced together a lot about what went on since that day you came to the boat, but you and I never talked, not really. What happened to you? Where have you been?' I realized he'd read me all too accurately. He knew part of me wanted to tell my story. His voice became mellifluous. 'You really should stay and talk.'

'About what?'

Anna, I expected him to say. I needed to hear her name from someone else's lips. *Anna*. Instead he made an offer. 'Why don't you come and see me in London?'

'Why?'

'Come on, Chris. Don't be such a spoilsport.'

'Mike,' I said, walking away, 'my name's Mike.' I turned down a side-street that led in the opposite direction from the bookshop.

Half-way along it I ducked into a narrow lane and waited in a doorway. When I was certain he hadn't followed me, I doubled back towards Pelham's. The streets and the shoppers felt remote, as if they were on the other side of a pane of glass.

At the bookshop, I turned the sign on the door to 'closed' and wondered, for the first time, about running. I'd done it before. I imagined packing a case, heading to an airport. There was money in our joint bank account. How long would it last me in Asia, in South America? The idea of leaving Sam and Miranda was unthinkable. I sat frozen in God's worn leather wing-backed chair, trying to work out the angles. What did Miles want? What did it have to do with Anna? I knew that if I was to save myself, I'd need to face certain things I'd always avoided; I'd need to go over it all again. There was an unsorted box in the basement I'd looked into just once, then ignored. I went down to fetch it. Underneath a layer of old sociology textbooks and blue-spined Pelican paperbacks was a cache of pamphlets and yellowing newspapers that I tipped out on to one of the frayed Persian rugs. There were copies of *International Times* and *Frendz* and *Black Dwarf*, flyers for meetings and demonstrations. In a slew of broadsheets and pamphlets, I found what I'd been looking for: traces of myself. There were several copies of *Red Vanguard*, a socialist paper that had, for a few issues, been printed in a workshop below the room where I slept. They'd run one of our communiqués, an early one, written before we got tangled up in self-justification. I remember lying with Anna on the mattresses at Thirteen, drafting it in a notebook:

```
CONFRONTATION! CONFRONTATION! CONFRONTATION!

CONFRONTATION dramatizes our condition, which is
struggle.
CONFRONTATION gives a lead to the apathetic.
CONFRONTATION is a revolutionary role model for
disaffected youth.
```

```
CONFRONTATION is a bridge from protest to resist-
ance.
CONFRONTATION helps combat so-called mental
illness and disorders of the will.
CONFRONTATION gives you insight.
CONFRONTATION is your path to revolutionary self-
transformation.

Action is movement, movement is change and
process. Accelerate the process:
CHOOSE YOUR TARGETS! ACT NOW!
CONFRONTATION! CONFRONTATION! CONFRONTATION!
```

We worked together, scrawling phrases, calling them out to one another, little fragments of polemic we delivered like orators, taking pleasure in the force of the words, their potential to make change. Often these documents were just a record of arguments, each line bitterly fought over, picked to pieces and reconstructed. This one had come easily, I remember, like making up a song.

On the evening of the riot at Grosvenor Square, I was moved to a cell of my own. Wrapped in a thin, scratchy blanket, I spent the night dozing fitfully. In the morning I was given a fried-egg roll and a cup of tea, then transferred to Bow Street magistrates' court. My trial, such as it was, lasted under five minutes. A dog-faced policeman described how he'd bravely tackled me as I was running towards the embassy to throw a missile. I was, he said, looking savage and shouting words it would embarrass him to repeat before the court. When he attempted to effect an arrest, I had punched him in the face. I shouted out that he was a liar. The judge, a lantern-jawed man with a drinker's swollen nose, sentenced me to six weeks' imprisonment. I was taken directly to HMP Pentonville.

* * *

Cold spray spatters against my face as I lean over the side rail of the ferry. The water, far below, is grey and choppy. Beside me a pair of girls, Sam's age or a little younger, are telling each other how sick they feel, taking drags on a shared cigarette. By now Miranda and Sam will know there's something wrong. Miranda will be phoning the bookshop, trying to get God to pick up. Walking carefully so as not to slip on the wet metal of the deck, I go inside, where it smells like all cross-Channel ferries, that queasy cocktail of lager and snack foods and exhaust fumes and cleaning products that doesn't quite mask the acid stink of vomit seeping from the toilets.

On impulse I feed some change into one of the arcade games in the corridor. Lights flash and writing races across the screen, too fast to read. The rules are incomprehensible. Coloured blobs race around. Little dots and spinning things, which look to me like pieces of fruit, blip in and out of existence, seemingly at random. I press buttons, push and pull the joystick. It's impossible to tell what I'm controlling, which of the little creatures is me. YOU DIE! says the machine. YOU DIE! TRY AGAIN!

The last time I played a computer game was at Christmas, when Sam's not-boyfriend Kenny came over with a PlayStation. I've always liked Kenny. He's awkward and slightly nerdy, which is why he'll never ascend to the position in Sam's affections he so transparently craves. Sam likes sporty boys – uncomplicated squash or tennis players who can drive her to the pub and talk to her about jobs or holidays. Kenny has a mop of dyed hair and a collection of T-shirts bearing the names of Japanese garage bands. Occasionally Sam allows him to escort her to the cinema, but whenever I ask if they're 'together', she rolls her eyes and adopts a long-suffering expression.

When am I going to see you again, Sam? And what will you think of me when I do? You've always lived in a bounded, knowable world: a triumph for Miranda, I suppose, keeping you safe all these years. I find it very hard to think of you as nineteen; that's almost the age I was when I went to prison. You seem so young, young enough for me to wish I wasn't the one smashing up your happy home. I can't ask you not to hate me, or not to be frightened. I think the best I can hope for is that one day I'll be able to sit down with you and explain. You're too old to be saying to me, as you did recently, that you weren't 'interested in politics'. You want to be a lawyer. Well, a lawyer needs to know something about politics, even a corporate lawyer who just wants to climb the ladder, to buy the things her friends buy and go to the places they go. You're lucky that politics feels optional, something it's safe to ignore. Most people in the world have it forced on them. To be fair, I suppose you're just a child of your time. Thatcher's gone, the Berlin wall's down, and unless you're in Bosnia, the most pressing issue of the nineties appears to be interior design. It's supposed to be the triumph of capitalism – the end of history and the glorious beginning of the age of shopping. But politics is still here, Sam, even in 1998. It may be in abeyance, at least in your world. But it's lurking round the edges. It'll be back. You ought to give Kenny a chance, by the way. He's a decent kid.

I realize I'm forming words with my mouth, muttering to Sam under my breath as I feed the last of my change into the machine. A voice comes over the ship's public-address system, saying we're entering port. We've arrived in France. As I line up on the narrow stairs down to the car deck, I still can't stop myself. Explanations, justifications, like a crazy old man. Logic says there has to be a beginning, a first moment of refusal. I'm not sure. There's the usual Oedipal tangle: Mummy-Daddy-me. There was my brother and Kavanagh the junk man, the Russians and nuclear war. There was my need to be better, more decent, to *deserve*. None of these. All of them.

My earliest memories are of red bricks and high green hedges, of being walked past endless garden walls down roads that always brought us to the shop or the white pebbledash and well-oiled gate of our house, *number-three-avon-close*. Depending on how you looked at it, we were either on the way into or out of London, part of its great westward sprawl. In the mornings a line of men walked past the end of our street on their way to the station. In the evenings they walked back again. On Saturday mornings the men came into our shop, Parker's Electrical, to buy fuses and lightbulbs, staying to turn over the price tags on transistor radios and what Dad always called 'labour-saving devices': vacuum-cleaners and kettles, gadgets for the wives. I remember feeling slightly cheated that Dad didn't go into London to work. I wanted to have more to do with 'town', where things mattered, where the goods we sold were made.

I often asked why we didn't change the name of the shop. Our name was Carver. Why wasn't it Carver's Electrical? Dad told me it would only cause confusion. Litter, teddy-boys, sons who asked stupid questions: confusion could take many forms and my father was enemy to them all. It was, I think, the reason he moved Mum out of Kennington when he came home from the war. Ruislip was, above all, an orderly place.

Where we lived was distinctive for only one reason: the airfield. During the war, as I learned at school, gallant Polish airmen had flown out of RAF Northolt to fight the Germans. Down by Western Avenue there was a memorial to them, with lists of battles and difficult names, all *z*s and *w*s. A little further away was the Amer-ican airbase, USAF South Ruislip. When you went past on the 158 bus, the conductor sometimes called out, 'Next stop Texas!' as a joke. Every day military transport planes flew directly over our house, the rumble of their engines cutting through the sound of the Light Programme as we ate our tea in the kitchen. Like the other Avon Close children, I sometimes went out to watch them land, taking turns at peering through a hole in the hedge that masked the airfield from the road.

As I watched the planes I would think about war. War was the midnight raids and lost patrols I read about in *Adventure* and *Wizard*. It was *Banzai!* and *Hande hoch!* and being wounded but still crawling forward to lob your grenade into the machine-gun nest. It made boys like me into men like my teachers and the shopkeepers of North End Parade, who'd all seen and done wartime things yet mysteriously chose to mark physics homework or sell pork chops to my mother. All the fathers carried war around with them every day, buttoned up tight inside their shirts. War was secret knowledge. But war had changed since the fathers went to fight. Now it was about the planes that made the cutlery rattle on our Formica kitchen table, planes that flew so high they couldn't be seen or heard from the ground.

I had good ears; Mum always told me so. Perhaps I'd be the first to hear it: a drone, a faint humming in the empty sky, out of which would tumble the Bomb. I tried to picture *everything*, which I hoped might be done by listing all the things there were until they ran out. I always failed, which made it even scarier. Each time you thought of anything, anything at all, you discovered it, too, was part of *everything*, which was what would blow up if they dropped the Bomb. I tried out survival techniques in my imagination. Ducking, crawling under the kitchen table, running down into the cellar we didn't have. Even the tube trains went above ground at Ruislip. Where would we go?

My dad was frustratingly inscrutable on the topic of how we'd survive the Bomb. Whenever I asked (which was often) he told me not to worry and went back to the paper. I interpreted this as courage, but wasn't reassured. There was something closed about my dad, and it made me think he knew more than he was saying. What little I learned about his own war was extracted from my mum. He'd served on corvettes, escorting convoys across the North Atlantic. His ship was called HMS *Primrose*, which sounded disappointing to me, un-martial. He didn't like to be seen without his shirt, even at home, because of the smear of livid red scar tissue that covered his left side, from hip to chest. There was a fire at sea, was all Mum would say. I could never get her to tell me any more. I imagined my dad's skin melting from the effects of the Bomb. *Its searing fireball is as hot as the sun's interior . . . Radiation is particularly dangerous because it cannot be felt or smelled, tasted, heard or seen . . .*

As I got older, I roamed around on my bike, discovering a world with no obvious centre, an unfocused sprawl of 1930s houses that gave way in surprising places to open fields where cows grazed or football goals stood waiting for Saturday league matches. The boundaries of this world were main roads. You'd come up hard against them, screaming with traffic, intimidating, uncrossable. The planes took off and landed. Sometimes I got up at night and opened kitchen cupboards to see if my mum was stockpiling enough canned food.

Parker's Electrical stood at the end of a parade on a long straight road, next to a butcher, a florist, a funeral director and a junk shop, whose window was almost obscured by clutter. The junk shop was run by an Irishman called Kavanagh, who, for reasons I never discovered but probably amounted to nothing more than the standard English stew of race and class prejudice, was roundly hated by the other shopkeepers. Kavanagh was scruffy. His horse left droppings on the pavement. He was rumoured to deal in stolen goods or pornographic pictures. When Dad came home from meetings of the North End Parade Traders Association, Mum would ask if they'd 'come to any conclusions' about him. There was something sinister in her tone.

My brother Brian heard what was said about Kavanagh. Brian was two years older than me and I did what he said. One night, under his direction, I sneaked out of the house to the lock-ups round the back of the parade. Kavanagh's was at the end and its wooden door was half rotten, a sad contrast to ours, which was royal blue and had the words 'No Parking In Constant Use' neatly painted across it in white letters. Brian put his hands on his hips and used one of Dad's words. 'Disgraceful,' he said. He made me hold the torch while he wrenched out one of the rotten planks and poured something from a bottle through the hole. I had to light the matches. It took two or three goes. As we ran away, a faint orange glow was coming from inside.

I lay awake listening for the fire engines, but they never came. The next day we went to see what we'd achieved. I was nervous. If there was a detective, he might be waiting for us to return to the scene of the crime. The door was charred, but otherwise the lock-up was intact. There was no sign of a detective, or of the devastation I was expecting. Brian was disappointed. I pretended I was too.

A couple of months later, just after my thirteenth birthday, Kavanagh's closed down. The man and his junk disappeared, leaving an empty shopfront, its glass whitened by smeared arcs of window-cleaner's soap. I had visions, influenced by Saturday matinées, of my father and the other shopkeepers taking Kavanagh 'for a ride'. An unshaven man in a greasy grey jacket, falling to his knees out in the woods.

Kavanagh's departure did nothing to appease my father's anger. He was always up in arms about something or other – rude customers, articles in the paper. It was a trait my brother had inherited. Brian became a very angry man, a shouter in saloon-bars, a puncher of walls. There were evenings when we'd sit round the kitchen table, eating the food Mum had cooked, and she would try to listen to *The Archers* while Dad held forth about Malaya or the West Indians or de Gaulle, banging the table with the heel of his hand while Brian and I competed to express our vocal agreement.

Then there was Mum, who had her good days and the other kind. One weekend I stood in the garden with a spool of copper wire in my hand. My father, cigarette hanging out of the corner of his mouth, was up a step-ladder by the back fence. I remember him silhouetted against the sun, a smoky black outline, the wire gleaming as he looped it over the trellis. Mum ran out of the house, wiping her hands on her apron and shouting at us in a high, strained voice: 'What are you doing? For the love of God, what are you doing?'

'It's for my radio, Mum,' I told her. 'We're testing my radio.' The wire hung slack over the bare branch of the elder tree, running back down into the spool, into my hands. Crystal sets needed long aerials. We were going to set it up so I could listen in my bedroom; it had to go all the way back to the house and through the upstairs window. My mother snatched the spool from me. Strands of hair fell across her face, which was red. So were her hands, from the washing-up. She was red and white, her breath making a little cloud in the cold as she screamed at me. Another smoking head. 'You'll electrocute someone! Burn the whole house down! We'd be trapped! Don't think you'll get away with this!' This last sentence was spat at my father, who climbed down the step-ladder, telling her to shut up and go inside. Grabbing her by the arm, he pushed her back into the house. It was no use telling her my crystal set didn't use electricity, just the energy of the radio waves. When Mum was in one of her moods, she didn't listen. She broke things in the kitchen. She went to bed and cried. Twice that year (the year I was nine) she phoned the police and told them stories about Dad. The first time, when they got to our house, they wanted him to go with them. He had to explain for ages before they went away.

Nothing was ever said in our house about my mum's 'moods'. As far as I know, she'd never seen a psychiatrist or talked to anyone else about why she found the world such a hostile place. She didn't really have friends, at least not the kind who did more than say good morning when they saw her at the front gate. The local GP kept her supplied with pills, a row of little bottles that took up a whole shelf in the bathroom cupboard. On a good day she'd go about her business with slow deliberation, like someone moving under water. On a bad one I'd sometimes find her stalled completely, staring straight ahead, a wooden spoon or a tea-towel in hand and an expression of bafflement on her face. Speak to her and she'd come to life again, shuffling round the kitchen as if nothing had happened.

On a typical Sunday, Mum would be lying in bed, listening for the rats and cockroaches she suspected were scuttling about in the attic over her head. Dad would sit downstairs with the newspaper and I'd be in my bedroom, attempting to summon the outside world. The first time I fitted the pink moulded earpiece of the crystal set into my ear, I heard a tiny crackle, then, very faintly, a voice singing a few words in a foreign language, accompanied by a violin. Like all first things these sounds were powerful. I felt they were being born out of the noise just for me, as if I was creating them through some special skill, coaxing them out of formlessness.

As a hobby, crystal sets occupied me for a year or so. Then, as a birthday present, my parents bought me a Japanese transistor radio. It was like hearing the world think. There were stations on pirate ships out at sea, stations playing advertising jingles and pop music and sports matches. Stern voices read out news items or religious texts, spoke terse messages in accents from the other side of the Iron Curtain. On short wave there were mysterious phenomena, urgent bursts of Morse code, mechanical voices reciting meaningless lists of numbers. I heard whispering, women crying, once a pilot or lost sailor calling, 'Come in, please, come in.' There was something angelic in the surf-sound of white noise between stations, the whoop and whine of travel across the bands of the spectrum.

The radio was a way to escape from downstairs, from my deep-sea diving mother, wading in lead boots towards the sink. Aged fourteen, I tuned in to the missile crisis. *I call upon Chairman Khrushchev to halt and eliminate this clandestine, reckless, and provocative threat to world peace and to stable relations between our two nations. I call upon him further to abandon this course of world domination, and to join in an historic effort to end the perilous arms race and to transform the history of man.* This was it. The Bomb was coming. Making the most of what I thought were my last few hours on earth, I stayed up all night, listening to short-wave artefacts, the noise between stations. Afterwards, noise would be all that was left.

After thirty-eight days the crisis ended, and I was still there, lying in bed with my radio. The following year the leaders signed a treaty saying they wouldn't test nuclear weapons in space or the earth's atmosphere or the sea; people acted as if this was some kind of victory. But what about the missiles? I wanted to scream. They're still there, pointing at my house. So when I ran into the couple outside the tube station, with their painter's table and their coloured leaflets weighted down with seaside pebbles, it felt as if I'd found the only other sane humans on the planet. They were old, in their mid-twenties. Colin had a scraggly blond beard and a CND badge pinned to the lapel of his pea-coat. Maggie wore a long peasant skirt at which I stared intently, because each time I glanced up at her face, I started to blush. She looked like Leslie Caron, an actress whose picture had recently joined a growing collage on the wall above my bed. Beat-band singers, models, artists: people from the *Sunday Times* colour section, from the new world growing a few miles away in town.

Maggie chatted to an old lady, trying to get her to sign a petition, while I hovered around, reading a leaflet about the government's advice to householders on protection against nuclear attack. We were to survive using whitewash, brown paper and dustbin lids. Colin introduced himself, made a joke about what he'd really do if the air-raid warning sounded. I liked him. He didn't speak to me as if I was a child. Nor did Maggie. When I said I wished I could do something, they told me I wasn't alone. Millions felt the same. If I really wanted to make a difference, I should come over to their house the next day. There would be a meeting. 'It'll be very informal,' said Maggie, 'but you'll get a feel for what's going on.'

I left with a copy of their newspaper and an armful of leaflets, which I promised to put through doors in Avon Close. That night I read about Distant Early Warning Stations: tropospheric scanners, enormous parabolic dishes looking out over the Yorkshire moors. Two minutes was all they'd give us. Two minutes to do what? Make love to Maggie. As I fell asleep I worked it all out, in the weird, narcissistic fashion of teenage boys. We'd be on a hill. I had an American accent. Where Colin was in all this I can't remember.

I also can't remember much about that first meeting. It must have been taken up with routine administration. Collecting dues. Arranging a speaker. I probably spent most of it staring at Maggie, at the way her mouth moved when she spoke, the shape of her breasts under her sweater. The other members of Ruislip and Northwood CND were a spooky bunch. Elderly Quakers, a vegetarian ex-fighter-pilot. It didn't matter to me. Thursday evenings now belonged to Maggie and the Bomb, in that order.

Soon I was knocking on doors to tell people about first strikes and secret NATO exercises, fall-out and megatonnage, all the thrilling science-fiction pornography of nuclear war. I handed out pamphlets with titles like *Six Reasons Why Britain Must Give Up the Bomb*, and *H-bomb War: What Would It Be Like?* For the first time I had arguments with adults in which I wasn't always told to be quiet and respect my elders. Women shut the door in my face and men told me I was a little fool, but sometimes they argued back, shaking their heads as I described the deformities of Hiroshima children, the underground bunkers to which key government personnel would be removed when the sirens sounded. People invited me inside, old people who wanted company, a man who put his hand on my knee and told me I was a likely-looking fellow.

The following Easter, a month or two before my sixteenth birthday, I marched to Trafalgar Square, part of a crowd (much smaller, I heard, than previous years, but to me still vast) who felt what I did; who had the imagination to look beyond their never-had-it-so-good daily lives to the threat that lay just over the horizon. We waved placards saying *No Polaris*. We sang 'We Shall Overcome' and 'Down By the Riverside'. Mothers wheeled their children in push-chairs. Bands played trad jazz, because trad was authentic. Authenticity meant roots and honesty, but according to Colin it also meant the reality of your death. If you knew – really held it in your mind – that one day you'd die, then the value of life would be clear, and you'd live fully, deeply. Most people found the thought of death unbearable and fled into the everyday, so most people were only half alive. Colin felt this was why the majority of them seemed to be learning to live with the nuclear threat. That seemed logical to me. If your Being was already infected with Nothingness, annihilation probably didn't seem so bad.

Authenticity was just one of the things I learned about from Maggie and Colin. They lived in a way I'd never even imagined. Their house, which from the outside looked just like ours, was open to all, and in contrast to the frozen routine of Avon Close, had a joyous and unpredictable rhythm. Even if Colin was working he was happy to open the door and let you make tea in the kitchen, with its jar of spaghetti on the counter and poster of a Picasso dove pinned above the hob. Colin was writing plays. I don't know how far he ever got, but he'd sit and bang away at an old Remington typewriter on the dining-table, making occasional contributions to whatever was happening around him, which might include four or five friends singing and playing guitar, or having a loud debate about Algeria. Maggie would 'clear him away' when she wanted to serve dinner, which she did for however many happened to be there, pushing his papers to one side and clattering cutlery on to the typewriter keys to indicate that it was time to lay the table.

Maggie was the magnet that drew people to the house. Though Colin's writing was the official centre of things, it was her determination and her adventurousness, not the way he'd sometimes talk excitedly of 'having a breakthrough' or sit around dejectedly when not having one, that gave the place its charged, purposeful atmosphere. She seemed inexhaustible, working as a teacher to support Colin's literary ambitions and coming home every day to an establishment that at times seemed part boarding-house and part fall-out shelter. There would often be someone sleeping on the sofa, and one or two others on mats on the floor. Usually they were other activists, men with rucksacks and pipes, pairs of tanned young women just returned from camps and congresses in exotic-sounding places.

Maggie's frank bossiness, her sudden inspirations, her willingness to put her shoulder to the wheel whenever there was something to be done infused the CND group with a sense of direction it would otherwise entirely have lacked. She listened patiently to my half formed opinions, and took me canvassing with her on the Saturdays when Colin was 'trying to get something done' and needed peace and quiet. We'd get a lift from Squadron Leader Myers, who had a car, and set up the table in our regular spot outside the station. We'd eat a packed lunch, and if I was lucky she would chat about herself. She told me she dreamed about 'doing something really useful' with her teaching. Volunteering, going abroad. I began to understand, dimly, that she wasn't happy; the thought both shocked and thrilled me.

At first I tried to keep Colin and Maggie a secret from my family. One Sunday Brian, always looking to stir up trouble, told Dad I was 'hanging around with some beatniks' and there was a terrible row. My father threatened all the customary things. I stormed upstairs, leaving him shouting in the living room while my mum mumbled and wrung her hands. Slamming my bedroom door, I found Brian standing on my desk, holding the old suitcase in which I kept all my CND stuff, the cuttings and souvenirs and supplies of leaflets for canvassing. He'd dragged it from its hiding-place under my bed and emptied the contents out of the window. Pieces of paper were turning end over end all down Avon Close, caught in hedges, silting up the gutters in little piles.

My professed non-violence didn't hold me up for a second. By that time I was as tall as Brian, though more lightly built, and he had an older brother's complacency. My attack took him by surprise, and I soon had him wedged in the corner by the bedside table, his lip bleeding, covering his face to ward off my flailing fists. My dad pulled me away, pinning my arms to my sides until I stopped struggling.

The incident was judged to be my fault. Mum took to her bed and Dad forbade me to see Colin and Maggie again. My CND membership card, which I'd retrieved from the garden, was torn up in front of my eyes. Shaken and furtive, Brian avoided any obvious triumphalism. I caught him smiling slyly to himself when he thought no one could see. That day was the end of something in our family. I couldn't give it a name, but after that it had gone.

* * *

Leaving Dieppe, I'm exhorted by signs to remember to drive on the right-hand side of the road. I crawl along in a train of British cars, past industrial estates and big-box hypermarkets advertising cheap deals on alcohol. Gradually the country opens up into farmland, interspersed with gloomy towns overseen by brick church towers and war memorials.

I support Kenny's cause with Sam for the simplest of reasons – he reminds me of myself. He's a painfully serious boy, just as I was in my teens. One afternoon, about six months ago, he was mooching about the house after my stepdaughter, vainly trying to interest her in a vinyl record he was carrying. 'Listen to the lyrics,' I overheard him say. 'And the guitar on track three.' She was sending a text message on her phone. It was like watching a depressive footman hovering behind the queen.

Later that day, I tried to talk to Sam, to tell her that if she didn't like him, she ought to put him out of his misery. 'You're being cruel,' I said.

'He's here of his own free will,' she replied primly. 'Anyway, what do you know about relationships? You've only ever been with Mum.'

She said it with such certainty. Suddenly I could see very clearly the unbroken borders of her world, the world of a child. She'd always treated me as a kind of country bumpkin when it came to feminine topics; amused, I'd accepted it as part of my fatherly identity. But her lack of imagination now struck me as odd, blinkered.

'Why do you think that?'

It was stupid of me. She looked up sharply. 'You've never talked about anyone else. And you were a monk before, so I just thought . . .' She trailed off. I was in too deep, and retreated to wash up. She followed me into the kitchen. 'You and Mum.'

'Yes?'

'You're all right, aren't you?'

I hugged her. 'Of course we are.'

So I never solved the problem of Kenny, and he's still hanging around, yearning for Sam just as hopelessly as I yearned for Maggie. After my fight with Brian and the ban on seeing her, I stayed away for three days, then went round to see her on my way home from school. As usual Colin was typing, Maggie sitting opposite him marking books. In melodramatic terms, I described what had happened, hoping they'd be able to help. Maggie gave my shoulder a squeeze and told me it was good to stand up for what I believed in, but I shouldn't have lashed out at my brother. Dr King had withstood much greater provocation. Colin frowned and asked whether my dad knew their address. They fed me bean soup and sent me home, Maggie's goodbye kiss burning on my cheek.

After a few months things were much as they'd been before. I'd avoid confrontations, lying about after-school activities, even inventing a fictitious youth club at which I played ping-pong once a week. If I ate at Maggie and Colin's I'd force myself to swallow another dinner at home. Dad knew I was still seeing the beatniks, but had more pressing things to worry about. Brian had abruptly left school and started work in the sales department of an engineering company. He was spending most of his salary in the pub and came home drunk several nights a week, tripping over the furniture and leaving marks on the wall as he staggered upstairs. His confrontations with Dad were much worse than my own, and he had no patience with my mother, jeering at her as a mad cow, a mental case. In response, Mum grew ever more anxious. Soon after my seventeenth birthday she was committed.

I'm ashamed to say I only went to visit her once in the three months she was in St Bernard's. It was a large Victorian institution, a cluster of imposing Gothic buildings surrounded by a high perimeter wall. Inside, orderlies pushed trolleys and escorted patients down long, echoing corridors. She was on a ward named after some royal personage, which smelled of urine and boiled cabbage. The beds were like little iron islands on the scuffed lino.

Brian had refused to come, saying he had better things to do with his weekend than go to a nuthouse. A nurse took Dad and me past a row of women sitting in vinyl-covered armchairs or lying in their beds. Mum had been given a course of ECT. She seemed not to know who we were. Trussed up in an unfamiliar flannelette dressing-gown she smiled uncertainly as my father tried to summon some gentleness into his voice. 'How are you bearing up, Angela?'

She pointed out of the window. 'You can see the birds,' she said.

Dad nodded encouragingly, then looked at his feet, unsure how to go on. There was a terrible silence. My eyes kept straying back to Mum's hair, which was messy, tangled up in knots at the back of her head. This was what I found most upsetting. She was particular about her hair. She'd spend hours at her dressing-table, piling it up, freezing it into gâteau-like shapes with cans of lacquer.

Under Maggie and Colin's influence I was reading books and working hard for my A levels. With my new confidence I'd acquired a new group of friends, boys my own age, with whom I listened to folk and modern jazz records, smoking cigarettes out of bedroom windows and talking about our various plans of escape from Ruislip. I'd applied to the London School of Economics: if I got in, I'd be able to go and live in hall.

As my exams came up, things at home got worse. Dad brought Mum home in a new hat with matching handbag, talking loudly and laughing a shiny, high-pitched laugh. Her brightness had something brittle about it, as if she were only performing her newly learned happiness, acting it out for our benefit. She had new pills too, which kept her awake. I'd hear noises in the kitchen at unearthly hours, three or four in the morning, and go down to find her rummaging in the cutlery drawer or polishing glasses.

Hello, dear, would you like some breakfast? For all her energy, she didn't seem able to cook any more, something about the complexity of it, the timing. There were small disasters, charred joints of meat, eggs at the bottom of pans brimful of cold water. Soon we were subsisting on a scavenger's diet of tinned food and fish and chips. Brian and Dad diverted themselves from their panic with breakages and shouting.

I spent as much time as possible out of the house, working in the public library or wandering around the West End, a habit I'd gradually developed since I first started taking the train into town for CND events. In draughty church halls I attended screenings of *Bicycle Thieves* and *The World of Apu*, accompanied by Czech cartoons in which people built walls and then all the flowers in the garden died. Soon I progressed to less elevated pursuits. Soho fascinated me, with its secret alleys and women sitting at upstairs windows, smoking and looking down at the street. There were coffee bars with rows of scooters parked outside. The amplified clatter of beat bands punched its way out of cellars. I didn't dare go into these places. Sometimes I bought a frothy coffee in one of the quieter caffs and sat in a corner watching girls, hoping to be noticed.

I'd begun to despair of CND. There was something antique about it, something hopelessly polite. The year the Mods and Rockers fought on Margate beach, CND youth groups were up on the pier, offering donkey-rides and a 'non-violent Punch and Judy show'. 'Don't shout slogans as you march,' advised one of our leaflets. 'This sounds ugly. Join in the singing, which sounds good and helps marchers along the road.' The warlords were trying to kill us but we had to be cheerful and take our litter home: good little citizens, asking nicely not to be irradiated. On the day I went on my first Easter march, the Committee of 100 held a sit-down demo at USAF Ruislip, just up the road from my house. I only heard about it afterwards. Hundreds of people were arrested. While I was strolling around the West End singing 'If I Had A Hammer', people had been blocking the airbase gates.

Colin and Maggie disapproved of breaking the law. They said we had to show we were a responsible, rational part of society. If we were perceived as wreckers or undesirables, how could we hope to have an effect? We'd begun spending time at a folk club, held above a pub in Shepherd's Bush. Maggie and I would watch as Colin, who'd been taking guitar lessons, went up to take his turn with the other amateurs before the professional singers did their sets. Sitting next to Maggie in the smoky darkness, I absorbed her high-mindedness and her optimism. I thought things were going to change; I was young enough to think the very strength of my desire for change would be enough.

Then came the 1964 election. The prime minister we derided as Homeosaurus ('Too much armour, too little brain, now he's extinct') was booted out and a Labour government came in. At meeting after meeting, speakers had assured me that once Labour were in power, they'd disarm. I believed them: the Labour Party stood for international brotherhood and peace. I was too young to vote, but I thought a Labour victory meant I was living in a country that made sense, a rational country where people knew that one day they'd die and until that day wanted to live, as fully as they could. Instead, the new prime minister, Mr Wilson, made speeches about economic progress, the white heat of technology. We would be keeping our nuclear weapons and getting more. After all my efforts, all the lost Saturday afternoons and the boring meetings, 'we' had won and still nothing was going to change.

I lost faith in CND and Maggie with it, as if somehow Wilson was her fault. With the discovery of her feet of clay, my idol became incapable of absorbing any more adoration. I had no vocabulary for what I was feeling, and such a hopelessly low self-image that had she ever shown any signs of reciprocating, I wouldn't have dared touch her, but all the same I knew my chaste knight-errancy – one part Tennyson to two parts song lyrics – was no longer sustaining me.

One day I was in the West End, listlessly handing out CND leaflets outside a theatre in Drury Lane, when a pair of Danish students stopped to ask directions. Freja and Sofie were both pretty, one dark and one fair, over to see the galleries and tick off sites of historical interest in their guidebook. I soon realized they didn't want to hear about the amount of strontium-90 in the bones of children under one year of age and began to brag about how well I knew Soho. This was only partly true. I'd never actually been through the doors of the fashionable places I was boasting about. Luckily the girls had as little money as I did, so I was saved the humiliation of being turned away from the Scene or the Flamingo. They said they wanted to hear some music, so I stuffed my leaflets back into my satchel and took them to Beak Street, where there was a basement club little bigger than my living room at Avon Close, a cheap dark cellar where the management weren't particular about the age of their clientele. I'd been there once or twice to lean against the back wall and smoke an affected cigarette. It was a place where I judged I wouldn't be out of my depth.

Though it was early, the basement was packed with people watching a band playing covers of American rhythm-and-blues songs. At first we stood by a pillar, sipping our drinks to make them last. Then I danced, first with Sofie, then Freja, pressed close together by the jostling crowd. The place was unbelievably hot. Within minutes sweat was running down our faces and soaking our clothes. Droplets of moisture dripped from the ceiling, barely a foot above our heads. I danced with my eyes closed, dizzy and ecstatic. Freja draped her arms round my neck and I squeezed her against me, feeling her thighs moving under her damp cotton dress, the ridge of the bra-line bisecting her back. Then, as the band sang *uh uh yeah yeah do you like it like that* we were kissing, her fingers scraping away strings of wet blonde hair from her mouth as we crushed our faces together and my hands travelled over the curve of her buttocks, the slippery nape of her neck. The hour of the last tube was edging closer and with it would have to come some kind of decision, but there was no contest, not really, because Freja was smiling and grazing my cheek with her knuckles and conferring with Sofie, giggling and whispering as I stood apart and nodded my head to the music, lighting a cigarette, tapping my foot *yeah baby oh baby oh* in time and just to make sure taking off my watch and slipping it into my pocket.

By the time we left it was very late. We sat in a coffee bar and ate toasted sandwiches, smiling conspiratorially at one another. Sofie drew fingertip patterns in spilt tea on the Formica tabletop while Freja and I played footsie until there was no money left for drinks and all three of us started to yawn. Finally I confessed I had no way to get home, and they both laughed, as if I was being sly. Freja told me they'd try to sneak me into their hotel, and led me by the hand into Fitzrovia, to a town-house in one of the bigger squares with an illuminated sign above the door saying the Richmond or the Windsor or something House. We hung around outside, prevaricating. Freja and I kissed and ran our hands over one another, almost clawing each other in desperation. Sofie hopped up and down a discreet distance away, hugging herself against the cold.

As they rang the bell for the porter, I hid out of sight. After a minute or two someone came to the door and they disappeared inside. I waited for a long time, crouching behind a pillar-box across the street. I began to feel lonely, suspecting that all the earlier discussion at the club had been about how to get rid of me. The stars were faint in a sky that was now turning from black to a washed-out purple-grey. On the other side of the square a car started up and pulled away, its engine sounding loud and hollow in the silence.

I must have been dozing when Freja came back down to let me in, because the first thing I heard was her voice hissing my name. She was standing in the doorway, waving frantically. I ran over and she pulled me up several flights of thickly carpeted stairs to a little room with two single beds and a huge mirrored wardrobe, a looming Formica block that dominated the far wall like a prehistoric monument. The lights were off and the curtains half drawn, letting through a dribble of pre-dawn light that fell across Sofie, just a mound under the covers, pretending to be asleep.

Without looking at me Freja started to undress, stepping out of her skirt and carefully folding it over the back of a chair. Too shy to watch, I turned away and found myself confronted with her double image in the wardrobe doors: the curve of her back, her bird-like shoulders. She unhooked her bra, struggled into a long cotton nightie, and dived into bed. 'Hurry up,' she whispered. 'Get undressed and get in.'

Grey hands unbuttoned a grey shirt. I was self-conscious: though I couldn't see her eyes in the half-light, I knew she was watching me. I got down to my underwear and crawled beneath the blankets and we tried to stifle our laughter as we wrapped ourselves around each other. She smelled of sweat and cigarette smoke. I kissed her salty face and her tongue darted out from her hot dry mouth. My body was a single nerve, thrumming with each small urgent movement, each shift in position. Her mouth at my ear. Her exploring hand.

Several times in my life I've gone through long periods without sex or any other kind of physical contact. The hunger it produces is deep and low; it's possible to lose track of it, to forget or fail to perceive how it's emptied everything out of you and made the world papery and thin. Touch-starved, you brush against existence like a stick against dry leaves. You become insubstantial yourself, a hungry ghost.

I found the hard points of her nipples with my mouth, sliding a hand into the extraordinary slipperiness between her legs. Her nightdress rucked up round her waist, then, as I pushed it higher, became a solid wad round her neck. I felt her lift up her arms and snake out of it, a sudden rush of cold air sweeping in as her movement dislodged the blankets. Then her miraculous hand was on my cock, slithering me into her as the covers fell away completely. The cold somehow added to my excitement as I arched myself back and forth. 'Don't squirt your stuff inside me,' she warned, and I pulled out and came copiously on to the sheets. My moan produced a kind of answering sigh in her, a long exhalation that might have been melancholic or relieved or regretful or satisfied, all or none, I had no idea. I saw Sofie was awake, watching us. Her mouth was slack, her eyes glittering.

We rearranged the blankets and lay silently on the narrow bed. I reached for Freja again but time had somehow passed and her breathing was even and the light coming through the chink in the grubby curtains was hard and strong, strong enough for me to see that Sofie was still watching. 'You've got to go,' she said. 'People will wake up soon, and they can't find you here.'

My head was swimming with lack of sleep. The daylight made everything complicated; guilt lurked in the corners of the room. I foraged for my clothes on the floor and, with a quick glance at the two girls, one asleep, the other staring, I tiptoed downstairs. From behind the frosted-glass door in Reception came the sound of someone moving around. I fumbled with the front-door latch, and all at once I was standing outside in early-morning London, a place of sunlight and milk floats and street sweepers, tucking my shirt in and realizing that I was miles from home and hadn't even got enough money for a bus fare.

There was a huge row, of course, but I didn't much care. I retreated to my bedroom to trace and retrace every minute of my night, the quickly fading loops and whorls of happiness.

There were times like that later on, with Anna. In the squat, in various shared beds and shared houses. Watching and being watched. We had abolished privacy: we hoped guilt would go with it. Watching could become anything. Mechanical or transcendent. It could leave you open-mouthed, touching yourself. It could make you curl up defensively, resenting the selfish animal sounds, the smell of other people on the pillow into which you were pressing your face.

Brian moved out. Mum went back to hospital, after she had scratched a lot of skin off her arms. While she was away, I moved around the house in a strange cramped dance with Dad, trying never to be in the same room. I could feel he wanted to talk to me, which made me all the more intent on avoiding him. Above all, I didn't want him to try to make friends, not now I was finally about to get away.

When my exam results came out, the first people I went to tell were Maggie and Colin. I wanted Maggie to share my happiness: I had my place at the LSE, my ticket out.

When Colin opened the door I waved my results paper at him. 'Hi, Colin. Guess where I'm going.'

He just stood there on the doorstep, staring blankly at me. 'What do you want?' he asked curtly. He didn't invite me in.

'I just came over to tell you I got in.' I was hurt by his abruptness. He hadn't said anything, hadn't reacted at all to my wonderful news. 'And,' I added, trying to be polite, 'to – to see how you are.'

'Well, I'm bloody awful, if you're interested.'

'Where's Maggie?'

'Where's Maggie? How the hell should I know?'

I was floored by this response. He had a strange, twisted expression on his face. I couldn't think of anything to say and it must have shown.

He snorted and let out a humourless staccato laugh. 'Sorry to disappoint you, Christopher, but she's not here. She's gone and she's not bloody coming back, or at least that's what she said in her letter. So now you can turn round and piss off home. I never liked you sniffing round her anyway. All that wide-eyed admiration rubbish.'

'But – I never –'

'Oh, you never, all right. Not for want of trying, you dirty little sod.'

'I didn't, I swear . . . What happened, Colin? Where did she go?'

He mimicked my voice. 'Where did she go? She left me, you ass. She buggered off to Ghana or Bongo-Bongo Land or somewhere to go and save the little black babies. So no more CND, no more free food, no more singalongs, no nothing, *comprende*? It's over. Now fuck off and leave me alone.'

And he slammed the door in my face.

I've often wondered what happened to Maggie. I can never

picture her. Perhaps she's still in a classroom in Africa, the head-mistress, the director of the orphanage. Perhaps she's dead. And then there's Freja and Sofie and all the others my daughter can't imagine, all the threats to the charmed circle of her-and-Mummy-and-me. Which of them am I driving towards now? Is it really just Anna?

* * *

By the time I reach the Paris *périphérique* I've fallen into a trance of headlights and signage. Round I drive. Porte d'Orléans, Port d'Ivry. Blossoming red lights, brake sharply, traffic suddenly filtering in from a hidden slip-road, brake again. The road's like a go-kart track, one damn thing after another, running in and out of orange-lit tunnels, through billboard-lined trenches and elevations. Was that my exit? My eyes are tired of squinting into the darkness for – what am I looking for? Porte d'Orléans. Didn't I pass that already? I have no idea of the time: Miranda never set the dashboard clock. Thirty thousand pounds' worth of high-status German engineering, but she doesn't set the clock. Round and round. Though I'm dog-tired, I can't face the complexity involved in turning off and looking for somewhere to sleep. So I carry on, round and round, Porte des Lilas, Porte de Montreuil, right shoulder inwards, circumambu-lating the large *stupa* at Wat Tham Nok, following the line of chanting monks, the tea-light in its little clay bowl warming my hands. Circling in the Aegean, the taste of salt on my lips, blank and free. Round and round. Porte de Charenton. Trudging round the yard at morning exercise. My revolutions: a hundred of us walking, two abreast, inner ring clockwise, outer ring counter-clockwise. Back in the days when Pentonville was the gateway to transportation, the builders constructed an endless double path of flagstones, two snakes eating their own tails, set into the black tar. The regime was designed to isolate prisoners from all human contact. Face-masks, enforced silence. Round and round, a folk dance or a fairground ride. Very important, they thought, never to give the scum a sense of achievement.

I never found out why I came to be sent to HMP Pentonville. It was the recidivists' prison. Remand prisoners went to Brixton, first-timers like me to the Scrubs. It had a bad reputation, which a police constable gleefully told me all about as he led me out to the 'meat wagon', a Black Maria with metal-grilled windows. 'The lags'll have you for breakfast, you hippie cunt,' he told me cheerfully, as he locked me in.

As we got down from the van a gang of prison officers descended on us, screaming like squaddies performing a bayonet charge. We were doubled into a low hall, searched, and assembled into a ragged line. The screws marched up and down, shouting at us to stand up straight, poking us in the ribs and asking rhetorically if we knew where we were. They locked us into small wooden cubicles, where we stood in semi-darkness while one of them read out the rules. The purpose of prison was to encourage and assist us to lead a good and useful life. We were to address all prison officers as 'sir'. We would be required to perform useful work for not more than ten hours a day. Failure to obey an officer would be punished with removal of privileges. The list went on. When we could receive visits. When we could receive letters. More rules were written on a card pasted to the wall in front of me in the coffin-like cubicle. I peered at them as I waited. I was not to fight or set fires. I was not to possess a greater quantity of any article than I was authorized to possess.

I was pulled out of the cubicle by a pair of POs, and taken to the desks at the end of the room. Behind each desk sat a trusty with a red armband, writing in a ledger. I was ordered to stand on a set of scales and my weight was written down, along with my age and occupation. 'Religion?'

'None,' I answered.

'C of E, then,' said the prisoner-clerk.

'No, none,' I insisted. 'I don't believe in God.'

'That comes under C of E.'

I was frogmarched into a second room to stand before a PO who occupied a stool behind a high desk, like a Dickensian clerk. He ordered me to undress and as I took off my clothes, they were itemized and dropped into a cardboard box. I had to bend over and spread my buttocks, then show the soles of my feet. Afterwards I was given a dressing-gown and taken to the showers, where the two POs escorting me shoved me into a stall and gave me an unhurried beating. Thought I was Fidel Castro? Long-haired wanker, I looked like a girl. They bet I took it like a girl. After a while it didn't hurt so much. Water spattered over me as I pressed my cheek against the cold white tiles of the wall.

Round and round. Porte d'Orléans. Porte d'Orléans? Turning circles in the sea. Walking round the *stupa*, mindfully placing one foot in front of the other, counting my breaths. Round and round, circling the Old Building steps, under a banner that read, archly, BEWARE THE PEDAGOGIC GERONTOCRACY. Exactly the kind of thing non-students sneered at as *studenty*. It had taken only a few weeks at the LSE for that clever-clever tone to wear thin. Still, I knelt under that same banner to have my picture taken for the newspaper, along with all the other sitters-in, clever young people trying to look serious and committed and political, which would have been easier if they'd stopped grinning like chimps.

We were in occupation. Smile! Speak into the mike. 'It's not even about Adams *per se*, it's what he represents. In Rhodesia he did nothing. He didn't oppose the UDI, didn't speak out when they started to arrest his students. The administration paints a picture of him as oh-so-brave, keeping his mixed college open while the Fascist, racist regime was consolidating power. But what's that? Just collusion, as far as we're concerned. Now he's foisted on us as LSE director and we're supposed to accept it without question.' It was freezing at night. None of us was prepared for a sit-in. No sleeping-bags, no food. They locked the doors open, hoping that would be enough to get rid of us. A lot of people did slope off home.

There are moments from those eight days of occupation that stand out, images that over time have become unmoored from their context, floating free in my memory. Rolling a joint and passing it round with three friends as we sat by an open upstairs window, listening to a police inspector barking orders through a megaphone. Two students from my year busking folk songs and rattling a tin. I had sex with a girl called Tricia in the toilets of the administration building. She wasn't anything to do with the university, just one of the people who'd appeared out of the woodwork, attracted by the spark of possibility flitting temporarily around our stuffy college. There were mysterious middle-aged men with flasks of tea and sheaves of self-printed leaflets, feral-looking hippies, delinquent teens, raggedy thirties Marxists looking to warm their hands at the revolutionary fire.

You could make something out, dimly, through the blizzard of opinion that seemed to surround even the simplest question of right and wrong: change, the sense that everything was in play, all verities suspended. We were getting telegrams from the CGT union in Barcelona, from Bertrand Russell. We were a sign of something, the canaries in the capitalist coal mine, the Vanguard. We issued self-important statements: 'WE HAVE CHALLENGED AND CONTINUE TO CHALLENGE THE WAY IN WHICH LSE SERVES THE NEEDS OF THE RULING CLASS IN PROVIDING THE RIGHT MANPOWER, STRONGER IDEOLOGY AND RESEARCH THAT MAKES EXPLOITATION AND OPPRESSION OF THE WORKING CLASSES MORE EFFICIENT.' Early one morning we broke into the administration building, barging past the night-porter when he opened the door. We milled around in the corridor outside the director's office, built barricades of chairs and desks and metal shelving, scribbled on the backs of notices, trying to formulate a statement for the press. I slept for a few hours, curled up with Tricia on the floor by a radiator. After a while I felt her get up. 'Got to go toilet,' she said. 'Go toilet', like a child. She never came back. A week or two after the occupation I started to itch and went to visit the doctor, who gave a short speech about living in an era of moral confusion and used Latin to tell me I had crabs. Pacing up and down in my room, slathered in white cream from knee to chest, I read a letter from the university authorities saying that as a result of my participation in the sit-in I would be fined, but no further action would be taken.

Round and round. Did I agree with the written record of my personal effects? The deputy governor's Home Counties voice was crisp with authority regularly exercised and obeyed. Club tie, thick plastic-rimmed glasses, pompous donkey-face made longer by its mutton-chop sideburns. Beside him, shuffling papers and glowering at me, sat the stern, crop-haired chaplain in the role of the Church Militant. The welfare officer was asleep, from the look of him, hunched over his notes like a great black beetle. He didn't move at all during the interview, presenting me with his balding crown, a featureless pink oval that I gradually came to think of as his face.

Yes, I said. I agreed with the written record of my personal effects.

The chaplain said he believed I was Church of England, and looked forward to seeing me in chapel. I'd derive much sustenance from attending services. The deputy governor wanted me to take the opportunity to ask myself some hard questions. I was an educated fellow. He hoped I'd come to see that my posture of rebellion was essentially immature. We were living in changing times, which made it all the more regrettable that certain irresponsible social elements were leading some of our best and brightest to squander their advantages, advantages most of the young lads in this place would give their eye teeth for. Watching one hand seamlessly over to the other, I started, for the first time since my trial, to recover myself. God-man and state-man, working in concert, indistinguishable in their pose of bland benevolence. When I moved I could feel the bruises from the previous day's beating. Fuck you, I thought. Fuck you and your polite, civilized tone. Fuck your unearned air of authority, your smug talk about advantages, as if the world is some kind of game you're refereeing.

Round and round. Miles's question. What would freedom look like? That first university summer, instead of going home, I'd crashed on the sofa of a friend's house in Muswell Hill. I found a temporary job at a small factory in Archway, which made control panels for industrial equipment. I had to sit at a bench, screwing glass dial-facings and Bakelite knobs to anodized aluminium plates.

It was easy enough work, and well paid. After a month I had enough money to travel, and set off for Europe. It was my first time abroad. I sat on the ferry's rear deck, watching the coast of England recede behind me. In Ostend I showed my brand new passport to a smiling immigration official, who waved me through into Belgium with such warmth that I felt I'd been given the keys to the kingdom. Soon I was on a sleeper train heading south. I lay awake for hours in my upper berth, listening to the whistles and slamming doors of night-time stations, the laboured breathing of the middle-aged Dutch businessman in the bunk below.

I spent a month and a half sleeping in youth hostels or on station platforms, making fleeting alliances with other travellers to share a ride or a meal or an evening in a bar. I went to sleep in one country and was woken up by the border police of the next, fumbling blearily for my documents as another unfamiliar land-scape took shape through the window. I wanted to travel far and fast and rarely stayed anywhere for longer than a night, passing through Berlin, Vienna and Rome without really seeing them. When I arrived in a new place there was always a moment of choice, of having to find something to do with myself. I had very little money. I saw a lot of parks. I was most content listening to wheels on a track, the sound that confirmed I was going further on, further out. Finally I found myself swimming off a beach on a rocky Greek island, turning circles in the water, my world reduced to a dazzle of white light. If someone were to ask me when and where I was happiest, I'd describe that afternoon swim.

Circle the yard then back up to the threes, walkways above and below, a palimpsest of girders and wire netting. My cell had a single grilled window high up on the wall, made of little four-inch panes of muddy glass. Sit, stare, eat slops from a pressed metal tray. Nine thirty sharp, lights out. Bad dreams on a narrow bed, cut through by the reveille bell. The best moment of the day was the first step on to the landing, where there was light and space, a distance on which to fix your eyes. At morning employment we sat, elbow to elbow, in a low-roofed atelier, dismantling old electrical equipment.

Radios, televisions. It was like being in the back of Parker's, with my dad. Once we were given a pile of Second World War gas-masks and spent a couple of days unscrewing the filters, cutting the glass eye-panels away from the rubber. I never found out what happened to the parts we salvaged. I suspect they were just thrown away.

Lunch in the cell. Three slops in the moulded metal tray and a cup of stewed tea. Afterwards, locked in. For an hour or two after a meal, the sharp tang of boiled cabbage hung over the wing. Once every few days a trusty pushed a library cart along the landings. Usually it had nothing on it but religious tracts or textbooks, but for a while I lived with a tattered old copy of *The Scarlet Pimpernel*, its green cloth binding shiny with years of use. I'd never liked fiction, never seen the point in something that wasn't real; Baroness Orczy's class-ridden Paris did nothing to change that. Her heroes were blameless gentry and the common people were 'human only in name, for to the eye and ear they seemed naught but savage creatures, animated by vile passions and by the lust of vengeance and of hate'. Disgusted, I started to imagine another book, the mirror-image of the one I was reading, peopled by greedy, vicious aristocrats and starving *sans-culottes* dreaming of a better world.

Harris, the man who sat beside me in the dismantling shop, liked to gossip. Who owed money or cigarettes. Who'd got a new radio or a rug in their cell. After the first few days I stopped listening, but the details of Harris's life had got in by osmosis, the wife who was definitely waiting but hadn't visited for the last three months, the mate who was going to give him a job when he got out. He kept offering me things – cigarettes, girlie mags, once a pair of shoes he said he didn't want. I always refused, though I was tempted by the shoes. My prison-issue boots were moulded to the shape of their previous owner's feet, the heels worn down in a way that forced me to walk with a strange pigeon-toed roll.

After a couple of weeks I was transferred to cleaning duty, scrubbing floors, mopping spilled tea and soup off staircases and landings. After the dismantling shop it felt liberating, even luxurious. Pushing a mop my mind could leave my body. I barely heard the screws shouting at me when I dawdled. Round and round. I rocked back and forth on my worn heels and dreamed of the island, of turning in the water, the horizon stretching away from me in an infinity of blue.

One night, in a room above a noisy taverna, I'd counted my money and realized I had barely enough to get back to England. I would have to leave the next day, or the day after. Three nights later I ate a dinner of dolmades and grilled fish and drank a bottle of red wine and three glasses of ouzo and decided to stay for good. What did I have in England? I'd get one of the crumbling little houses by the harbour and do it up. I'd learn to fish. I tried to talk to the taverna-owner about it as he played dominoes with his friends at a back table. I was drunker than I thought. Angry with me for interrupting his game and unable to understand what I was saying, he waved me away. I insisted, grabbing his shoulder and babbling about fish and houses and a local girl I'd spotted outside the church. Eventually a couple of the players pushed me outside. Like a fool, I tried to fight them. Bruised and hung-over, I left the island the next morning.

On the overnight train trip from Bari to Milan I was joined in my compartment by a man in a well-cut suit, who said he was from Rimini and worked in local government. We talked for a while, mostly about football. His English was stilted, but he knew the names of all the current Spurs squad, reciting them one by one, as if telling a rosary. He rummaged in his bag and pulled out a bottle of a nasty-looking orange drink. I sipped some, just to be polite. 'Please, take more,' he said, smiling. 'Please.' The next thing I knew, it was daylight, I was alone, and the train was pulling into a siding. The carriage was stiflingly hot. I stumbled out into the corridor and came face to face with a cleaner, who gesticulated and shouted at me in Italian. The train was completely empty. Sick and disoriented, I had to walk down the tracks back to the station. Only when I tried to buy a ticket for my next journey did I realize my camera had gone, along with the small amount of cash I had left in my money-belt.

I ended up begging from a middle-aged English couple who were sitting at the station café. The wife believed my story. The husband patently thought I was a liar, but handed over enough money for a ticket to Calais, along with their address, 'In case,' as he told me drily, 'you intend to do the decent thing.' At Calais I had to beg again and this time wasn't so lucky. I hung around in the ferry terminal for hours, approaching every likely-looking person. *Are you English? Sorry to bother you*. Eventually I was arrested. At the *gendarmerie* they checked my documents, searched me and let me go again. By that time I hadn't eaten for two days.

I was saved by a middle-aged homosexual who stood me a beer and a sandwich in the terminal café. Wretchedly I told him my story, and to my surprise he bought me a ferry ticket. On the crossing he fussed over me, treating me to more drinks and food. He had a racing green MG parked at Dover and I gratefully accepted a lift to London. Eventually we drew up outside a mews house in Chelsea and he said, enunciating pointedly, that he thought we should have a little *cock*tail together. I let him unload my pack from the boot, then staggered away down the street, while he tugged at my sleeve and swore at me in a sort of stage-whisper so as not to wake the neighbours. I walked all the way to Muswell Hill and, after emptying my friend Alan's fridge, lay down on his sofa and slept twenty straight hours, waking up with a start in the middle of the night in the deluded belief that I was still on a train.

Round and round. The rhythm of wheels on a track. With about twenty hours of solitude a day, I had plenty of time to think in prison. If Pentonville was a factory, what would it make? If it was a machine, what was it designed to do? I spent hours running through my memories. I thought about when I'd been happy and unhappy, the times when I'd been closest to feeling there was a future. The more I thought, the clearer the moral landscape appeared. There seemed to be two worlds. One was basic and sensual, a human-scale place of small tasks and pleasures, building things and eating good food, lying in the sun, making love. In this world, human relations were very simple. The desire to dominate, to own and to control, just didn't arise. The other world, the world of Law and War and Institutions, was a strange and abstract place. In this mirror-world I was a violent person and had to be punished because violence was a monopoly of the state. I'd somehow authorized the British government to distribute violence on my behalf, which it did through various branches of officialdom – the army, the police, the Pentonville screws. The problem was that I couldn't remember giving my consent. What paper had I signed? Where had I said I wished to regulate my habits and govern my sexual behaviour and strive for advancement in various abstract games whose terms had been set before I was born? The state claimed it was an expression of the democratic will of the people. But what if it wasn't? What if it was just a parasite, a vampire sustaining itself on our collective life, on my life in particular?

* * *

I was released in the last week of April 1968. No one was there to meet me. I was relieved not to see Dad or Brian, whose single visit had been as bad as anything else that had happened to me in prison, but I'd hoped some of my Vietnam Action Group friends would be at the gate. So much, I thought, for solidarity. But I'd had a short letter from Alan in Muswell Hill, saying he was storing my stuff and I should go over there when I got out, so that was where I headed.

I bought a paper from a newsagent and read it as I waited for the bus. I found it hard to concentrate on the news. It felt too good to be wearing my own clothes, my own shoes, standing on the Caledonian Road looking at rows of houses blackened with grime from the railway yards. Beautiful pigeons, beautiful old man in his vest, smoking a fag and watching the beautiful street from an upstairs window.

Back at the Muswell Hill house Alan shook my hand and asked how I was. I didn't know what to say, so I told him I was OK. We drank tea, standing in the overgrown garden, where one of his housemates was storing a partially dismantled scooter. I expected Alan to be curious about prison, but he didn't ask any questions at all. He seemed fidgety and distracted. 'They've suspended you,' he told me. If I wanted to continue at university I'd have to begin my second year again in the autumn. I asked him what was being done. Were any of the activist groups at the LSE going to support me? He looked uncomfortable and wouldn't meet my eye. 'The thing is, you were convicted of a crime. That doesn't make it very easy, politically.'

I took in this unwelcome information as he told me his news, which consisted of gossip about various LSE factions, who'd slept with whose girlfriend, who'd taken what line on the Powellite dockers' march. As he chattered, I realized he hadn't the slightest conception of what had happened to me. As soon as I'd disappeared into the police van, he'd more or less forgotten my existence. The last straw was his announcement that he'd 'something rather delicate to discuss'. His housemates had told him they'd rather I didn't stay there. They were worried about police attention, didn't want to jeopardize their degrees. He was sorry. Naturally he'd argued, but it was a democratic household. He'd been outvoted.

I couldn't believe my ears. My so-called comrades were washing their hands of me, self-proclaimed revolutionaries so timid that at the first sign of trouble they were running away. Without raising my voice I told Alan he was a coward, a middle-class fraud. He'd been with me on that demo: it could have been him who'd got arrested. I'd just spent a month in jail, I had about ten bob in my pocket and he wasn't even going to let me kip on his couch? He mumbled something about there being hash in the house. But did I need money? My lip curled. Money, of course. The bourgeois solution. I extended my hand. He couldn't get his wallet out fast enough.

I took the bus into town and went to a steak house just off Leicester Square, where I ordered all the most expensive things on the menu and drank a bottle of red wine. The waiters looked at me uneasily until I actually waved a banknote at them. From a phone booth outside I rang a girl I knew called Vicky, who lived in her parents' basement in Holland Park. Yes, she said, I could stay with her.

I took a taxi, giving the driver a tip to get rid of the last of Alan's cash. Vicky seemed excited to see me. Her place was impressive, a self-contained garden flat on a winding side-street of elegant Victorian houses. I found out later that her father was on the board of a mining company with interests in southern Africa. She was riddled with guilt about where her money came from and did all she could to antagonize her family while still living under their roof. I was part of that strategy.

We talked and smoked a joint and she asked all the questions about prison I'd expected from Alan. I told her a little of what had happened, in a series of rambling and elliptical answers, which she broke short by taking me to bed. Later I lay awake and listened to her breathing. We didn't know each other well and I'd gone round there for the most cynical reasons: I knew she liked me; I knew she had her own place. Still, it felt good to lie beside her in the darkness, even if I couldn't sleep.

I stayed at Vicky's for a week or so, smoking her dope and playing her LPs. She had a job volunteering with a playgroup on Portobello Road and left me alone during the day. I spent my time lying on her floor looking at the patterns the light made as it filtered through the branches of the monkey-puzzle tree in the garden. If Vicky minded my lethargy, she didn't show it. I think she could see how low I was feeling. I only left the flat to go walking in Holland Park, long, aimless afternoon meanderings through the formal gardens, during which I looked at my feet and kept as far away from other people as possible. Elsewhere, Parisians were building barricades. I wandered around and listened to music and ignored the washing-up. At the weekend Vicky told me she was driving to the country and asked if I wanted to come. I said no. Alone in her flat, I spent a day and night completely motionless in a chair, not thinking about anything in particular, just cradling myself inside a sort of glacial depression. I felt as if I was mummified, living inside some kind of membrane that formed a final and definitive barrier to human contact. The bright light outside was a mockery: energy radiating across the whole world, none of it for me.

* * *

I knew Miles wouldn't leave me alone. Two days after I'd seen him at the Market Cross, I answered the phone in the kitchen. I'd been filling the dishwasher, while Miranda sat at the table flicking through a gardening catalogue. 'Hello, Chris,' said the voice at the other end. Reflexively, I hung up.

'Who was that?' asked Miranda.

'Wrong number.'

The phone rang again. I stood there, paralysed.

'Aren't you going to answer it?'

I picked up. I had no choice.

'Listen to me, Chris,' said the voice. I assumed it was Miles. It didn't sound like him.

'I think you have the wrong number.'

'Don't be stupid about this.'

'I told you, you have the wrong number. Don't call here again.'

I slammed the phone down, trying to master the tide of adrenalin rising through my body.

'Who were you talking to?'

'Just some guy. He thinks this is his friend's place. He sounds strange.'

'You were very aggressive with him.'

I shrugged noncommittally. Again, the phone rang. Miranda got up to answer it. 'Don't,' I told her sharply. She put up her hands in mock-surrender. The phone carried on ringing. After a while it clicked through to the answering-machine.

'This is a message for Chris,' said the voice. 'Listen, mate, don't piss about. You need to phone me. For your own good, you should phone me.' He left a mobile number.

'You'd think people would actually listen to the message,' said Miranda, vaguely. 'It says quite clearly "Miranda and Michael Frame".'

My throat was dry. I poured a glass of water from the filter jug. 'Yes,' I said. 'You'd think they would.'

After Miranda went to bed, I slipped out and drove over to the shop. God wasn't there, so I was able to sit for a while in comforting darkness, huddling into my jacket and rubbing my hands as I waited for the gas-heater to cut through the cold. I was thinking seriously about leaving. How far would I get if I made a run? If I went straight to the airport, would I be able to board a plane?

I switched on the ancient Anglepoise on the desk and sifted listlessly through a pile of Left Book Club volumes. The dreams of the thirties and forties; Spain and the hunger marches. They were fragile objects, those books, their yellowing pages flaky and brittle, about ten years away from dust. Soon, as I knew I would, I found myself taking another look through the unsorted sixties and seventies box. I opened copies of *Socialist Worker* to read about Grunwick and Blair Peach, events I'd missed because I was in Thailand. Why had God even bought all that stuff? As far as I knew, he was an old-fashioned Tory. Englishman's home is his castle, the whole bit. I was about to put the box away when I found a copy of the *International Times*, which fell open to a collage of a jazz-age figure in a sweater and plus-fours operating a hand-cranked camera. The man's head had been replaced by a fist. Out of the camera lens spilled a cornucopia of bodies and flowers and abstract forms. Rifles and feathers and half-tone dots. Biafran children, Chairman Mao. I knew that image. It had been on a flyer someone had handed me on Portobello Road, the day I finally roused myself and walked out of Vicky's basement:

FREE PICTURES

No politics but the politics of experience!

Towards a revolutionary reconstruction of society.

Construct zones of liberation, counter-institutions, alternative systems of exchange.

Reject the bankrupt logic of submission and domination.

Saturday Free Pictures 21 Albany Square
London W11

Shoeless, I wandered down into Notting Hill. The streets were lined with decaying mansion houses, peeling and sooty, with rubbish piled up in their once-elegant porches. Here and there West Indian men sat out on the steps enjoying the weather, talking or slamming down dominoes. Gangs of wild children ran between the parked cars. On some streets, half the houses were empty, their boarded-up windows like sightless eyes. I sat in a pub for much of that afternoon, listening to the sounds of the street-market winding down outside. The public bar was populated by old boys who sat silently smoking and watching their pints fall inch by inch in their glasses. The fruit machine chirruped the fake promise of money. I was backing Britain. We were all backing Britain. The good times were coming our way. If I didn't leave immediately, I knew I'd end up another lost soul, my arse moistening the leatherette for ever.

Out in the world, it was getting late. The light had softened and the Portobello Road was carpeted with rotting vegetables. I wandered northwards, ignoring the people who called out at me or stared at my bare feet. In side-streets, music filtered out of upstairs windows and young white girls talked to black men in smart cars. In a quiet square I found myself outside a disused cinema, a shabby deco façade tacked on to a red-brick building that had probably once been a church meeting-hall. The doors were covered with sheets of corrugated iron and a sign warned of dire penalties for trespassers. From the pavement the place looked deserted. On the unlit marquee, the word FREE had been spelled out in red letters.

Clutching the flyer, I banged on the sheeting. There was no answer. I banged some more. Eventually, a voice on the other side asked who I was.

'My name's Chris,' I said. 'Is there a – a happening here?'

The person on the other side did something with bolts and padlocks. The door opened a crack and I stepped into a darkened foyer smelling of cigarettes and stale beer.

All I could see was a silhouette. Jacket. Curly hair sprouting from the sides of a peaked usher's cap. 'Who do you know?' he asked.

'No one, really. This is it, right? Free Pictures?'

He thought for a while, examined me. 'You'd better come in. Everyone's on the roof. Watch your step, there are holes. Also rats.'

Underfoot the carpet was sticky. The usher, who'd completed his outfit with army boots and what looked like an old-fashioned floral skirt, shambled ahead of me into the auditorium, a murky, crypt-like space. The air was tinged with damp. From the ceiling, just visible in the gloom, hung an unlit chandelier, an ominous mass festooned with cobwebs, like a prop from a horror movie. The electricity was obviously borrowed from elsewhere; just above head-height sagged runs of cable, looping round sconces, draped over the plaster cherubs on the little balcony. Here and there light fittings had been wired up, bare bulbs hanging down to brighten little circles of moth-eaten red plush. The usher took me behind the screen, where a narrow staircase led into a dusty gallery. From there we climbed a ladder out on to the flat roof.

In the afternoon sunlight, a young woman was reading from a typescript to a crowd of about thirty people, who lounged around on rugs and broken plush seats. She spoke with a seriousness accentuated by her extreme pallor and by her clothes, a shapeless man's sweater and a headscarf that dragged her hair severely back from her scalp. It was an appearance that suggested a punishing lack of self-regard. 'More,' she was saying, 'is not the issue. We

86

have more cars and fridges, more summer holidays in Fascist Spain. In fact, we have more of everything except life and freedom.' She spoke about the pressure to compete, how it was destroying basic social formations. Atomized workers were convenient for capital, free of attachments to each other, to place, even to time.

As she spoke it dawned on me gradually that I recognized her. Eventually I was certain she was the girl I'd seen throwing the stone at Grosvenor Square. She looked haunted, as if she hadn't slept for days. I thought she was beautiful. She sat down and was immediately succeeded by a guy with a messy Afro and a German accent, who told us it was no good to talk theoretically, or to make a politics on the basis of a theory – any theory whatsoever. That would just mean swapping one set of masters for another. It was time to throw everything up in the air, to live in a radically different way. Out of that would come a politics based on material conditions.

Someone handed me a joint. I found a place to sit where I could rest my back against the parapet wall and check out the girl, who was sitting with a group of friends, nervously jigging one foot up and down and smoking a cigarette. These people were wilder and more ragged-looking than student crowds, where you'd still see sports jackets, combed hair. Most political meetings I'd attended happened against a background of whispering and poorly masked boredom. This had a different atmosphere, intense and anxious. 'Freedom begins with the self,' called out a woman from the floor, and the freedom she was speaking about seemed to be present up there on the cinema roof, a fierce astringent energy, a flensing away of the past.

A man got to his feet and started stabbing a finger at the speakers. 'Bullshit!' he snarled. 'Total bullshit! Everything you said is stupid and naïve. You're fools if you imagine revolution is going to happen in the way you just described – like some kind of light-show. Blobs joining together to make bigger blobs? It's just crap!'

He was a menacing presence, piratically bearded, listing to star-board, a lit cigarette stuck to his bottom lip. From behind me someone called out to him not to be insulting. He turned round, spreading his arms. 'Why not? If you talk shit you deserve to be insulted. It's not about the self. The self is reactionary crap. It's about mass mobilization.' Someone else yelled out in agreement and suddenly the thing was a free-for-all. A bespectacled guy in a sort of shapeless smock was shouted down when he accused everyone else of being repressed. The ascetic young woman told the pirate his mass line was boring. The pirate told her to grow up. Revolution wasn't going to happen without someone seizing power. It was going to take struggle. It was going to be violent. The woman shook her head vehemently. She was opposed to all forms of violence. It made no sense to her to employ violence to end violence. The pirate, unusually for a pirate, quoted Mao: 'We are advocates of the abolition of war, we do not want war. But war can only be abolished through war, and in order to get rid of the gun, it is necessary to take up the gun.' There were cheers. He seemed exasperated. 'Just use your heads!' he spat. 'As soon as the workers' state becomes even a distant possibility, they'll try to crush it. What do you imagine? That they'll let your amorphous liberated blobs incorporate factories and army barracks?'

The ascetic woman called him a casuist. 'Get back in the kitchen!' shouted a male voice. 'Leave the revolution to people who understand politics!' That caused a proper row. An avenger threw some sort of liquid over the misogynist, a skinny, shirtless boy who had to be restrained from throwing punches. The fight disturbed the transvestite usher, who disappeared downstairs. Meanwhile the verbal tanks rolled back and forth. Look at the Soviet Union. But that's not Communism. Immediate union with the working class! War on the nuclear family! Gradually the light failed and people started to slip off, as the hard core wrapped themselves in coats and blankets against the chill.

Seize power, abolish power. Which did I want? I spoke only once, to make some kind of call for immediate action. I don't remember what I said, just what I felt as I said it. There was an energy up on that roof, an urgency I didn't understand at the time.

* * *

At God's desk I fell asleep for an hour or two and dreamed Anna Addison was standing by a window, looking at me. I woke up in freezing darkness and stumbled around disoriented until I remembered where I was. I locked up the shop and drove home in a bizarrely altered state, dazzled by sleet and memory and oncoming headlights. I undressed in the bathroom and crept into bed beside Miranda, who grumbled and shifted over, her naked side hot as a ham against my hand.

The next morning I got up late. Miranda had already left for work. I made myself breakfast and ate it standing up, staring out of the kitchen window. I went for a long walk, which didn't solve anything. I didn't call the number on the answering-machine.

The day after that, Sam came home from university. I picked her up from the station and was almost overcome by her breezy hug. My eyes watery, I told her I loved her and she patted me complacently on the knee, already deep into a story about someone called Susanna, who had an orange Beetle and wanted to take her horse-riding in Wales. The girl with the neat row of teddies waiting on her bed had acquired a nose-stud and a noticeably different accent, a layer of London posh sprinkled over her ordinary voice. She was, she said, a bit disappointed with law. She was thinking of switching to psychology. It was all too much to absorb at once, this sudden fluidity, these changes. She seemed so happy. I was so happy for her.

I dropped her at home and while she unpacked I went out to buy something for lunch. When I got back, I heard voices in the kitchen.

'Hello, Dad. I've been hearing *all* about *you*.'

I froze in the doorway. It took me a moment to assemble the

scene. Miles at the kitchen table, his black coat draped over the chair-back, a mug of coffee in his hands. He smirked and raised an eyebrow. 'Hi, Mike,' he said, emphasizing the name slightly, just enough so I'd pick up on it. 'I came by on the off-chance.'

'I see.'

Sam laughed. 'Miles says he knew you in the old days. He says you weren't always such a goody-goody.'

'Is that what he says?'

Her tone wouldn't have been so light if he'd told her anything serious. I put the shopping down. They were, I saw, both smoking cigarettes. I lit one too. Miles sat back in his chair, enjoying himself. Sam adopted a conspiratorial tone. 'Miles says you got arrested together. Protesting against the war, *man!*' She made a peace sign at me, giggling.

'What else does he say?'

'Oh, don't worry,' drawled Miles. 'I haven't been telling her about the really naughty stuff.' Sam's grin faltered a little when she saw the look on my face. Miles distracted her by telling a tall story about how he and I had supposedly spent an evening with the Rolling Stones. His anecdote had a rehearsed quality. It was, at least as far as my involvement in it was concerned, a complete fabrication. Miles evidently assumed Sam would be impressed by the mention of the Stones, but she listened with a polite, slightly puzzled expression. It was possible she didn't know who they were.

How was I going to get him out of my house? I asked whether he'd like to go for a walk. 'Pub?' he suggested, then theatrically corrected himself. 'Oh, yes, I forgot. You don't drink.'

'We could go to the pub if you like,' I told him. His smile broadened. He knew I was begging. 'It's a bit cold out,' he said, warming his hands on his coffee cup. 'Much more cosy in here.'

Just then I heard the sound of the key in the front door. Miranda smelled the smoke before she even entered the room. 'What on earth are you doing?' she asked me angrily, flinging open the back door and letting in a blast of icy air. Then she noticed Sam and Miles. 'Hello, darling. And – hello.'

Miles got up from his seat. 'Miles Bridgeman. Old friend of Mike's.'

'Miranda Martin.'

They shook hands and she turned to me in genuine surprise. 'You didn't say you had anyone – I mean –'

Sam stood up and embraced her. 'Hello, Mum.'

'Hello, darling. You stink of cigarettes.'

'That's a nice welcome.'

'Well, you do. It's disgusting. I'm sorry, Mr Bridgeman. I don't like smoking in the house.'

'I'm so sorry. Mike, you should have told me. Now I've gone and embarrassed myself. And please, Miranda, call me Miles.'

'Of course. I'm sorry – were we, I mean – I was – was Mike expecting you? I didn't know. He never tells me anything.'

Miles adopted a raffish expression. 'No, I think I came as a surprise. You know, we haven't seen each other for years. I was visiting friends near here and thought I'd look him up. You have a beautiful house, by the way. I love what you've done to this kitchen So real. What gorgeous flooring. Is it slate?'

'Yes. Welsh slate.'

'Beautiful colours.'

'Exactly'

Soon Miles was asking her about the old glass medicine bottles and the bunches of herbs drying over the hearth, demonstrating a suspiciously perfect knowledge of the properties of lemon verbena. Miranda chattered to him, so taken with my charming friend that before I knew it she'd invited him to stay for dinner. I sat at the table while she cooked a risotto, and he bared his teeth without mirth, toasting me ironically with his glass of elderflower cordial. 'Next time,' he said, 'I'll bring a bottle.'

'So what kind of work do you do, Miles?' asked Miranda, as we sat down to eat.

'Consultancy.'

'What kind?'

'Public affairs. I spend a lot of time at Westminster, doing strategy work for various people, generally oiling the wheels of democracy.'

'Sounds exciting.'

'It's very dull.'

'So are you Labour or Tory?' asked Sam.

'Neither. I'm my own man. I like to think of myself as a progressive.'

His own man. Whatever Miles was it wasn't that. Miles Bridgeman would always be someone's creature. To Sam and Miranda's delight, he told more anecdotes about our supposed exploits back in the old days, slaloming in and out of the truth, adding deft little touches, hidden allusions, subtle reminders to me of all the other things he wasn't telling. I was completely powerless, as removed from the situation as an accident victim, floating above the scene, looking down.

He made a few slip-ups, such as telling Miranda we'd known each other at university. Unlike Chris Carver, Michael Frame hadn't gone to university. I improvised. 'I was only there for that one term, remember? Then I dropped out.' He was quick to take the hint and I had the disturbing sense that we were now colluding with one another, jointly spinning a yarn. It was a story tailored to its audience, a confection of swinging London and San Francisco flower-power, as phoney as one of those television nostalgia shows where they soundtrack archive footage with old Top 40 hits. Miranda and Sam lapped it up.

'It's so great you came, Miles,' said Miranda. 'Mike never talks about any of this. I had no idea he was so involved in that sixties milieu.' She made it sound remote, historical. Waterloo or the Armada. Miranda's youth was all punk bands and cider, or whatever they had to drink in Hendon. Sam's primary reference point was probably Austin Powers. 'You know, Mike doesn't have any photos from back then,' mused Miranda. 'He barely mentions it at all. He's so unsentimental. Actually, I think you're the first person I've met . . .' She trailed off.

I knew exactly what she was thinking. Miles was the first person she'd *ever* met who'd known me for longer than she had. I could see the starkness of it clouding her mind, an oddity about her life that she hadn't noticed before.

'So you haven't kept in touch with the old gang?' Miles asked me sweetly. I shook my head. 'Not even Anna and Sean?'

'Who are Anna and Sean?' asked Sam.

My mouth was dry. Miles left me on the hook for a while, cocking his head to one side and examining me with a vaguely scientific air. Then he answered himself: 'Just a couple we knew. Although – weren't you and Anna, you know? Didn't you have a thing for a while?'

Now Miranda and Sam were all ears.

'She was your girlfriend?'

'You've never spoken about any Anna.'

Sam smelled gossip. 'What was she like?'

'Go on,' says Miles. 'Tell her.'

'She wasn't my girlfriend. I haven't heard anything about either of them.'

Sam frowned at me.

Miles rubbed his chin. 'Shame,' he said.

Miranda was frustrated. 'I don't know why you're being so tight-lipped, Mike. I'm not going to be jealous of some lover you had thirty years ago. It's part of *you*.' She patted my hand, made big eyes. How hungry she was for this. How I'd starved her.

'Did you go travelling together?' she asked peevishly, when it became clear I wasn't going to say anything voluntarily.

'No. We last saw each other just before I left.'

Miles served himself another scoop of ice cream. 'So where did you go, Mike? India, was it? You never told me at the time.'

'I was in India for a while. I went overland through Asia. I spent several years in Thailand.'

'How very interesting. Bangkok?'

'For a while.'

Miranda cued up her favourite line. 'Mike was in a monastery.'

Miles looked wry. 'Really, Mike? That surprises me.'

'Why?' asked Miranda.

'Well, he was never really into the spiritual side of things. He was more of a political animal. So you became a Buddhist, Mike?'

'Yes.'

'And you're still a Buddhist?'

'No – at least, not in any meaningful way.'

'But you don't eat meat.'

'Neither of us does,' said Miranda.

'Simplicity. Non-violence. I admire you.' Again that predatory grin.

It dragged on for hours, but at last Miles looked at his watch and decided it was over. He had, he said, a long drive back to London. He ought to get going. Miranda hugged him and gave him some samples of the new Bountessence men's line. Sam kissed him on the cheek. He handed me a card. 'In case you lost the last one,' he said. I walked him to his car, which was parked on the street outside.

'So, you'll come and see me.'

I nodded, defeated. 'When?'

'I'll let you know. I'll phone you. Don't let me down, Chris. You won't let me down, will you?'

No, I said, I wouldn't let him down.

'You're such a dark horse,' murmured Miranda, as we lay in bed. She snuggled closer to me, eager to explore our new intimacy. Thankfully she wasn't confident enough to say Anna's name.

* * *

Round and round. The sky's getting lighter. I'm experiencing
momentary drop-outs, instants when my mind is completely blank.
When I finally turn off the *périphérique* I have a near-miss as
someone unexpectedly pulls out in front of me. Overreacting, I
jerk the wheel and scrape the near-side wing against the crash-
barrier. That's it. No more. I need to sleep, or at least close my
eyes. I think I'm on the right route now, somewhere in the south-
eastern sprawl of the Paris suburbs, heading out of the city. I pull
into a lay-by, where I piss into a dark corner, broken glass crunching
under my feet. Leaning out of the passenger door, I splash my face
with bottled water, recline the car seat as far back as it will go and
lie down. For a while, headlights continue to pass behind my eyelids.
Then they stop.

I'm woken by a gloved hand tapping on the window. Daylight.
A pair of policemen are peering at me through the steamed-up
glass. I sit up with a jolt and open the door, rubbing my eyes.
There's a certain amount of confusion, but the general gist is that
they want to see my passport. I dig through my luggage, wondering
if they're going to arrest me. Perhaps I'm on some kind of list. As
they check my details, I get out and look around at the desolate
place where I've spent the night. Above me looms a row of huge
housing blocks, slabs of seventies concrete faced with cheerless
primary-coloured panels. The lay-by is a dumping ground for HGV
tyres and building waste. The policemen ask me to walk up and
down, checking, I think, to see if I'm drunk. I see a row of long
black scratches on the car's paintwork where I hit the barrier. So
do they, but finally they let me go, repeating the word *hôtel*, clearly
and patiently, as one would to a child.

I drive away, checking in the rear-view mirror to see if they're following me. A few kilometres down the road I stop at a service station to fill the tank. In the brightly lit café I drink a coffee and eat some kind of plastic-wrapped pastry, all sugar and synthetic apple jam. I watch a truck driver flicking through a selection of pornography at the news concession, carefully making his choice. The sugar gives me a rush of clarity. Out of habit, I just paid for the petrol with my credit card. I'm angry with myself. So stupid, leaving a trail.

Does it really matter? Perhaps not. They're going to find me, however careful I am. I have no resources. My choices are limited. I want to speak to Anna before they catch up with me. I want to hear how it was for her. I want her to say my name. After that, they can do what they like.

I take a swig of bottled water, start the engine, and swing back out on to the road. Round and round.

As that first afternoon at Free Pictures turned into evening, people started to drift off to their next destinations and the usher was kept busy climbing up and down the ladder to let them out. The girl who threw the stone left with a black man in a leather jacket. I would have followed her, but I was reluctant to leave the roof, knowing that as soon as I stepped on to the street I'd be back on my own, in depressive limbo. The pirate who'd argued with the other speakers also seemed annoyed to see her go. Sprawled next to me, apparently exhausted, he swore under his breath, then propped himself up on his elbows and announced that he was hungry. I said I was too. 'So,' he suggested, 'let's go get something to eat.'

Even now it's hard to talk about Sean Ward without romanticizing him. He was a handsome bastard, with a fine, rather delicate jaw-line he hid with a full beard, a crooked nose, wavy dark hair and heavy-lidded brown eyes. His looks were the first thing everyone noticed about him and he knew what to do with them. Red Sean, fucker of the unfuckable, charmer of the barmaid and the arresting officer. To those who just remember him in the early days, or who take their history from some of the frothier journalism about Anna, the romance is all that survives. I'm almost invisible in those books, a bearded oval in a couple of fuzzy group photos. Sean is omnipresent – but somehow simplified, bleached out into some kind of revolutionary rock star. The pictures (of which there are surprisingly few) tend to show him with rock-star accoutrements, dark glasses, his battered biker jacket. There he is, smoking a cigarette, throwing an arm casually over Anna's shoulders. There he is, standing on a hillside in Wales, waving a huge flag. As far as the world's concerned (if it's concerned at all any more), he's just a footnote to Anna's story, and since she's been so distorted, it's as if the real Sean, the Sean who was paranoid and generous and self-denying and confrontational and just vain enough to have liked those rock-star photos, has almost vanished behind a haze of Byronic bullshit.

The other cardboard cut-out of Sean is, of course, the social deviant, a member of the criminal classes led astray by a superficial engagement with politics. The stories about his hard knock upbringing aren't exaggerated. He was from a sprawling London-Irish clan that had disintegrated when he was a kid, spitting him into a series of foster-homes from which he ran away, then borstal, from which he couldn't. He'd stolen a car, or rather many cars, but the one they got him for was a Jag he drove into a lamp-post during some kind of police chase, aged fifteen. Even when I knew him, he had a thing about fast cars, the more expensive the better. I think there was an element of revenge, of abusing rich men's toys. Yes, he had no education in the traditional sense, except what he'd given himself. Yes, he was impatient with theorizing, but it was an earned impatience, one I came to share. When I first met him at Free Pictures, all he wanted to talk about was books. It still makes me angry to see him painted as some kind of noble savage, a thug who didn't know what he was doing.

Sean had drifted around. He'd done part of a plumbing apprenticeship, which he gave up, he told me, when he realized he wasn't prepared to spend his life sticking his hand into other people's toilets. At one point he'd thought of joining the army. By the time I met him, he'd been in Notting Hill for a couple of years, making a living in a variety of ways – a little carpentry, a little hash-dealing, delivering furniture in Rosa, a ten-year-old combi-van he'd painted a sickly shade of flesh-pink. In search of food, he led me through the frosted-glass door of a café on the All Saints Road. 'Hello, Gloria,' he said cheerfully, striding up to the counter and grinning at the stout black woman behind it. I followed him gingerly, feeling as if I'd stepped into the saloon-bar scene in a western. Men in work clothes or suits and skinny-brim hats were hunched over the Formica tables, narrowing their eyes and kissing their teeth at us. The hostility was almost palpable.

'You have to go eat it at home,' Gloria told us. 'We very busy tonight.'

'It's all right, Gloria darling,' wheedled Sean. 'We can just take it upstairs.'

She shook her head. 'It's Saturday night. You go upstairs it always upsets some people. I won't have it, not on a Saturday.'

'But –'

'Not on a Saturday. Anyway, how I know your friend been brought up to mind his business? You tell me that.'

Sean put on a particularly winning smile. 'It's all right. He's not about to cause any aggravation.' Gloria shook her head definitively. We ordered and hung around, waiting for her to finish shouting at whoever was doing the cooking. Her customers went back to their suppers. At the time I was confused by their resentment. I was, as I thought of it, 'on their side'. Having said that, I still remember my shamefully instinctive recoil, my little moment of panic at the sight of all those black faces staring at me.

Gloria started wrapping up our food, but Sean kept hassling her to let us join in with whatever was happening upstairs. It looked as if she was about to relent until she noticed my bare and by now rather dirty feet. After that it was definitely no dice. Sean was told never to bring such a filthy good-for-nothing (her word) into her establishment (also her word) again. We took our supper and left in a hurry, me rattled, Sean laughing. A month or so later we were finally allowed upstairs, though not on a Saturday night, and I caught a glimpse of another of London's many undergrounds, Gloria's miniature shebeen, where in her packed living room grizzled old men bet on cards and young ones smoked reefer out of the window, a scene of minor debauchery acted out to the terrible Jim Reeves records she played on her old Dansette.

We took our goat curry back to Vicky's flat. On the way, Sean stopped off at a house under the shadow of the half-built flyover, rang the bell and in a brief transaction conducted through a barely cracked front door took possession of a bottle of Wray & Nephew's rum and a quarter of powerful-smelling weed. After we'd eaten I lounged around on the rug as Sean unsuccessfully mined Vicky's record collection for rock music. Within an hour or so we were back on the road, several shots into our game and walking with a swagger that, while not yet a stagger, was already showing transitional signs. Just after eleven Sean handed me a tiny barrel-shaped tablet and some time around midnight I came up on my first ever acid trip.

We were back in the flat and I was telling Sean how pathetic it was to be grateful for gammon and boiled potatoes, when I noticed the paint was starting to peel off the wall behind his head. Gammon and potatoes was what Vicky could cook – and had – three times in the previous week. It was better than the food in prison, though that wasn't saying much. At that point in my life it wouldn't have occurred to me to make a meal for myself when there was a woman around to do it, and I was presenting myself to Sean as a sailor on the culinary seas of fate, doomed to wander oceans of blandness until I came upon the 'islands of curried goat', a phrase I found unaccountably entertaining – and odd, if I was honest, part of a general sharpening of words and things that I'd just begun to notice. Sean grinned, looking at me with an inscrutable glint in his eye. The paint really was coming off, whole patches of it cracking and bubbling, giving the wall a scaly appearance disturbingly suggestive of giant reptilian life. The light in the room, and now I came to think of it *everything else*, my entire evening, seemed to have been refracted through some sort of transforming prism, every object in my field of vision revealing itself with startling exactness, not just visually but *in itself*, a sort of ontological clarity that led me to look around and think, Yes, *this* table, *this* rug, which I'm stroking with my fingertips. I had a sudden sense of the incredible connectedness of things and soon afterwards my environment transformed itself into something rich and radically strange.

Other people's acid stories are always dull, I know. *And then I thought, What if we're all just grains of sand and each grain of sand* and so on and so forth. But that trip with Sean accelerated something. Afterwards we were close friends, as if we'd known each other for ever. It was as if we'd skipped a bit, leaped over a whole period of time.

My memories of the middle section of that night are fragmented. I've no sense of the order of things, just a series of random snapshots. Sean dancing dreamily in the back garden, Sean as professor of the Faculty of Better Living, explaining the future with the aid of a diagram drawn on the bubbling white wall. During a period in which I seemed to be naked, apart from some of Vicky's costume jewellery, I spent a long time looking in her bedroom mirror. How many eyes? Was I sure? Sean brooded in an armchair, his skin an unhealthy yellow.

The light was harsh. We began to fidget and pace. It was ridiculous to be cooped up in a basement, a little hutch carrying the whole weight of a town-house on its back. It was such a big rich house, so substantial, so groaning with *things* that I felt it was crushing me beneath its weight. Sean was crying and laughing in short experimental bursts. We got ourselves up in a jumble of weird clothes, including a cloche hat and some sort of big silk scarf scavenged from Vicky's wardrobe. Sean insisted on taking the sheepskin rug with us, which was how we came to leave it on a bench in Holland Park. Locking up took ages, because the logic of keys was beyond comprehension, but before too long we were on the march, the night air good in our lungs, stepping between the streetlights, whose spooky cones of phosphorescence looked too bright to risk trespassing into.

The business of getting over the fence into Holland Park was confusing and messy enough for us not to want to go through it again until we were straighter, which meant that we spent several hours wandering through a landscape of ponds, statues, twenty-storey boxes of filigreed golden light, flowerbeds and other phenomena. It was quite cold. Sean, who seemed much better than me at doing things, who to my admiration could exhibit sophisticated goal-oriented behaviour, saw I was shivering and wrapped the rug round me.

'Always stay in your movie,' he advised.

'I'm in my movie.'

'Don't fall out of it.'

'Don't worry.'

'Stay in!'

'Sure. I'm in my movie, you're in yours. It's our movie.'

'The same movie?'

'The same movie.'

When daylight established itself, we climbed out of the park and walked through the deserted Sunday-morning streets to a greasy spoon in Shepherd's Bush. We hung around outside, waiting for the owner to open up. Then I watched Sean put away bacon, sausage, egg and beans, several cups of tea and three cadged cigarettes while I stared at the swamp-like mass of disturbing textures on my plate and took tiny sips of coffee.

'Food not the thing?' he asked, in a solicitous tone.

I shook my head.

'Can I have yours, then?'

I pushed the plate over to him. I felt like hell. Come-down had firmly nailed the centre of things, though the corners were still displaying a tendency to fly away. The caff was a place of flickering shadows, loud noises.

'I reckon I should go to bed,' I told Sean.

'You won't sleep,' he warned.

'All the same.'

I got up to go. He wiped his mouth with the back of his hand and smiled at me. 'OK, well, come over to mine if you get bored.' He gave me the address.

Trudging barefoot down Holland Park Avenue I felt scoured, wiped clean. It was as if my mental scaffolding had been swept away. I could build again from scratch.

Then I saw the state of Vicky's flat. There was something black crushed into the carpet. Her clothes were everywhere, the dresses she'd carefully hung in the wardrobe tangled up together with shoes and – oh, God – underwear. What had we been doing with her underwear? Where was the rug? A diagram of some kind had been drawn on the wall in what appeared to be red lipstick. It was a complex mess of arrows and little bubbles. I found it hard to say what it represented. I had a dim memory of Sean explaining his plan for a space colony. I'd have to get paint. Paint on a Sunday.

I made my way back to the park and found the rug, dew-soaked and dirty, but otherwise undamaged. Returning elated by this initial success I decided to have a quick lie-down and burrowed under a heap of clothes. I didn't sleep, as Sean had warned, just spent an indeterminate period in a state of jerky dislocation, chasing thought-rabbits down burrows and failing to follow the million simultaneous skeins of logic offered up by my hyperactive mind. I wished my brain would shut up and knew that soon I'd have to start tidying, but first I needed to rest, so I tried to quell the point-less churn behind my eyes and kept on trying (in a *minute*) until Vicky came back home.

I think she thought she'd been burgled, because when she came into the bedroom she was carrying the hockey stick she usually kept in the umbrella-stand in the hall. Seeing me looking up at her from beneath a pile of her evening dresses she quickly realized some kind of party had taken place. So what the bloody hell had happened, Christopher? There were cigarette burns on the rug, Christopher. She'd trusted me, Christopher. She'd Christopher taken me in. I told her to 'be cool', which didn't go down well. She hustled me to the door and threw my shoes after me. I dressed on the pavement outside the house, feeling like a human shell, a zombie whose voodoo was wearing off.

I didn't know where to go, so I ended up at Sean's place, a tall crumbling town-house on Lansdowne Road with a front garden overgrown by weeds. To my surprise, the door was answered by the Afro-haired German guy Sean had berated so fiercely the previous night. He seemed happy enough to let me in, and I clambered through a forest of bicycles into the sitting room, where I fell straight to sleep on a broken-down chesterfield.

I stayed at Sean's for several days. It was a place with a floating population. Charlie Collinson, the owner, spent six months of the year in India, where he bought textiles and leather sandals, selling them in London to finance his next trip. At any given time several of the other tenants would be travelling too, subletting their rooms or inviting their friends to stay there. Sean, who lived rent-free, was supposed to act as a sort of house manager, but being philosophically opposed to private property, he was happy for the place to be a crash-pad for more or less anyone who didn't work for the authorities. It was a chaotic arrangement, made more so by the comings and goings of various groups, sects and gangs, mostly political, though it wasn't unusual for a band to be rehearsing in the basement or stage-lighting to be stored in one of the bedrooms. Some people handled the lack of routine better than others. Matthias, who answered the door, had been there for a few months with his girlfriend Helen, a slight, red-haired girl I'd also seen at Free Pictures. For all their earnest talk of dismantling their social conditioning, they were shy and rather private people. Living there was driving them crazy.

Though chaotic, Charlie's was never the kind of stoner household that had people and their ashtrays frozen into position on the sofas. Life was lived in an atmosphere of frenzied communal preparation. Something was happening in the world and, whatever it was, we were going to be in the middle of it. It was time to get ready. People got ready by waking up at five a.m. to join picket lines, by writing leaflets, folding leaflets, organizing fund-raisers, getting pushed around by the cops, folding more leaflets, going to court, getting up at two a.m. to write slogans on walls on Golborne Road and talking, above all, talking. One morning I went to sleep in someone's bed and woke up a few hours later in the middle of a reading group, eight people sitting on the floor picking through Hegel. I was just beginning to get involved in a discussion about the master-slave dialectic when Sean put his head round the door to ask if I wanted to go and 'do the food run'. The word *food* was enough. I couldn't remember the last time I'd got it together to eat.

We climbed into Rosa and parked just off Portobello Road. Sean seemed to know most of the stall-holders, and as we made our way through the market, he bantered and wheedled and was told to cut his hair a dozen times, but by the time we got to the far end we were carrying two large boxes filled with fruit and vegetables. There also seemed to be a butcher who had a bag of chops that needed eating up and a Portuguese grocer who owed him a bag of rice. It was an impressive haul. 'And that's just the leavings,' Sean said, a note of disgust in his voice. 'Think what we could do if we got organized.'

We went back to Charlie's and handed the food over to a couple of women from a Cuban Solidarity group, who happened to be chatting near the door. They headed into the kitchen and we sprawled on the sofas in the living room, listening to the peevish rattle of pans.

'Primitive Communism,' explained Sean, skinning up. 'You hunt, you gather. You work for the group.'

'There's more food than we can eat. There's only about six of us in at the moment.'

'More will turn up. We could invite more.'

'You think they're OK in the kitchen?'

'Sure, mate, they're fine.'

Some time later, about twelve people sat down to eat and Sean and I told them about the plan we'd just formulated to run a free shop. It would be an event, a one-day action. Systematic collection – go early to all the markets: Billingsgate, the Borough, Covent Garden. Box it up, then just give the stuff away outside Free Pictures. People could hand out literature. We'd feed a few people and make a political point: it would be an example of practical redistribution, a condemnation of consumer society.

We stayed up late, smoking cigarettes and making a list of people who might help out. I say we, but I knew nobody. Sean, on the other hand, seemed to know everyone in W11. By the time we went to sleep we had dozens of names – people who worked on legal or housing issues, members of Big Flame and the IMG, some Spanish Black Cross anarchists who lived above our local betting shop. He had friends who worked at Release and the BIT information service. There was someone who wrote regularly for the underground press and a household of self-styled Diggers, who'd declared themselves the Albion Free State. The BIT people had an office round the corner. They'd probably let us use their phone.

The next morning I woke up on the sitting-room floor to find myself staring at a pair of long, tanned, female legs, which culminated in sandalled feet with chipped black varnish on the toenails.

'Anyone in there?'

I looked up to see the stone-throwing girl. From the floor she looked startlingly tall and slender, beautiful enough to make me feel conscious of being naked inside the sleeping-bag. She had high, almost Slavic cheekbones, green eyes and straight brown hair that fell round her face like a curtain as she stared down at me. She wore denim shorts and a sleeveless black vest, no jewellery, no adornment at all except a black and white *keffiyeh* thrown round her shoulders. 'Is Sean around?' she asked abruptly.

'No idea. He was here last night.'

'I need to talk to him.'

I noticed that she was with someone. A thick-set, handsome man with curly dark hair and a flourishing, almost biblical beard was leaning on the back of one of the sofas. He looked like a boxer or a rock-climber, someone used to physical endurance, an impression emphasized by a number of fresh cuts on his face.

'I don't know where Sean is,' I told the woman. 'I was asleep.'

'I suppose you think you're living here.'

I disliked her tone. 'What's it to you?'

'I actually *do* live here.'

'I see. And you are?'

'God, what the fuck is your problem?' asked the man. He had an American accent.

I noticed they'd dumped backpacks on the floor, amid the remains of last night's planning session, a jumble of papers and dinner plates used as ashtrays. I propped myself against the wall and rubbed my eyes. 'I don't like being hassled when I'm half asleep. That's my problem. If you want to leave a message for Sean, I'll give it to him. He's probably gone to Free Pictures. What time is it?'

'It's eleven,' said the woman, her tone softening slightly. 'I'm going to make tea. Is there milk?'

'Yeah, probably.'

'Do you want a cup?'

'OK. Thanks.'

'How do you take it?'

And so I ended up sitting round the kitchen table listening to Anna Addison and Saul Kleeman talk about Paris. For three weeks we'd been reading about the strikes, the students fighting the police in the Latin Quarter, but the reports were so confused and partisan that it was impossible to make out what was happening. They'd actually been there. Their stories were incredible. Groups of people who'd never met each other forming chains to build barricades. The CRS launching tear-gas grenades, then charging the protesters. They'd met in the doorway of an apartment building, desperately ringing doorbells, trying to get someone to let them in after the CRS overran the rue Gay-Lussac. With the cops tramping up and down the stairs outside, a girl had hidden twenty of them in her place overnight. The next morning, a friendly workman had driven them through the police cordon, hidden in his *camionette*. There had been mass arrests, terrible violence. They'd seen a police squad corner two Algerians, leaving them both for dead.

It was obvious they were lovers. As they told their tale, Saul draped an arm over the back of Anna's chair and played with her hair. The cuts were souvenirs of a beating he'd taken on a demo outside the Renault factory. He'd narrowly escaped getting arrested and deported, which, since he'd fled the States after drawing a low number in the draft lottery, would have meant either prison or Vietnam. He was going to apply to stay in Sweden, unless 'something serious' happened in London, in which case he thought he might hang around. I couldn't tell whether he meant something serious politically, or with Anna.

I heard the front door slam upstairs, then Sean came bounding down into the kitchen. 'Anna,' he shouted, gathering her up into his arms and kissing her full on the mouth. I noticed she responded. So did Saul. He didn't look pleased.

That night, as people were sorting out where they'd sleep, Anna asked Sean casually whether a particular room was free. He said it was. 'See you in the morning, then,' she told him, taking Saul's hand and leading him upstairs. Sean watched them inscrutably, then unhooked his jacket from the back of his chair and left the house.

So much has been written about Anna, almost all of it wrong. She's been reduced to the woman in the Copenhagen photo, with her fist raised out of the embassy window. It's impossible, I suppose, to separate who she became from who she was in 1968, but that masked figure is as much of a cartoon as Byronic Sean Ward. The Copenhagen woman stands for death, death to the pig state, death to the hostages. If I say I think Anna was motivated by love, it sounds banal, an old hippie talking. Or an old lover, blinded by sentiment.

We had so many questions about Paris. Why were the unions asking their members to go back to work? Why was it all falling apart? The next day at Free Pictures, Anna ran a question-and-answer session for an audience of almost a hundred people, drawn from every niche in the feral ecology of the London underground. Pure word of mouth, as far as I could tell. Bush telegraph. Sean pointed out a who's who of local activists. The Black Power crowd, the neatly dressed Leninists from the orthodox Communist Party. Anna was an eloquent speaker. She'd arrived in time to participate in the enormous street demonstrations of early May and 'both personally and politically' the previous six weeks had 'felt like a lifetime'. The situation was now very uncertain. De Gaulle had called an election. Yes, some of the immediate revolutionary potential had dissipated.

As she spoke I peered at her. Under the bare bulb her head was a collection of angles, futurist splinters of cheek and brow. Her voice was made to sway a crowd. As she talked she leaned on a chair, using its back as a lectern and sweeping the darkened room with one hand, gathering us all up into her intensity. I thought that gesture was the most graceful, truthful thing I'd ever seen. When she smiled, which she did often, I wanted her so much I could have cried.

* * *

The area around Notting Hill was a crappy part of town in those days, a couple of square miles of rotten ghetto housing cut through by a half-built flyover, but it supported a ramshackle counter-culture made up of hundreds of cliques and groups and communes, little magazines, support groups, co-ops, bands. By finding my way to Free Pictures I'd fallen straight into the middle of a place with its own geography, an anti-city of bed-sitters and bookshops, rehearsal rooms and cramped offices.

I'd also stumbled into the middle of an elliptical game that Sean and Anna were playing with one another. For the rest of that summer everything happening in the world, however big – Czechoslovakia, Bobby Kennedy's assassination – was, if not exactly subordinate, then wrapped up with what was taking place between them. Like a fool I became willingly, even eagerly entangled. Poor Saul Kleeman was in as deep as me: we'd both fallen out of our own movies into theirs.

Sean and Anna had been together before she went away, but monogamy was never part of their arrangement. This was both a personal and a political decision. Like many of us, they were moving towards the view that the building blocks of the oppression we all felt, the molecules that made up the vast body of the capitalist state, were psychological ones. A revolutionary transformation of society would require a transformation of social life, a transmutation of ourselves. Everything about my own family confirmed this. If I was to be free, I had to be free of them. But I also had to recognize that they were prisoners too. It wouldn't be enough to kill Daddy and marry Mummy. We had to kill the engine that generated all the daddies and mummies, throw a clog into the big machine.

In the meantime, Sean and Saul were going to compete for Anna. I think she set it up: a lesson or an experiment. Of all of us, she was the only one who had real experience of the world. She was in her late twenties. At one time she'd been married to a photographer, running around in Chelsea wearing fake eyelashes and A-line dresses. The marriage had lasted only eighteen months but remained with her as a kind of hinterland, an intolerance of certain things and people, an address book filled with scribbled-out names. 'It's OK being put on a pedestal,' she once told me, 'until it's built so high they start to feel afraid of you. Then they hate you and after that it's all they really want to do, the hating.' One of the many striking things about Anna was her indifference to her own happiness and comfort, even her personal safety. I think she came increasingly to consider herself unimportant, except as a vehicle for the revolution. The rest of us tried to cultivate the same selflessness, the same erasure of personal preference, but Anna could always go further, could always get closer to absolute zero.

If Anna was self-negating, Sean was fiercely present. He wanted Anna. He didn't want Saul to have her. But Sean wanted a lot of things. Did he love her? That depends, I suppose, on what one means by love. Sean would use the word in a way that made it seem like a kind of freedom, a moral energy he intended to project through the world by sheer force of will. Love was freedom, so love had to be free. It was all walls and bars and cages with Sean. It was all breaking things open, smashing them apart.

If you believe in free love – not in the sense of promiscuity, but in its true sense – as the release of libidinal energies from any restraint, any check whatsoever, the barrier between desire and action becomes terrifyingly thin and permeable. *I take my desires for reality because I believe in the reality of my desires.* How many of us could actually live like that? Is it even possible? We all tried, and both Sean and Anna got closer than I did. I can say that about them. At least I can say that. So yes, *love*. Love firing off in all directions.

Saul never stood a chance. If I fared better, it was only because it was a long time before I even admitted I was in the game.

Sean's first tactic in his offensive against the invader was blitz-krieg household disruption. The next day he rousted Anna and Saul out of bed so he could replaster a section of bedroom wall that, until then, he'd been perfectly happy to leave to crumble behind the paper. In subsequent days he took up floorboards, moved people and furniture in and out of the house, creating a sort of permanent domestic revolution, a constant flux designed to unsettle everyone as much as possible. Once he'd filled the place to bursting, he took the door off the toilet and started forcing people to share rooms, accusing anyone who argued with him of bourgeois individualism. There was to be no privacy. Helen and Matthias had to sleep alongside two anti-apartheid activists from Birmingham. I spent a night wide awake on a mattress in a corner of the largest bedroom, watching Saul and Anna fuck in the orange glow of the streetlight outside the window. Once or twice her eyes caught mine.

Initially, Saul was happy enough to put up with Sean's dislike of him, even to take a little pleasure in the chaos he was causing, as long as he had Anna. On the surface, he and Sean were quite friendly with one another. Then one weekend Sean held an impromptu party that started on Friday afternoon with three friends and a bottle of Dexedrine and ended thirty-six hours later with half the transient population of Ladbroke Grove inside the house. By the end of the first day Sean was higher than I'd ever seen him before, a ragged ringmaster goading people on to perilous heights of excess. Someone had rigged up a PA in the kitchen, which played a mixture of ska and R & B and acid rock, depending on which faction had seized control.

The first most of us knew about the raid was when the police pulled the plug, shorting the electrics and plunging the place into darkness. I was upstairs, arguing about something or other with Matthias, when everything went black. There were sounds of panic from the hall and someone called out, 'Pigs! Pigs!' which cued general swearing, hiding of stashes, tripping over and crashing around. A minute or two later a torch was shone in my face. I was told to leave the premises immediately and not to cause any trouble while I was about it.

Several people were arrested, all of them black. Saul had a close call: he was one of a dozen or so partygoers who escaped over the back fence and were chased by police through neighbouring gardens. Earlier in the evening, Sean had been feeding him whole handfuls of drugs. When the raid happened, Saul couldn't understand what was going on. The police were already in the room when he worked out what the blue uniforms were all about. He spent the rest of the night hiding in a flowerbed. Afterwards, sleep-deprived and paranoid, he accused Sean of engineering the bust. 'You wanted me put away, you bastard! Don't deny it! You wanted those motherfuckers to get me.' Sean sneered at him, needling him with a mocking cowboy mime, blowing on six-gun fingers and adjusting an imaginary hat.

They were squaring up to one another when Anna arrived back from the phone-box. A friend had been charged with possession. She'd been trying to get him a lawyer. Saul and Sean both switched gear and started to outline competing schemes for dealing with the situation. She seemed angry with both of them. Turning her back on Sean, she asked me what I thought. I told her the truth – I didn't know. At that moment I didn't care. I was sick of everyone and wanted to be alone. Anna looked over at me, smiling curiously. I felt I was being assessed. I went to the pub and sat out Sunday evening with the old men, staring into my pint and trying to ignore unwanted flashes of her naked torso rocking backwards and forwards under orange light.

＊ ＊ ＊

In my opinion, the Free Shop was a success. About twenty people foraged through London markets, from Billingsgate to Covent Garden, bringing back piles of food that we laid out on a stall outside Free Pictures. Anna wrote a leaflet explaining the action, giving definitions of 'waste', 'redistribution' and 'socialism'. I provided some ideas, a few words and phrases, a little historical context about English civil-war radicals. It was the first time the two of us worked together, sitting round the big wooden table at Charlie's, scribbling in a notebook. I asked her where she'd learned so much political theory. 'Secretarial college,' she told me tartly.

Along with our material, the Free Shop displayed handouts from a dozen organizations, promoting everything from veganism to a united Ireland. The shambolic usher from Free Pictures, who gloried in the name of Uther Pendragon, changed the lettering on the marquee to read: FREE ALL PEOPLE ALL FREE. Customers flocked to the stall. Most, I saw, were young, long-haired and fashionably dressed. I noticed Sean staring coldly at a pair of couture hippies as they picked fastidiously through a box of bananas. Later, a few of us walked round the streets with baskets, offering food to anyone who passed by. Most people were suspicious. 'What have you done to it?' was the most common question. Though younger ones took the food willingly, older ones seemed to think there was something shameful about it. One or two women poked and sniffed at the produce, then furtively slipped things into their bags, hurrying off as if they'd transacted a drug deal.

Late in the afternoon, Sean and I divided up what was left into boxes and drove Rosa to the top end of the Grove, where we parked and started knocking on doors near the Harrow Road. We had them slammed in our face a couple of times. A stern-faced West Indian church lady got really angry. How dared we offer her charity? How dared we come round there with our filthy clothes and nappy hair and act like we were better than her?

We were invited in by a young Irish couple, who were living in two rooms on the top floor of a rotting town-house. The place should have been condemned. Damp was streaming down the walls. The toilet was on the landing, and the shared bathroom all the way downstairs. The wife, who had a persistent cough, attended to a baby while we drank tea with the husband, trying to get him to stop apologizing for not offering us a biscuit. They'd been in London just under a year. He was making a little money from building work, but the rent was high and at the end of the month, there wasn't always enough. We left promising we'd be back.

'That was the kind of place my mum had in Hammersmith,' said Sean, as we went downstairs. 'Trying to cook our tea on the landing while everyone else was waiting their turn on the hob.'

'Is she still there, your mum?'

He ignored the question. 'Round here the landlords can charge what they fucking like. The tenants don't complain because they're grateful to have anywhere at all. You should hear Gloria tell about what it was like when she first came. No one would rent to her. She won't have a word said against Rachman, says at least he didn't care what colour you were, long as you paid.'

'So what can we do?'

'Fuck knows. The bastards who own it all now are ten times worse than he ever was.'

That night at Charlie's, the Free Shop collective discussed the action. Sean saw it as a total failure. The people who'd taken our food could fend for themselves. They *ought* to fend for themselves or, better still, join with us in helping others. Anna agreed. She said she wasn't interested in symbolic gestures. The point was to channel resources to people who were in genuine need, not subsidize middle-class parasites. It was the first time I'd heard either of them so bitter. I decided they were right. It wasn't enough. We had to do better.

While I tried to sort out the problems of the world, I'd been neglecting my own. I was broke and homeless. Since no one had come to see me while I was in prison, I had to assume I couldn't rely on family or old friends. I went to sign on.

The very architecture of the dole office was humiliating. Hard benches, cubicles made from grubby prefabricated panels. I took a number and sat down opposite a poster promising *Good News For Claimants*. After an hour or so, I was called for an interview with a man who seemed so beaten down by his work that it was all he could do to lift a pen and fill in my form. We had a desultory conversation, then he flicked through a card index of vacancies. To my relief he decided he didn't have *anything suitable* for me *at the present time*. I should *monitor the boards* in the office *on a daily basis*, because things often *came up at short notice*. I should also consider *working on my personal presentation*, which was often a *surprisingly important factor* in employers' minds.

I looked at him, this bedraggled claims officer with his polyester jacket and his hair plastered over his scalp. I thought I should at least give him a chance. 'You ever fantasize about burning this place down?'

'I'm sorry, Mr Carver, I'm not sure I follow you.'

'Burning it down.'

He looked up from his papers. 'Is that some kind of threat?'

'No, not me. I'm talking about you. Surely you must think about it once in a while. You know, when you're on your own, late at night, glass of whisky in your hand.'

'I'm not sure I like your tone. I've tried to be as courteous as possible, so I don't see why you should adopt an aggressive attitude.'

I took that as a no.

Afterwards I decided to go to see Vicky. I needed an endearing prop, so I stole some flowers from the park. It was one of Vicky's volunteering days. I hung around outside the playgroup and caught her when she went for lunch. I told her the truth, which was that I was sorry about her flat and knew she probably didn't want to see me but I'd needed an address to give to the dole office and, to put it bluntly, I'd used hers. She was furious, but not as furious as when I asked if she'd lend me some money. She wasn't so much mollified by the flowers as astounded. She stared at them for a moment (they were blue flowers, hyacinths, I think) then got out her purse. I told her I'd pop by every week to get my cheque.

Tensions between Sean and Saul got worse. Anna fanned the flames by spending the night after the Free Shop action with Sean, while Saul sat up late in the kitchen, drinking despondently with Jay Marks, an artist who was one of the long-term residents. Jay was an openly gay man, an unusual thing for those days. He sometimes worked with a street-theatre troupe, performing political plays in tourist spots, all white-face and agit-prop slogans and cardboard planes. He and Saul had developed an uneasy friendship, based on banter about Saul's discomfort with his homosexuality. As the level in the rum bottle dropped, their sarcastic jokes gradually flagged and Saul started to slump despairingly on Jay's shoulder. Tentatively, Jay stroked his hair. I decided it was time to go to bed.

Everyone was in a bad mood the next day. Helen and Matthias were threatening to move out unless the door to the toilet was replaced. Jay was locked in his room. Over breakfast Saul called Anna a bitch and Anna called Saul a misogynist. Sean gave a smug lecture on possessiveness, playing to a captive audience in the kitchen, where we were trying to get ready for a demonstration at South Africa House. Anna threw a coffee mug at him, which smashed on the wall by his head. 'Don't you ever fucking act like you own me,' she warned. Anna's rare displays of temper were shocking, not just because she was normally so controlled but because they didn't appear to have a limit. When she was angry, it didn't matter where she was or who was present. Context just disappeared.

Later that day, Sean suggested we rob the supermarket. Not shoplifting – a commando raid. Empty the place overnight, distribute a meal to every poor household in Notting Hill. Most people wanted to talk about apartheid, because of the demonstration (something to do with cricket, I think), but Sean carried on, expounding his theme as we got on the bus with our placards, carrying on as we walked back through the park. Principle number one: if we wanted to call ourselves revolutionaries, we had to be prepared to break the law. This wasn't just a gesture, or a bonding ritual. The experience of transgression was part of our formation as revolutionary subjects. It would change us, change our relationship to power. Principle number two: it was our food already. Deep down anyone who argued against stealing was motivated by guilt and fear, all the apparatus that had been installed in us by the ruling class for the purposes of social control. The truth of the situation was the exact opposite of the picture offered by the power structure. That food was the product of ordinary working people's labour. It belonged to us already. *They* had stolen it from *us*.

It was directed at Saul, which worried me. A challenge. A dare. I think I called the idea adventurist. I remember Anna attacked me ferociously. 'So that's how it is? I had hopes of you. You say things like "The truly revolutionary line on such and such is such and such." But I think when it comes to actual revolution, you'll hate it. You'll hate the noise. You'll hate the people. I think you're a *theorist*.'

She'd hit on my weak spot, my secret fear. I don't really know if Anna convinced me or just wore me down, but a few days later I found myself climbing into the back of Sean's van. She and Sean were in front. Saul was next to me, nervously chewing his beard but determined not to back down, draft or no draft.

As would so often happen, Anna had taken on one of Sean's projects, meticulously planning what we were about to do and transforming it from a piece of Errol-Flynnery into something like a military operation. We had a second vehicle, a Luton van usually used by Jay's theatre group. Jay had already gone ahead and was parked across the street from the supermarket. Someone had a friend who'd worked there stacking shelves. Around four, before the early-morning deliveries started, there would apparently be no one in the building. As far as he knew there wasn't an alarm. We'd climb the fence, force the doors to the loading bay and drive the Luton van right in.

I'd taken a French blue and the world was pinned down. Sharp edges, hard clean light. I watched the others swarm over the high fence, using a bit of carpet to cross the tangle of barbed wire that ran along the top. Sean went first, carrying the bag of tools. Saul and Anna followed him, dropping down into the darkness of the yard.

It seemed to take them for ever to cut the chain on the gates. I sat there with Rosa's engine running, looking in the wing mirror to see if anyone was coming. At last the gates swung open. Jay backed the Luton van into the yard and reversed it into the loading bay. I followed him in and Sean closed the roller door behind us. The next few minutes were insane. We ran round the building like television prize-winners, pulling stuff off shelves and slinging it into the vans. We'd only brought two torches, so several people were always stumbling around in the dark. In the freezer room I grabbed chicken after chicken. Sean and Anna were chucking in sacks of potatoes, jars of coffee, whole pallets of canned vegetables. Soon enough we were back on the road, skidding northwards up Ladbroke Grove towards Free Pictures. I was whooping and shouting, laughing like a maniac.

Anna's true genius showed itself in the set-up at Free Pictures. In the dank cinema, Uther, Matthias, Helen and about ten others were ready with tape and cardboard boxes. We formed a human chain to get the stuff upstairs and by the time it was properly light, people across the area were waking up to find several days' groceries on their doorstep. In each box was a slip of paper:

After the revolution there will be enough for all.

It was a weird, apocalyptic summer. Things seemed to be collapsing: tower blocks, foreign governments. Sean and I went to a meeting of something called the London Irish Civil Rights Solidarity Campaign, where I heard new and ominous words: *Bogside*,

Orangemen, B-Specials. Hoping for Paris, we traipsed up to Hornsey, where there was a sit-in at the art school. We found a lot of students discussing the meaning of design, eating in the canteen under a banner that read BUREAUCRACY MAKES PARASITES OF US ALL. Other things were more fun. We disrupted property auctions by making false bids. A group of our friends dressed up in animal costumes and broke into the private gardens in the square opposite Free Pictures, opening them up as a playground for the local children. Just before he left for Sweden, Saul ran a training session at a local Vietnam Solidarity Campaign meeting. He'd been at the big Washington demos, the ones we'd seen pictures of, with people putting flowers in the barrels of guns and trying to levitate the Pentagon. He showed us various physical tactics, how to make yourself difficult to dislodge, how to 'unarrest' someone without getting arrested yourself. He kept emphasizing the need for collect- ive action. Nothing would work unless it was practised by disciplined groups of people, who were aware of each other's strengths and weaknesses, the level of risk they were individually prepared to take.

One night we got caught up in a violent bust at a basement bar off Westbourne Grove called the Island Breeze. We'd gone there to meet activists from a group called the African Liberation Caucus, a fancy name for a group of young men who gave out political leaflets outside the tube station and faced down the local mods. The ALC wanted to talk to us about the police. The Notting Hill force had always had a bad reputation, but now they seemed to be running amok. Black people were finding it impossible to drive a car down Ladbroke Grove after dark without getting pulled over. They were being beaten up in custody. Everyone agreed there was a problem; the trouble was that some of the ALC didn't like involving whites in the issue. There was an ugly row, some name-calling; we were about to leave when the police came charging down the stairs. No one resisted, but they smashed up the chairs and tables anyway, broke all the bottles behind the bar. Sean and I were held overnight, then released without charge. Everyone else had to go to court. A rumour went round that a white informant had told them about the meeting. An edge of paranoia was creeping in.

Though much of our energy was directed at local issues, we had connections to the wider political world. In the messy aftermath of Paris we went to a rally at the LSE, where student leaders from around Europe had been invited to speak. French friends of Anna were there. Matthias knew delegates from the German SDS. The occasion was the foundation of something called the Revolutionary Socialist Students' Federation. It was the first time I'd been back at the LSE since March; the place felt like a relic of a past life. The rally was a fiasco. For all the rhetorical imperatives – the *urgent need* to constitute an extra-parliamentary opposition, the *urgent need* to form red bases and commit as a bloc to all anti-Imperialist and anti-Fascist struggles around the world – it was just another sectarian talking shop. Crop-haired delegates from the Socialist Labour League sprayed invective at their rivals. Some fool got up to explain why the thoughts of Chairman Mao were essentially revisionist in character and had to be seen as contrary to the strict principles of Marxist-Leninism.

'So much for the new vanguard,' scoffed Anna. We were bored and disgusted. Eventually we started throwing things at the platform and shouting abuse at the speakers until some of the stewards tried to remove us from the hall. Among them was my old friend Alan. As we pushed and shoved, I jeered at him. He was dressed in a Chinese tunic, the height of revolutionary chic. 'No more Carnaby Street shirts, Alan? Worker-peasant now, are we?' Around us people laughed.

'What happened to you?' he snarled.

'I went to prison, remember, *comrade.*'

Eventually we were frogmarched towards the doors. And that was when I met Miles Bridgeman for the second time, perched on a chair at the back of the hall, panning an 8mm camera across the crowd. As we were hustled past he called out to me. Beside him, sitting on the floor in the aisle, was a pale young girl in a big floppy straw hat, smoking a cigarette and staring abstractedly at the ceiling.

He followed us on to the street with his camera and filmed us continuing our argument with the stewards. Various groups had set up tables outside the hall to hawk literature and solicit donations. Some onlookers joined in on our side and eventually Alan and the others, most of whom I knew, retreated back indoors. The rest of us went to the pub.

I introduced Miles to the others, only to find some of them already knew him. He introduced me to his friend, whose name was Ursula. She asked me what star sign I was and seemed very put out when Anna told her all mysticism was inherently Fascist. Miles kept filming us as we walked, until he irritated Sean by putting the camera in his face, for which he almost got it knocked on to the pavement. I asked how he'd got on after Grosvenor Square.

'They didn't have anything on me,' he said. 'They let me go.'

I told him he was lucky. They hadn't had anything on me either.

For whatever reason, the others peeled off and I ended up spending the rest of the day drifting around Covent Garden with Miles and Ursula. Miles told me about his latest project, documenting the lifestyles of revolutionary youth around the world. He was planning to go to Cuba. By early evening, we were lying around on mattresses at the Arts Lab watching a film of people's faces as they had orgasms. Ursula told me I had a muddy aura. She rolled joints and passed them to Miles to light.

After that Miles always seemed to be around. He'd drop into Lansdowne Road and Free Pictures and hang about with his camera. Not everyone was pleased to see him. Sean never liked him, despite Miles's sycophantic efforts to get on his good side. Chelsea poseur, he called him. Super-hippie.

I always felt a bit awkward about Miles, as if I was responsible for him. He'd irritate me, then do something generous, something that made it hard to get rid of him. I remember he always seemed to have drugs, even when no one else was holding.

One night he took me to a party in a flat on the Cromwell Road, a high-ceilinged place decorated with big brass Buddhas and cane furniture. It belonged to a theatre director and was full of expensively dressed people drinking white wine and eating macrobiotic snacks out of delicate Chinese bowls. I was sitting against the wall with Ursula, whom, for reasons no longer clear to me, I'd started sleeping with. Ursula's conversation was mostly about her past incarnations, which included an iron-age priestess, Charlotte Brontë and a peasant girl who'd died in a workhouse. She had a rage for systems, the more complex the better. Every time I saw her she'd half learned another chunk of tarot or the *I Ching*. I put up with it because she never wore any knickers under her beaded twenties dresses. We'd done it in a rowing-boat, on a bench on the Embankment. 'It's about your brain blood volume,' she was telling me. 'Animals hold their necks horizontally. We've evolved into an upright position, but there are real disadvantages in that, from the consciousness point of view. Your level of consciousness is entirely related to brain blood volume. Once your cranium hardens, there's no room for your brain to breathe. So you drill a small hole. It's the most ancient surgical procedure known to man.'

I wasn't really listening, occupied in watching the other guests. They were people on whom the Age of Aquarius was sitting uncomfortably, the men all polo-necks and half grown-out hair, the women caught between matronly respectability and tentative essays at hippiedom. Looming over us as we sat was a group of academic-looking men. While two of them made loud and rather ostentatious conversation about the *Kama Sutra*, the third was staring fixedly at a point somewhere between Ursula's legs.

I went to find Miles, to ask if he was ready to leave. To my surprise I found him in the kitchen with Anna. I had no idea she'd be there. She was dressed with deliberate sloppiness, in tennis shoes and a pair of old paint-spattered jeans. Nevertheless she seemed to be at home, dangling a wine-glass in her fingers and making some conversational point to Miles, who was vigorously shaking his head. When she saw me, she frowned. 'What are you doing here?'

'I could ask you the same thing.'

She shrugged. I thought uncomfortably about Ursula. I hadn't mentioned to Anna I was seeing her. Actually, we almost always stayed at hers – the one time she'd slept over at Lansdowne Road, I'd more or less sneaked her in and out of the house. Just then she came into the kitchen and draped herself possessively round me. Anna raised an eyebrow. Embarrassed, I shook Ursula off and she angrily flounced into the other room, followed by Miles. I watched him skilfully steering her towards a group of actors; she was soon happily reading someone's palm.

'I hope for your sake she's a good fuck,' said Anna.

I must have blushed, because she laughed heartily, spilling a little wine out of her glass. I tried to cover my annoyance. 'How come you're here?' I asked. 'I thought you despised the decadent pastimes of the bourgeoisie.'

'I thought you did too.'

'I came with Miles.'

'Good for you.'

'You seem to know him.'

'He's a friend of my ex-husband. Jeremy will probably be here himself, unless he's found somewhere with more fashion models. You know, it's odd to see Miles at Charlie's. I never thought of him as the slightest bit political. Not like your little friend, eh, Chris?'

'That's right, she's not political.'

'So you're just fucking her?'

'Why are you here, Anna? I thought Jeremy was supposed to be a pig.'

'Jeremy is a pig. Look, I know people, OK? Just because you're the tortured introvert. Besides, I needed to be out of the house.'

She didn't have to say any more. Sean and Saul had been at each other's throats all day. The pretext was some abstruse point about workers' councils.

She took a drag on her cigarette. 'The sooner he goes to Sweden the better.'

'If you think that, why don't you just tell him?'

'Because it's nothing to do with me.'

'Oh, come on, it's everything to do with you.'

'Not really. If it wasn't me it would be someone else. Something else. Something.'

Around us the alcohol level was peaking. Voices were raised. Rhetoric flew messily around the kitchen. A woman I recognized from some late-night discussion programme on the BBC was holding forth to a little group by the sink. 'If you mean that by honouring my feminine side, I'm honouring the divine within myself and elevating non-material values over the consumer culture, then I'd have to say you're substantially correct.'

'That's just crap, Maria.'

'But why is it crap?' The woman camped up her incomprehension. 'Just tell me why.'

I never knew much about what it was like for Anna when she was married to Jeremy Wilson. East End chancers and aristocratic junkies; everyone up for a free ride. She was only twenty, divorced by twenty-two. I looked at the television woman, at her careful makeup and amber jewellery. In other circumstances, could Anna have turned into her?

We drifted into the main room where the host was fiddling with an expensive hi-fi. Ursula was dancing with a good-looking young man.

'He's an actor,' Anna told me. 'He's in something somewhere and he's a great success.'

Ursula looked sulkily over. I was obviously being punished. The actor eyed me warily. 'So,' asked Anna, 'are you going to do something about it?'

'Like what?'

'I thought you were with that girl. Look at where his hands are.'

'I don't care. She's a free person. We're all free people.'

'You mean you don't care, or you're afraid?'

'I'm not afraid of him.'

She laughed, and appraised me. 'Yes, you are. Maybe not of him in particular, but of this.'

'Anna. I don't give a damn. She's pissing me off anyway.'

'Oh, is she? Poor you. But you're not taking my point.'

'I don't know what your point is.'

'I'm saying you respect it too much. This party. These people. These sophisticated people.'

'I've got no respect for them at all. They're smug. They're bourgeois.'

'You're lying, Chris. You want them to love you. You follow all their rules. Politeness, acceptable behaviour. My mother would adore you.'

'What rules? And I still don't understand what your problem is. We're both at this party. We've both chosen to come here. It's just a party.'

'The difference is that you couldn't step outside it, if you chose. Look at these people. Look at them, Chris. They're blind. They're happy to ignore everything around them, just pleased to be having a good time. And, as far as I'm concerned, that makes them culpable. It makes them complicit in everything they're ignoring. Vietnam, the lot. It makes them pigs.'

'So what? You want to leave? I agree. Let's get out of here.'

'Run away?'

'Christ, Anna! Run away from what?'

'Why not confront them? If they're pigs, why not tell them to their faces?'

'If they piss you off so much, why don't you?'

Without a word, Anna went over to a middle aged man in a velvet jacket, who was talking to the host. As she approached, he smiled reflexively, wondering if he knew her. She leaned forward and tightened his tie until it started to constrict his neck. Then, as he scrabbled ineffectually at his collar, she dashed the wine-glass out of his hand and screamed at him, 'You pig! You fucking baby-killing pig!' The music was quite loud and not everyone could hear, but the room was instantly energized.

People stared. The man cowered, his hands up, ready to ward off another attack.

Anna turned to me and inclined her head. The blood was pumping in my ears. I felt sick, as if there was a physical weight on my chest. She was right. I was scared of those people. I valued their good opinion. I envied their confidence, their social position.

I took a step forward. Then another. In front of me was the BBC woman. I batted a bowl out of her hand, spraying rice salad over the people around her. I screamed at her, 'Pig! Fucking pig!' Anna went up to another woman, spilling wine on to her blouse. I pushed the actor who was dancing with Ursula. For the next few minutes we shouldered through the party performing small acts of transgression, breaking things, screaming obscenities and feeling people up, until the place was in a state of uproar. People shouted at us. One man slapped Anna's face, the macho movie hero dealing with the hysteric.

I remember Miles's horrified expression as we were pushed out of the door.

On the street, taxis streamed past, carrying people back to the suburbs. The host was apparently calling the police. We ran off towards the tube station.

When we clattered down the stairs, we found the platform was deserted, and since she was laughing and I was on a high, I pushed her against a pillar and put my face close to hers. I could feel her back, slick with perspiration under her thin T-shirt. She didn't pull away. When I kissed her, she responded passionately, or so it seemed to me, until I tried to slip my hand between her thighs, at which point she pushed me off and held me at arm's length, smiling and shaking her head. 'Fuck off, Chris,' she panted. 'You don't get to drag me back to your cave. I'm not your reward, your gold star.' Then, while I tried to digest what had just happened, she playfully slapped my cheek and hopped on to a train, waving to me as the carriage doors closed. I watched her take a seat and fish a book out of her jacket pocket as it pulled away.

Was that party the turning-point, the most important moment

of my summer? Or was it when Jay came to find me in the pub? I remember he'd acquired a large fedora hat from somewhere. It made him look like a theatrical villain, off for a touch of opium and some white slavery, then home in time for tea.

'There's a guy in the living room,' he whispered ominously. 'You've got to come and deal with him. He's fucking awful, mate. Harshing the vibe. Says he's your brother.'

By the time I arrived, Brian had been there almost an hour. He'd refused tea. He'd refused to sit down. Fear of contamination? It was hard to say why. Maybe he thought he'd get spiked, believe he could fly. I found him standing to attention by the living-room door, like a furious standard lamp.

'Where the hell have you been?' was his greeting. It was months since we'd seen each other.

It wasn't merely that I hadn't thought about Brian for a while. I'd blocked him out. But there he was, a presence from another life, a scowling, sandy-haired man whose meaty back and shoulders were hunched inside a shiny grey suit jacket, a tie knotted under his jowl like a big floral noose. My brother. Make the sounds with your mouth and see if they conjure up a feeling.

'Hello, Brian.'

'Christ almighty, it's taken me three days to track you down.'

'I see.'

'What are you doing here? This house is revolting.'

I'd already had enough. 'You spent three days looking for me just to tell me you don't like where I live? If you can't be friendly, just go, OK?'

'Don't give me any of your lip. Of course I didn't come for that.'

'You're sure, Brian? You always had strong opinions about décor.'

I heard Jay snigger behind me. Among other things, Brian lacked a sense of humour and, like most humourless people, he was always watching out beadily for perceived slights, the jokes he knew he wasn't getting.

'Don't talk to me that way. I'm your elder brother.'

'Fuck off, Brian. I didn't ask you to come here.'

'Is there somewhere private we can talk?' He gestured at Jay, who was hovering in the doorway. Matthias was in the background, wrapped in a blanket. I think he was hoping Brian would leave so he could go back to sleep. My brother adopted an air of high seriousness. 'I don't want to discuss family business in front of people like that.'

'Like what?' asked Jay, mock-innocently.

'You know exactly what,' growled Brian.

'Right,' I told him. 'Get out. I don't know why you came here, but now I want you to piss off back to your office. Haven't you got customers to rob or something?'

I didn't think it was possible for his colour to deepen any further. 'You're so bloody arrogant,' he spat. 'Look at yourself. Got up in those wretched clothes, hair all over the place.'

'Don't know if it's a boy or a girl,' tutted Jay. Brian turned on him. 'Just helping you with your lines,' Jay offered.

At that point Brian almost lost control. I had to step between them. 'Don't you dare.'

'Get that – creature out of here.'

'Jay, I'm sorry. Leave it to me. I'll get rid of him.'

Brian put his face very close to mine. 'I don't know what Dad's going to say when he sees you.'

'I don't give a damn what he says. And I don't give a damn what you say either. Fuck off, Brian. Fuck off and leave me in peace.'

'So you're going to force me to do this in public?'

'Force you? What the hell are you on about? What are you doing here?'

'Mum's dead.'

Brian's little triumph. You could see the poorly concealed pleasure on his face. Living the scene as if it were some ghastly Victorian genre painting. *The prodigal brother chastised*. The extent of his self-righteousness rolled out in front of me like a carpet. I was furious. The way he'd come: unasked, wreathed in sanctimony.

I *bet* he'd spent three days looking for me, the sick bastard. I bet it was worth it to him.

'How?' I asked, making my voice as flat as I could.

'The hospital say she had a stroke. I thought maybe you still cared enough to want to come to the funeral.'

I fought back my anger. I had no room, really, to think about Mum. It was all Brian.

* * *

At the crematorium, no one spoke to me. My father saw my jeans and refused to shake my hand. Of course I'd done it on purpose. The battered leather flying jacket with the tear in the back. The unwashed hair. The building was neutral and discreet. A few middle-aged people in sober clothes had come to pay their respects, filling the pews so that later on someone would fill the pews for them. There was a representative from the hospital, a couple of neighbours. It was just another transaction to most of them, conducted in the same detached manner as one might renew a passport or open a savings account. Hats for most of the women. Cigarettes smoked outside, at a discreet distance from the hearse. None of them had really cared about her. How could I not hate it? How could I not hate myself for being part of it?

Brian hadn't trusted me to make it on my own. He was right: if he hadn't sent his friend to pick me up, I wouldn't have gone. The friend was called Bob or Dave or Phil. He looked just like Brian: sideburns, drinker's red chops. 'Are you coming like that?' he'd asked, winding down the window of his Cortina.

When he saw me Brian hissed at Bob-Dave-Phil, who blocked his way with a raised arm. Go on, I thought. Take a swing. You want to so much, but it wouldn't do. *Decorum.* Disrespectful to Mum.

The curtain was operated by some kind of automated pulley system. To the sound of a crackly recording of organ music, it jerked its arthritic way along a brass rail, concealing the coffin from view. As an attempt to shield us from the finality of death it was ineffective. When it was over I tried to speak to Dad. One last chance for us. I touched him on the shoulder.

'You did this,' he told me. He meant Mum.

His petty, vicious tone still transmits clearly to me today. I didn't answer, 'What about you, Dad?' or any of the other things it has since occurred to me I could have said. And because I couldn't find any words, I walked away. I suppose it goes without saying that I never saw him again. Or Brian. After that, there was just me.

Collectivity. That's what Saul called for in his speech to the VSC activists. That's what he said the British lacked. A couple of days later he was gone, his bedroll and kit-bag packed and shifted, his argumentative bulk absent from the kitchen. But he left that point of view behind him. No one had wanted to hear it. I listened to a cacophony of voices, all shouting that *their* particular project, *their* thing was a genuine example of community, throwing a lot of jargon at Saul to prove that he was wrong and, anyway, they were cleverer than he was. I thought he had it about right. Perhaps it wasn't our fault. We were in a church hall and somehow that made everything we were doing absurd, just a bunch of people pushing each other around, like a Scout troop. How could we even think of making something new for ourselves when there were metal-framed chairs stacked at the sides of the room and a piano under a canvas cover in the corner? In England the power structure had fastened its roots right down to the bedrock; every inch of land, every object on which you rested your eyes spoke about the past, about how many people had gone before you and how insignificant their individual efforts had proved. It was all designed to stop us coming together. All of it. And that meant it couldn't be rejected partially. If it was going to be changed, it would have to be changed beyond all recognition.

That October, I decided I wasn't going back to university and would dedicate myself full time to political work. A second large anti-war demonstration was planned. After my arrest in the spring I wasn't sure I wanted to attend, but my friends persuaded me it was important. Displaying solidarity on the streets was a way to make our politics visible to the masses. Every day, how many thousands of pounds of bombs? How much napalm? How many burned children? How many villages destroyed? They said I shouldn't allow myself to be intimidated.

At a planning meeting there was a bad-tempered argument about the proposed route. The organizers insisted that a repeat of the violence in March would be counter-productive so it was moved that we'd walk along the Embankment to Whitehall, staying well away from Grosvenor Square and the US embassy. A lot of us weren't happy about that. Surely the point wasn't to lobby the British government but to send a message to the Americans, to show that even in a country that was supposedly their ally, the people supported a Vietnamese victory. Wrong, said others. A riot would dominate the news coverage at the expense of the issues. Personally, I thought the papers would be against us whatever we did. There were already hysterical articles running almost every day, building up the march as a full-scale insurrection. Despite my militancy, I was privately pessimistic. I didn't believe that a protest, violent or not, would change anything. British men weren't getting drafted, let alone fighting for their freedom. People seemed half asleep. My sense of futility was deepened by the group of neatly dressed men sitting at the back of the meeting, taking notes. They were obviously from the police or secret service. What was the point of making plans that would be immediately relayed to the authorities?

On the day of the march my mood oscillated wildly. The Lansdowne Road group took a vote and decided as a bloc that if there was a move to divert to Grosvenor Square we'd go along. We put on heavy shoes, extra layers of clothes, padding our bodies in case there was a fight. Sean filled his pockets with marbles. 'For the horses,' he said. For a while, as we walked along Fleet Street, I felt OK. The crowd stretched away as far as the eye could see and the chants of 'US out!' reverberated in the enclosed space. The newspapers had taken their own dire warnings seriously: we passed rows of boarded-up office windows. I looked around at Anna and Sean and the others and felt I was part of something, that perhaps together we could make a difference. At Trafalgar Square, as the stewards shepherded the march in the direction of Whitehall ('Turn left! Turn left!'), thousands of us broke away, running through the streets, shouting and letting off fire-crackers. At Grosvenor Square the police were waiting. As we reached it we saw an enormous cordon in front of the embassy. Various groups had decided to leave the main march: there were anarchists, Maoists, non-sectarian people we knew from Notting Hill. Together we linked arms and charged the police line, but time and again they repelled us. Just as we'd become more disciplined, so had they. In the end we forced them back through sheer weight of numbers. After that, as I'd feared, it degenerated. They started using their truncheons. They charged us with horses. It became a repeat of the March demonstration, with one significant difference: this time my friends stayed with me. Everyone from Charlie's – a group of about twenty of us – kept as closely together as we could. We ran together. We stood together. And we fought. We threw stones and distress flares and marbles. When a policeman tried to grab Anna, we rushed in and tore her free.

Afterwards, back at Lansdowne Road, bruised and crushingly tired, we watched ourselves on television, soundtracked by a disapproving commentary. The home secretary came on to praise the Whitehall protesters for their 'self-control'. 'I doubt,' he said, 'if this kind of demonstration could have taken place so peacefully anywhere else in the world.'

'Can someone tell me what the hell the point of today was?' I asked. No one replied.

* * *

After Miles came to dinner, I couldn't sleep. I got up and made a cup of camomile tea, which I held as I sat awake in the study, looking out at the lawn, the skeletal branches of the pear tree silhouetted against the sky. On the second night it was the same. On the third night, as I lay rigid in bed, imagining the phone call that hadn't come, Miranda noticed and solicitously dropped lavender oil on my pillow, offering me a tincture of valerian to drink, a sample of a new Bountessence product she was thinking of calling 'Lethe Water'.

Ever since then – four months now – when I haven't been able to sleep I've sneaked out and let myself into the shop, where I spend the night sifting through old books and papers, only coming home as the dawn breaks to 'wake up' in bed next to Miranda. I do that two, maybe three times a week. The other nights I drink. There's not too much of a smell with vodka. I keep it in a filing cabinet in the study. I haven't drunk alcohol since Thailand. It works well enough as a sedative, but it scares me, because it reminds me that what I'd really like to do is score. What I'd like to do is sit at night in the study and fix up and look at the pear-tree, wrapped in total indifference: mine to the world, its to me.

At first I thought I'd find something in God's books. Perhaps a clue to what Miles wanted. It wasn't logical. I was like the drunk who loses his keys on the way home from the pub and looks for them under the streetlight, because that's where it's easiest to see.

In the glass case where God keeps his more valuable stock is a folio of Jeremy Wilson pictures. Complete, *Modern People* has become a collector's item, its black-and-white photographs of musicians, artists and other taste-makers of mid-sixties London reproduced in numerous books and magazines. God's copy has

John Lennon missing, but is still worth a couple of hundred quid. Looking through it one night I spotted Anna, in the background of a shot of a famous gallerist. She was leaning against a pillar in a white-walled studio peopled by serious-looking hipsters holding dramatic props – an ear-trumpet, a classical bust. In her shiny plastic mac and heavy makeup she was barely recognizable as the woman I knew a few years later. Exactly ten years separated that and the second photo, the figure leaning out of the embassy window in Copenhagen. She'd moved so quickly to the end of her journey.

Except it wasn't the end. I'd seen her. I'd seen her swinging her arms, smoking a cigarette. Little by little I identified what I felt: jealousy, a slow, viscous panic seeping out of my bones. She was alive. She'd been alive all the time. Without my knowledge we'd swapped places. I was the dead one, the old photograph, frozen in time, my blacks turning brown, my whites yellowing with age. And what about Miles? From the start he'd been deader than I could ever be and now he was walking abroad with his rictus grin, lumbering through the tissue-paper screen of my life with Miranda. Miles was after Anna. Surely that was it. The Michael Frame identity was blown and must have been blown for some time, but there was no urgency in the way I was being approached. I was being coaxed, handled. If I'd been important in my own right, armed police would have been at my door: the house surrounded, four in the morning when the body is at its lowest. After so many years, it felt strange to find out I mattered so little.

Whatever Miles needed me for, it seemed to be worth taking care over. Meanwhile he left me entirely alone. I drank in secret; I jumped every time I heard the phone. Otherwise, strange to say, it was a good Christmas. Sam, Miranda and I did the things people do, ate too much, sat in our pyjamas watching *It's a Wonderful Life* on television. It was as if we had an understanding, a pact not to shatter the sugar-glass of our holiday. Over the years, the pagan solstice Miranda was celebrating when I first knew her, an awkward personal substitute for her parents' Judaism, had gradually been sprinkled in style-magazine Scandinavian kitsch. In the front room stood an enormous tree decorated with rustic straw ornaments she'd bought in London. Every surface twinkled with tea-lights. Sam, queen of pester-power, had always craved the Christmas advertised on television, the big family party shot in golden soft focus, the turkey and the plastic snow. So it was amusing to see her roll her eyes at her mother's 'commercialism'. Miranda was confused, wrong-footed by her daughter. I could see her wondering how Sam had changed so effortlessly in two short months away from us.

'She's growing up,' I whispered, as we picked at leftovers in the kitchen. 'That's all.'

Miranda shook her head, annoyed. 'Do you see how she's dressed? She's plaited beads into her hair.'

'Listen to you.'

'I don't mean that, Mike. It's just she was always so conservative.'

'If she thinks we're talking about her, she'll be furious.'

We hugged. Guiltily I kneaded her shoulders, ran my fingers down the ridge of her spine. Perhaps there's a finite amount of reality in the world, only so much energy flowing round in the circuit. The more I'd thought about Anna, about Sean and Lansdowne Road and all the rest of it, the less real Miranda had come to seem. Despite her physical presence, her body pressed against mine as we stood there in the kitchen, for weeks she'd been most clearly present to me in her traces, the plume of blood in the toilet when she had her period, the underwear puddled on her side of the bed. I tried to suppress the urgency I felt as I held her, the need for greater contact. I was afraid she'd pick up on it and ask questions.

New Year's Eve was hard. Miranda had invited friends to dinner. Oliver and Rose ran a specialist organic farm and had a *völkisch* rude health about them that I'd always found slightly sinister. As an antidote to Rose's braying laugh and Oliver's fatuous opinions about the world beyond his orchard walls, I invited God, telling Miranda that otherwise he'd be on his own (which was true) and would feel lonely (which I very much doubted). The others were all settled with drinks and snacks when he shambled in, bundled up in a thick overcoat and carrying his customary burden – twin plastic carrier-bags stuffed with mysterious papers. Reluctantly he let Miranda prise them from his hands and store them in the hall cupboard, along with his coat, which she held as if it was potentially infectious. Collapsing into an armchair, he accepted a whisky and looked at me with heartfelt gratitude when I discreetly put the bottle next to him on the side-table.

Sam went off to a house-party with Kenny and some other friends, kissing everyone good night and wishing them a happy new year. During dinner I savoured God's table-talk, intemperate monologues featuring the local council, people who phoned up to sell office supplies, and the makers of television game-shows, against whom he nurtured a particular animus. He told us frankly that he despised vegetarians, then without missing a beat complimented Miranda on the risotto. He used the word 'cunt' in a variety of inventive contexts. Oliver and Rose were cowed into submissive silence, exchanging panicked glances whenever God's language became more than averagely degenerate. They took their revenge over coffee by instituting a game of charades. Miranda was already furious with me, so saying no was not an option. As God pretended to doze on the sofa, I found myself trying to mime the title of some American romantic comedy I'd never heard of, while Rose giggled behind her hand with moronic glee.

At midnight we sang a self-conscious verse of 'Auld Lang Syne'. The party broke up soon afterwards; Miranda stalked off to bed and I drove God home. Much later I was woken by Sam, who'd had a minor disaster, a flat battery, which meant she was stranded at her house-party. I pulled some clothes over my pyjamas and drove out to pick her up. The music was still booming, and through the door I had a brief glimpse of celebratory carnage, bodies and ashtrays and beer cans. She came running out to meet me, leaving some boy on the doorstep. As we drove home, scattering rabbits on the narrow country lanes, she told me she loved me and I told her I loved her too and felt sick because it was yet another reminder of what was broken and couldn't be fixed. Sure enough, when the phone rang the next day it was Miles. I was to meet him in London the following week. It would be an overnight visit; I should dress smartly. He made it sound like a job interview.

I spent the next few days craving heroin in a way I hadn't for many years. The weather was atrocious. Rain beat down on the garden, leaving pools of water on the terrace. Three nights in a row I drank and watched daylight assemble itself behind the pear tree. New Year's Eve had broken my truce with Miranda, and after Sam had taken the train back to Bristol we collapsed into the atmosphere of sullen hostility that had prevailed before she came home. On the morning of my trip, I watched Miranda standing at the kitchen counter eating a bowl of cereal and talking on the phone, trapping the handset between shoulder and jaw as she discussed packaging. If she noticed my combed hair or the jacket I'd retrieved from the back of the wardrobe, she didn't comment.

'You're not wearing a tie,' Miles pointed out, when he met me at Victoria.

I shrugged. 'I don't think I own one.'

'You're just saying that to annoy me. Still, you'll have to do, I suppose.' We got into a taxi and he gave the address of a conference centre just off Parliament Square.

'Are you going to tell me what we're doing?' I asked.

'Patience is a virtue, Chris.'

'Oh, fuck off.'

It was a short journey, passed in silence. Outside the conference centre Miles paid the driver and walked me through the foyer into a room set up for a press event. It was already half full of journalists and political staffers. Photographers were pacing about, talking into mobile phones. TV crews hefted cameras on to tripods. Miles steered me towards the reserved seating in the front row. We were directly in front of the podium, where a long table was set up in front of a screen bearing the logo of the Home Office.

My nerves were on edge. I fidgeted in my seat and played with the cuff buttons on my jacket. Just when I thought I couldn't stand it any more, the buzz of conversation died down.

A lot can change in thirty years. People who sat around at Lansdowne Road preaching revolution can start to speak the language of choice and competition. They can come to take an interest in efficiency, in productivity, in getting things done. The Right Honourable Patricia Ellis MP, Minister of State for Police and Security, was apparently here to make an announcement about crime figures. The overall trend was positive, thanks in large sum to measures she'd instituted, giving the cops greater resources and discretion and something else, to which I didn't pay any attention because I was too busy looking at her, taking in all the ways she'd changed, the lines around her eyes, the crisp suit, the sensible middle-aged perm. What, I wondered, does Miles want with you, Patty Ellis? And how long is it, with all your rhetoric about cracking down and hitting targets and the challenges of the imminent new century, since you thought about the past, about the changes in a face you'd never expected to see again?

She scanned the room, making professional, impersonal eye-contact, modulating her voice and illustrating her various successes with emphatic chopping hand gestures, like a martial artist breaking roof tiles. The people alongside her, civil servants, a ministerial junior, looked on with the requisite expressions of bovine admiration. Miles had positioned me so I was directly in her line of vision. Once, twice, she looked directly at me, but there was no flicker of recognition.

* * *

OCCUPATION OF CHATSWORTH MANSIONS:
HOUSE THE HOMELESS!

Nowhere to live? Come to Chatsworth Mansions: 120
luxury flats built three years ago are lying
empty while thousands in this country are homeless or live in slums.

1868: The Workhouse
1968: Local Government Hostels

Some things never change unless you force them.

Across Britain speculators are keeping buildings
empty to make vast profits. We say this is wrong.

We have occupied this building to protest at a
system which deprives some of shelter while
others wallow in money. Though it is a symbolic
gesture and we will leave after 24 hours our
anger is real.

HOUSE THE HOMELESS! HOUSE THE HOMELESS!
HOUSE THE HOMELESS!

Patty and I stood on the roof of the block and looked down at the
crowd. A couple of police cars had arrived and a man with
the pinched look of a local news photographer was perched on a
wall, trying to take our picture.

140

'He'll need a longer lens,' she noted drily. 'He'll never get anywhere with that.'

'Do you think there's enough of a crowd?' I asked.

'Not yet.' She peered over the parapet. 'I don't see many press people.'

I blew on my hands. It was a freezing November morning. We'd been up there for two hours. There were about fifty of us. Hats and gloves, Thermos flasks, red noses. We were waiting for something to happen, poking the city's corpse a little to see if it moved. In front of us, east London stretched away into the distance, the grey expanse of Hackney Marshes pocked with chimneys and skeletal Victorian gas towers. The block had been built with a flat roof, and we'd draped a banner across the façade.

HOMELESS? COME HERE!

As I watched, another couple of cars drew up.

'Might as well drop some more leaflets.' Patty reached into the box, took a handful and threw them over the side, where they fluttered down into the street. Behind us, Anna paced up and down, her hands clasped behind her back, like a general.

Chatsworth Mansions was part of a battle with abstraction. We'd been talking for weeks about our disillusionment with the anti-war movement and our feeling that the only political way forward was through practical action: building the new world, not marching for it. The Free Food had encouraged us, but the task seemed too difficult. Housing was an area in which we knew we could make a difference. As the warmth faded from the air, so did the atmosphere of playfulness that had cocooned our little group. London felt tenuous, poised. I couldn't tell what was making me so edgy – the sense that things were about to change or the fear that they wouldn't. If there wasn't a transformation, what would I do? I brushed the idea aside. We were living through a historic upheaval, a time of chance.

Patty and her husband Gavin were newly qualified lawyers,

volunteering at an advice centre in the East End. They were a pleasant couple, serious about their work, politically committed in the way a lot of – what do estate agents call them? – *young professionals* were back then. I liked Patty. She worked hard for her clients. We'd met at some talk or other and soon the two of them were coming over regularly to Lansdowne Road. They were, by temperament, less intense than our group, more rooted in the world as it was than the one they said they wanted to see. Compared to us, they lived a conventional life, paying rent, going to the office. I remember them as people who knew how things functioned. They talked about using the system for progressive ends. In retrospect, I think their politics were entirely fluid, their professed radicalism a product of the time and place, rather than any deep dissatisfaction with the order of things. Anna, I remember, never found them convincing. At the time, I thought she was just jealous, because Patty and Gavin were devoted to one another, while Sean had met a young Irishwoman called Claire, whom he'd moved into Lansdowne Road and was pushing as a full member of the collective.

I thought reflexively of Anna and Sean as a couple though, looking back, my story about jealousy seems wildly off the mark. They slept together sometimes. Otherwise they didn't behave like a couple at all. Nevertheless it was obvious they shared some kind of past, some experience that gave them rights over one another. I found out Sean had helped Anna tunnel her way out of Chelsea; if you believed his version, she'd more or less got on to the back of his bike one day and left her husband. If anyone was jealous it was me, acutely conscious of the electricity in Sean and Anna's detachment from one another.

Claire, Sean's new chick, was a pale, rather sepulchral blonde with long hands and an oval face that made her resemble a figure in an early medieval painting. It was a look she emphasized with shawls and long, flowing dresses. Anna quickly went to war against her, criticizing her for various social and political faults in the long and often bruising group arguments that were becoming a regular

Lansdowne Road ritual. To my surprise, Claire didn't buckle, but often gave as good as she got. She cut her hair and started to wear work clothes. Anna backed down. Anna's own hair was now very short, almost shaved to her scalp. I'd watched her do it, rolling myself a joint at the kitchen table as she leaned over some sheets of newspaper and hacked away with a pair of scissors. Now she looked like one of the mod girls you saw down in Shepherd's Bush, smoking fags and waiting for their boyfriends.

Everyone from Lansdowne Road was up on that roof, lying on their stomachs and looking over the parapet. There were people from Pat Ellis's committee, whatever it was called, from three or four east London communes and activist groups. Miles was there with his camera, showing off to one of his teenage Guineveres. Uther, the usher from Free Pictures, was there too, waving a wand at Hackney Marshes, trying to chant the gas towers down. It's amazing to think Pat Ellis could ever have been part of the same enterprise as Uther Pendragon.

For the site of our next action we chose a boarded-up terraced house near the flyover in Ladbroke Grove, one of a row that had been forcibly purchased by the council when the street was cut in two to build the road. Connections were growing. Our nameless Lansdowne Road group was now part of a spidery network. A lot of people seemed to be thinking as we did.

We worked on the house like maniacs. In the run-up to Christmas Eve we spent more than a week replacing rotten floorboards, painting walls and reconnecting the water and electricity. I wired up lights. A plumber friend installed a bath and toilet salvaged from a bombsite near Free Pictures. With Anna I travelled round in Rosa, skip-raiding and picking up donated furniture. By the time we'd finished, the house looked great. Not luxurious, but spick and span. A home for a homeless family.

Once we had the renovation under way, the big question was who should live there. We wanted to do something that was practical as well as symbolic and for that we needed a family which was indisputably in need. At the time local-government hostels were more like barracks than homes. They were run along the lines of Victorian poor-houses and the people staying in them were treated like morally dubious dirt. They were grim, overcrowded and over-regulated. Many only admitted women and children, husbands having to fend for themselves. Families who complained or 'misbehaved' would be summarily evicted, at which point social workers would often take the children into care. They were cruel and coercive. We saw them as a tool the state used to discipline the poor.

We found a couple called the Castles, who'd been in a shelter for a year. They had three young children, the oldest of whom was seven. Bill Castle had been laid off from a bed factory; he was a sallow Brummie with a persistent cough and an air of utter defeat. His wife Ivy was visibly the stronger of the two. Anna took me to meet her in a caff somewhere up near Wormwood Scrubs. As she talked, her two little boys played with the salt and pepper, opening sugar sachets and tugging at her coat as she tried to manage the baby and concentrate on what we were asking her to do. As far as she was concerned, she told us warily, anything would be better than where they were.

I got to know the Castles much better when the occupation started. Early in the morning on Christmas Eve, we picked up Ivy and the kids from the hostel, bursting through the front door past the warden and the woman from the welfare office. We were deliberately confrontational, swarming through the building and making lots of noise, trying to break down the oppressive air of the place. The warden was furious, telephoning his bosses as soon as we were inside. One or two of the staff tried to block our way. Nevertheless, I remember the action as a festive affair. Jay was dressed as Santa Claus. I gave sweets out to the kids. It was like a kidnap in reverse. The two little Castle boys had a great time, chattering and making pow-pow fingers out of the window.

We calculated that if we raised enough fuss, the council would be shamed into rehousing the Castles. Even if they didn't, we were determined to occupy the place at least until the new year. Since we weren't certain how the authorities would react, we kept the boards on the downstairs windows and barricaded the front door. We draped a banner across the front, Pat Ellis rang the press and by lunchtime we had a crowd of supporters on the street outside, singing carols and waving banners and giving interviews to newspaper hacks while photographers snapped pictures of masked protesters waving from the upstairs windows. We'd written a statement informing people that we'd housed a homeless family in protest at the council's policy of keeping usable buildings empty, their inaction on social problems and the inhumanity of government hostels. We demanded that the Castles should either be immediately rehoused or allowed to remain in the place we'd found for them.

After lunch a pair of council officials turned up, along with a vanload of workmen from the housing department and about a dozen police constables, who positioned themselves on the far side of the road and did a little shuffling dance in the cold. The council officials demanded we let them in. We refused. They threatened us with legal consequences. We asked them whether they were ashamed of what they did for a living. In the middle of this, Ivy Castle leaned out of the bedroom window and gave them a piece of her mind. It was, in the end, Ivy's towering rage that carried the day. She told them she'd had enough. She told them she wasn't going to put up with it any more. The men from the council couldn't take the pressure for very long. They got back into their van and left.

On Christmas morning we celebrated with the Castle children. Someone had donated a tree. Ivy cried and hugged people indiscriminately. The stand-off continued into the new year. While her husband retreated into the background, smoking roll-ups and moaning that the house was cold, Ivy found a vocation. Everyone who stood in front of her, whether journalist, councillor or pompous local MP, received the same full-in-the-face torrent of indignation. Sometimes we had to restrain her, nervous that years of pent-up frustration were leading the stabbing cigarette too close to an official face, or tempting the right hand into an administrative slap. I saw in 1969 in the boarded-up living room. Three days later someone pushed a rent book through the letterbox. The Castles could stay put. We'd won.

Late that night, after a riotous victory party, Anna dragged me into the deserted street outside the Castles' house. We were drunk. The flyover loomed above us. Her normal reserve had dissolved completely, replaced with a fierce libidinal intensity. 'Come on, Chrissy-boy,' she told me. 'Now's your chance.' Pressed into a doorway like a couple of teenagers, we mashed our faces together and fumbled at each other's clothes, icy fingers digging under coats and jumpers, our breath misting in the freezing night air.

That night we slept together on her mattress at Lansdowne Road, in the room she'd painted white and emptied of every possession but a battered metal trunk of clothes and books. The room was cold and we were high and sometimes I'd briefly hallucinate that we were statues or corpses, an instant of lost time before I was jolted back to the slick panting tangle of our fucking, her mouth on my cock, my tongue lapping and sucking at her breasts, her cunt. It was these words she wanted to say and for me to say to her, *cunt*, *spunk*, *asshole*, as if to scrape the act bare, purify it of sentiment.

It felt like a coronation, such a violent release from the frustration of wanting her. Afterwards she lay in my arms and I felt, narcissistically, that we'd sealed some kind of bargain.

Early the next morning I woke up to find Sean sitting at the end of the bed, shirtless, smoking a roach he'd fished out of last night's overflowing ashtray. Anna was asleep next to me, one arm thrown over my chest. He was examining us, a curious look on his face. In the grey half-light the blurred tattoo on his chest was an amorphous stain, a Rorschach blot. I asked him where he'd left Claire and he grinned humourlessly. After that something changed between the two of us. I was no longer an observer of the game he was playing with Anna. I'd earned full participant status. Being Sean's rival (the term seems archaic, with its overtones of chivalry, and somehow coy, evasive) committed me to something. To the group. To whatever it was we were all daring one another to do. I'd thought of leaving once or twice, of going travelling or just finding somewhere else to live. Now I put those ideas from my mind.

A month or so later, as we were planning our next action, Charlie Collinson turned up. He was making one of his periodic visits back home to sell the rugs and jewellery (and the *charras*) he'd picked up in India. It was the first time I'd met the owner of the Lansdowne Road house. With his long, matted hair, his beads and mirror-work waistcoats, he was an alien presence in our increasingly puritanical group. By early 1969, Lands End, as we'd started to call it, had more or less become a formal commune, with an exclusive and fairly stable membership, a habit of collective decision-making and a gruelling schedule of meetings at which personal and political issues were debated with a sort of Möbius-strip logic that made them indistinguishable from one another. Charlie was a lotus-eater, rich and not particularly bright. He was unselfconscious about his status as landlord, moving his things back into 'his' room and expecting the people staying there to make themselves scarce. He was obviously used to having his banalities about love and peace taken seriously and was shocked when Anna called him a 'neo-colonialist parasite' as he was showing off a batch of silver necklaces he'd bought in Ladakh. The atmosphere of round-the-clock revolutionary preparation freaked him out. He'd left behind a scene of genteel Bohemianism, but things had moved on, fast.

Above all, Charlie wanted the printing press gone. Sean and Jay had moved an ancient offset machine into the sitting room, a monstrous thing that was kept working by a mixture of improvisation and brute force; at most times of the day or night someone was tending it, doing repairs or running off leaflets. Stakhanovite slogans were painted on the wall behind it. The floorboards were stained with ink. Charlie wanted it out. He also wanted at least half the residents out. He wanted the women's group to stop using the place for teach-ins. 'It's my own fucking house,' I overheard

147

him complain to someone on the phone, 'and these dykes want me to leave whenever they're hanging about in the kitchen.'

One day, Sean called a meeting. Charlie had indicated that he wasn't happy. How were we going to accommodate ourselves to his wishes? Should we move the press, ask the women to meet somewhere else? We decided that to make any concessions would be objectively Imperialist. The fault lay with Charlie, not us. He was politically backward. He needed re-education. When he came home he was told that if he wanted to participate in the household he would be welcome to do so, but he had to commit, as we were committed, to the project of forming a disciplined vanguard, to being one of an exemplary group of people who could credibly go out to the workers, raise consciousness through agitation and prop-aganda and grow the movement to the point where overthrow of the capitalist state would become feasible. He was told he fell short in several ways. There was the whole area of individualism. There was the implicit racism of his business activities.

'A pig?' he shouted. 'You're in my house and you're calling me a pig?'

'You never let anyone forget that you own the house. That's one of the things which makes you a pig. You think you deserve more respect because you're a property owner.'

'It's my fucking house.'

'Why should that give you a greater say than any other resi-dent?'

'It's not – for Christ's sake, you're not even paying me rent. I don't even know most of you people.'

I have to say I never expected Charlie to call the police. He didn't even tell us. The first we knew about it was when a patrol car pulled up outside. Sean was so livid that he punched Charlie in the face. People were scaling the back fence. Sitting on the kitchen floor clutching his jaw, Charlie suddenly remembered the five pounds of hash stashed in his room, sewn up in leather cushion-covers. He spent the next twenty minutes on the doorstep trying to get them to go away again.

After that, for obvious reasons, we had to leave.

For the next couple of months the group was forcibly split up. I drifted around, sleeping on floors and sofas, sometimes with Anna, but often not, which upset me more than I let on. Without even telling me, she went to Ireland for a week with Sean. For a few days I stayed with Pat and Gavin Ellis up in north London. I remember Pat cooking pasta, working on papers at the kitchen table. I stayed at Free Pictures for a while, trying to look after Uther. Free Pictures was a good place to sulk.

In addition to being the guardian of Free Pictures, Uther was the local shaman. Pretty much everyone had their Uther story. He was our talisman, the guy who once painted himself red with household gloss because he was thinking about colour. As the most visible freak in the area, he acted as a lightning-rod for neighbourhood feelings about hippies. He was regularly beaten up; teenagers would follow him around, imitating his complicated, bustling walk. He collected junk, pulling it back on a home-made trailer he'd welded to his bicycle; when it was stolen, he roamed the locality day and night, hairy and tragic, like a despondent wolfhound. The police loathed him. One night, when I wasn't there, they broke down the cinema door and arrested him. They held him for twenty-four hours and asked him a lot of questions, then released him without charge. Uther swore he'd been cooking and the detectives had tipped the contents of his pan into a bag 'for use as evidence'.

After the raid, the doors to Free Pictures were left hanging open. Kids got in and broke the place up. They smashed all the toilet bowls, ripped most of the seats to pieces. Within days the place had been taken over by a group of Italian junkies, who sat squabbling round a fire on the roof. Stinking rubbish silted up in the corners and there was a scorched patch on the floor where someone had started a fire. Uther refused to move out, more or less living behind the screen in the auditorium, wrapped in a blanket and surrounded by the box files containing his most precious possession, an enormous collection of postcards he liked to arrange in occult sequences on the floor. I tried to chase the junkies off, and I managed it for a while, but Uther was slipping into a state of full-blown paranoia. When he was dancing on the roof of Chatsworth Mansions, he'd already begun to hint at a vast conspiracy, involving the Queen, the Labour Party and the makers of a particular brand of breakfast cereal whose packet was illustrated with a picture of a glowing child. Later he started to spot threats in newspaper headlines and the licence plates of parked cars. His garbled explanations would go on for hours, always arriving at the same conclusion – that he was at risk from some elusive but diabolical force.

One afternoon a friend dropped in to tell me he'd seen Uther being picked up by the police. At one in the afternoon, with hundreds of people walking by, he'd decided to share with the world the genius of William Blake by painting THE ROAD OF EXCESS LEADS TO THE PALACE OF WISDOM in foot-high letters on the side of a building just off the Harrow Road. He'd got as far as LEADS.

What bothers me is that we lost track of him. He disappeared into the system and never resurfaced. As soon as we heard of his arrest we tried to bail him out, but before we could get a lawyer to the police station he was sectioned and taken to a hospital out in the north London suburbs. I hated the idea of Uther on a locked ward, but after Mum I had such a horror of mental institutions that it was almost a month before I steeled myself to visit him. I found him morose and suspicious, sitting in front of the television in the common room, watching the news through a haze of medication. After a few minutes of awkward conversation he accused me of being an agent of the Queen and refused to speak any more.

I told myself that sooner or later Uther would come back, happy and cured. Instead they moved him to another hospital, then another, out of London. There was so much else happening, so many battles to fight, that Uther was left along the way. I'd like to imagine he got out and found a better, easier place for himself, that even now he's on a beach, gnarly and wrinkled, standing on his head and spooking backpackers. All I know is, without him things got cold. Cold and hard.

Finally our homeless commune found the Victorian sweatshop that became Workshop Thirteen, a name that (as Anna pointed out) was almost as bad as the 'Imperial War Museum' in its combination of negative associations. Thirteen was an old light-industrial unit in Hackney, on a back-street near a forlorn patch of park, a place that had once been a garment factory in a row of other garment factories, crammed with Jewish tailors sewing cheap shirts and trousers for the market stalls of the East End. By the time we found it, it had been empty for years. The machines were long gone and the building was just a thin skin of bricks and rotting floorboards, so bowed and warped with age that the whole structure appeared to twist on its axis and the floor sloped in a sharp diagonal from one corner to another. It was draughty in winter and baking in summer. The upper storey had been roosted by generations of pigeons; we found it caked with an acrid white carpet of their shit.

The name started as a sort of shorthand. It had none of the complicated meanings I've heard ascribed to it. The address was 13 Moreno Street and on the brick façade was painted some kind of advertisement, which had faded so much over the years that only the single word *workshop* was still legible. Thirteen was cheap. As in free, once we'd broken the lock and put on our own. No one ever turned up claiming to be the landlord; there were no immediate neighbours. For a long time I don't think anyone even knew we were there. At first the place saw a rapid turnover of people who used it as a crash-pad, staying for a night or two, or a week, or a month. All that had to stop when security became an issue, but for a while Thirteen was a bizarre mix of encounter session, politburo meeting and house-party. We cleaned and scrubbed upstairs and pushed mattresses together to make a large soft area, piled with blankets and sleeping-bags. If people wanted to go to bed they just grabbed a space. You got used to falling asleep with people fucking right next to you, or rolling on to sleeping people as you fucked. Downstairs we built kitchen units and a long refectory table and partitioned a bathroom with sheets of plasterboard. We pulled desks and chairs out of skips, rigged lights and switched the water back on, heating it in a tank we ripped out of a house someone had been squatting in Bow. Finally we screwed a thick reinforcing sheet of scrap iron to the door and moved in the printing press, which had been mouldering in Charlie's garden, making Thirteen a propaganda centre as well as a living space, a laboratory (or so we intended) for the new society.

The question of violence had started to raise its head. We wanted change. We felt it was part of our duty to sharpen contradictions, to make the difference between the rulers and the ruled glaring and unambiguous, impossible to ignore. This meant confrontation. At meetings or demos we adopted a deliberately aggressive attitude, trying to provoke people and intensify whatever was going on. Our behaviour often brought us up against other activists. If they criticized us, we were sarcastic and patronizing; we'd question their courage, the extent of their commitment to the revolution. We began to judge ourselves by our willingness to take risks. I was arrested on a demonstration in Brixton after a young West Indian died in custody. Anna and Helen were wrestled to the floor in a department store when they smashed up a lingerie display. After any action, we'd meet up at Thirteen for what we'd started to call Criticism-Self-Criticism, each of us pointing out moments when we felt we'd failed, when we'd been too conciliatory or someone else's behaviour had fallen short of our increasingly high standards.

There was an anarchist bookshop in Whitechapel where we'd sometimes go to listen to foreign speakers, anti-Franco Spaniards, Greeks on the run from the Colonels. Half of Europe was still Fascist and secretly our own government was collaborating with them, sharing information with their police forces. I heard about things that weren't reported in the papers – bombs in airline offices, assassination attempts against European leftists. In the East End we had our own Nazi problem. I can't remember if we were already calling them skinheads. They were crop-haired mods out of Hoxton or Bethnal Green, kids who beat up immigrants, put lighted rags through their letterboxes. The police didn't do much because many of them were sympathetic to the attackers. I'd started to do odd jobs to make money, casual work on building sites. I'd hear the same thing everywhere, how the Pakis were moving in, breeding like flies. Historically they'd always stayed further south, near the Thames in an area the Spitalfields boys called Brown Town, but now the council was redeveloping it and suddenly little knots of dark-skinned men were standing on street corners they had no business to stand on, corners that had always belonged to white people.

Though much of the violence was random, some of it was organized. There was a pub in Cheshire Street, which over the years had become a kind of Fascist shrine, a place where Nazi splinter groups went to form new parties or sniff Eva Braun's knickers or whatever it was they got up to when they weren't marching around saluting the Union Jack. I heard about it from Leo Ring, the leader of a group who were living in one of the semi-derelict squares in Stepney. Leo, at twenty-four, was tall and dark, with a head of curly black hair and a past as a member of the Firm, a gang of Barking mods who'd once terrorized every blues and R&B club in London. Leo's friends had got into acid, then the revolution. They talked about 'street politics', about 'keeping it low to the ground'. The idea that a cabal of Mosleyites could hold meetings in the saloon bar of their local was an affront and they wanted to do something about it.

At Workshop Thirteen I reported Leo's plan to the others. Should we get involved? Some of us were very much against it. A suggestion was made (by Sean, I think) to exclude the women, but was rejected as chauvinist. We were in or out as a group. I said we should be in. Anna agreed. Sean asked me whether I had the stomach for it. Secretly, I wasn't sure, but of course I said yes. The logic of confrontation started to do its work. I cycled over to Leo's to give him the news.

It's a strange thing to walk out of your front door on your way to a fight. There's something disconnected about it, something about the collision of routine with its opposite that renders the world temporarily unreal. For some people, violence is easy, even familiar. For a few, it's actively pleasurable. For most of us at Thirteen it meant overcoming almost insurmountable barriers, mental and physical. We were afraid. Everything about our backgrounds, our conditioning, the ideals we professed in our politics screamed at us not to go through with it. As we prepared to meet Leo, I watched Helen throw up into the toilet. Matthias was holding her head. 'I don't think I can,' she was saying. 'I just don't think I can.' Helen was tiny, barely five feet tall. Until we'd brow-beaten her into abandoning her position, she'd always considered herself a pacifist. She'd been pushed around in marches, but that was all. She was a sociology graduate, a doctor's daughter.

Me, I had the metallic taste in my mouth that always came before I did anything dangerous. I wasn't like Helen. Neither was Sean. He and I were buzzing on the drama we'd created for ourselves, eager to be off. I could see something in Anna's eyes too. Not avidity, exactly. Clarity. She spoke to Helen with exaggerated gentleness. 'What are you afraid of?' she asked. 'It doesn't matter, honey. Getting hurt doesn't matter. Nothing that happens to any one of us matters, because what we're doing is right.' I watched her, gaunt and tender, a crash-helmet on the floor beside her, like a figure from a medieval altar-piece.

We had spanners, pipes, bats. We wore bandanas and hard hats. We met up in a park near the pub. There were perhaps fifty of us: Leo's people, others who'd come from south or west London. There wasn't much talking. Just before closing time, one of Leo's friends stuck his head round the door to confirm that the pub was full and some kind of meeting was going on upstairs.

We started jogging down the narrow cobbled street towards the pub. Someone blew a whistle. Leo had a sailor's distress flare, which he lit and threw through the front door. We aimed bricks and dug-up cobbles at the windows. Soon orange smoke was billowing out of the pub and choking men were staggering out to be met by a rain of blows. Most were thoroughly disoriented. One or two fought back. I swung the plank I was carrying, felt it connect once, twice. It was a hit-and-run action, all over in five minutes. Beside me, Anna was battering someone with an iron bar. We attacked anyone who came out. Bodies staggering, crawling, lying still on the ground. As arranged, when the whistle was blown a second time we ran off into the side-streets, helping anyone who couldn't walk unaided.

One of Leo's friends had been stabbed. I drove him to hospital, along with another boy who had a broken arm. No one from Thirteen was seriously hurt. That night we held a party; in an atmosphere of borderline hysteria, most of us drank ourselves senseless while a few, like Helen, sat around in a state of mute shock.

Two days later a car stopped beside Jay and Matthias as they walked up Bethnal Green Road. Four men got out and beat them so badly that both had to go to hospital. I spent the evening driving around in Sean's van, looking for the people who had done it. The next night, someone fire-bombed a Sylheti-owned shop on Brick Lane. We responded in kind, by burning out three black cabs at a railway-arch garage owned by Gordon Webster, self-appointed 'commissioner' of the British Patriots League. By the beginning of July a small unreported war had started in the East End, one that was still going on ten, even fifteen years later, long after we'd all gone.

Leo and several of his friends started living at Thirteen. We now had a reputation in the underground, a notoriety that was making us nervous. People we didn't know were starting to turn up, expecting to stay. There were always too many strangers in the building, people we didn't recognize, who didn't quite fit. One night in a pub, a long-haired man approached me and Sean and told us he'd heard we wanted to buy a gun. We said we didn't know what he was talking about and walked home, looking behind us all the way to see if we were being followed. We were sure Thirteen was either going to get busted or attacked by the Nazis. We decided to shut it down, at least temporarily, and join an occupation that was in progress a few miles away in Leyton.

Sylvan Close was an ironically named spot, a melancholy cul-de-sac of boarded-up terraced houses on the site of a proposed dual-carriageway. When I first went there we broke a hole and climbed through it to take a look around. Two rows of five and a couple more at the end, windows and doorways blocked by sheets of corrugated iron. The occupation was centred around Alex Hill, a tall, rake-thin man with thick corrective glasses and a lugubrious manner that concealed a sly sense of humour. He was of indeterminate age and always wore the same rather grubby black trench-coat, which made him look like an out-of-work *film noir* detective. His plan for the derelict houses was nothing if not ambitious. It involved secretly renovating the whole street, replacing rotten floorboards and missing windows, reconnecting plumbing and electricity, then moving in a whole population of homeless people from various local hostels. Eventually he assembled a committee, including Pat and Gavin Ellis, who arranged things with military precision. Building materials were stored in someone's garden. Everything from printing to fund-raising was deputized to separate work groups. Somehow the secret was kept. The job got done.

At Thirteen we initially dismissed Hill's plan as impractical. We were involved in what we euphemistically called our 'community-defence work' and were debating whether to move to Dagenham and take jobs in the Ford factory, in order to organize the car workers. Still, we helped the Sylvan Close lot in peripheral ways and when, on the appointed day, the fence at the front was torn down and it was officially reopened we attended their street party. They had balloons, paper hats, cake, the whole thing. Someone had even managed to scrape together a ramshackle brass band, which farted its way through a few military marches until the bandsmen were distracted by the keg of beer donated by a local pub. It was the end of June, high summer, and the sun beat down optimistically as the police arrived and were officially informed of the situation.

I remember it as one of those days when the future didn't seem to require such an effort of will to imagine. It was right in front of us, an autonomous terrace of houses, organizing its own affairs. A little community. I remember sitting with Sean and Anna in the middle of the street, lounging on canvas deckchairs and surveying our undiscovered country while a gang of children with clown-like smears of orange juice round their mouths played a rough-and-tumble game in and out of the houses. The things we could do! Knock some walls together to make a library. Open a space up as a crèche. We could convert one area into a communal laundry, another into a bake-house. Helen joined us and collectivized our imaginary gardens, planting vegetables and fruit trees, planning a compost heap, a pool, glasshouses, swings. It would be a life of luxury. We'd have saunas and windmills, solar panels, looms.

In the real world what we got was Keith Mallory. Mallory's firm, New City Investigations, had a frightening reputation in east London. Some of Leo's friends had been on the receiving end of a New City eviction in Stepney, which had left one of them with a fractured skull. Within a couple of days Mallory's men were banging on doors in Sylvan Close, trying to wheedle their way inside. They shouted threats through letterboxes. They parked their van so it blocked the end of the street. For some reason the press weren't paying much attention and the papers that covered the story were just reproducing the council's hysterical denunciations. The occupiers were delinquents, criminals, social deviants perversely helping people jump the housing queue.

The occupiers got increasingly panicky about eviction. There were several pre-dawn false alarms. Sleep-deprived, tempers started to fray. Groups had formed around different houses; some wanted to strengthen their fortifications in case of an eviction attempt; others thought this would create a bad impression. As a result, when Mallory's men did attack, some places were much better barricaded than others. There were more than a hundred bailiffs.

Only three houses held out; by the time we heard about it, the families occupying the others were already back in their hostels.

The occupiers were terrified. One by one, over the next two days, the remaining homeless families dropped out. After that very few of the activists were prepared to carry on. The moderate faction, led by the Ellises, felt that without the families, it had become meaningless. This was when the Thirteen collective decided to move to Sylvan Close. We announced that we intended to hold the last three houses, whatever happened. We would make Sylvan Close the site of an open confrontation with the State.

If I say that for me the moon landing didn't happen, I don't mean I believe the conspiracy theories – the studio in Burbank, the misaligned shadows or the unaccountably waving flags – just that the spasm of technocratic pride that apparently shuddered through the television-watching world didn't penetrate the walls of the barricaded terraced house where I spent most of that month. As Neil Armstrong fumbled his pre-scripted line, I was on guard duty, blearily watching the street.

Mallory's thugs left us alone for more than a week. Early one morning I was asleep upstairs in number thirty when I heard noise outside. I poked my head out of the window and saw men in army-surplus tin hats smashing windows and pushing ladders up against walls. In the middle of the street was Mallory, a stocky man in a sheepskin coat directing operations like a general at a siege. At the end of the road stood half a dozen policemen, observing.

The house was barricaded downstairs with heavy wooden beams. We'd installed a trapdoor, which allowed us to block off the first floor. As we watched, two bailiffs started to swing a battering ram against the front door, while two more tried to get a ladder up to the bedroom window. We emptied buckets of water and cans of paint over them, pushing the ladder away with sticks and metal scaffolding poles. Angry and keyed-up, they started to scrabble around for missiles to throw at us. Milk bottles and bricks came flying up. The police did nothing.

I watched the bailiffs force their way into the house next door. Leo, Alex Hill and some others were inside. Mallory's coat got spattered with paint and he flew into a rage, producing a cosh from his coat pocket and laying into a young guy called Milo, who must have been dragged on to the street straight out of his sleeping-bag. Wearing nothing but a pair of underpants he crouched on the ground, trying to protect his head with his arms. We shouted at the police, pointing out what was happening. They ignored Mallory and arrested the other people who were being pushed or dragged out.

When our front door gave way, we scrambled upstairs and dragged weights over the trapdoor. For a while the bailiffs tried to batter their way through, without success. Then they stopped. We couldn't understand why until we noticed little plumes of smoke rising up through the gaps in the floorboards and realized they'd lit a fire downstairs. There were eight of us trapped up there. They were shouting at us from the street, daring us to jump out of the window. We had a couple of jerry-cans full of drinking water, so we soaked rags and tied them round our faces. Pushing open the hatch to the attic, we were lifting Sean up so he could smash an escape hole in the roof when the police finally intervened. I think it was because some reporters had arrived. The fire was put out and Mallory's thugs were forced to leave. As they got back into their bus we sang the 'Bandiera Rossa'. '*Avanti, popolo! Alla riscossa . . .*'

We'd held two of the three houses. As soon as the bailiffs left we split into teams. People were sent for building materials, others for food and water, to organize lawyers for the people who'd been arrested.

Surrounded by the debris of battle, Anna and I smoked cigarettes and brewed tea on a Primus stove.

'What do you think?' she asked me.

'I think it's like the Alamo.'

July was a heavy, muggy month. As we waited to be attacked, it was impossible to stay inside the stuffy little houses. Anna and I made a kind of den in one of the unoccupied buildings, a roofless upstairs room, which we swept and furnished with a mattress and some rugs. It was open to the air but completely private, a secret place where we sunbathed and smoked dope and at night, by candlelight, acted out a series of increasingly confrontational and fetishistic sexual encounters. Anna gave orders. Hit me. Come on my face. I had the sense that my levers were being pulled, that I was the subject of one of her personal experiments: *an analysis of the pathways between violence and sexual arousal in the white male.* I slapped her and she thanked me. I was disturbed to discover how angry I was with her, with women, with the world. Disturbed and turned on, just as she wanted. Sex for Anna was always an assault – on comfort, on the thing in herself she was trying to eradicate. Me, I wanted to smash myself up, to get rid of structure altogether.

One evening I was standing over her as she knelt, naked, on the floor, when we noticed Claire watching us from the doorway, open-mouthed with shock. Anna's reaction was instant. 'Get out!' she screamed. As Claire fled, she hurriedly got dressed. For the first time since I'd known her, she seemed ashamed, humiliated. Claire lost no time in calling a meeting to spread the news of Anna's hypocrisy. Oh, yes, the woman who'd forced her to cut her hair, who'd reduced her to tears by calling her a slave to patriarchy, had been grovelling on her knees to a man. Organization sex. Capitalist perversion.

For me it was a disaster. It spelt the end not just of our private meetings but of all intimacy between us. It was as if Anna slammed a door shut. I'd had a glimpse of something I shouldn't. Now she would eradicate her deviation, without interference. I felt confused, bereft.

The morning after Claire's denunciation I went out to the end of the street in search of fresh air and time to think. To my astonishment, I found Miles Bridgeman filming the houses. 'I've come to join up.' he told me, indicating his camera. 'I've brought my truth-machine.'

I was surprisingly glad to see him. Just then it would have been good to see anyone from the world outside Sylvan Close. Miles's urbanity and his silly surface Chelsea cool were exactly what I needed.

He told me he wanted to document the occupation. It was, he said pompously, a historic confrontation. He asked a lot of questions. Who'd been around? Who was in favour of the new hard line? I was happy enough to chat. Besides, he'd brought a bottle of Scotch and some blues and I'd been subsisting for days on adrenalin and watery vegetable stew. As ever, Miles's studiedly casual clothes, like his studiedly revolutionary attitude, betrayed a hint of flash that made him stand out against his surroundings. When he asked if there was enough hot water for him to take a bath, it was my pleasure to reveal there wasn't even a functioning toilet.

The first sour note came from Sean. 'Who let the spiv in?' he asked sarcastically. I told him the spiv was with me, which calmed him down until Miles took out his camera. Sean immediately threatened to smash it. 'We don't want any pig reporters in here,' he said. 'No fucking observers. Are you here to take part or just watch?'

I told Miles to ignore him. The two of us sat up late, sharing his whisky and talking about what had happened in the months since we'd last seen each other. He'd been in California, filming for the BBC. He'd picked up a lot of new jargon about Gestalts and Rolfing. Ursula had been sleeping with a German bass-player, but was now with a guy who worked at the zoo. The last thing I remembered was the light streaming through the window as Miles described an orgy he'd attended at some hot springs.

When the fight broke out I was asleep. I had a splitting headache and the mid-morning light was making me nauseous, so it took a while before I could make sense of the shouting in the street. It seemed Claire had woken up to find Miles going through her things. She'd alerted some of the others and they'd thrown him out. Miles was still talking, trying to get back into the house, but Sean and Claire were blocking his way. Sean was throwing punches. I leaned out of the window and Miles shouted up, pleading with me: 'Chris, it was a misunderstanding. I thought it was my bag.' He wanted his camera, which he'd left upstairs. Eventually I threw the thing to him and watched him jog off down the street, casting little nervous glances behind him.

Why did I vouch for Miles? Because I wanted to. Because I didn't believe there was anything sinister about him. Claire said she'd found him looking through her address book. Though I told her she was being paranoid, I didn't really know what to think. I didn't have much time or mental space for Miles. Sylvan Close was obviously going to end badly. We were down to ten people and there seemed to be very little support for our cause. No press, no demonstrations. We retreated into one house and spent the next twenty-four hours working continuously, building a wall of breeze-blocks downstairs, filling buckets with sand and water, constructing an escape route across the roofs. We decided there was no point in everyone getting arrested. Six people should go back and reopen Workshop Thirteen. The others should stay. Sean, Claire, Anna and I volunteered.

As we waited for the final assault, the Apollo 11 crew landed on the moon. Tranquillity base. Up there the crew-cut astronauts could see the whole world as a blue-green disc. Down below, we were in our bunker. We stayed awake for forty-eight straight hours before the attack came. A massive battalion of police blocked the end of the street, guarding vanloads of council workmen. There was no sign of Mallory: it was obviously going to be a completely different operation. As a small group of supporters shouted slogans from behind a cordon, an inspector with a sergeant-major's penetrating tone told us through a loud-hailer that we had twenty minutes to get out. We refused and they moved forwards, forming a ring that closed in through the backyards until number thirty-four was surrounded by a triple row of uniformed officers. We had a huge red and black flag, which we waved out of the window as the workmen swarmed into the empty houses around us with crow-bars and sledge-hammers.

Within half an hour most of Sylvan Close had been rendered uninhabitable. Floors were torn up, toilets smashed, pipes and cables pulled out of walls. The council was evidently determined that, whatever else happened, we weren't going to be able to move back in. Watching the ruin of the rest of the street was somehow more frightening than listening to the bailiffs breaking down our barricade. They weren't just smashing up our crude repair-work but all the things we'd imagined: the long refectory table, the kindergarten, the workshops. When they finally broke through the wall we retreated to the roof. My lasting memory of that day is the shudder of the bricks under my hands as I clung to the chimney, watching the black slates tremble and spray upwards as the council workmen battered their way through.

* * *

Sylvan Close was on Miles's mind too as Pat Ellis left the room after her press conference. I craned my neck to watch her leave, followed by a train of advisers and assistants. Miles studied my perspiring face. 'She did legal work for you after Leyton, didn't she?'

'That's right.' I felt like a lab animal, skull shaved for the probe.

'So now you've performed your little experiment, you can tell me the results.'

'What?'

'Stop baiting me and tell me what you want. What have I got to do with Pat Ellis? I haven't seen her since – for longer than I haven't seen you. You know she had nothing to do with anything. Whatever you're involved with, I won't be part of it. It's not my business. I just want to be left alone.'

'For God's sake, Chris. Let's at least get out of the building. Stop raising your voice and we'll go and find something to eat. Eat, then we'll talk, I promise.' He gripped my elbow and steered me outside. On the street he hailed a taxi, giving the driver the address of a members' club in Soho.

All four of us pleaded not guilty. Hoping to turn our trial towards some political purpose, we disrupted the proceedings, shouted at the bailiffs and policemen who were giving evidence. Sean and I were given short prison sentences. Claire and Anna were fined; I think the judge was feeling chivalrous. While I was locked up in Brixton there were riots in Northern Ireland and British troops were sent over to keep the peace. I heard later the soldiers were welcomed by the Catholics, who thought they were going to protect them against a police force staffed and controlled by their Protestant neighbours. To the Thirteen collective it looked like one thing only: the British state was beginning to make war on its own people. Tanks on working-class streets. Soldiers taking aim behind garden hedges. Our boys, the Fascist regime. The Prince of Wales's Own went in on 14 August 1969. It became a kind of shorthand for us, *14 August*, proof that the logic of confrontation was being followed by the other side too.

Miles's club was in a Georgian town-house. We climbed a flight of narrow stairs and Miles signed us in, flirting with the young woman at the front desk. Heavily, deliberately, I wrote *Michael Frame* in the register. We sat on broken-down leather armchairs and I squirmed agitatedly around, trying to brace myself against sinking. The room projected an artful air of shabby comfort. Discreet waiting staff, discreet touch-screens to process your order. It wasn't one of those places where they make you wear a tie; if Miles had taken me somewhere like that I'd have been less disoriented.

'Would you like something to eat, Chris?'

'What exactly is it you do, Miles? I've never known what you do.'

'You wouldn't like to see the menu?'

'Not really. I want to know who you work for.'

'Christ, Chris, you might as well get lunch out of it. I'm not going to pretend this is all fun and games for you. I know what's at stake.'

'You're a consultant. That's what you said. A political consultant. So who are your clients?'

'Like I said, I know what's at stake. You've got a nice niche down there in Sussex. I can understand you want to hang on to it. And if you want this done with the minimum fuss, you need to get it into your head that I'm not going to answer all or even most of your questions, so you might as well calm the fuck down and order some lunch. Everybody needs to eat. I certainly need to eat.'

He realized the waitress was hovering, nervously. 'Oh, hi. Let's get two large gin and tonics and then I'll have the fish pie. Glass of sauvignon with the pie.'

She turned to me.

'You have a vegetarian option? Fine. I'll take that.'

The waitress left. Miles nodded gnomically. 'OK,' he said. 'Now we've actually taken a breath, maybe we can do this in a civilized fashion. In answer to your question, I work for myself.'

'You're lying already.'

'I own and run a public-affairs consultancy, which has a number of clients, some of whom you no doubt disapprove of. I've worked for multinationals. I've worked for various special-interest groups. Trade associations, that kind of thing. I help them get what they want from the political system. In the seventies I spent some time working in the media. You remember I was interested in film-making?'

'I remember that.'

'I ended up in television for a while. Current affairs.'

'You were a journalist?'

'Briefly. Mostly management. I had contacts. I got to know how things work.'

'And now?'

'Now I want to know what you thought of Patricia Ellis.'

'She's doing very well.' I shrugged. 'She seemed to have a lot of flunkeys.'

'She used to be a real fire-brand, remember?'

'Did she?'

'Oh, come on. What about during all that Leyton business? Quoting Mao in meetings. Talking about expropriating this and smashing that.'

'I don't remember you being at any meetings, Miles. I remember you turning up one day out of the blue and asking a lot of questions. I remember you getting thrown out. I remember Sean Ward punching you. Do you remember all that?'

'It was a misunderstanding.'

'Of course. And is this a misunderstanding too?'

'This is lunch, Chris.'

'At least call me Mike.'

The waitress came with our drinks. Without thinking, I gulped my gin and tonic. Miles looked at me, his lopsided smile creeping across his face. 'Well that seemed to go down easily. I knew your whole teetotal Buddhist thing was a con.'

I felt I'd tripped up. 'It's not a con. At least it wasn't, not at the time. I don't consider myself a Buddhist now, but I was. I'd be dead otherwise.'

'What happened to you?'

'When?'

'After you left.'

'I couldn't deal with – anything. What had happened, anything. I drifted around in Asia, did too many drugs. It got very bad. Someone scraped me off the street in Bangkok and took me to a monastery. The monks used to treat addicts.'

'And they cured you.'

'That's right.'

'They cured you and along the way they made you into a believer. So God got you in the end!' He did a little trumpet call, trilling his fingers in front of his face. 'After all that!'

'Buddhists don't believe in God.'

'But a believer, nonetheless.'

I had no come-back to that. First the revolution, then the Four Noble Truths. A compulsive believer, always mistaking my ideas for the world. 'Wisdom is not scholarship,' said the monks. How I'd studied that saying!

The waitress returned with our food. I watched Miles fork fish pie into his mouth. It was frightening to hear my life tossed about in trite phrases, a joke to be capped with a punchline. It made me feel temporary, disposable.

His long jaw, masticating and grinding.

At Wat Tham Nok we stayed in huts, a wretched, emaciated crew, our jaundiced skins crossed with track-marks and blackened by tattoos. We pottered about in our red pyjamas, Thais and bird-shit foreigners together, looking at the floor, racked by withdrawal. The village of the damned. 'Drink, drink.' Every morning, kneeling before a bucket, we downed a beaker of the mixture and waited for the spasms to come. The acid reek of my vomit. The sounds of the men beside me, groaning and cursing. 'Drink, drink.' The monks paced up and down behind us like drill instructors. The whole bucket of water was to be ingested, then spewed into the trough. Hard men, the monks. In their quarters they had pictures of accident victims, syphilitics, horribly mutilated corpses. Aids to contemplation.

'You know,' Miles was saying, 'I've thought about you quite a lot over the years. I always felt you got caught up in something you had no control over. You didn't seem like the others. You didn't seem like an extremist.'

I had to smile at that. Miles was still the same, untroubled by doubt or hope and incapable of understanding it in others. He could live in the world as it is, which (depending on your point of view) is either pragmatism, coarseness or a particular kind of heroism. Whatever it is, I've never been able to do it. The world has always seemed unbearable to me.

He called over the waitress to ask for a second glass of wine. 'Sentiment aside,' he said abruptly, 'you've made a mess of your life. You had brains and a certain amount of talent, unlike – let's just take an example at random – the Minister for Police and Security, who's generally considered around Westminster to be a dull biddy whose main talent is for worming her way up the greasy pole.'

'I don't really follow politics, these days.'

'Is that so? You must admit it's strange. To think about what she once believed and the job she does now.'

'She's not the only one to have changed, is she?'

'We've all changed, but she's the one in charge of a major Home Office portfolio. And when her boss is forced to drink hemlock, which can surely be no more than a few months away, she's odds-on favourite to become Home Secretary. I mean, for Christ's sake, be as zen as you like, but you have to see that's some career trajectory. She was a self-proclaimed revolutionary. She was plotting the violent overthrow of the State.'

'No, she wasn't. She was a voguish liberal who went with the flow. She was following fashion.'

'I'm sorry to say not everyone shares your sanguine view.'

'Meaning?'

'Meaning there's a public-interest question.'

'Speak English, Miles.'

'It's the Home Office, not Culture, Media and Sport. There's a feeling that someone with her background isn't suitable for the job. A former revolutionary in charge of the security services? That's a little too much baggage, don't you think? She's not a safe pair of hands.'

'So she's not a safe pair of hands. What of it?'

'It's a widely shared opinion.'

'She must have been security-vetted. Isn't that what you do?'

'Oh, absolutely, but vetting committees can make mistakes. They found no connection between her and the fourteenth of August actions, for example. Completely in the clear. But there were dissenting voices. Some people don't think the checks were thorough enough.'

'I'm telling you, she had nothing to do with fourteenth August.'

'Let's take it by stages. When did you last meet her? You saw her after you got out of prison, didn't you?'

'Yes, I think so.'

'Did she come to your squat?'

'I suppose she must have done. I have a picture of her at the women's group, but that might have been earlier on.'

They picked me up outside the prison, Leo, Anna and Claire. I was expecting Sean's old van. Instead they were driving a big blue Rover, an expensive car.

Anna kissed me on the mouth. 'We got rid of Rosa,' she explained.

It was about time. Back in Notting Hill the van's loud exhaust and distinctive pink paint-job had become a liability. By the time we moved out of Charlie's we were spending half our time by the side of the road, watching sour-faced constables kick her tyres and poke around under the seats. Eventually we'd taken her to a friend's garage in Shepherd's Bush and had her sprayed white, but it was a sloppy job. You could always see a faint pink sheen on the bonnet and the back doors.

'Where did you get this from?' I asked, running my hands over the car's creamy upholstery.

'Somewhere in Belgravia,' said Anna.

'I thought Sean was still in prison.'

'He is.'

'Anna and Claire took it,' muttered Leo.

'Leo says it's too flashy, but really he hates it because stealing cars is man's work.'

'You should bloody get rid of it.'

'Oh, calm down.'

We parked the car in the yard behind Workshop Thirteen and covered it with a tarpaulin. I found the place full of people I barely knew. Two or three agit-prop friends of Jay's were lounging around, bumming cigarettes and waiting for someone to cook. A young black woman was running off leaflets on the printing press.

In the Brixton prison rec room there had been a television. The news pictures seemed to tell a simple, chilling story. Glass on the streets of the Bogside. Blazing cars. 'We have to fight back,' I told Leo that night. It was late and we were whispering. Everyone around us on the mattresses was asleep, bundled in blankets and sleeping-bags. Nearby Anna spooned closer to Shirley, the young black woman. I was expecting to be with Anna on my first night of freedom. Either her or Claire. I was angry. Leo was too, though for different reasons.

'They're ganging up on me,' he hissed, 'calling me a misogynist. Anna said I was unable to distinguish rape from ordinary sexual relations. Fucking bitch.'

There was always a lot of tension at Thirteen. I think that was partly because so many things weren't said. I wanted to talk privately, not least with Anna, but it was impossible. With Sean still away in prison, Anna had exerted control over the collective. She'd become the advocate of a policy of absolute openness. The individual was a politically suspect category; privacy was just another name for isolation; the atomized worker was subject to feelings of depression and alienation that could only be cured by participation in an authentically communal experience. It was as if she subsumed herself entirely into Thirteen. Everything she did, whether it was washing herself or going to the toilet, she did in the presence, at least potentially, of someone else. And somehow she succeeded in placing herself entirely on the surface. Her naked-ness became meaningless, even to me. It was as if she had no inner life at all. But that totalitarian sharing became the rule for every one of us that winter, not just Anna, and in most of us it bred furtiveness. It was easier not to speak about your feelings to anyone than be forced to offer them up to everyone, yet another sacrifice on the bonfire of openness.

Soon after I got out of prison, there was an argument among the women involving Leo's traditionally minded girlfriend Cynthia, who rolled his joints, did his laundry and looked at him with big eyes when he spoke at our meetings. Cynthia was told she was politically backward. She was informed that she was no longer welcome. Leo was furious at her expulsion and moved out with her to stay in a huge unruly commune that had been set up in an empty mansion in Piccadilly. When I went to visit I found more than a hundred people dossing down in high-ceilinged reception rooms, climbing on the roof and shouting down from the windows at a besieging crowd of police and hostile gawpers. You had to get in and out using a makeshift drawbridge. After a couple of weeks, the place was stormed. Leo came back. Cynthia didn't. Was Pat Ellis there when they expelled Cynthia? I think she was. I remember her face, twisted, shouting. I was upstairs, dozing on the mattresses. I went down to watch. Pat was listing Cynthia's faults. Other women were joining in. Cynthia was whimpering. 'You just aren't human, you people. What's so bloody revolutionary about being cruel?'

That would have been just after we burned down the first army recruitment office.

The noise of chatter in Miles's Soho club was increasing, forcing us to raise our voices. 'Are you telling me,' he said, draining his second glass of wine, 'that Pat was completely unaware of what you were doing?'

'We weren't exactly advertising it.'

'Not at first.'

'She was part of the women's group. Most of them split off and set up some kind of commune in Tufnell Park.'

'She didn't go, though.'

'She was married.'

'But she didn't go. She wanted to be in the action faction, not the sisterhood.'

'Where did you get that? You sound like someone's uncle trying to talk jive. She wasn't part of either. The feminists thought she was soft because she wasn't prepared to leave her husband. We thought she was just another *bourgeoise*. She was useful because she was a lawyer, but we didn't trust her.'

'Regardless. She must have known.'

'Known? Why? She hardly ever came to Thirteen.'

'I'm not sure you're remembering correctly.'

How is my memory? When Leo showed me the crate of petrol bombs it made sense. I didn't discuss it. I didn't really stop to think very much at all. Milk bottles filled with four-star and engine oil, ballasted with sand, stoppered with wadding. We drove the Rover down to a recruitment office in Blackheath where the two of us broke a window and threw a couple of our crude devices through the hole. As we drove away all I could think about was Kavanagh the junk man, me and Brian setting fire to his garage as kids.

When Anna found out, she was furious. We hadn't consulted the group, meaning we hadn't consulted *her*. 'How could we?' I hissed. As we argued, Shirley was lounging nearby on the mattresses, pretending to read Régis Debray. The place was full of people I

172

didn't know and didn't trust. That evening, we told the various interlopers and sexual partners and hangers-on that they needed to find somewhere else to sleep. We shuttered the doors and held a closed meeting.

Q. Why have you done this?

We felt it was the only adequate response to the presence of the army on British streets.

Q. What political purpose does this serve?

It reminds people the system isn't invulnerable. It has a small practical effect on the machinery of the military.

Q. Shouldn't it have been a group decision?

It was spontaneous. Besides, all action seems equally meaningless in our alienated state. Why focus on this in particular? What's special about it?

Q. How do you justify putting the collective at risk?

It was a provocation. We want to force you, our comrades, to think.

Q. What are we to think about?

Your quietism.

Your continuing collaboration with Imperialism.

Q. Can you promise you won't take such unilateral action again?

No. Why should we promise? Why would you want to extract such a promise? Is that you setting a limit, or the voice of some power that has a hold over you?

Q. Your gesture is infantile. The revolution will be led by the working class. A terrorist is just a liberal with a bomb, arrogantly presuming to lead the way.

Rubbish. You're covering up your cowardice with quotations Change is imminent. It's happening around the world. The slightest pressure will tip the balance in our favour.

One spark, a thousand fires burning.

We were so impatient. We wanted the time to be now. Of the core group, only Matthias and Helen remained seriously troubled by what we'd done. We were supposed to be protesting against war. Surely a peaceful gesture would have been better? I accused them of fetishizing non-violence, telling them they'd just internalized the state's distinction between legitimate protest and criminality. Leo and I were censured for our individualism, but the logic of confrontation did its work. By the end of the meeting, everyone was in agreement. We would go further.

That night I slid into bed beside Anna and asked her why she was ignoring me. I told her she was beautiful, and she asked how I'd feel if someone threw acid on her face. Then I pushed too hard and said I loved her, which made her pull my hair and hiss at me, tears of rage and frustration in her eyes. How could I be such a pig-thick *bourgeois*? Why didn't I get it? Unless we were prepared to do something, we were just another part of it, more dead weight on the shoulders of the world's poor. Our precious individuality was oppressive precisely because we found ourselves so special. To give ourselves pleasure, we'd countenance all sorts of horror, as long as it happened far away. So why didn't I get it? Why didn't I get that my stupid narcissistic idea of love made her sick?

The night after that, we drove to Chelmsford, then Colchester, setting fire to a recruitment office and a Territorial Army storage depot. At each site we scattered leaflets.

FOR QUEEN AND COUNTRY

Great prospects! See the world!

What will YOU be doing in Northern Ireland?
They tell you it's for your country. They're
lying. You'll be breaking down working-class
doors, trampling on people like yourself and your
family. They want you to kill and die for their
profits. We're fighting back against their power.

Rise up! Remember 14 August!

We made it back to London as dawn broke, still wired on the amphetamines we'd taken to get through the night. The Rover stank of petrol. Its upholstery was smeared and grubby. We drove it on to some wasteground near Hackney Wick and burned it out. Anna insisted we should steal another car immediately, but we couldn't get into any of the vehicles parked on nearby streets and ended up trudging several miles home through freezing fog.

For several days we looked through the newspapers, expecting to see our actions reported. There was nothing. We read that BBC1 had just started broadcasting in colour; an actor from *Coronation Street* had got married. No real news, just distraction. A couple of days later we stole another car and drove to Chelmsford to check our work. There it was: a blackened building like a missing tooth in a jaw of shuttered shop-fronts.

New Year came and went. A new decade. Thirteen was so cold that milk froze in bottles on the windowsill and a film of ice coated the inside of the bathroom window. A dozen of us slept close together on the mattresses, a rat-king in a midden of sleeping-bags. None of us was working. We had problems with dole claims, fines, probation, unpaid debts. I wanted a life free of money, but it seemed to be plucking at me, its tendrils curling round my ankles as I shivered in my sleep. I developed a rash, which left clusters of tiny lesions round my mouth and between my thighs. It was several weeks before we realized that we were all suffering from it, scratching at our armpits, our pubic hair, infecting and reinfecting one another. We burned the bedding and got more.

We went out looking for work, pooling whatever money we could get. I laboured on building sites. Leo and I stole tools and used them to open up empty houses, leaving a trail of flapping doors around the East End. We joked about setting up a squatters' estate agency. In the face of hostility from the other women, Anna got a job in Soho, first as a cocktail waitress, then as a stripper. I think the work was important to her, part of her project. Once, or at least once that I know about, she accepted money for sex from a man she met at the club. She told me she did it to see what it was like to become a commodity. Self-denial would be the wrong term for what she was doing. It wasn't some kind of religious bargain: Anna certainly didn't believe in a reward in the hereafter. She was mounting yet another assault on her own sense of privilege and entitlement, on what she considered the 'excessive value' she'd been brought up to place on her life.

Sometimes I went to pick her up from the club, hanging around on the pavement outside because the doorman wouldn't let me in. She'd come and find me and we'd go to drink frothy coffee at an Italian place on Old Compton Street. I'd surreptitiously examine her for signs of change, beyond the unfamiliar traces of makeup round her eyes and mouth. We'd talk a little, laugh about inconsequential things. It felt good, a moment of relief from the struggle. I knew she enjoyed it too, so I was shocked when she denounced our meetings in Criticism-Self-Criticism, accusing me of deviation, of clinging to the luxury of bourgeois leisure.

Someone brought a plastic bag of mushrooms back from Wales. We tripped and argued and shivered under the covers and scraped the huge pan of vegetable stew, endless vegetable stew made with whatever we could buy or scavenge, tasteless however much curry powder we added to the mix. We wrote position papers and smashed monogamy and once in a while we burned something down. Then Sean was released from prison and our hibernation came to an end.

* * *

As I watched Miles eat fish pie, it occurred to me that we were sitting more or less across the road from the coffee bar where I used to meet Anna. When I went to use the toilet I looked out of the window. The café had gone, turned into a Thai restaurant. The club was gradually filling up, the sofas now tenanted by well-dressed after-work drinkers. In the toilet I splashed water on my face and tried to work out where Miles was leading. I expected him to make a proposition, a demand of some kind, but when I got back to the table he'd called for the bill.

'I think that's enough for now,' he told me. 'I have things to do. I'll drop you at your hotel.'

'So that's it? You've finally got it into your head that Pat Ellis wasn't involved?'

'Whatever, Chris. We'll talk about it tomorrow. There's some where I need to be, but I'll come in the cab with you. I'll pick you up at eight tomorrow morning.'

We drove to a dingy town-house in Fitzrovia, with a card in the window saying *No Vacancies*.

Miles left me in the care of an elderly landlady with a floral housecoat and no small-talk. Both she and her nameless establishment seemed like survivals from an earlier era, before new-fangled notions of comfort or hospitality took hold in the British hotel trade. The lobby smelled of cigarettes and carpet-cleaner. The leaflets in the rack by the reception desk advertised shows and exhibitions that had long since closed. There was no sign of any other staff or guests. The woman gave me a key on a heavy brass fob and walked me arthritically upstairs to a room decorated with hunting prints and the kind of geometric-patterned wallpaper last current thirty years previously.

'What time's breakfast?' I asked.

'I understand you'll be taking it out. Mr Carter's company specified when they made the booking.'

'Mr Carter?'

'The gentleman you were just with.'

'His name's Bridgeman.'

'I wouldn't know about that. Will you be going out at all?'

'Yes,' I said.

'Front door's locked after ten.'

Grudgingly she accepted that the night porter would let me in if I was late, then quit the room, shutting the door smartly behind her. Contemplating the hospital corners on the bedsheets, the small cake of soap and the paper-wrapped tooth-mug on the basin, I was filled with foreboding. All British state institutions, whatever their purpose, share an atmosphere. When I was growing up they used to share a smell too, an alkaline reek that united school and hospital and prison and dole office, and always triggered in me a kind of cellular-level panic, a fight-or-flight reflex. The smell has gone, abolished along with so many of the visible signs of power (in dark moments I think it's all my generation achieved, killing that smell), but even without it the atmosphere remains and that room had it: old and cold and abstractedly cruel.

I grabbed my coat and half-ran down the stairs, ignoring the landlady's barked inquiry about the key. The evening had turned cold and the few people on the street were hurrying along, hunched into coats and scarves. I headed for the tube station. At that moment my plan, in so far as I had one, was to get on a train, any train. I had a cash card. I could withdraw some money, go somewhere, start again. How far would I get on two hundred quid? Little by little, I slowed my pace. I knew I was panicking, not thinking clearly. On impulse I turned a corner. Up ahead I saw the lights of Oxford Street. Basics, Chris, I told myself. Remember the basics. Miles will have you followed.

The wind whipped at my face. I lingered outside a cinema on the Tottenham Court Road, using the glass window to watch the street behind me. Then I made my way into Soho, loitering in alleyways, ducking in and out of video stores and bookshops, trying to spot my tail. In a basement, as I pretended to browse bondage magazines alongside a row of suburban commuters, I finally picked him out, a young guy in jeans and a hooded sweatshirt who looked out of place among the briefcases and thinning hair. I led him towards Regent Street and lost him in a department store, shouldering my way back out through the late-night shoppers and jumping on a bus outside. It was only then, as I sat on the top deck, breathless, eye-level with the advertising hoardings of Piccadilly, that I realized how I'd been addressing myself. Turn left, Chris. Don't look behind you, Chris. For years I'd trained myself to be Mike Frame. I'd settled down in him, ceased even to think of who I'd been before, but Miles had uprooted me with a few short conversations. In itself that didn't matter, except that if Mike Frame went, Miranda and Sam would go with him.

Oh, Sam.

Once upon a time I'd been prepared. When I worked at Olla's new-age shop I'd kept a metal cash-box hidden in the store-room, containing money and an American passport I'd bought on the street in Bangkok. Then Miranda and her fatherless baby had come into my life. Mike Frame had applied for a bank account, a national-insurance number. The identity held up. After a couple of years he renewed his British passport to go on a camping holiday in Spain, where he baffled his partner with his nervousness at the airport and his interest in relics of the Civil War. Chris Carver had tried to escape the state, but Mike Frame eagerly embraced it. Each database record, each countersigned form confirmed his reality, put flesh on his bones. Little by little, the running money got spent. The American passport expired. Michael Frame started to seem like an end, a final destination. Looking back, I think I closed my escape routes deliberately. I didn't have it in me to run again; which is, I suppose, another way of saying I'd got old.

I stepped off the bus near Victoria station. In a brightly lit Indian restaurant tricked out with laminate flooring and contract furniture, totally unlike the flock-wallpapered haven I'd hoped for, I ate chick-peas and drank several pints of lager. I paid the bill and stood swaying slightly on the pavement, knowing that I was going to have to face whatever Miles had in store for me. I went into an off-licence and bought a half-bottle of vodka, then hailed a cab and went back to the hotel, where I lay on the bed and drank shots out of the tooth-mug, embalmed in the swirling patterns and petrol fumes of 1970.

* * *

Sean raced out of prison like a greyhound chasing a hare. Before we'd even got him back to Thirteen he was making war plans. The Tupamaros had shown the way in Uruguay. Urban guerrilla: a small band, operating in the city, using the terrain to our advantage like peasant revolutionaries used the mountains. Street corners and tower blocks our Sierra Maestra. And cars. Cars featured heavily in Sean's plans for our future.

We were the vanguard party in embryo. We would lead the way. We'd be exemplary and we'd be self-sustaining. So there would be fast cars, stolen and stored in lock-ups or sold on to get money. There would be money and with the money we'd buy arms. There would, above all, be no more waiting, no more frustrating attempts to persuade others of the urgency for change.

It felt like spring twice over. Without Sean, Anna's intense cold had spread through all of us, sealing us into a sort of mute despair. Now the ice had gone from the windows at Thirteen. At the back of my mind there was a twinge of resentment at the way Sean could push things forward so easily. He and Anna spent long hours on the mattresses, plotting and whispering to one another. In Criticism-Self-Criticism I chipped away at their exclusivity. We were still opposed to monogamy, weren't we? Anna accused me of being manipulative. I had a misogynistic desire to dominate. I was trying to force her back into my bed. I told her she was being arrogant. My only concerns were political.

We got the explosives out of the phone-book. Sean had formulated a baroque plan to stake out construction sites and mines, then follow lorries to find out where they went. Without directly contradicting him, Anna visited the local library and came back with a list of ten demolition contractors, all within fifty miles of

London. The theft went smoothly enough. There was a company out in Grays, along the Thames estuary, which had a yard by the river, at the end of a desolate lane strewn with car tyres. The only guard was an old man who sat and read model-railway magazines in a hut by the gate, his head framed in a little yellow square of electric light. We parked on a patch of wasteground and watched the oily black water, waiting for a cloud to obscure the moon.

I remember the sound of my breathing, ragged and heavy and somehow detached from my body as I carried a wooden box across the yard towards the hole we'd cut in the fence. Light rain falling on my face, the endlessness of the space between the warehouse and the gap in the wire. The open steppe.

Back at Thirteen we sat around the kitchen table, staring at our haul. It looked like bars of some kind of confectionery, each yellow block wrapped individually in waxed paper. We had a hundred and fifty charges of nitroglycerine gel, a spool of safety fuse and fifty PETN detonators. I don't think any one of us knew what to say. There was no exultation, no sudden release of tension. We just sat there. I don't know about the others, but I didn't sleep that night. The mere presence of the stuff, hidden in a metal box under the floorboards, imposed a density, a pressure on the atmosphere that made it impossible.

Since none of us knew anything about explosives, our plan was to do some tests, drop a stick down a hole somewhere and see how big a bang it made. We told ourselves we'd proceed slowly. We'd take care.

Richard Nixon put paid to that. On May Day we woke up to his announcement that he was sending US combat troops into Cambodia. It was a massive escalation of the conflict. 'This is not an invasion,' said the President, describing the movement of several thousand troops across the border. America couldn't be a pitiful helpless giant while the forces of totalitarianism and anarchy were threatening free nations everywhere. Here was the man who'd told voters he had a 'secret plan to end the war', shuffling his notes and gesturing vaguely at a map on an easel as he told us why more killing was the right thing for everyone.

We had to respond. He'd given us no choice.

In principle the device was straightforward. An electric current initiated the detonator. The detonator initiated the gel. A kitchen timer from Woolworths would close the circuit. The timer was shoddy and imprecise, but as long as you didn't set it too short, it would do the job. I was the one who knew about electricity, so I was the one who sat down at our long wooden table and spread out tape and tools and wire and batteries and made a bomb. I told the others to go out for the afternoon. As I worked, all I could think about was what would happen if I made a mistake. I could already feel the explosion welling up inside me, as if merely thinking about it tapped a disintegration already latent in my body. Only a month previously, a group of New York radicals had blown themselves up in a Greenwich Village town-house. Rich kids, said the newspapers. Stupid nihilistic rich kids who got themselves killed. Nothing was mentioned in the articles about their politics.

Stripping the plastic coating from the wire to expose the core, twisting the ends. My hands shaking. It was, essentially, no more complex than wiring a plug, but it seemed to take for ever.

Late that night we put the bomb in a blue leather handbag (a jumble-sale purchase of Helen's) and left it against the front door of an American bank near the Mansion House. It was a weekend and the City of London was deserted. A stage set, waiting for the play to begin.

A BOMB TO HALT THE MONEY MACHINE

Nixon invades Cambodia. More blood on his hands.
Bankers and arms companies pull the levers.

THEY profit. WE die.

US trade supports mass murder. UK government
wants a piece of the action.

It's time to RESIST.

Numbers for Nixon:
US military spending 1968, 9.4% of GDP.
US soldiers killed last year 9,414 killed, 55,390
wounded.
Vietnamese and Cambodian dead are not counted,
hundreds of thousands so far, maybe millions.

We are acting in solidarity with all oppressed
people across the world. Our attack is violent
because violence is the only language THEY
understand.

RISE UP!

MAY DAY 1970

We posted copies of our communiqué to mainstream newspapers and the underground press. From callboxes we phoned the
BBC and ITV, claiming responsibility. Then we waited. Three days
later there had been no response. No news reports. No commentary. No acknowledgement at all. It was as if the bomb hadn't
detonated. But we'd heard the sound, a muffled crump. We'd seen
emergency vehicles racing towards the scene. The day afterwards
the bank was closed. Wooden boards covered the building's ground-
floor façade.

Does something exist if it's unobserved? Does something happen
if it is not reported?

***

Renounce anger, forsake pride. Sorrow cannot touch the man who is not in thrall to anything, who owns nothing. This car, with its silt of water bottles and maps and fast-food packaging in the footwell. This body.

It smells, this body that is not my body. These unwashed clothes, these furred teeth. This face coated with grime and sweat.

South of Paris the country has changed. The air is warm and pine trees line the road. I catch a glimpse of a river, a flash of blue water scattered with white boulders. On impulse I take the next turning and make my way down towards it. Leaving the car in a clearing carpeted with pine needles and scraps of blue plastic, I pick my way to the water, where the light is harsh and bright. I take off my shirt and shoes. The stones are painfully hot, a bed of coals for me to walk across. No one seems to be around, so I strip naked and wade into the deepest part of the river, where it's slimy underfoot and the shock of the cold, up to my knees, thighs, chest, persuades me that I'm still more or less alive. I stay in until I'm shivering, then clamber on to a large flat boulder and lie down. The sun quickly begins to dry off my skin.

I'm exhausted.

An orange bloom of light on my closed eyelids. Orange wallpaper in a hotel room, nauseating op art swirls rotating as I drink and fret and wait for Miles. Heat like the fierce heat of the dry season at Wat Tham Nok, when the ground hardens and the grass underfoot is parched and brittle. The lizard that squats for hours on the wall of my cell. It's there when I go out to do my chores, still in the same spot when I get back. I sprinkle water on the ground in front of the *farang* block to lay the dust, sweep the flagstones, line up the battered metal buckets for the morning purge, then walk over to the monastery office to help Phra Anan with the accounts and the registration letters. Translating the letters, learning scraps of French and Dutch and German: *I pray for you to help my son with his addiction. I feel you are his last chance* . . . Every day the lizard is waiting for me, judging me with its little liquid eyes. How have I done? Have I trodden lightly? The tinselly promise of religion: follow the instructions, find the exit. Orange, fading to guilty red, flaring up to an unbearable dazzling white as I open my eyes, then fading again as I drowse, watching seven-year-old Sam playing with a bucket and spade, pottering around and chattering to some invisible friend. Her arms and legs are less chubby than last year, her game more organized. My daughter, not by blood but because I notice such changes. My daughter because I love. Miranda, some way down the beach, looking for fossils, stooping to examine a find. Anna, walking away up the hill. Tall, rangy Anna, smoking a cigarette. What will I say to you? I'm driving south because I have something to ask you, but do I know what it is? I think I want to ask why you carried on, even when you must have known the revolution wasn't getting any closer, when it must have been obvious you weren't changing anything, just piling up horror. Did you still have a choice, by then? Grainy photographs of the burning embassy building. Uniformed police gesturing, looking up at the balcony. How did you survive? Who was the dead woman if it wasn't you? And who helped you, Anna? What deals did you have to make to be allowed to live in peace in your little village, to walk up the hill carrying a string bag of melons, smoking a cigarette? When you cut up the fruit at your table, what do you feel? When you look back at your life, does it make sense? That's what I want to know. That's the answer I need from you.

For a year after that bombing, we fought a strange, silent war. Our first targets were corporate, because we believed corporations were pulling the strings of government. After the bank bomb, we attacked a chemical company, a subsidiary of a group that sold defoliants and white phosphorous to the American army. VICTORY

TO THE NLF AND ALL THIRD WORLD REVOLUTIONARIES. We bombed the head office of a construction firm with a contract to build new prisons. We bombed a bank that financed the regime in South Africa. WE ARE EVERYWHERE, we wrote. WE ARE IN YOUR OFFICES YOUR FACTORIES WE ARE THE MAN AND WOMAN NEXT TO YOU ON THE TUBE THE BUS THE TRAIN. Anna and I composed them together, lying on the floor or sitting at a rickety Formica table in one of the flats we rented after we closed down Thirteen.

```
Their school is a concentration camp.
Their factory is a concentration camp.
Their prison is a concentration camp.
Their hospital is a concentration camp.

Concentration Camp Britain.

We are the Jews.
Can you smell smoke?
```

We'd argue about the tone, veering between a terse, tabloid style we hoped would speak to the masses and the technicalities of an argument we wanted to make to other revolutionaries. As we wrote them, our statements felt reasoned and sober. If they sounded harsh or hysterical, we felt it was only because we were speaking truth to power and the truth was bleak. We drafted them in a notebook, then made copies with a child's printing set, sealing them and giving them to militant friends to circulate to the media.

```
Lessons: how to police each other, how to
persecute the weak. State machine, making the
citizens it needs. Bells telling you when to
sit, when to stand. Can you handle it? Always
productive, always on time. Ring ring! Mummy,
```

Daddy, Janet and John. Open up, pop it in. The
State installs the cop in your head.

SMASH THE STATE! OFF THE PIG!

The silence was eerie, absolute. Nothing in the papers, nothing on
the TV. We tried to seed rumours, put out feelers to the underground
press, who were running lurid stories about the Brigate Rossi in Italy,
the German RAF, the PLO, the Weathermen. Nothing came of it,
nothing reflected back to us at all. It was obvious the mainstream
media had been instructed not to run the story, but why was
no one else asking questions? How many accidental fires and
midnight gas explosions would people accept? Richest one thousand have more than poorest two billion. A billion
live and die on a dollar a day. It was as if we were
shouting into a vacuum. I began to wonder what else took place in
this silence, how much dark matter there really was in the universe.

Our lives changed very rapidly that year. We moved out of
Thirteen, splitting up to stay in rented flats, two in London, the
other in Manchester. I cut my hair and started to dress conserva-
tively, something I found oddly wrenching. I hadn't realized how
attached I was to my Bohemian self-image, how empty it would
feel to be a man in slacks and a drip-dry shirt. Passing other young
people on the street, I'd feel angry and envious. In Criticism-Self-
Criticism I was diagnosed as a closet élitist, still trying to set myself
apart from the proletariat. Since we'd stopped organizing or partic-
ipating in mass actions, I knew the others were just as isolated as
I was. We saw no one, spoke to no one who wasn't part of an
increasingly narrow and rarified network. What, I wondered, was
the difference between a vanguard and an élite?

Discipline, certainty: the way they seem to bleed into one
another, to blur at their borders. Because I am disciplined I am
certain. Because I am certain, I am disciplined.

Sean pinned a magazine picture to the kitchen wall, a NASA
image of the earth seen from space. It was the only decoration in

the tiny Kentish Town flat and it wormed its way into our heads. A green and blue disc surrounded by infinite blackness. The shortest of shorthands. We were on the world's side, the side of life.

WE ARE EVERYWHERE. We needed funds. Our best source of money was cars, luxury models we stole from quiet streets in Mayfair and Belgravia. The market is not nature. The ruling classes are not invulnerable. They have no immutable right to power. First comes refusal, then resistance. Fumble with the lock, break open the plastic housing round the ignition and yank out the cable. Touch the wires together, then listen for the starter motor. We sold the cars to a connection of Leo's, a feral-looking ex-con called Fenwick who ran a garage out of a railway arch in Bethnal Green. It wasn't an arrangement I felt happy about. Fenwick had little reason to be loyal to us, still less the pair of black mechanics he had working for him. I never knew their names and they never asked questions, but they were always checking us out. They knew there was something odd about us. Our accents, our manner. We didn't fit. I hoped Fenwick was spreading a little of his profit around.

Pigs, know that we can get to you behind your high walls, your mock-Tudor mansions, your barracks, your police stations, your plush offices. There is nowhere to hide. Sean and Leo went to meet a Spanish contact in Earls Court, someone connected with the anti-Franco resistance. They took elaborate precautions, getting on and off buses and trains, watching, doubling back. They came back with two hand-guns, snub black Czech pistols that they proudly unwrapped on the kitchen table. The guns looked brand new.

'What are we going to do with these?' I asked.

'Expropriations,' said Sean, pointing one at the wall and squeezing the trigger. 'And self-defence, of course.'

'It's a serious business,' said Leo, pointing the other at Sean. He swung round, so the muzzle was pointing at me. 'Have a go?'

We had a rule. We'd all agreed. We would attack property but never people. That was supposed to be an absolute prohibition, a line we would never cross. What good, I wanted to know, was a gun against a building? Sean told me to relax. It was all spectacle. We had no reason to use them.

As it turned out, I wasn't the only one with misgivings. A few days later Sean went over to the other London flat. He arrived back a couple of hours later, swearing and slamming the door. I'd never seen him so angry. 'I'll kill them,' he said. 'I'll fucking kill them.' He picked up a coffee mug and smashed it against a wall. 'Fucking cowards. Can you believe it?'

It was a while before I could get any sense out of him. Helen and Matthias had disappeared. They'd packed their things and left. They hadn't communicated with anyone. Jay, who'd been staying with them, thought they'd seemed unhappy, but hadn't noticed anything out of the ordinary. The news provoked a flurry of paranoia. We wondered if they'd informed on us, if perhaps we were about to be raided by the police. In the next few hours, we moved the guns and explosives out of their hiding-place under the floorboards and left London.

Through Claire, we'd found ourselves a bolt-hole, a tumbledown farmhouse in North Wales that we could use in emergencies. Driving there, behind the wheel of a stolen Ford Cortina, I tried to work out what had happened. The last Criticism-Self-Criticism had been particularly hard on Helen. She'd admitted she was missing the work she used to do, the women's group, the housing activism. Though Matthias had covered for her, it was obvious she was losing faith. Anna told her bluntly that her problem was psychological. If she agreed in theory that we had to resist the power of the state, it must be the reality she found disturbing. Leo joined in. He'd said he'd always thought of her as a typical intellectual, happiest with ideas, so nice and neat and antiseptic. Why couldn't she admit that real people disgusted her, that she wished she was back in the library? When Matthias tried to defend her, he too was accused of harbouring reactionary tendencies. The whole tenor of their relationship was suspect. Monogamy was tied up with all sorts of other capitalist formations. If they couldn't bring themselves to reject that particular residue of the old world, who knew what other sentiments they might be harbouring? After a couple more hours, Helen was in tears. Matthias tried angrily to leave, but we prevented him, blocking the door. It was one of our new rules that no one could leave a Criticism-Self-Criticism session until the group agreed it was finished. Nothing could be broken off. Every interaction, every interrogation, had to run until the bitter end.

So instead of complying with the will of the collective, Matthias and Helen had run away. The rest of us – eight or nine people, as I remember – met up in Wales, more or less convinced none of us had been followed. Outside, rain lashed at the windows as we tried to light a fire in the damp hearth. In the corner of the room a hold-all contained the guns and explosives. Everyone was nervous and depressed, except Anna, who chain-smoked cigarettes and stared into the fire and talked, half to herself, half to the room. She approached the situation methodically. This wasn't a problem. It was an opportunity, a chance for us to confirm our commitment to the armed struggle. Matthias and Helen had shown us they were objectively reactionary. Of course it was hard for us to accept. We'd loved them, treated them as our brother and sister, but they were pigs, end of story. They were pigs and now they'd gone. Things like this were to be expected. As revolutionaries, worse misfortunes would happen to us than losing a weak comrade like Helen. Once we became a serious threat to the state, we shouldn't expect it to show us any mercy. It was important to know this, to know how strong we had to be. She proposed an answer. We should conduct a Criticism-Self-Criticism session to discover if anyone else was thinking of leaving or, worse, was working for the enemy. We had to nip our paranoia in the bud. Sean caught on quickly. We had to trust one another. It was, he agreed, the only way. That night he and Anna seemed to be marching in lock-step. They were thinking with one mind, finishing each other's sentences.

Sean produced a sheet of blotter acid. By then the only drug we used with any regularity was speed and none of the rest of us liked the idea of tripping in our anxious, mistrustful state. Sean argued that this was exactly why it was necessary. If we were going to break down barriers, everything had to be in play, everything out in the open. So we sat round the fire and swallowed our hits, washing them down with gulps of ice-cold water, drawn from the pump outside the kitchen door. Then, to my horror, Sean loaded a round into one of the pistols and put it on the rug in front of the fire, smiling beatifically.

'Now you're just being stupid,' I told him.

'Why do you say that, Chris? Afraid you might use it? Afraid it might get used on you?'

'Of course I'm afraid.'

'He's right,' said Anna. 'Enough macho bullshit. It's not going to help anything.'

But no one made a move to take the thing away, so it sat there on the rug and we stared at it until Anna told Leo she didn't think he really believed in building the revolution and Leo defended himself and made a counter-accusation and gradually we were all drawn in, pointing, shouting, putting one another to the question, everyone an inquisitor, a Dzherzhinsky, a Beria strutting about in our psychedelic Lubyanka basement. I don't remember much about what happened, except that it was frightening and sometimes physical and all night the gun sat there in the middle of the floor, radiating malevolent potential. We ruthlessly hunted down every molecule of Fascism and Imperialism in one another until at last it was daylight and we were all exhausted, shaking with come-down, finally convinced there were no traitors, that we were all committed and prepared to carry on. Claire made strong sweet tea and it tasted like life itself. I remember looking out of the window, feeling scoured, purified, my hands trembling as I held the mug.

That afternoon we went out walking across the hills, following a ridge-line high above the scribble of stone walls and sheepfolds around the farmhouse. I was beside Anna, the others straggling out ahead of us, making for a cairn of stones marking a nearby peak. We'd said very little, each lost in thought. On impulse I asked her the question that kept echoing back to me. Miles's question in the cells at Bow Street.

'What do you think it will look like?'

'What?'

'After the revolution. What kind of place will this be?'

'That's not for us to know.'

'What do you mean, not for us to know? That just sounds like mysticism.'

'Not mysticism, historical process. It doesn't matter what we think, because the future will be determined by the will of the masses, not a few individuals.'

'Sure, but you must think about it. What do you imagine, when you imagine it?'

'I don't, Chris.'

'Why not?'

'Because I won't see it, and thinking about it would make me sad.'

A couple of months later, we got a letter from Helen, postmarked Frankfurt, West Germany. It said she and Matthias had moved there to live in a *Sponti* commune. She was involved with a *Kinderladen* and Matthias was working for a magazine. They wanted us to know that in their opinion we'd started to reproduce all the worst forms of hegemonic domination in our conditioning. We should reconnect with the working class or risk succumbing to our latent group Fascism. Helen also wrote that she was pregnant. She hoped her child would be brought up in an atmosphere free of nihilism, safe from our perverse fascination with horror.

Pigs, I thought. Traitors.

* * *

The more the worker expends himself in work, the more powerful becomes the world of objects, which he creates in the face of himself, and the poorer he himself becomes in his inner life, the less he belongs to himself. Anna and I stand in a lift on our way up the tallest building in Britain. It's five hundred and eighty feet high. The lift is travelling at a thousand feet a minute. I know a great deal about this building, the Post Office Tower. I know about the TV and telephone traffic it routes through powerful microwave transmitters. I know about the radar aerial at the top, designed for short-range weather forecasting. I know something about the layout of the upper floors, where this lift is taking us. If I stare straight forward, my view of the steel lift doors is barred at the periphery by the unfamiliar black plastic frames of a pair of glasses. I can see my reflection in the polished metal, not clearly, but as a kind of fuzzy impressionistic blur. The dyed reddish-brown hair, the grey smudge of my suit. Beside me Anna shifts from foot to foot, uncomfortable in her high heels. Her face is obscured by her wig, a curtain of long blonde hair cut into a severe, unfashionable bob.

We have a dinner reservation at the Topofthetower revolving restaurant. Name of Beresford. I've eaten there once before. I've been to the viewing gallery and the cocktail bar. I've seen the arc of tables on the revolve next to the plate-glass windows, the three-tiered buffet displays in the centre, stacked with dramatically lit piles of fruit and crudités. I know the location of the toilets and the emergency stairs. I know that this is the restaurant's busiest night of the week.

The lift stops at the thirty-fourth floor and we step out on to an expanse of lurid blue and red carpet, woven with the restaurant's logo. The whole place is blue and red. Red vinyl banquettes. Blue curtains. Blue tablecloths with red borders. We're shown to our table by a man with a phoney French accent who introduces himself as Gustav. The menu is also phoney and French, snobbishly printed without translation. Screw you if you don't know the difference between *consommé au paillettes* and *créme à la reine*. All the luxuries can be had at the top of the tower. Oysters and caviar. Sole in a champagne and lobster sauce.

The waiter hands me the wine list and does fussy things with the napkins. Anna looks out of the window. She's wearing heavy makeup. Lots of blue eye-shadow and burgundy lips, a face to match the décor.

We sit in silence, revolving slowly over Fitzrovia. The sun has gone down and the buildings are constellations of lighted windows, a vertical column of lights marking Centre Point, a black void the open space of Regent's Park. Remembering how we're supposed to be behaving, I take out my camera and click the shutter pointlessly into the darkness outside. Then, impulsively, I take a picture of Anna.

'Don't do that,' she snaps. The waiter comes back, pours the wine for me to taste, takes our order. We do our best to appear animated, the young married couple from the suburbs, up in London for a special night out. We're good at it. I almost believe in us. What, I wonder, if we were what we appear to be? What if we could just sit here and hold hands, toasting one another and looking out over London?

'I'm going to do it now,' she says. Without waiting for me to reply, she slides her bag from its position under the table, picks it up and heads in the direction of the toilet. I try not to stare. I don't want anyone to follow my eyeline. I sit, looking fixedly out of the window. One full revolution takes twenty-two minutes. I have completed an arc of perhaps a hundred and twenty degrees when Anna returns, still carrying the bag.

'It's locked,' she says. At that moment the waiter returns,

carrying two bowls of clear soup. We fall silent as he pours more wine into our glasses.

I wait until he's out of earshot again. 'It shouldn't be.'

'Well, it is.'

'Did you try the observation deck?'

'We don't know anything about who's down there.'

'It'll be empty.'

'We don't know that for certain.'

'I tell you, there's no one there, not at this time. I'll go, if you won't.'

This is bad. We're not doing it properly. The Beresfords shouldn't be arguing with one another over their romantic dinner. Near the toilets, behind a thick blue curtain, there's a fire-door opening on to a narrow set of concrete stairs that leads to the observation deck and from there to floor thirty-two, where there's a storeroom right beside the emergency exit. On thirty-two there's also a lot of switching equipment: a bomb placed there could shut down phone service for the whole of London. But they've locked the door. They've locked the door, which was supposed to be open.

Our information came from a friend of a friend, a girl who used to have a secretarial job at the GPO. At night, she said, the only person on the upper floors was a watchman. Jay and Leo checked it out. One evening Jay wandered around the building for almost half an hour without being challenged. He was the one who found the storeroom.

But the door's locked.

What a farce. The door's locked and there are gun battles on the streets of Belfast and children are dying in Biafra and in their infinite wisdom the British people have elected themselves a Conservative government. The right-wing press is whispering to its readers about the enemy within, but despite our best efforts we're still just a rumour, part of the toxic atmosphere of this old, cold, grey little country. Not for long. This action will make us real. Undeniable and real. But the door's locked.

Here I am, surrounded by bovine executives and their

frozen-haired mistresses, proud members of the ruling class squatting in a hermetically sealed revolving bubble, chowing down on duck à l'orange: bland and selfish, totally unconcerned with all the horror inflicted in their name. I've made hating them into such a habit that I don't really see them any more, don't regard any one of these rich white people as more or less attractive or clever or cultured or better-dressed than the others. They're an abstraction, a quantity of power that has to be moved from one side of the balance sheet to the other. As individuals, they have no substance for me at all.

But we are agreed. We respect human life. That's the difference between us and them. We've taken care not to hurt anyone with our bombs. But we need to make a point. It's time to put an end to the silence. In Britain, established power likes things discreet. Confrontation is always a sign of failure. When the system's working, the energies of those who resist it are always diffused, our anger spiralling down into some soft and foggy place where there's no obvious enemy, just a row of civil-service desks and a faint, receding peal of trumpets.

I can't taste my soup. Mechanically I spoon it into my mouth. The door. The fucking door.

'Give me the bag,' I say to Anna.

'You can't carry a woman's bag through the restaurant. People will notice. It'll be too obvious.'

'Just give me the fucking bag.'

I have to do something. I can't sit and eat. My stomach has cramped up.

'I'll do it,' she says, and gets up again, toting the heavy bag over her shoulder. I'm left in my seat, slowly revolving. I try to control my breathing. In through the nose, out through the mouth.

'Is everything all right, sir?' asks the waiter, and I stare at him as if he's speaking a foreign language.

I don't want death. I try to remember that. I'm twenty-two and I want life. Life for myself, life for the world, all the people of this fragile blue and green disc. This is my hope, as I sit at the table, scraping breadcrumbs into patterns with the side of my knife: that the revolution can happen through an accretion of small actions, like moth holes on a suit left too long in a cupboard. Because what's the alternative? 1917. Executions and prison camps and civil war and tens of thousands dead.

Cleansing, Anna calls it. I hate that word.

I wish she'd come back. Panic is bubbling up inside me, a primal scream, all the psychic pain knotted into my muscles. Just as sitting still is about to become intolerable, she slides back into her seat. She hasn't got the bag with her. At the same time the waiter arrives with our main course. In answer to my unspoken question she just nods.

I stare down at my plate. A fussy little pile of mashed potato. Green beans. A pork chop.

At three a.m we phoned in a warning. At four thirty our bomb blew up part of the thirty-first floor of the Post Office Tower, sending chunks of concrete and shards of glass showering over the roofs of Cleveland Street. By morning we were the lead item on BBC News. *London landmark a target.* No one was hurt, though the night watchman phlegmatically reported being 'lifted two or three inches' out of his armchair. A government minister gave a statement calling it an act of insanity.

```
SHUT DOWN THE SPECTACLE!

Last night Post Office Tower bombed.
Because it is the lobotomy machine
the pacifier
Microwaves sent out across Britain
Television transmission
the dead hand of technology
their means of control
their communications
their message
```

```
fairy stories to distract you
REALITY: Imperialism, Colonialism, Dictatorship
REALITY: troops on British streets
REALITY: an international state of war
REALITY: the mental patient spasms with
electricity
REALITY: dead-eyed mothers on Merseyside streets

REALITY: not a GAME SHOW

We demand complete withdrawal of American troops
from Indochina, British troops off British
streets.

WE ARE EVERYWHERE

SHUT DOWN THE SPECTACLE
DESTROY THE RULE OF CAPITAL
ARMED RESISTANCE NOW!
```

Even though the news report didn't quote our communiqué I was still ecstatic, hugging the others, even punching the air, the idiotic gesture of a football player celebrating a goal. For a day or two I felt slightly manic and walked the streets in an attempt to calm myself. I covered miles of pavement, feeling the world had subtly changed. Faintly but unmistakably our idea had been absorbed into the air. Every passer-by had been touched by it. There we were, a headline behind the grille of the news-stand outside the tube. There we were, propagating through the radio spectrum. Eventually my euphoria dissipated and I found myself on London Bridge, pushing feebly against a pin-striped tide of evening commuters, feeling naked, surveilled. I went home and slept, the covers pulled over my head.

I was in a Camden café with Sean when an unfamiliar face appeared on the television above the counter. The man was a chief superintendent in the Met, an unremarkable-looking official in his fifties or sixties, with thick-framed glasses and greying combed-over hair. It was hard to catch what he was saying over the noise of the diners. He stood outside Scotland Yard and spoke to an interviewer in an unhurried, languorous voice, 'educated' vowels pasted over a Black Country accent . . . *Entirely in hand . . . the object of attention . . . who sees anything suspicious is urged to come forward . . .* I examined him, this bomb-squad detective, soothing a troubled situation with the balm of euphemism. Business-like and professionally unemotional, a man who'd never understand that his own impersonality was at the root of our so-called crime, that we'd placed our bombs to destroy the rule of men who'd evacuated themselves of their humanity, functional men like him. The enemy.

The police acted quickly. Within the next day or two, we started hearing about busts. In Notting Hill detectives turned over every underground household in the area. During the next few weeks, it seemed as if every squat and commune in London got raided. Bizarre tales filtered back: a feminist bookshop in Stoke Newington whose entire stock was confiscated, an International Marxist Group organizer taken for questioning because he had fencing equipment in his room. We'd got what we wanted. Reality. War on the state. War, or at least talk. We were being talked about all over Britain.

the saturation of our minds with the poison of subversion has become so constant that we are no longer even aware you say we can support the aim while disagreeing on methods but they should think about the damage they're causing to legitimate organizations trying to do real creative grassroots work opinions that once would have been thought frankly treasonous are openly as a tactic it's useless actively promoted by at least thirty known Communist organizations and many thousands of unassociated do these bombings ever connect anyone from different struggles? No. Pretty much the opposite. Have they moved any of the struggles (Ireland etc.) on to a higher level of awareness or activity? One is continually confronted by (occasionally well-meaning but always blinkered and immature) there is cowboys and indians glamour and then there is getting real often members of the privileged middle classes, who seem to believe that by the endless repetition of slogans don't seem to know the difference between some kind of improvement an analysis and that's better than nothing they should consider the effects/ ineffectiveness of what slightest criticism of their reasoning, let alone the suggestion that they might be fellow travellers with totalitarianism, is met by denunciations of the most hysterical end up busted or worse in the general crackdown only the most closed of closed minds could have perpetrated the latest outrage in London. The bombing of an important economic target and familiar landmark should be roundly condemned by all who have I wonder if the people doing these acts of so-called armed struggle ever opened up wide discussions with other militants? further proof, if proof were needed, that a climate exists in this country that might best be described as a terrorist has Britain's best interests at heart a bomb, said Lenin penetration by subversives of the trade unions and shop floors has led to widespread industrial strife and demoralization we lost leaflets, copying equipment, stencils. And they took our membership list, diaries, personal papers etc. the unprincipled exploitation of largely imaginary grievances by wreckers and state-subsidized layabouts threatens to undermine the values and ideals that we cherish as a nation exactly what they say they're against but they're provoking not soon to find ourselves minions of Moscow, we must meet the threat of the bombers with the utmost firmness and moral clarity

The only thing the commentators and letter-writers seemed to agree on was that we were wrong. We were mindless and evil. We were probably mad. I was shaken by the reaction – not by the condemnation, which I'd expected, but by the fact that most people seemed not to understand why we'd done it. I thought our action was so pure in motive and clear in intent that no one could fail to understand it. I thought we were a spark. My expectations seem extraordinary to me now.

I tried to hide my disappointment from the others, but it came out as a bitter rant against our supposed fellow-revolutionaries. Their reaction smelt, I said, like fear. Secretly they didn't want anything to change. They were just having a good time playing Che and pushing policemen at demos. There was more, which I didn't say, about my own fear – that we were the fools who'd believed, poor political Tommies, who'd charged over the top with nobody following.

We had supporters: no group like ours could exist in total isolation. Though we'd severed many of our connections with the overground Left, we had contacts, people who believed in the armed struggle and were prepared to help us with logistics, but we had no one to speak out in public. Our own words were still missing.

So it became real, our fight. Or did it? We were already floating free, as removed from the experience of the average worker as the diners in the restaurant at the top of the tower. After that, the insidious message of the spectacle – that nothing takes place, even for the participants, unless it's electronically witnessed and played back – took us over. We thought we were striking a blow against it, the hypnotic dream-show of fuckable bodies and consumer goods. Instead we fell into the screen. Our world became television.

* * *

Orange wallpaper. Nauseating swirls. Gummed eyes, sticky mouth and the sound of insistent knocking on the door. I pulled a sheet round me and went to answer it. Outside I found the landlady. 'Mr Carter is downstairs,' she told me, a look of pure hostility on her face. 'You're late.' Obviously I'd caused her some trouble.

Miles was waiting outside, slouched in the back of a large black Mercedes. The driver, a middle-aged Nigerian, greeted me politely. He was playing some kind of handheld computer game, which he put away in the glove-box as I got in. Miles looked run-down. He had bags under his eyes, patches of shaving rash on his chin.

'Have a nice time last night?' he asked peevishly.

'You look unwell.'

'So do you. Put this on.'

He handed me a tie, an old-fashioned item with some sort of crest repeated on a green background.

'What is it? Grenadier Guards? Old Wykehamists?'

'Just put it on. You look like you slept in that jacket.'

I knotted the tie round my neck.

'Fuck's sake, you're even scruffier now. Take it off.'

We inched through the morning rush-hour, the driver lurching forward into each gap, then braking sharply. I opened the window, hoping the fresh air would make me feel less sick. Near Regent's Park, Miles directed the driver to pull up outside a terrace of elegant Regency houses. A man was waiting for us, pacing up and down on the corner, his hands jammed into the trouser pockets of a grey suit. He was in his late twenties or early thirties, with floppy blond hair and a scattering of freckles on his face, looks that would have been charmingly boyish were it not for the crude jaw and the unfriendly grey eyes he passed over me as he opened the front passenger door. He had what is euphemistically termed an athletic build, a square head rooted in a thick neck, shoulders that strained against the fabric of his jacket as he settled himself in his seat.

'Good morning, Mr Carter,' he said, in a public-school accent. He didn't introduce himself to me. Miles shot a significant look in my direction. Through my hangover I smiled back. I felt I'd achieved something. We'd come to the edge of civility, the point beyond which force would be used. I'd pushed him thus far, at least.

We made our way up Euston Road, slowing to a crawl outside the grimy façade of St Pancras station.

'Where are we going, Miles?'

'Don't worry. Just a business breakfast. If you relax, we'll be out of there in half an hour and I won't be bothering you again for a while.'

'Really?'

'Yes, really.'

We turned into a side-street near King's Cross and parked outside an office building, some kind of recent warehouse conversion, all sandblasted bricks and plate glass, fashionably facing the canal. The driver opened the glove-box and retrieved his computer game, placidly resuming the arrangement of little falling bricks into a wall. The big man disappeared inside the building and came out again with a set of laminated visitor passes.

'Now,' said Miles, 'this is an informal, walk-around event. Just let me guide you. I'll be right beside you. You don't have to do anything at all. You don't even have to speak.'

We walked past the front desk into a large function room, which had been laid out as some kind of exhibition space. A girl handed us each a folder, pointing us towards a table laid with coffee urns and jugs of juice and platters of large, rubbery-looking croissants. We wandered around, past photographic displays and architectural models presented on felt-covered tables. Little prison wings. Little model figures banged up in little cells, playing ping-pong with one another in little rec rooms.

'Architects,' said Miles, gesturing at the people around us, who were balancing cups and saucers and peering surreptitiously at one another's name-tags as they made conversation. 'Architects and detention-centre contractors. And Home Office people, of course.'

Pat Ellis was at the centre of a knot of acolytes, who were listening to her with rapt attention, first nodding in agreement, then laughing doggedly at a joke. Without preamble, Miles gripped my arm and steered me towards her, pushing his way into the circle.

'How nice to see you, Minister,' he said, cutting through the laughter.

Pat Ellis looked momentarily nonplussed, then nodded curtly and continued her anecdote. She was talking about a visit she'd made to some facility in Holland, what she'd said to the director, what he'd said to her. The young man at her side, obviously some kind of aide, frowned at us.

Miles ploughed on. 'You remember Chris Carver, don't you?'

The minister broke off again and smiled at us, a neat and practised smile, which gave the impression of warmth without masking her irritation. 'No, I'm sorry. You'll have to remind me.'

'Chris Carver,' repeated Miles. 'Think back.'

I looked at Pat. She used to have long chestnut hair, which she often wore in a scarf. It was grey now, bunched up in a tight, unflattering perm. She was dressed in business uniform, like all the people around her, a dark suit, a string of pearls doubled over the mottled skin of her neck. I'd seen her the previous day, of course, and before that on television, but I was unnerved to find myself so close to her. I couldn't find a trace of the nervous, hard-working young woman I'd once known – crushingly sincere, easily moved to tears. The features were the same, the long nose and the large widely spaced eyes, but the thin-lipped mouth (which I'd kissed once, in the middle of a drunken party) had a twist of placid vanity, the curdled self-assurance of the professional politician. She looked at me blankly, complacently, not recognizing me. Then she made the connection. I could see it happen, the loss of traction, the sudden skid on the ice.

'No, I'm sorry, Mr – uh . . .'

'Carver,' repeated Miles.

For a moment she was completely speechless. She looked at the floor, then at her assistant. Everyone was waiting for her to say something. Reluctantly she turned her eyes back to me and her expression was momentarily unguarded, almost warm. I realized, bizarrely, that somewhere inside she was pleased to see me. Then a flash went off. Miles's young thug had taken a picture. Instantly, the barriers slammed down. She looked about, coldly furious, trying to spot the photographer. I opened and closed my mouth. I wanted to say something, to disrupt the trap Miles was setting.

'Sorry, Pat,' I said. 'I'm really sorry.'

'Yes,' interrupted Miles. 'My apologies, Minister. I thought you knew one another.'

He grabbed my elbow and steered me away, leaving Pat Ellis behind us, hissing into her assistant's ear. Miles's thug was on the other side of me, his hand on the small of my back, propelling me discreetly but firmly towards the exit. Angrily, I shook them both off, a violent gesture that made people turn and watch. 'Excuse me, are you with the press?' asked one of the PR women, when we reached the door. 'This is a private event. There's no photography.' Miles made an inconclusive hand gesture at her as we brushed past.

We got into the car. The driver put away his game and pulled out on to the street. 'Well,' said Miles, keying a text message into his mobile phone, 'a bit crude, but we'll just have to see if she takes the hint, won't we?'

While I tried to understand what had just taken place, Miles relaxed into his seat, received an answer to his text, read it and slipped the phone into a jacket pocket.

'What hint?' I asked quietly.

'Put it this way. There are some people it's just not appropriate for the next Home Secretary to know. That is, if she wants to be the next Home Secretary.'

'I keep telling you, she had nothing to do with anything. I didn't see her or Gavin after 1969.'

'Well, you say that, Chris. And, of course, you could well be telling the truth. But if you were a journalist, the possibility would certainly be worth following up, wouldn't it?'

'You can't give this to the press.'

'Why not? I'd say it was in the public interest.'

'Why not? Please, Miles, you keep saying you're my friend. Think about my – my wife. Our daughter. Our daughter knows nothing about any bombings. Think what this would do to her.'

'Yes, I do understand. You're Michael Frame, suburban family man, and you were rather hoping it would stay that way. But you must have known, Chris. Sooner or later it was going to come out.'

'But why? You're not the police. This isn't about bringing me to justice or anything straightforward like that. Whatever job you're doing, I know you don't give a shit about justice. What did Pat Ellis do to you, Miles? She must have done something.'

'To me? Nothing at all. It's just politics, Chris. Real, grown-up politics, not the kind that starts by carving out a Utopia and then hammering at the world, trying to make it fit. If she's going to get the top job, she'll have to make sure all the stakeholders are satisfied. Simple as that. No mystery. No conspiracy theory. If everyone's happy, then this all goes away. There'll be no need to bring you any deeper into it and you can fuck off back to Sussex. But if Mrs Ellis doesn't play ball, she'll find the media beginning to focus on certain issues of character.'

I stared out of the window, and Marylebone Road was just a jumble of planes and reflections. Miles sighed, adopted an avuncular expression and squeezed my shoulder, one – two – three, an autistic mime of sincerity. 'I am your friend, Chris. Really. And as your friend, I think you should tell your family. They deserve to be let into this as gently as possible.'

I wanted to kill him, to smash his face to a bloody pulp. 'And what am I going to let them into, exactly? That Daddy's a terrorist and he's going to prison?'

He shrugged blandly. 'Not necessarily. Everyone knows this all happened a long time ago. Yes, you did certain things, but – well, the context has changed. People are quite pragmatic, these days. I won't pretend that there won't be pressure for an – um, judicial dimension, but there are ways you could make the climate as favourable as possible. If you had something to give, for example.'

'Give?'

'Oh, God, Chris, don't be obtuse. If you could find something a little more concrete to say about Pat Ellis, you could help yourself considerably.' He looked sharply at me. 'Unless you have something else?'

'Such as?'

'It might help for you to tell me what happened. In your own words. Who did what. A lot of that period is still rather murky.'

I said nothing, though Anna's name was hanging in the air.

Miles put me on a train at Victoria. I slumped in a window-seat and was pulled out of London, mouldering suburban stations scrolling past as I ate a clammy sandwich and thought about powerlessness. Not about abolishing power, let alone seizing it. Having it trample over you, take the substance of your life and grind it between its teeth. Miles demanded a burnt offering: Pat Ellis or Anna or me. Because he was powerful he would have one. Heart and entrails, sizzling on the fire. I scrunched up the sandwich packaging, stuffed it into the bin behind my seat. Seeing Pat Ellis had taken me back into our own private grey area. Of course there was one: in every situation involving two or more people, there's always a grey area, a few half-tone specks at the border of the black and the white. 1969 wasn't the last time I'd seen her. It was late in the summer of 1971.

I don't know what kind of figure I must have presented. When she answered the door of her basement flat, in one of the hilly streets around Tufnell Park, she looked shocked. I'd turned up unannounced. Someone had been watching the place for a few days and we knew Gavin would be at his chambers. We'd judged her the more sympathetic of the two, the one more likely to help.

She invited me in, not without a trace of reluctance, and we drank mint tea, sitting on her sofa in front of a rug littered with wooden blocks and rattles and stuffed toys. She introduced me to her son, Robin, who was almost a year old. I played with him for a while, making faces and letting him grip my fingers. Pat asked what I'd been up to and I asked her if she still considered herself a revolutionary. I can't remember what formulation she used in her reply, but she was noncommittal. I got the impression I was making her nervous, because she kept finding excuses to get up and walk around, fetching things from the kitchen, fussing with Robin. She asked again what I'd been doing and I told her (as planned) that I was living in Leeds and was in contact with certain comrades who were facing criminal charges arising out of their clandestine work. The baby began to cry and she picked him up, walking up and down, rubbing his back. She asked what kind of charges.

'Armed robbery,' I told her.

Expropriation was logistically correct, since we needed a better way of financing ourselves than car theft. It was politically correct because it was an act of dispossession. It was tactically correct because it was proletarian, the method of people who owned nothing, who had no stake in the system. But our first attempt had gone badly wrong. For once, I hadn't been directly involved. It was Sean's project. Anna was out of the country meeting some of her Paris contacts and he'd put it together with Leo, whose idea of planning was as vague as his own. Accompanied by Ferdy and Quinn, two of Leo's old friends from the Firm, they'd gone into a bank in Reading and held it up. Sean had fired a shot into the ceiling, cowboy-style. According to Leo, he'd even insisted on wearing a Stetson over his stocking mask. They'd got away with a fair amount of money, but somehow Ferdy was left behind, tackled by a passer-by as they ran to the car. Though Sean had threatened to shoot him, the man wouldn't let go and Sean hadn't been prepared to pull the trigger.

I told a version of this story to Pat. Though there was no chance of acquittal, Ferdy wanted to plead not guilty. We needed lawyers who could run a political trial, who could use the court to propagate our message; in that way we thought we could salvage something from a disastrous situation. Pat heard me out, jiggling up and down on the rug as she tried to soothe her baby. She told me she didn't want any part of it. She didn't believe there was anything to be gained from that kind of politics. She used the same words I'd heard from so many of our supposed allies. *Adventurist*, *counter-productive*. I argued with her for a while and eventually she agreed to write down some names, people she knew who might take the case. I gave her a phone number, told her she should ring if she changed her mind. I knew she wouldn't. Why did she help at all? Out of friendship? To get rid of me? I suppose one could find some ambiguity in it, space enough for Miles to live and thrive. I next saw her when she popped up on TV some time in the early nineties and I discovered that she'd become an MP. The idea of a political trial soon faded away and Ferdy, who refused to name his accomplices, was sentenced to eight years in prison, without the question of his political motivation even being raised.

When I got off the train at Chichester I went straight to God's and drank myself into a stupor, sitting in front of the gas fire with a bottle of supermarket Scotch. He must have come downstairs and found me, because when I woke up the next morning, feeling shaky and bleak, I found a blanket thrown over me and a glass of water and a foil strip of paracetamol waiting on the desk. God wasn't given to making conversation, least of all in the morning. As I tried to gather myself to leave, he shuffled around the shop and pretended to look for something in the theology section, working up courage to speak.

'I don't like to pry, Mike,' he said gruffly, after several minutes of inner struggle, 'but is everything all right at home?'

'Don't worry, God. I'll be fine.'

He looked immensely relieved that I wasn't going to force any intimacies on him. I was touched. I knew what it had cost him even to broach the subject. A great respecter of the private pain of others, Godfrey.

* * *

I must have fallen asleep, because when I open my eyes the sun is low and my skin feels hot and tight around my face. I sit up, watched suspiciously by a family of picnickers who've set themselves up elaborately on the riverbank, a small brightly coloured complex of windbreaks and umbrellas and barbecue equipment. My head is swimming. I'm very dehydrated. I dress and pick my way back across the rocks and up the path to the car, where I change my shirt and gulp down half a bottle of warm water. Then I sit on a bench, listening to the buzzing of the flies round the overflowing litter-bins. The air is fragrant, heavy as lead.

I drive through the evening, passing Bordeaux just as the light fails. The radio chatters and spits out pop songs and the road climbs through foothills into the darkness. Little by little, my skin exhales heat and the bends sharpen into hairpins, dented metal barriers gleaming suddenly in the headlights. I'm close now. Only another hour to Sainte-Anne. I don't feel ready. I want to swing the car round, to defer the moment when I'll find myself face to face with Anna.

After the Post Office Tower, the conflict escalated. We began to hear rumours of other actions, ones we hadn't carried out. Someone blew up a railway line in Ayrshire, near the Cairnryan ferry to Northern Ireland. They phoned in a warning to British Rail, told them not to allow their trains to be used as troop transports. There were attacks on electrical installations, airline offices and embassies. Some of our friends were arrested, notably Alex Hill from the Sylvan Close occupation, who apparently had a copy of one of our communiqués in his flat. Many more had their homes raided and their possessions smashed or taken away for examination. I remember Sean remarking sarcastically that if having your record collection trashed was sufficient to radicalize someone, a revolutionary situation would exist in Britain within weeks.

We responded with two further actions. Leo and Claire planted a bomb in a gambling club patronized by senior American officers, which demolished the entire rear elevation of the building, a mansion house in St James's. Because of Agent Orange leaching into the earth of Cambodia, because of white phosphorus burning through the skin of small children. Britain is not a safe haven for the strategists of extermination. Nowhere in the world will they be protected from the guerrilla, acting in support of the people of Indochina. We phoned in a warning and the place was cleared, though we heard the next day that two people had been hurt by flying glass. They were our first casualties, but I don't remember any particular discussion about them. I think we blamed it on the police. A second bomb, placed outside an air-force base, failed to detonate. It was suggested in the underground press that the attacks were the work of neo-Fascists, trying to discredit the Left. We read a dozen theoretical demonstrations of the objectively counter-revolutionary nature of our actions, a dozen more of the historical inevitability of our failure, but it seemed to us that history was on our side. Every week there were more strikes. Dockers, car workers. Ninety Soviet diplomats had been expelled from Britain, accused of spying. An anti-Communist panic was sweeping the country, which seemed to be completely polarized between those who were more terrified of Moscow and those who were more terrified by the binary madness of the Cold War. It was a question of gut feeling: you chose one kind of fear or the other. Not being afraid wasn't an option.

A message to all those comrades who feel that revolutionary action is not appropriate in the UK because this is a place where the forces of reaction are strong. If you believe, as we do, that Imperialism is a paper tiger, then nowhere can be excluded as the site of struggle. You say we are

squandering revolutionary energy, that adventurism
is a characteristic deviation in times of weakness.
We say agitation and propaganda are insufficient.
If that's the sum of your ambitions, you should be
ashamed.

Sometimes it felt as if we were spending more time arguing
about money than about strategy. Like our failure to discuss the
injuries at the gambling club, this should have been a warning to
me, a sign that things were beginning to degenerate, but we were
desperate for funding and prepared to do more or less anything to
get it. A friend of Jay's worked for a record company. Through him
we were introduced to an underground character called Nice Mike,
who wanted to score fifty thousand hits of acid off some Liverpool
gangsters who had a lab down in Devon, at a farmhouse out on
Exmoor. Nice Mike didn't trust the people he was involved with
and wanted to take along some protection. Jay suggested us.

It was risky. We knew nothing about Nice Mike's contacts. We
didn't know a great deal about Nice Mike himself. I disliked him
on sight, an overweight south Londoner with shoulder-length hair
and loud Carnaby Street clothes, who set up our first meeting in
a trendy bar and seemed incapable of answering direct questions.
He laid out his proposition in an exaggeratedly soothing tone, as
if lulling children to sleep. We told him nothing about our political
activities; he seemed satisfied with the story that we were ordinary
criminals, connected with some unspecified east-London gang. He
was prepared to pay cash up front plus more when he'd sold the
drugs on. Despite our misgivings, we agreed.

He wanted to drive down to Devon, which was fine, but on
the appointed day he turned up in an absurdly conspicuous car,
a bright blue Bentley, loaded with gadgets that he insisted on
demonstrating to us, like a salesman. The heated leather seats,
the eight-track built into the dashboard. On the road he played
acid rock and clicked his many elaborate silver rings on the
steering-wheel, bragging about the famous groups he dealt to
when they were passing through London. It was all birds and

backstage and Jimmy this and Mick that, clicking his damn rings on the wheel in time to the beat.

It soon became apparent that Mike was very nervous. As he drove he smoked joints, stubbing them out in the ashtray, weaving alarmingly in and out of the traffic, occasionally freaking himself out about phantom objects in his peripheral vision and pulling the wheel round to avoid them. Luckily the car handled like a boat or I swear he would have spun it. He wasn't helped by his glasses, big octagonal things with a heavy blue tint that must have increased the weirdness several-fold. When we passed Stonehenge he insisted on stopping, as if we were on some kind of excursion. The three of us – Sean, Jay and I – trailed after him while he wandered round the stones, waving his arms and intoning a lot of *faux*-Druidic nonsense, invoking the pagan gods to bless our endeavour and promising to 'make a sacrifice upon our return'.

When we got back into the car, which was parked on the grass verge by the roadside, Mike scrabbled around in the glove-box and pulled out a plastic bag of pills. 'Want anything? We need to maintain our edge, yeah?' I told him I thought what we needed was to keep our shit together and he got very defensive. Who was I to say who did or didn't have their shit together? Who the fuck was I? He kept repeating it, his tone increasingly self-righteous. 'I mean, who the fuck *are* you? How do I even know *you* have your shit together?'

We ate a tense fry-up at a Little Chef somewhere in Somerset, wreathed in cigarette smoke and mutual distrust. In the middle of the crowded diner, Mike decided to start talking about guns. We'd brought guns, right? We were packing, because we needed to be packing, because he hadn't paid for fucking amateurs, OK? He'd thought we were going to look heavier. We didn't look heavy enough. He was speaking very loudly. The subject of guns seemed to tug his accent part-way across the Atlantic. People were staring. Young families, lorry drivers.

The only way to shut him up was to walk out, so that was what we did, leaving our plates of food half finished on the table. When we got back to the car, I took his keys and Sean shoved him into the back seat of the Bentley, still protesting about his eggs and his second cup of tea. Jay kept watch, leaning on the car, as Sean and I got in beside him and shut the door.

Sean was direct. 'Now, look here, you decadent little fucker. If this goes bad I'm going to cut your balls off and make you eat them, you understand?'

Nice Mike's eyes narrowed in suspicion. 'Don't you dare rip me off. If you rip me off you'll regret it. I've got friends, man. You touch any of my money and I'm telling you right here and now that you'll regret it.'

We quizzed him again about the people we were going to meet, what he knew of their background, who else he'd told about the deal. He was evasive, panicky. Then we locked him in the car while we went for a quick walk round the forecourt.

'You know what?' said Sean. 'We should just dump the cunt. Take the money, take the car and have done with it. We don't need to go to Devon.'

'It'll come back to us,' argued Jay. 'He's not kidding about having friends.'

Like Sean, I'd had enough of Nice Mike. 'Fuck his friends,' I said. It was two to one, so we went back to the Bentley and told him how it was going to be. When he argued, Sean stuck a gun in his mouth, to prove he was 'packing'. We took Mike's briefcase of cash and his bag of pills and drove away in his ridiculous car, leaving him kneeling by the side of the road, his eyes tightly shut and his hands clasped in front of him, as if in prayer. If he had friends, they never found us.

Was that before or after Anna went to Paris? I'm honestly not sure. Maybe it's the stress we were living under or maybe it's just too long ago, but that year exists for me only as a series of fragments, shards of memory I can't fit together and don't quite trust. I know my mind is capable of playing tricks, not just in sequencing but in deeper, more subtle ways. For example, I remember daffodils in the graveyard where I walked with Anna, looking for dead babies.

It was a little Norman church with a lychgate and moss-covered gravestones leaning at drunken angles. The light of my memory is golden-hour light, warm and diffuse. Sunshine-yellow daffodils are scattered in the long grass. Sunshine-yellow and paper-white. But that would place it in early spring, and it was certainly later than that, months later.

I remember, very clearly it seems to me, what she looked like and how she was dressed. Her hair was cropped short, her arms and legs bare. There was a softness about her body that I associate with periods when she was happy, when she allowed herself to be less rigorous and austere. We were laughing, strolling through the churchyard like conventionalized lovers, bathed in the yellow light that's now eternally the light of 1971, not just for me but for everyone who saw a film or looked at a magazine that year. Dazzle and softness and lens-flare.

We held hands. I can't have concocted that. She talked about her childhood. For most children, the world is defined by the sensory; by likes and dislikes, favourite smells and tastes. Anna's narrative was mostly about ideas. Witness, duty. It's the only time I remember hearing her speak about her family. She was an only child, hot-housed and diligent, the repository of all her Quaker parents' wishes for the future. She didn't say much about her mother, but spoke of her father with respect and what sounded like regret. He'd been, she said, like an exam board, asking her general-knowledge questions at the dinner-table, testing her on her memory for various prayers and catechisms. She recited for me, in an ironic sing-song voice: *We utterly deny all outward wars and strife, and fightings with outward weapons, for any end or under any pretence whatever; this is our testimony to the whole world.*

'He knows someone has to fight,' she told me. 'That's what makes him unforgivable. He's just too finicky to do it himself.'

Later, I saw a picture of her father, a gaunt man in an old-fashioned woollen waistcoat, staring defiantly at the camera as he defended his dead terrorist daughter to a magazine journalist. He'd taken her on demonstrations, taught her that it was sometimes necessary to exercise dissent if one wanted to have a conscience void of offence towards God and towards men. The journalist described him as a religious zealot.

Anna remembered playing at the back of meeting halls during lectures, whispering to her doll. She looked so lonely, as she told me that; I reached for her instinctively. I was hurt when she started to speak to me in the jargon of Criticism-Self-Criticism, reproaching me for allowing myself to get distracted. 'What about pleasure?' I asked, trying to sound sarcastic. She told me flatly that our pleasure wasn't relevant to the struggle. It was only through the struggle that we could materialize ourselves in a meaningful way. If I wanted to fuck, she said, we could fuck; but politically she was sick of fucking.

I was so angry that I couldn't speak. Was that what she thought? That I only wanted to fuck? She walked a few feet away, looking down at the line of headstones.

'Here's one,' she said.

And there it was, in gold letters on a little white marble slab.

MICHAEL DAVID FRAME

10.4.48–12.1.50

'RESTING WHERE NO SHADOWS FALL'

'That could do for you.' She got out a notebook and started taking down the details.

In the car on the way back to London she told me, almost casually, that she'd been approached, through one of her Paris friends, by the Popular Front for the Liberation of Palestine. The PFLP had offered us funds and training. She was going to Paris to meet one of their representatives.

I was stunned. Why hadn't I been told? This was the most important news imaginable and she hadn't even discussed it with the rest of us before agreeing to a meeting. There were a thousand political questions. There were security issues. I started to argue with her but she brought me up short by telling me that the others had already agreed. She and Sean had discussed it in some detail, she said. Sean thought it was the right move. Leo and Jay were in agreement too.

'The revolutionary is a doomed man,' wrote Nechayev. 'He has no interests of his own, no affairs, no feelings, no belongings, not even a name.' The monks at Wat Tham Nok would recognize that, I think. If to be a revolutionary is to be nameless, without attachments, then a revolutionary is simply a person who has understood the first three of the Four Noble Truths of Buddhism. He sees suffering, sees that its cause lies in greed and craving; he also sees that it could potentially come to an end. But what's the right way to end suffering? The revolution, giving yourself up to history? Or Nibbana, giving yourself up to transcendence? Phra Anan, whose English was good enough to discuss such things with me, had no time for history. 'Too much history in Indochina,' he'd say, shaking his stubbly head. 'Less history needed, not more.'

After so long living as Mike Frame, it's sometimes hard to find my way back to Chris Carver, to remember why he made the choices he did. There seems such an obvious split between how I wanted things to be and how they actually were, not just in the world but in our group, our little cell. We were supposed to be a band of equals, committed to abolishing every trace of power in our relationships with one another. But once Anna and Sean started taking decisions on their own, that was self-evidently no longer true. I was twenty-three by then. Not so young. Old enough to know that taking your desires for reality wasn't a straightforward answer to anything.

With the benefit of hindsight, it's easy to see that Anna and Sean had always been in front, daring one another to go further out on to the ledge. In a way it seems extraordinary that they took so long to fuse together, to start acting in concert. When they did, they ran the rest of us off our feet. The PFLP contact was the first incontrovertible sign that I was no longer in control of my life. I should have seen I was heading into the darkness. I should have got off the bus.

At the time I got bogged down in detail, I knew very little about the Middle East and, unlike a lot of my friends, I had an instinctive sympathy with the Israelis. After the concentration camps, who could deny them a home? On the other hand, the cruelties inflicted on the Palestinians were undeniable. Anna poured scorn on my confusion. The PFLP were Marxist-Leninists. They were fighting Imperialism. That should be enough. It wasn't necessary to get into the intricacies of their political position, or to agree with everything they did. It would be a pragmatic alliance. Their contact in Paris would pay us three thousand US dollars a month, which would solve our money worries at a stroke. Our people could go out to Lebanon and receive proper weapons and explosives training. We'd become an effective fighting force. What was there to discuss?

So Anna disappeared to Paris and stayed away for weeks. Sean organized his disastrous bank raid. I sent off for a birth certificate in the name of Michael Frame and used it to apply for a passport. We were all doing the same thing, developing aliases, preparing to go underground.

* * *

Finally I turn off the main road and start to pick my way up the pass towards Sainte-Anne-de-la-Garrigue. It's after midnight and the petrol gauge has dipped into the red. I drive very slowly; my tired eyes are producing phantoms, shadows that race across the road and flicker in the rear-view mirror.

I crest the col and see that the tower is illuminated, its blocky form like a lighthouse guiding me in. I bump my way over the cobbles into the main square, where I park in front of the church, on the spot where the righteous Christian knights burned the heretics on their pyre. Miranda: *Why should I care what happened here? . . . It's just a pretty little village square on a very hot day.* Well, it's cold now, the air whipping round me in icy gusts as I get out of the car and stretch, trying to work the cramp of two days' driving out of my body. Though there's a light in the Bar des Sports, the door is locked and no one answers when I knock. I had some idea of getting a drink, perhaps a sandwich. Now I'm here I don't know what to do. I fish a sweater out of my bag and walk around, feeling the blood gradually returning to my legs. I peer up at the looming frontage of the church, with its massive bolted wooden doors; I run my hands over the cold lip of the drinking fountain, a carved stone bowl with a copper spout, dribbling away in front of the *mairie*. Finally I force myself to head up the steep street that leads to the tower. The houses are mute, shuttered; there's not a radio, not a chink of light to indicate occupation. I can't remember which of the line of identical doors is Anna's and something in me recoils from the idea of knocking. When I see her, it ought to be in daylight, so there can be no mistake, no misrecognition. As I hesitate, a cat emerges from the shadows. I watch it stalk down the hill, the only sign of life in a scene as desolate and hermetic as a de Chirico piazza. Inevitably, I end up climbing towards the tower, wreathed in a jaundiced yellow glow at the summit of the hill.

After my trip to London I didn't hear from Miles for a long time. It seemed that Pat Ellis had decided to comply with the demands of her 'stakeholders', whoever they were.

At home things had reached a new low. I'd given up hiding my drinking and sometimes brought home bottles of wine to nurse in the study or in front of the TV. Miranda didn't comment; she'd more or less stopped speaking to me. We moved around the house in a strange silent dance, trying as far as possible to stay in separate rooms. At God's, I leafed through old pamphlets and thought with increasing regularity about heroin. I'd noticed a drop-in centre near the leisure park, a nondescript building where the county Drug and Alcohol Services ran a methadone clinic. Two or three shell-suited men were always leaning against the wall outside, slouching in the unmistakable lizard posture of dealers. It would take half an hour at most to score and make it back to God's. I could sit and smoke and think without having to care about what I was thinking. If the dealers at the drop-in centre couldn't help me, Portsmouth, a few miles away, was teeming with junkies. You saw heroin faces everywhere, shuffling about behind shopping centres, sitting disconsolately on garden walls. No problem scoring in Portsmouth. It was Oblivion-on-Sea.

I kept answering the phone to someone named Carl, who needed to talk to Miranda about business. She'd always take the calls upstairs in the bedroom. As I put down the receiver I'd hear her greet him, an unfamiliar warmth in her voice, a breathiness. Was he her lover? It wouldn't have surprised me. There were so many secrets between us that one more wouldn't really have made a difference. I felt happy for her: she deserved someone who could share her ambitions, her hopes for the future. She certainly deserved better than me. Yet this new mystery, this sense of possibilities away from our shared life, suddenly made her seem desirable again. It was like some bad behaviourist joke: me in the dunce's cap, salivating on cue. I found myself watching her as she dressed to go to the office, her trim bottom wiggling into a pencil skirt, the nape of her neck as she twisted sideways to brush her hair.

One evening I was in the living room, half watching Pat Ellis on the news. I had a bottle in front of me on the coffee-table, a Portuguese red that I was trying to make last. Miranda came in and sat down beside me on the sofa.

'Want one?' I asked, trying to sound playful.

She shrugged. 'Why not?'

'Really?'

She nodded. I muted the TV and went to fetch her a glass. She took a couple of sips and set it down on the coffee-table. She looked very tired. A sudden deep silence fell between us, a mutual ease I didn't want to break.

'How was London?'

'Fine. Busy.'

'I can't remember who you were meeting.'

'No reason for you to remember. Someone was showing me retail units.'

'Retail?'

'I haven't decided yet, but I think we'll open a little boutique. Somewhere to showcase the new range.'

'That's a big step.'

'Not so big. Not since the investors came on board.'

'Where would it be?'

'I was thinking the King's Road, but Carl says Notting Hill would be better.'

'So was it Carl who was showing you the shop?'

'Carl Palmer. I've told you about him.'

'No, I don't think so.'

'He's in property. He's been very helpful.'

'He rings here a lot, your Carl Palmer.'

She looked defiant. 'Does he?'

I held up my hands. 'Forget it. Sorry.'

Anger and hopelessness played over her face. She took a deliberate gulp of her wine. 'We've got a lot to sort out, Mike. But let's not get into accusations. Not when we're actually having a nice time.'

'You're right.'

'Look, why don't we go out for once? I feel like I'm suffocating.'

We drove to a Greek restaurant where we treated one another with such care and formality that we eventually made ourselves laugh. Carl Palmer was with us at the table, floating beside Anna Addison, balancing her, giving our conversation the brittle lightness that comes when two people are colluding with one another, working hard on the deferral of pain.

The next morning we woke up wrapped round each other in bed. Miranda smiled at me warily. We had a truce. It was soon afterwards that she first mentioned the idea of a birthday party.

October from the study window: Miranda brutally stabbing at the garden with a trowel. February brought her a reward of daffodils, great clumps of them lining the beds, paper-white and sunshine-yellow. I spent hours at my desk, the desk I didn't use for anything any more, watching them quiver in the rain. In the evenings I followed Pat Ellis on the news. There she was, nine months into the new era, standing beside her leader wearing a scarlet jacket and an optimistic smile, like some kind of political redcoat. There she was, surrounded by hand-picked representatives of the topic of the day, addressing the concerns of Junior Police Officers or Minority Community Representatives or Victims of Antisocial Behaviour. Whatever her gang was up to, she was right in the middle of it, retailing euphoria, glad-handing rock stars.

When the telly started spewing pictures of fox-hunters pushing policeman in Parliament Square, I laughed so hard I almost fell off the couch. Oh, I was living in a topsy-turvy world all right, a mirror world of flash and spin and graphic design. Politics was just lifestyle. Even the scandals seemed to be about home improvement. Miles's taunt came back to me: yes, this was the opposite of carving out a Utopia, the opposite of whatever I'd been fumbling for all those years ago. Thoroughly pragmatic, blandly ruthless, always up for a cocktail party. The bloody prime minister was five years younger than me, whichever birthday I counted from.

Then the Home Secretary got himself in a pickle over immigration and the pundits started mentioning Pat Ellis as the coming woman. One day I was half listening to the radio at God's, watching that rare thing, an actual customer, scanning the poetry section, when I realized Pat was talking in my ear. It had long been her belief, it transpired, that the end of the Cold War necessitated a change of focus in Britain's intelligence services. She buried it in jargon, smoothing the edges with euphemism and talking with great seriousness about people-trafficking and animal-rights activists and other contemporary threats to state security, but the underlying message was a budget cut, a reduction of influence for the spooks.

People think Fascism doesn't exist any more. It's just a cartoon perversion, a repertoire of sketch show mannerisms: uniform fetishism, short hair, lining your pencils up in a row on your desk. But the Fascists didn't go away after the Second World War. I don't just mean skinheads, though even they've burrowed underground, talking about multiculturalism, dressing like breakfast-television presenters. There's always been a part of the British establishment that identifies its own interests with the interests of the state. They're unsentimental about human life. They have creatures like Miles to do their bidding.

Whoever Miles represented, whichever clique or tendency or faction, I knew that to them, someone like Pat Ellis was just a blow-in, a temporary occupant of a chair. They wouldn't hesitate to remove her if they thought she was a threat. The only question was whether they took her speech seriously.

Back in 1971, the defenders of British liberty didn't bother to camouflage themselves. As union unrest grew and middle-class leftists talked about revolution around Hampstead supper-tables, there were rumours of an imminent military coup. In Northern Ireland, young men and boys were being rounded up and placed in camps. Detainees spent hours or days hooded and shackled in stress positions while loudspeakers played white noise into their cells. There were stories of mock-execution, prisoners forced to run gauntlets of baton-wielding soldiers.

In a peculiar way, I felt relieved by the news from Ireland. Internment confirmed what I'd always felt was true: inside the democratic velvet glove there was an iron fist. To the imperial dreamers who still ran our country, this was just another colonial police action, rounding up a few natives to keep the rest in line. To us it looked like the beginning of the slide towards the gas chamber.

Sean's anger knew no bounds. He wanted to act as soon as he heard the news and it was all I could do to stop him walking out of the door, looking for someone to shoot. He talked about kidnapping, about bombs under cars. He'd always been volatile, but since the débâcle of the bank raid, his anger had grown uncontrollable, bitter. He kept talking about how he'd failed to 'save' Ferdy, how he should have fired. With Anna away there was no one to counterbalance his self-disgust. He barely listened to the rest of us, even Claire, who could sometimes talk him down. Strangely, for someone who seemed to have trouble concentrating and whose consumption of amphetamines meant that he sometimes went several nights without sleep, he'd taken to reading. He attacked books; after he'd been at one it would look as if it had been through a storm, brutally battered, whole pages underlined in thick pen strokes. To everyone's annoyance he'd scrawled a quote from Mao on the wall of the room where he was sleeping. *We are advocates of the abolition of war. We do not want war; but war can only be abolished through war, and in order to get rid of the gun, it is necessary to take up the gun.* It was Sean's old favourite line; I didn't like to think of it running round his head when he was wired, late at night.

The problem was that there was very little we could do. We'd almost used up the explosives we'd stolen from the demolition contractor. The rest of our arsenal consisted of three pistols and an old Sten gun, which was so rusty I doubted it could be fired.

Thankfully, the plan we came up with was simple, if risky, and the only casualty had been dead for three hundred years. Late at night, with Sean on pillion, Leo drove a motorbike into Parliament Square. While he pretended to break down, Sean ran into the darkness and planted a bomb on a short fuse beneath the statue of Oliver Cromwell that stood outside the Palace of Westminster. As they accelerated away down the Embankment, the explosion blew the old butcher into little pieces there is no point trying to explain right and wrong to cowards and crooks and part-timers we are sick of justifying ourselves to you our so-called masters or to you liberal dilettante scum who wring your hands and say oh no not this way not now not yet not ever if it was up to you not while british troops are setting up concentration camps in ireland three hundred years after cromwells army raped and pillaged across Two days later the inspector from the bomb squad came on the TV to announce he'd made arrests in connection with the so-called '14 August' group. We saw blurry photographs of people we'd never heard of, who were described as dangerous seditionaries. The policeman was confident their 'dangerous antics' had now been brought to an end we are talking to those of you who get it already who are sick of the endless talk which never brings anything into reality we are talking to those of you who know we are all in prison and want to break out go and explain to the people it is time to put an end to the pig state they have looked their whole lives into the lying eyes of judges and social workers and managers and teachers and foremen and doctors and local councillors and still the only ones they fear are the police WE ARE EVERYWHERE we are the man standing next to you on the station platform the woman cleaning your kitchen floor. I tried to speak to Anna. I had to leave a coded message with a contact in Paris, who called back several days later asking me to wait beside a telephone at a certain time. Since I was staying in a flat with no phone, I'd persuaded a friend to let me use hers. This friend, a girl I knew from Notting Hill, had no idea I was involved in anything illegal. When Anna's call came through she was in her living room, drinking and playing records with some friends. I sat on her bedroom floor in a tangle of tights and paperbacks and ashtrays and listened to the party on the other side of the door and the crackle on the line and an operator's voice speaking in a language I thought must be Arabic and then came Anna's voice, cosmically distant, saying, 'Hello.' Our conversation was stilted and telegraphic. I didn't want to risk discussing Sean. I asked how she was and she said she was fine. There was a long pause, then she asked if Grandma was all right, our code for an emergency. I didn't dare say that my main reason for calling was to hear her voice. I pretended to have a logistical question, a query about a vehicle we'd left in the long-term car park at Heathrow airport. I didn't ask where she was. I knew it wasn't France.

Three weeks later. An indeterminate landscape, neither land nor sea; the light a uniform grey dazzle. I drove a brand new VW camper van over endless mudflats, the only sign of my passing a pair of tyre tracks, abstract lines in the rear-view mirror. It was impossible to tell where the sky began.

I was still on the German side of the border. Up the coast a mile or two was Denmark. The Holstein marshes appeared primeval, almost empty of human life. Up ahead the mudflats folded themselves into low dunes crested with grey-green sea grass. Huge flocks of migratory birds wheeled overhead.

There it was, the place I was looking for – a boat-house with a red roof. I drew up, parked beside it on a patch of broken concrete, listened into the wind. A series of muffled stuttering reports. Silence, then the same sound again. Short bursts of automatic-weapon fire, coming from some distance away. I got out and walked round the boat-house, rattling the big double doors, trying to see in through the smeared glass of the windows. Muffled as it was, the sound put me on edge. An animal reaction. Fight or flight. As I looked round, someone grabbed me from behind, pinning my arms to my sides. I struggled and found myself face to face with Sean, who seemed to find my violent thrashing very funny. When I shook him off, he raised his hands in pretend-surrender.

'Hold on there, cowboy. I saw you drive up. I came to find you.'

'Get off. Get the fuck away from me.'

'Calm down, *amigo*. Bad journey?'

'It was OK.'

'We're over in the dunes, shooting targets.'

I'd followed Anna's instructions. A Middle Eastern man in a café on the Edgware Road. An envelope of money. I'd bought the van, taken it to be modified. Now there were secret compartments behind the door panels and between the front and rear axles, ready to transport the equipment back to the UK. We'd all made our way to the marshes in ones and twos, disguised as tourists exploring the national park. As money was no longer a problem I'd bought myself new camping equipment, an expensive tent and sleeping-bag. I told Sean I'd follow on and pitched it some distance away from the boat-house. I wanted to wake up in the morning and see the horizon. I wanted to watch the flight of the birds.

For that week we knew each other only by single names. The instructors were Khaled and Johnny. There were the Germans, Jochen, Conny, Frank and Julia. Paul, I think, was French. Some had been in southern Lebanon, training in a PFLP camp. For others, like me, this was the first contact with what Khaled called 'the organization'. I watched Anna skilfully stripping and rebuilding a 7.65mm Skorpion machine pistol. She demonstrated how to reduce the rate of fire, how the stock folded so it could be carried under a jacket or a coat. Khaled stood beside her, nodding approvingly, his eyes fading from view behind his Polaroid sunglasses whenever the sun emerged from behind a cloud.

A gun, an animal weight in my hands, warm and snakily alive. Anna repeating Arabic words from a phrasebook. Johnny picking his way over the dunes, the sand filling his city shoes. No one disturbed us. No one came. In the evenings, after the light had failed and we'd eaten a tasteless meal of canned soup and bread, discussions were held in the dank boat-house. Ideas were debated in a patchwork of languages. Plans were formed. People spoke of a strategy for victory. They spoke about the end of Imperialism. They could have been talking about anything. Road resurfacing, waste disposal. Out in the marshes, I thought. We're out in the marshes at the edge of the sea, miles from the nearest other human beings, talking about who we're going to kill to demonstrate our organic connection to the masses. I'd light my way back to my tent with a little pocket torch, a bright speck in the enormous darkness.

Johnny and Khaled never let us forget where the money came from, whose agenda took priority. Whatever we'd been doing before, whichever acronymic jumble of letters represented our particular hopes, we were now part of something much larger than ourselves, an international network with nodes in Frankfurt, Milan, Beirut, Bilbao. They talked about targets in London, people and places that had no connection with anything I cared about. They talked obsessively about Zionism. The weapons were new, some of them still in their packing grease. They were all of Eastern-bloc manufacture: Makarovs and Tokarevs, the Czech Skorpion machine pistols. This should have told us all we needed to know. We weren't autonomous any more. Far from it. Yet none of the others, these people I knew as Sean and Leo and Anna and Jay and Claire but who now had other names, seemed to want to be reminded of the way we'd talked to one another only a few months previously, how we'd intended to escape the binary madness of East and West, how we respected human life. Armed love, we'd said. In order to get rid of the gun it is necessary to take up the gun. I fired off rounds into a paper target, and with each bullet I believed a little less. Quietly, privately, I began to wonder how I could get away.

Oh, Sam. It was arrogance, I suppose. We thought we'd stepped outside. We thought it had been given to us to kick-start the new world. Can you understand that? Does wanting to be a corporate lawyer count as a dream? For the first time in many years I celebrated my birthday, Chris Carver's birthday, a few weeks before that of Michael Frame. I sat in the study with an expensive bottle of Burgundy and looked back at my fifty years and felt so fucking disappointed, Sam. I knew I needed to speak to you, to prepare you, however imperfectly, for what was about to happen. That was just last week, when I drove to Bristol to see you. You were shocked to find me on your doorstep. You opened the door a crack, your hair a mess, a sheet wrapped round your middle. It was past twelve. I could hear someone coughing in the background. You left the boy in your bed and made me coffee in the shared kitchen, shuffling past your neighbours as they boiled pasta and opened tins to make a sauce.

'What are you doing here, Dad?' As if I were a visitor from outer space, bug-eyed and slightly disgusting, come to earth to rupture your reality. I told you I needed to talk and you said you had a lecture. Couldn't I have rung first? I offered to occupy myself for an hour or two, meet you afterwards. I wandered round Clifton and, when you'd got yourself together, took you to lunch at a fancy French restaurant where I encouraged you to over-order and flourished the wine list and generally faked my way through the part of the jovial father who'd come down to uni to give his daughter a surprise. I tried to get you to eat. You just pushed your food around on your plate. You looked thin and I said so, and immediately you flew off the handle, telling me to mind my own business. That sort of remark was typical of me. It was typical of men. I asked what you meant and you raised your voice and demanded to know why it was that, unless you were totally stuffing yourself, men were always, like, were you some kind of anorexic. You used the word *fucking*. Miranda never liked you to swear. What, you asked, was I doing in Bristol anyway?

I told you there was something you needed to know about, and you immediately asked whether your mum and I were splitting up.

Such a direct question, it threw me. 'Of course not,' I said automatically. 'No, of course not.' You sat there, your face suspicious and expectant by turns. I was lost for words. I'd already gone wrong. You were so volatile, so unexpectedly bitter. In a bid to mark time, I heard myself say, yet again, that there was something I needed to discuss. I tried to push myself on by telling you there were things you and your mum didn't know about me.

You reacted with hair-trigger hostility. 'I knew it. You're sleeping around on Mum. You bastard.'

As much as I protested, you wouldn't listen. You were so absolute, so unwilling to be contradicted. You called me various names echoing things Miranda must have complained to you about. Why didn't I do something with my life? Why did I just mooch off other people?

You were impossible, Sam. You wouldn't let me get a word in. You'd sensed something and you knew you were at least half right, which gave you the confidence, the self-righteousness, to shut me down completely. Angry and hurt, I called for the bill. We didn't part as friends.

Miranda must have forced you to come home for the party. You didn't have much to say to me when you arrived that evening, just dropped your stuff and went out to the pub. Surely you must have told your mum I'd been to see you. She didn't bring it up. I decided she must be holding it in reserve. That was what I was thinking about when Miles arrived. Was it yesterday? The day before. I was in the study, watching the men from the marquee company fooling about on the lawn. I swivelled round on my chair and there he was, standing in the doorway.

'Hello, Chris. Sorry to call so unexpectedly. Door was open.'

My instinct, as ever, was to get him out of the house, so we walked into town and sat in a café, some hideous chain operation with prosthetic-pink iced buns lying like hospital patients under the glass of the counter and a bedraggled Eastern European girl making coffee that tasted of washing-up liquid. 'Will that be everything for you today?' she said mechanically, as we lined up to pay.

'Would you like to add an extra shot or a flavour for only fifty p?'

We sat in the window. Miles performed his usual fussy sitting-down routine, fiddling with his trouser legs and smoothing his jacket under his bottom. For a while he rambled on about his chiropodist. Miracle-worker, reasonable rates. Another carry-over from the old days. Miles always had an air of slight distraction, a vagueness that made it hard to tell where his attention was directed.

'I'm sorry, Chris,' he said eventually, with the compassionate expression of a doctor about to tell the patient his cancer had metastasized.

'What exactly are you sorry about?'

'In life, I always say, you start off somewhere and you end up somewhere, but the trouble is you don't begin with a clean slate. I think that's what we were after. A clean slate. Not much to ask, you would have thought. Take me, for instance. I realize everyone thought I had it very easy. Well, I didn't. My life wasn't simple at all.'

'Is that so?'

'You sound sceptical.'

'You seemed to be able to do what you wanted. You drifted around, made your films. You always had money.'

'Money wasn't really the issue.' He leaned back in his chair and stretched. I heard the joints in his arms and back make an unpleasant gristly sound. 'I was doing my best to look free. It was the fashion, wasn't it? You had to look free. And sincere! You had to be so crushingly sincere all the time! God help you if you weren't. Everyone jumped down your throat.'

'What do you want, Miles? I need to get back.'

He ignored me, fixated on his train of thought. 'I've given it a lot of input over the years and now I understand why everyone was so bloody boring. I think deep down we all knew we were doomed to be terribly disappointed, but we hated anyone bringing it up. If you brought it up, it messed with everyone's vibe.'

'Who's this "we" you keep talking about? I hardly knew you.'

'Do you remember the time we met in Wales?'

'Yes.'

'You were in too deep, by then. I could tell you were.'

That was true enough. I'd started to get eczema on my eyelids and on the backs of my hands. Whole days went by when I couldn't get out of bed. At other times I was possessed by an intense, restless energy. From the flat in Camden Town, I started to take long walks by the canal, picking my way along the towpath towards the rubble of the docklands, or into the West End, where I'd wander around staring at the bustling world as if it were behind glass, an expensive window display arranged for someone else's benefit, not mine.

After I got back from the training camp, I couldn't see what the future held. I felt like I'd cut myself off from everything meaningful. Other groups were continuing the political work we'd once done; they were still connected to the struggle, to something wider than themselves. Once I'd been surrounded by people. Where had they all gone?

One afternoon, as I was bustling purposelessly towards Camden Lock, someone called out to me. I didn't respond at first, but finally, after my name was shouted a second and a third time, I turned round and saw a girl I knew from Free Pictures. Alison had curly dark hair and a broad, gentle smile; I hadn't seen her since the last chaotic party at Lansdowne Road, during which, for an hour or two, I'd hoped we might go home together. She greeted me with a hug and asked what I'd been doing. I gave some noncommittal answer. She seemed almost absurdly excited and carefree, as if she were the inhabitant of a parallel world where young people were allowed to drift around on September afternoons without worrying about raids and explosives and surveillance and the secret state. She was living nearby. And me? 'Round about,' I said. 'Staying with friends.' Why hadn't she seen me? I shrugged. She gave me an appraising look. Then, as if struck by a sudden inspiration, she asked if I wanted to go to Wales with her and her friends. Right then, that afternoon. There was a free festival. There was space in the van.

I said yes instinctively, without thinking.

As I was driven out of London in someone's beaten-up Bedford, I started to think of all the reasons I shouldn't be going. The breach of security; the breach of discipline. But no one else had been in the flat where I was staying so there'd been no one to question me.

There were six of us. Though the others were all my age, they seemed incredibly young. The boys showed off, telling jokes and trying to impress each other. The girls giggled and rolled their eyes at Alison, who let them know I was her property, nestling herself beside me in the back and chattering away about things that seemed utterly foreign: the names of bands, the hassles of her part-time job.

By the time we reached the Welsh borders, a light rain had set in and the atmosphere in the van became more subdued. At last, after many hours' driving, we found ourselves crawling through tiny lanes in a remote spot on the Caernarfonshire coast, looking for the festival site. We found it by following a London taxi painted with Day-Glo orange and yellow swirls, which led us to a muddy patch of farmland by a river, set in a beautiful bowl of forested hills. The festival wasn't a huge event. The organizers had erected a small stage and a few hundred people had set up camp on the soggy land around it, a scattering of tents and trucks and tepees that looked like some sort of tribal encampment.

Ragged people moved through the forest foraging for firewood. Some had built shelters among the trees out of tarpaulins and artfully interwoven branches. As we pitched tents there was a moment of awkwardness until Alison made it clear I'd be staying with her. We went over to hear some music, stretching out on a rug listening to a group featuring a flautist who traded licks with a sitar, while their singer rhymed *getting straight* with *meditate*.

Lying down beside Alison, I let the sound wash over me. A jazz-rock band came on, all complicated riffage and polyrhythms. A gnome-like old guy, naked except for a loincloth, performed a shuffling shamanic hop at the front of the stage. Alison and I talked, or rather she talked and I listened, happy to hear her opinions about books and fashion and films. A kitchen was dispensing free food and as we lined up with our bowls I had to fight the urge to cry on her shoulder, to let all my troubles spill out. As night fell, people lit bonfires and someone passed round a tube of tiny red stars. As Alison came up on her trip she wanted to have sex but I couldn't and felt bad about it, which made her feel bad too. We stopped trusting each other and she retreated to her friends and eventually I left the circle of firelight and wandered around in the dark. Someone was playing a repetitive figure on an electric guitar, a jagged rasp that seemed vaguely threatening, like the shadows that loomed up around me as I stumbled through the damp woods, shadows that always resolved into the silhouettes of other festival-goers, lost souls too high and disoriented to get back to their friends. I fell asleep by someone else's fire and woke up very early in the morning to the sound of conversation.

For a long time I didn't move. I couldn't feel my arms and legs. In my confusion I wondered if I'd died. The light was very bright. A young girl with a disturbingly doll-like face was reaching down towards me, touching my face. Her blue eyes and white clothing triggered some Sunday-school routine in my brain: it was only when I noticed the muddy hem of her dress that I was finally convinced she was real.

'You're very cold,' she said, in a broad Yorkshire accent. I sat up stiffly, rubbing my eyes. She was right. My back had frozen into a painful block. She offered me a joint, which I waved away. Then, to my amazement, I noticed Miles Bridgeman sitting next to her, wrapped in a shaggy Afghan coat. His hair had grown and he had a full beard, plaited into twin strands held together by little glass beads.

'Chris?'

'Miles?'

'I couldn't decide if it was you. Someone had to move you in case you burned yourself. Man, what are you doing here?'

'I don't know. I came with some people.'

'You must be cold. Give him a blanket, Milly.'

Milly looked about thirteen, but there was something about the way she carried herself that made me think she must be a good deal older. She draped a patchwork quilt over my shoulders, looking at me incuriously with her ceramic blue eyes. Someone was building up the fire and within a few minutes I was huddled next to it, poking my feet as far forward as I could get without melting the soles of my boots.

'You fought them, you know.'

'What?'

Miles grinned. 'The people who tried to move you. You'd passed out completely, but you woke up and tried to fight them.'

'Shit.'

'You didn't hurt anyone.'

I watched Milly make tea and my mind raced as I tried to work out how much trouble I was in. I didn't think Alison had any connection with Miles. I saw no way he could have engineered this encounter unless Alison had been placed in the street, waiting for me to go by. But I hadn't seen him since he was kicked out of Sylvan Close. I knew I needed to be careful.

'It's been a long time,' he said. I nodded, looking over his shoulder to see if I could spot Alison in the crowd. People were milling about, looking for breakfast, making their way down to the river to wash.

'You were calling out, too, you know. When they were trying to move you.'

I must have looked worried, because he held up his hands and smiled. 'Impossible to tell what you were saying. Just noises.'

We sat for a while, poking the fire with sticks. I was beginning to warm up, to master my shivering.

'What have you been doing?'

'Not much. You know.'

'You're still in Hackney?'

'I'm staying with friends.'

'I've got a houseboat down in Chelsea. Just off Cheyne Walk.'

You should come and take a look at her one day. She's called the *Martha*. You can still see a place on the side where she got hit by a German shell at Dunkirk.'

'Very patriotic.'

'Goodness. Dirty words, coming from you.'

Milly made beans on toast, which I ate gratefully, the reviving warmth of the food doing what the fire hadn't quite managed. 'Very bad about Northern Ireland,' said Miles, as I scraped the plate with the side of my fork.

'Let's not discuss politics. Not today.'

'That's unlike you.'

'What?'

'Not to want to talk politics.'

'I feel like shit, Miles.'

'Of course. Sorry. How's Anna?'

'She's fine.'

'So you're still in touch?'

I was too tired to lie. 'Sure.'

'And Sean? I haven't seen him around.'

'Why would you? You're not exactly his favourite person.'

'I suppose you're right. Good to know you're all still together, though.'

There was a massive hinterland to his words, a realm of insinuation. He reached into a pocket and pulled out a pen and a little notebook. What kind of person carried a pen at a festival? He scribbled something down, tore out the sheet and handed it to me.

'Take this, while I remember.'

'What is it?'

'My address. The boat. I've put my phone number on it.'

'Thanks.'

'You really should come by. I always feel I ought to keep up with friends a little more than I do. People have missed you, Chris.'

'Oh, yeah? Like who?'

'Me, for one. But there are others. I'll be honest, people say things. What with all the raids and everything – well, when heavy people like you and Sean and Anna drop out of sight – you know. There's talk.' He left it hanging in the air. 'Chris, whatever you're into, you should be careful.'

I stood up and brushed myself down. I was covered with dried mud and bits of grass. 'I should find my friend Alison.'

'Really? Perhaps I'll see you later.'

'Maybe. Do you know her?'

'Alison?'

'Her surname's Jenner, I think. Dark hair. Used to work at BIT.'

'No, doesn't ring a bell.'

'I thought she might be a friend of yours.'

Miles stood up and put his hands on my shoulders. It was an oddly intimate gesture for such an unphysical, self-contained man. 'If I don't see you, call me when you get back to London. I mean it. If you ever need someone to talk to about anything. Anything at all.'

I waved to Milly, thanking her for the beans in a strained, over-cheerful voice. Then I went around the camp, trying not to get spotted by Alison as I hunted urgently for someone who was driving back to London. In the end I got a lift with a couple who said they could take me as far as Reading. I got into the back seat of their old Hillman Avenger and was half-way to Bristol before I realized I'd left my sleeping-bag in Alison's tent.

Miles remembered the festival as a bucolic moment, a highlight of our shared youth. It was evidence, he told me, that we'd once been friends. He hoped that even if I felt angry now, I appreciated that he'd acted in as decent a way as possible.

'Unfortunately,' he said, in a tone of infinite resignation, 'Mrs Ellis is being pigheaded. It was put to her that now might be an appropriate moment to step down from front-line politics and do something more suitable.'

'What does *suitable* mean?'

'Voluntary sector. Academia. The places they keep the more intractable old lefties.'

'And she refused.'

'Sadly.'

'Because your insinuations aren't true.'

'Yes, they are.'

'Who says?'

'You do.'

I watched the shoppers trudging past the café window.

'You're an evil bastard.'

Miles sighed. 'Chris, I'm not doing this to be vindictive. In fact, you shouldn't go away with the impression that I give a damn one way or the other, because quite frankly I don't. I don't care what you did thirty years ago, or what Pat Ellis did. Believe me, I'd rather be doing anything with my day but this. I realize how it's going to disrupt your life, but it's unavoidable. You'll be in the spotlight for a while, which is also unavoidable. The thing to remember is that it'll only be for a short time, the exposure. They get bored. It stops. And you won't be on your own while it's happening. We'll help you through. You've had a good run, but it's over. You have to understand that.'

'I'm not doing anything for you.'

'Chris, I'm sorry. But it'll be a lot better if we do it my way. The other way you wouldn't like. It's time to come out of hiding. It's time to tell your story.'

I asked him if he wanted another coffee. He shook his head. 'So,' I asked wearily, 'what are you proposing?'

'You'll give an interview to a journalist, a man called Gibbs. He's someone I've worked with before. Very reliable. An arsehole, of course, all those guys are, but he's not unpleasantly rabid. In it, you'll describe your remorse for your actions, your secret double life and so forth. Your "explosive revelation" – as their headline writer will no doubt dub it – is the fact that a serving government minister was present during the manufacture of the Post Office

Tower bomb. You'll throw yourself on the mercy of the British justice system. You'll be given the opportunity to remind readers how young you were. In return, I'll try to minimize the legal consequences. It's not something I'll be able to control entirely, but I promise I'll give it my best. Have you told your wife yet?'

'No.'

'I think it's time you did.'

'Don't fucking tell me what it is or isn't time to do. It's my life. My *life*, Miles. We've been together sixteen years. What do I have other than her and Sam? Fuck all, that's what. They're my life and the person who has that life is Mike Frame.'

He slammed his palm down on the table, making the coffee cups rattle. He looked exasperated. 'God, you make it fucking difficult, don't you? Think! Use your head! You *don't have a choice* about whether this is coming out. One way or the other it's going to happen. Your only choice is *how* it comes out. I'm asking you to think of your family. Make it easy for them, if you can't for yourself.'

We'd been raising our voices. The girl behind the counter was glancing around nervously, as if wondering whether she'd have to intervene.

'I'm going now.' I got up and walked out, cutting across the street and weaving through the Saturday shopping crowds. I didn't look behind but I knew Miles was following me. I could hear the sharp reports of his shoes on the flagstones. Metal heel protectors. What did we call them when I was a kid? Blakeys. He was wearing blakeys.

'Chris, stop.'

'Mike. I'm Mike, all right? Michael Frame.'

'It's over, Chris. All that's over. I told you Pat Ellis has decided to fight. Apparently she's contacted the police about you. She's made it official, so that if she's challenged she can say she took immediate action. They're circulating your old pictures.'

* * *

Shoot the messenger. That was it, partly. But there was also a deeper question, one of trust. I didn't blame them for their paranoia. I'd have been just as suspicious. I was cadre. I was supposed to be disciplined. Without warning I'd disappeared for a weekend, gone completely off the map. Then I'd come back with a story about Wales and Miles Bridgeman, who everyone already suspected was an informer. It was never going to look right.

There was a meeting. Hostile faces, searching looks. I was left in a room on my own and when they came back, they told me – or, rather, Anna told me, using her coldest and most impersonal tone – that Leo and Jay would take the train with me to Manchester, where we had a flat we'd kept empty for emergencies. We should phone in every day. We should wait for instructions.

Whether or not I'd been believed, my news precipitated a group transformation, a sudden shedding of skin. For some time we'd been laying paper trails around our new identities, breathing life into birth certificates and library cards and utility bills and fake letters of reference. We'd all practised changing our appearance. It was time to break with the past, to go completely underground.

From that day on my name was Michael Frame. I practised it. If Michael Frame was walking down the street and someone called out, he should turn round instantly, without hesitating. Michael Frame had short hair and a neatly trimmed moustache. He had no connection with politics of any kind. I rehearsed the names of his mother and father, his date of birth.

On the journey north, Leo and Jay behaved more like guards than comrades. I couldn't buy a newspaper at a kiosk or walk through the train to the buffet car without one of them accompanying me.

We didn't talk much. They both had trouble meeting my eye. I knew Leo was armed and that made me afraid.

The Manchester flat was on the sixteenth floor of a system-built block in Rusholme. It was almost bare of furniture, just a couple of mattresses and a little black-and-white telly balanced on an orange crate by the heater. We stayed there for almost two weeks, playing cards, smoking endless cigarettes. The weather was filthy. Wind drove dirty sleet against the windows. Once in a while the sun appeared, a bilious pale yellow ball like the yolk of a battery farm egg. If it hung around for more than an hour or two in the morning, it turned the treacherous film of ice on the pavement into a nasty grey slush.

A strike was on, so there were power cuts. When night fell, its reign was absolute. In the stairwell of Arkwright House, bobbing torch-beams; dishes of melted candlewax on the kitchen counter. Sixteen floors up and the lifts didn't work. Sixteen floors with crappy plastic shopping bags, which sagged and tore, sending cans and bottles crashing down the hard steps. When the wind was strong, rushing through the gaps between Arkwright and Stephenson and Cobden, the three towers groaned in pain.

One evening as I climbed the stairs with Jay, my pocket torch lit up an old man clinging to the hand rail. He was like a ghost from the industrial past: flat cap, scarf knotted round his neck, his jacket unbuttoned to reveal a woollen undershirt tucked into a pair of greasy trousers. He was in a bad way, breathing heavily, the sweat pouring down his unshaven cheeks. When I asked if he was all right he mutely shook his head. 'It's Mary,' he said, expelling the words with great effort, through a curtain of phlegm.

George was probably in his sixties but work had aged him brutally, scooping out his face and clogging his lungs with cotton dust. In August his wife had slipped and fallen; now she was too frail to leave the flat. For the last couple of days she hadn't stopped shivering, so he'd put on his shoes and gone downstairs to fetch a doctor. It had taken him the best part of an hour to make it as far as the seventh floor. We sat with him for a while, and when we realized his asthma wasn't getting any better, Jay went back down to the pay-phones in the hall to call an ambulance. Half an hour, they said. They'd had a lot of calls. I told George they were on their way and went to check on his wife.

'Don't frighten her,' he pleaded. 'Sing out before you go in, else she'll think you're a burglar.'

Up on the fourteenth floor, I knocked on the door and called through the letterbox. George couldn't remember if he'd locked up so he'd given me his key. Still calling out, I went inside. The flat smelled of bacon fat and was as cold as a tomb. The torch picked up patches of damp, a shelf of dusty china birds, an armchair with a stack of *Reader's Digest* magazines balanced on a footstool beside it. I found Mary bundled up in bed, her eyes shut and her mouth hanging open, a little grey-faced figure with a tuft of thin hair plastered across her scalp. The bedroom stank of stale urine. I wondered if she was already dead.

'Mary, I'm a neighbour. George sent me to see how you were.'

She moaned. I couldn't tell if she was aware of me, but at least she was alive. My foot hit an overflowing chamber-pot, sitting out on the rug by the bed; I tried to master an overpowering sense of disgust. How had they been left like this? Who was supposed to be looking after them? Eventually the ambulance men came; Jay and I made ourselves scarce. We stood on the landing, just out of sight, listening to them cursing and swearing as they carried Mary down the stairs. I expect it was the smell, rather than the weight. She must have been as light as a bird.

The next day I took George a bag of necessities: candles, toilet roll, tins of food. He was too proud to admit it, but there were obviously days when he and Mary ate nothing at all, when their pension money had run out or they hadn't been able to make it to the shops. I sat in the armchair and he shuffled around, making a slow-motion cup of tea. I listened to his laboured breathing, the squeak of his cane on the kitchen lino. It made me feel ordinary, human. I remember it as the one decent moment of my time in Manchester.

When I went back upstairs after taking George his food, Leo thrust a newspaper into my hand. Across the front page was splashed the story that a bomb had blown up part of the employment secretary's constituency home. A communiqué had been received from the bombers, which hadn't been reproduced.

'Was that us?' I asked. Leo nodded.

'Anyone hurt?'

'No, not that it says.'

'Why wasn't I told?'

He shrugged. 'Because you're a security risk,' he said flatly.

At last, to my face. I tried to make a joke of it. 'What are you going to do, Leo, put me on trial? A people's court? March me into the woods and shoot me in the back of the head?'

I wanted him to laugh. He didn't laugh. He told me to use his other name. Paul. I was to call him Paul Collins.

'Since when,' I asked, 'are we bombing people's houses? Did we know nobody was in there?'

'A risk assessment was made.'

'A risk assessment was made. You know what's going to happen, don't you, Leo? Someone's going to get killed.'

Again he shrugged, the same petulant, noncommittal shrug. 'Collateral damage,' he said. 'It's inevitable in war.'

'You sound like General Westmoreland.'

'What do you mean by that?'

'Callous, Leo. You sound callous.'

'Human being or pig. You make your choice.'

'So there's nothing in between?'

'No.'

'And the pigs have to die?'

He didn't reply, just stared at me angrily.

I gave him a slow round of applause. 'Well, good for you, mate. That's the kind of commitment I like.'

He chose to ignore my sarcasm. 'Sean's coming later. You can have it out with him.'

Soon enough came the death-rattle buzz of the doorbell. Sean wore a new grey suit and a hungry look. He was carrying, of all things, a leather attaché case, the kind with a combination lock and fancy metal clasps. He loped into the flat and filled the living room with misdirected energy. 'Hello, Mike,' he said.

I laughed involuntarily. I couldn't get used to the name. 'Christ, Sean, there's no one but us here.'

'Dennis Kilfoyle,' he said sharply. 'Dennis.' The case dangled awkwardly from his arm. It was the oddest thing for him to carry. Its effect was to render the rest of the disguise theatrical; the suit, the club tie, the badly shaved chin.

He walked past me into the bedroom, picking his way over the mess. As we had no table, we'd taken to eating our meals standing at the kitchen counter or sprawled on the living-room carpet, which was now pocked with stains and cigarette burns. I asked Sean if he wanted to go out and eat.

'No time,' he said. 'I'm here to drive you all to a meeting.'

I took this in. 'When?'

'Tonight. Now. You should get some things together.'

I found a sports bag and started stuffing dirty clothes into it. Sean lit a cigarette, turned over one of the books lying on the floor. The sky was a black square in the curtainless window.

'So, how have things been?' I asked.

'We're making progress.'

I waited for more. The silence spooled out like thread.

'You ready?' he asked eventually. I nodded. He was all business, ostentatiously checking his watch. Sean Ward, wearing a watch. We walked through the piss-stink of the lobby and into the night-time drizzle. Outside Arkwright House was parked a brand new Mercedes. He motioned me to get in.

'You're going up in the world,' I noted.

'It's a company car.'

All four of us broke into nervous laughter.

Sean drove out of the city, heading into the Peak District. It was drizzling and he was driving fast, too fast, as it turned out, for the traffic police. Flashing blue lights appeared in the rear window.

Under his breath, Sean swore, shifting around in his seat and loosening his jacket.

'Here,' he said. 'Take this.' He handed me a gun.

'What the fuck, Sean?'

'Dennis. It's fucking Dennis. If he asks me to get out of the car, you do him. Understand?'

I turned round. In the back, the other two were also readying weapons. Leo seemed to have one of the machine pistols.

'I'm going to pull over, OK? Everyone set?'

Oh, fuck, I thought. Fuck. Fuck. It seemed as if we sat there for eternity, hazard lights flashing, waiting for the tap on the window.

'Hello, sir? Could I see your driving-licence and the car's log book, please?'

He was young, a clean pink face peering into the car, shiny with rainwater. He played a torch over our faces.

'Sorry, Officer, I don't have them on me.'

'Your car, is it, sir?'

Stupidity. I tried to transmit it to the policeman by means of telepathy. Just be stupid, if you're not already. Be lazy.

Sean grinned. 'Like the car?'

'Very nice. Three hundred, is it?'

'That's right. Six point three litre.'

'Could you just tell me the registration number?'

Sean hesitated. Don't make me shoot him, I thought. Please don't make me fucking shoot him. It was as if I could already feel it, see it, the bloom of bone and blood, the bullet collapsing the planes of the young policeman's face. The silence was too long. Sean was taking too long. Fuck. Fuck.

Then he reeled it off. 'PWF 97K.'

The policeman hesitated. Leave it alone, I willed him. Go home out of the rain.

'Thank you, sir,' he said, after a silence of infinite weight and duration. 'I'll let you go now, but you'll have to produce your documents at a police station within the next five days.' He wrote something in his notebook. 'And if you could just watch your speed, visibility's not so good tonight. We don't want any accidents.'

We pulled away and drove for a long time without speaking.

'Is this stolen?' asked Jay.

Sean nodded, fiddling with the radio. 'It's all right. I changed the plates.'

I exhaled. 'And you memorized the new number.'

'What do you think I am? Some kind of cowboy? I'll have the gun back now, if you don't mind.'

We travelled through open countryside, listening to a stream of crackly pop songs that faded into static as we got up into the hills. The rain grew heavier, fat drops plashing on the windscreen. The headlights illuminated stone walls at the verge, rabbits scooting across the road. Finally Sean turned the Mercedes up a track that ran through a dense pine forest, coming to a halt in front of a rusty metal gate. I waited in the car as he ran to open it, holding his jacket over his head as an ineffectual shield against the water. We parked in front of an ugly grey stone building built, as far as I could see in the murk, around a little courtyard. The windows were covered with sheets of corrugated iron. Half the frontage was colonized by an enormous black ivy. It was a tumbledown place, the trees crowding in as if they were trying to reclaim it for the forest.

Soaked, Sean got back in, his hair plastered to his face.

'Where are we?' I asked.

'Somewhere to keep you on the straight and narrow.'

He bared his teeth mirthlessly, pointing at a weathered wooden board nailed above the gate.

TOIL HARD

FEAR GOD

BE HONEST

Sometimes I dream about that old workhouse. Its interior was as stark as the granite façade. Most of the fittings had been ripped out, leaving empty bathrooms whose skin of black-and-white tile was broken by the silhouettes of missing sinks and toilets, a foul-smelling workshop with painted-out windows and a raised invigilator's dais at one end. Our people had obviously been staying there for several days, sleeping on mats in a dusty dormitory that had a pile of iron bedsteads in one corner. They'd even rigged up a makeshift kitchen, with a low table of scavenged planks and a couple of rings running off bottled gas for cooking. Light came from oil lamps. A row of plastic buckets stood by a rainwater butt in the courtyard.

The smells of hash and vegetable stew mingled against a humid background of rotting wood. We ate, squatting on the floor by a heater. I asked Sean what was happening. When was the meeting? 'Tomorrow,' he said. So why had it been so important to drive two hours through the rain to get here? He shrugged and carried on spooning stew into his mouth. 'We wanted everyone in place,' he said. I caught an officious note in his voice, one of Anna's inflections. Someone handed me a glass of water. People moved through the room, materializing like wraiths out of the shadows. Leo's friend Quinn, a couple of others I didn't know. No one introduced me.

'Is Anna all right?' I asked. 'Nothing's happened to Anna?'

'Why do you say that?' asked Sean, sharply. After that no one made conversation. We just sat there in the half-darkness and waited.

'Is something about to happen?' I asked.

'Do you think it is?'

I turned round. It was Anna, dressed in jeans and a torn sweater. Even by the light of the oil lamp I could see how gaunt she was. Giacometti body, polished-bone head. She looked elevated, somehow *achieved*, as if she'd burned some final layer of indecision away from herself.

'Hello, Anna. I was worried about you.'

'No real names, please. Call me Christine, if you must call me anything.'

It wasn't just physical, what Anna had erased. She sounded uncannily detached, as if communicating from a great distance.

'If that's how you want it.'

'It's not a question of how I want it.'

'No, of course not. I'm sorry.'

I was beginning to feel uncomfortable; the atmosphere in the room was a physical weight pressing down on my shoulders.

'Are you expecting someone, Michael? You keep looking over my shoulder.'

'I can't see who's here.'

'Who's going to come through the door?'

'I don't know.'

'I'm sure you do. Tell me, what have you been up to?'

'You know what I've been up to. Hanging about in Manchester.'

'Hanging about in Manchester. What else?'

'I don't understand. Is this the meeting? Are we having the meeting now? Do you want to discuss targets?'

'I asked a simple question.'

I realized I was at the centre of a circle. People sat in the shadows, smoking, watching. 'Are you interrogating me?'

My words dropped thickly off my tongue. Anna's face was a yellow blur. Around it the flickering light had taken on an involuted quality; the whole room was pointing towards her face.

'Why do you say that?'

'I'm asking you a question.'

'Who have you been talking to?'

'Is this an interrogation?'

'Tell me who.'

'Nobody.'

'That's good, Michael.'

Is that what she said? Briefly, her face looked gentle again. Oh, Anna, I could have loved you. I could have tried to be perfect. I listened to myself talking. What had I been talking about? Nothing. Talking about nothing. Then I realized what was happening and a tendril of fear crept up into my chest. 'Did you spike me?'

I said the words and knew it was true. The dryness in my throat. The change in the quality of the shadows. My skin was tingling. My peripheral vision was just a puzzle, a palimpsest of sight. Suddenly I was very afraid. Please don't let me be coming up, not here in this terrible place. But I was. I was coming up. What was it? The glass of water, brought without me asking. So this was what it felt like to be a traitor, to be Kavanagh in the woods. Anna was still talking, asking a stream of questions. God, how much had they given me? Just out of eyeshot, it was getting busier. Teeming shadows, a cacophony of vision. The questions became sharper. It wasn't just Anna. They were all joining in. *Are you sure?* Sure of what? *Is there anything you need to tell us?* I don't think so. *Think so or know so?* We even had a name for it, a name from Criticism-Self-Criticism. They were bombing me. They were going to turn me inside out and pick over my head for the bad bits, like monkeys smashing a coconut to get at the flesh. How much had they given me? And why do it there, in that place? I said again, to them, to myself, that I had nothing to be scared of, nothing to hide. How much had they given me? Nothing to hide. I was a good person with nothing to hide. *Who do you work for?* Good, Chris. *Do you work for Miles?* Good, Mike. *Who is Miles?* Nothing to hide. And as I tried my best to fight my fear and answer their questions, reality slid away until there was no me, just a voice pleading with other voices. *How many voices? Tell us how many other voices?* They seemed to come from all sides asking *what are your real beliefs* an impossible question *answer* a human being for other human beings *that's no kind of answer* a man *only one way to free yourself michael you have to let it go this pretence* say what you want *it's in your head* in my head *say it down with the pig system this miles who is he* down with the pig system *twelve thousand a day* what is what *twelve thousand people die every day* twelve thousand every day *do you care or do you hate perhaps you're just a pig who wants a car holiday colour tv* no, that's not it, not it at all *come on pig sick pig let it all go* pig sick pig pig pig

Eventually they must have given me some kind of sedative, because the next thing I remember is waking in the late afternoon of the following day to find myself curled up in a sleeping-bag, my mouth dry and my head thick and pounding. The world still wasn't back to normal. It had an ugly slant to it, a sickening lean. Anna was kneeling down in front of me. She looked haggard and exhausted. I saw she had a cold sore on her bottom lip.

'Do you want some tea?'

I propped myself up on one elbow. I felt weak and slightly nauseous. The tea, which had a lot of sugar in it, tasted good. I noticed Anna's hands as she passed it to me. The chewed nails, the line of black scabs on her knuckles.

'Well done, Mike. I was so worried about you.'

I couldn't really speak, so I just nodded. She left me alone and I lay there, trying to piece together what had happened. Another hour or so passed. I could hear the sound of people moving around downstairs, birds singing outside the boarded-up window. I think I fell asleep again.

Later that night, as I lay awake in the dormitory, listening to people breathe and cough in the darkness, Anna came to crouch beside me. She smelled of the workhouse, of rotting wood and long-ago fear. She brought her face close to mine. 'It's good to have you back,' she whispered, kissing me.

What was this? A reward? Another interrogation? I traced with my fingers the winged ridges of her shoulder-blades, her ribcage, and as I touched her I felt a rising tide of horror. 'What would you have done?' I asked.

'What, baby?'

'If you'd found out I was a traitor.'

She tugged her T-shirt over her head. 'I'd have killed you,' she said, lifting her leg to straddle my hips.

* * *

Slipping on loose gravel, I pick my way up the path to the tower, which glows inscrutably above me like something from a science-fiction film. There's a cold wind up here on the hill, shuddering through the bushes, catching at my arms and legs. I sit down against the tower's blank stone wall and arrange myself into a comfortable position, straightening my back and resting my hands in my lap. There's nothing I can do now but wait until morning. Gradually I start to become aware of my breathing. How long since I last meditated? For years, while I was living at the monastery, I practised every day. I stopped as soon as I got back to Britain. The two things were connected, deciding to stop and going home. I was angry with the monks; that was part of it. I was sick of the pretence that I'd managed to renounce the world. Wat Tham Nok was a bustling place, a worldly place, for all the incense and chanting and saffron robes. I think the last straw was the ceremony the abbot performed to bless a certain Mr Boonmee's fleet of taxis. Boonmee was a gangster, as far as I could see, an oleaginous man who owned a brothel and a service station and various other businesses in the nearby town. I remember the gifts piling up, the vapid grin on Boonmee's face as he accepted congratulations on his public act of piety.

After a while, the spotlights switch off, cutting out with a click and a soft buzzing exhalation, like a sigh. I'm left in darkness, breathing in, breathing out. Gradually I'm able to make out the horizon, the point where the purple-blue sky is cut off by the denser black of the hills.

I shut my eyes.

There was to be another action. That was what they told me, after my interrogation. A job we were to do for Khaled. They laid out the details. Whether it was come-down or disorientation or simple shock, I was able to listen and show no emotion at what was being proposed; my horror existed in a small, locked-away place, far from the surface. Everyone was very friendly to me. Sean and Leo in particular went out of their way to be nice. As proof of my recuperation, I was given an important task. I would meet the PFLP contact in London and pick up our next tranche of funding.

I drove there overnight with Sean, half listening to his stream of fractured amphetamine jokes. He dropped me in the West End as dawn broke, where I hung around for a couple of hours, waiting for things to open and wishing I didn't feel so sick. Then I went to meet the man we knew as Yusef. In a Lebanese café that smelt of rosewater and cigarettes we drank cups of bitter coffee and I watched him adjust his tie and run his fingers over the lapels of his fashionable suit, caressing himself, stealing glances at his reflection in the plate glass of the window. He handed me a package containing five thousand pounds. He didn't seem to notice how my hands were shaking, the dusting of spilled sugar on the table.

I wasn't sure before. It was only when I stepped out on to the pavement that I knew what I was going to do. My Michael Frame passport was in my pocket. I had a bag full of money. I hailed a cab and twenty minutes later was standing on Cheyne Walk, looking at the little village of houseboats moored in front of the elegant town-houses. Low tide had exposed an oily swathe of black Thames mud, a cluster of peeling hulls and a wooden gangway butting up against a flight of weed-slathered concrete steps. The *Roaring Girl*, the *Linnet*, the *Annicka*, the *Lisboa Princess*. Some were shabby, others spick and span. Here and there were jolly touches: stripy life-rings, rows of pot plants. One or two boats were flying the Union Jack. A Bohemian slovenliness hung over the place, a mannered slouch.

The *Martha* was an old tug with a freshly painted nameplate and a little porch built in front of the wheelhouse. I spotted a patched section on the side, which I supposed was the shell-hole. The deck was cluttered with folding chairs and a bicycle was chained to the gangplank rail. I walked up and knocked on the cabin door. There was no reply. I knocked harder.

Miles had obviously been asleep. In his ratty check dressing-gown and scuffed leather slippers, he looked very young, almost like a schoolboy. 'Chris, what are you doing here?'

'I need to talk.'

He frowned. 'You'd better come in.'

He made coffee in the galley and I sat on a stool, wondering how to start. Miles kept his place very tidy. There were no piles of books, no dirty laundry on the floor. Everything was perfectly presented, from the row of gleaming copper pans hanging over the cooker to the Super 8 camera standing decoratively on a tripod by the bed.

'I need to tell you something, but before I do, you have to understand that I don't want to know what you'll do with the information. I don't want to know anything, Miles, about what you do or who you are. Do you understand?'

'I think so.'

'After this, you won't see me again. That's part of the deal. I tell you and then I disappear.'

'All right. I'm listening.'

'I'm telling you because it's gone too far. I can't justify it, not what's being proposed. Not politically – not *morally*, whatever that means. I want you to know that I'm not here because I've stopped believing in the need for a revolutionary politics. I haven't. I'll always work towards the revolution. I just need to stop this happening.'

'I understand.'

And then I told him. The names of the members of our group. The addresses of our safe-houses. I gave him what details I had of the next action. I told him where to find our cache of arms. At first he looked confused. It took him a while to realize what I was talking about. When he did, he looked ashen. After a while he began to take notes on a legal pad. When I'd finished, he breathed deeply and shook his head.

'And Anna Addison? You haven't mentioned her.'

'She's not involved.'

He looked as if he were about to contradict me, then stopped himself. Lighting a cigarette, he flicked through his notes. 'Where will you go?' he asked.

'It doesn't matter.' It didn't. Not then. Not for a long time.

Outside, the traffic was beginning to build up along the Embankment as commuters made their way to work.

Thirty years later, running down East Street, we were making a spectacle of ourselves. Two middle-aged men, pink-faced and out of breath. I slowed down and Miles slumped gratefully against a wall. Passers-by turned round to watch him, this dandyish man sitting on the concrete. He looked as if he were about to pass out.

'Last chance, Chris,' he choked. 'If you walk away from me again, I'll make a phone call and the tabloids will be on your doorstep by the end of the day. How do you think it'll go for you with them on your back?'

I shrugged.

'I'll tell you how. The police will be forced to act. There'll be an investigation. And – this is what you need to know – if there's an investigation they'll find something against you. Do you understand, Chris? If they search they will find. And it'll be serious, we'll make sure of that. You're fifty years old. What age do you think you'll be when you get out of prison?'

All the years. All the years, because of conversations with Miles Bridgeman. It crossed my mind that I could kill him. I could take him into the park, wring his scrawny neck like a chicken's. And then what? Then I'd be running. Did I really have the energy to run?

'And if I co-operate, what happens to Miranda?'

He laughed, standing up and brushing the seat of his trousers. 'She'll probably get a book deal.'

I pictured Miranda getting over the shock and finding herself the centre of attention. Miranda doing the rounds of the talk-shows, lunching with journalists from women's magazines. Miranda blossoming, finding someone with better hair and teeth to sit beside her on the interviewer's sofa.

'You'll need a lawyer.'

'Oh, of course, a lawyer.'

He was irritated by my sarcasm. 'Let's get out of the street, shall we? We could at least try to talk like grown-ups.'

We went into the nearest place, a chain pub with blond-wood furniture and a loud juke-box. One window was boarded up, presumably a souvenir of the previous night's chucking-out time. Miles bought beers and I asked him what I hadn't wanted to ask all those years previously, on his houseboat.

'Who are you, Miles?'

He pursed his lips in annoyance. 'Oh, God, Chris, don't get metaphysical. I couldn't bear it.'

When he spoke again, his voice was weary. 'OK. You want my story? Once upon a time I wasn't so far away from you, politically. Not as serious, no, but I did want things to change. Unfortunately I didn't have a choice about how I acted. They had me. They had me from before I first met you.'

'What? Recruited over sherry in your tutor's study? "Young fellow, how would you like to serve your country?"'

'Christ, you probably think that's really how it happens. That's the funny thing about you, Chris. After all this – all this madness you've been through – you're still peculiarly naïve. Amazing, really. No, I got busted. It was in 1966. I knew a man who ran a gallery, a little place in St James's that sold *objets d'art*. Oriental stuff, mostly. Pictures and vases, chinoiserie. He offered me a job. I'd been at school with his brother.'

I snorted derisively.

'Well, it turned out the pots and rugs were just a front for other business. I needed money. I wanted to make films. Do you have any idea how much stock costs? Processing? And it was only hash. Nothing that was going to do anybody any harm.'

'And you got caught.'

'My employer liked to boast at parties. They arrested me at Dover, picking up twenty pounds of Nepalese black. We were shipping it inside brass ornaments. I was terrified. I thought I was going to get ten years. And then some chap in a rumpled suit and a Balliol tie turned up and told me that if I helped him I might be able to sort out my problems. Work off my debt.'

'So you became an informer.'

'That's more or less it. They were desperate for people who could fit in. Everyone could always tell a policeman. Hair, shoes – they stuck out a mile. The bastards kept on at me. They always had something else for me to do, someone else for me to get to know. At first it was drugs, but pretty soon it was political stuff. Who was at what meeting. Who knew who.'

'Did they put you in that cell with me?'

He nodded. 'God, that was an awful job. All day on that march I felt like shit. Because I was against the war, you see. I really was. But each time I tried to drop out they threatened me. And what I was giving them seemed so innocuous. For Christ's sake, it *was* innocuous. There were all those pseudo-Trotskys yabbering away, but most of them didn't have a clue. All that revolutionary fervour – it was a sort of wishful thinking. Oh, I don't deny there were things that needed doing – I mean, Britain was a joyless hole of a place before our generation got hold of it – but no one could see further than the end of their noses. We thought it was all about us. Even Vietnam was about us. And there we were, in the middle of the Cold War.'

'At least some of us tried to do something. At least we stood up to them.'

'Can't you even admit it now? Anything that destabilized the British state was to the advantage of the USSR.'

He drained the rest of his pint.

'And since then?' I asked. 'Did they let you off the hook?'

'Eventually. But, oddly enough, by that time it had turned into a career. There was something called the Information Research Department. A Foreign Office set-up. They gave me a job in a press agency. They used it to place things in the newspapers.'

'Disinformation.'

'Propaganda, certainly. Things that made the other side look bad.'

'So much for wanting the world to change.'

'Oh, and you made the right choices, did you? "Trying to do something". You were irrelevant, don't you get that? History doesn't care about what you did. Who's even heard of you? Ideology's dead now. Everyone pretty much agrees on how to run things. And you know what, Chris? I don't mind. Let's all get on with gardening and watching the soaps and having kids and going shopping. You've done it. You've been able to lead a dull life because there's no real conflict any more. In a couple of years it'll be a new millennium and, with luck, nothing will bloody happen anywhere, nothing at all. That's what a good society looks like, Chris. Not perfect. Not filled with radiant angelic figures loving each other. Just mildly bored people, getting by.'

'How the hell do you face yourself in the morning?'

'Don't patronize me. I don't see you've any call to occupy the moral high ground.'

'No, I mean it. What's it like, trying to live like you do?'

'It's very simple. It's what most people do. You don't need to agree with me. You don't need to approve of me. But it's not people like me who are the problem. All right, let's say I don't believe in anything. Well, one great advantage of that is not wanting to blow anyone up.'

We sat there in front of our empty glasses.

'So,' he said, 'now that we're actually talking, what about you? What happened to you after you walked off the boat that afternoon?'

What happened to me? I did what you did in those days. I got on a bus. I had a passport and five thousand pounds, a huge sum of money, enough to keep me alive for several years if I lived cheaply. As far as I was concerned, my life in Britain was over. I didn't have any clear intention; I just wanted to move, as quickly as possible.

So I got on a bus at Victoria station and headed for the Continent. It was the beginning of a period of drifting through Europe that ended about three months later, in a street in Istanbul. I remember that time as a flip-book of cheap hotel rooms, a two-guilder dormitory in Amsterdam, a flophouse in Naples where you could hear cockroaches scuttling about on the tiled floor after they turned out the lights. At first, out of habit, I gravitated towards places with a counter-culture. I sat around on my bedroll in main squares, listening to long-haired kids playing guitars and hustling one another for dope. I went to gigs and lost myself in the amplified darkness, the anonymous strobing of the lights.

I don't remember much about what I thought or how I felt. I was treading water, turning round and round, existing rather than living. I had the idea that I'd try to find somewhere very beautiful and very simple and settle there, far away from all kinds of violence and destruction. To say I was disillusioned with politics would be too simple. I still hated the system, hated the cops in their grey or green or blue or brown uniforms, pushing people around, moving them on from the Damrak or St Pauli or the Strøget. But I didn't trust myself any more. I was suspicious of my instincts, my capacity for violence.

Khaled had ordered us to kill someone. His name was Gertler, a Jewish businessman who owned a supermarket chain. Gertler's crime was Zionism. He donated large sums to right-wing political groups. The British government had given him a knighthood. Every morning he took his nine-year-old daughter to school, waiting on the pavement outside his house for the driver to bring his Bentley round from the mews where it was garaged. The plan was to ambush him and shoot him dead.

I was confused about many things, but I knew what I thought about that. Perhaps Khaled and Yusef were justified in fighting the enemies of their people. Perhaps, having no army, they had no alternative but horrific, spectacular violence. But I couldn't see how it was justified for me, who'd never even been to Palestine, to kill a man out of some abstract sense of revolutionary solidarity or third-world internationalism. No matter how crisply logical the theory, no matter how tightly one blocked one's ears to the historical hiss of Zyklon B, on a simple human level Khaled's plan still meant killing a man in front of his child and that had nothing to do with what I believed in. I wanted an end to poverty, to carpet-bombing, to the numbness and corruption of the death-driven society I'd been born into. Instead it seemed death had corrupted me too.

Sooner or later, in every city I visited, I'd see someone I thought I knew. I would hide or walk the other way, but before long I'd start turning the incident over in my mind and decide they must have recognized me. I'd feel as if I were being followed. Eventually I'd pick up my things and run to the railway station, in the grip of a sweating, heart-racing paranoia.

All that came to a head in Istanbul. The city was seething with bad vibes. There had recently been a military coup and soldiers were patrolling the streets, grim men in fatigues who checked papers and lounged around contemptuously at intersections, watched by the sullen populace. People were always tugging at my sleeve in the bazaars, trying to sell me drugs or steer me into their shops. I was spending most of my days looking for someone to give me a ride further east, knocking on doors at my hostel, hanging around outside a café called the Pudding Shop, which had a traveller's noticeboard and a crudely painted mandala on the wall. One afternoon I picked up an eight-week-old copy of *The Times*, which had somehow survived, preserved with various other archaeological relics of the foreign media, on a stall just off the Grand Bazaar.

TWO DEAD, OTHERS SOUGHT AFTER LONDON TERRORIST RAIDS

The shopkeeper watched me curiously as I tore off the plastic wrapping and read. The article was frustratingly terse. Following a tip-off, police had raided premises in north and east London, looking for weapons and explosives. They'd arrested three men and two women and retrieved a number of small arms. On the same afternoon, armed police had been involved in a gun battle on a residential street in Shepherd's Bush, after a vehicle had failed to stop when requested. The occupants of the vehicle opened fire on the police, killing one, a Sergeant Terence Denham, aged thirty-two. One of the terrorists was also killed. Another, who was seriously wounded, surrendered. The dead gunman was named as Sean Michael Ward, of West Kensington. Police were seeking a twenty-six-year-old woman, Anna Louise Addison, who had fled the scene, hijacking a car that was later found abandoned in Camden Town. A watch on coastal ports and airports had so far failed to produce any results. Members of the public were warned not to approach her as she was believed to be armed.

Sean was dead. At first I flatly refused to accept it. I spent the next few days scouring every bookstall and hotel lobby in the city for English-language papers and magazines. Though I was half mad with guilt, I didn't dare ask other travellers directly, fearful of drawing attention to myself. I clung to the irrational hope that the *Times* article was wrong or would turn out to be some kind of police ploy. Eventually I found an old American news weekly, which confirmed the worst. It had happened a few days after I'd left. Leo had been shot in the stomach. The police were holding Jay, Claire, Quinn and several others, at least two of whom I didn't know. Nowhere was my name mentioned. And Sean Ward was dead. They'd printed a picture of the street, cordoned off with tape. A BMW was slewed across the pavement, its windows shattered, its doors hanging open, visibly punctured by nine-millimetre rounds. Beside the car lay a form covered with a white sheet. Sean was dead because I'd betrayed him. I'd killed him as surely as if I'd pulled the trigger myself. My feeble attempt to keep Anna out of it now just seemed ridiculous. I ought to have found another way – written a letter to the papers, warned Gertler. Anything but tell Miles. My emotions led me in all sorts of directions. I considered going to Lebanon, giving myself up to the PFLP. I thought of going home and surrendering to the authorities. I assessed various methods of killing myself. My only comfort, if such a word is appropriate, was that Anna had escaped. For the policeman, who was apparently a member of the Special Patrol Group and trained to use firearms, I had no feelings. A pig, to me, was just a pig.

I was sitting in the Pudding Shop, trying to work up the courage to go back and throw myself off the roof of my hotel, when a Dutch couple offered me a lift in their bus. They were heading for Erzerum, then Tehran. As it turned out, Peter and Justine were junkies. They showed me a way to sidestep the horror, an instant method of coming to terms with my confusion and guilt. We trundled up the rutted road into the mountains and gradually I made myself a stranger to the world. The wheels turned round and I disappeared.

Somewhere in Iran, I left my Dutch friends, who wanted to push on to India. I arrived, perhaps in a taxi or riding on the back of someone's truck, in a village whose name I never knew. It was an ancient and apparently timeless place, on which the world could surely never intrude. The fields were tilled with wooden ploughs. Old men in woollen caps sat in the doorways of crumbling houses. I made my wishes known by signs, finding a room with a packed earth floor and a neighbour who brought me food and enough opium to prevent me giving a damn about who'd lived and who'd died because of me. I spent my days with Abbas and Hamid, the layabouts who fed the fire for the village *hammam*, watching them lower themselves into a pit of bitumen, coming out black from the waist down. Together we sat and smoked and watched the snow on the mountain. The air was clean and pure, the sky a dome of blue tile.

All I'd wanted was certainty, a solid place to stand, but the more I'd tried to produce it, the more ambiguity had grown up in my life, choking it like pond-weed. Gertler the capitalist had lived. Sean Ward the terrorist had died. Accumulation, dissipation. I still wanted to kill myself, but I lacked the will. My self-disgust was total. Sucking the acrid smoke into my lungs, I was Darius the King of Kings, an ant crawling on the cracked wall. The Shah, about whom I'd once had an opinion, presided over my purgatory, nailed above the wooden boards of the table in the form of a hand-tinted print. Everything was connected to everything else and none of it was very important. Nothing was true. Nothing was good.

One day men came from the city in a dusty car. I hid in a sheep-fold on the hill above the village. 'America,' Abbas said, stabbing a finger at me. They'd been looking for the American. I moved on.

Yellow earth, a concrete ribbon of road. Men squatted at the verge to urinate. The next dusty village and the next. At the cara-vanserai, I sat in a crowd of truck drivers and watched a movie. The girl danced in an overdriven screech of violins. People were shouting at the screen. The smoke tasted like death inside me. A man with a hare-lip tried to sell me a watch. I grew thinner and more ragged and my hair and beard became a single tangled knot. I met a black American wearing a ruffled shirt and carrying a matching set of alligator luggage. I met a German boy who seemed to own nothing but a blanket. Pashtun tribesmen fired AK-47s into the air. Flies crawled across lambs' hearts. The German boy couldn't remember his own name. Death lay in the leaves at the bottom of my teacup, in the thud of the butcher's cleaver.

I cultivated absence. I dared myself to doubt further. What did it mean if nothing was real? What did it mean if there was nothing between people except a brutal, cynical commerce? Money from the money-changer, the red-striped pole that marked the border. White people begged from me. Just for the hell of it, I begged from them. I learned to feed myself and buy drugs in at least four languages, forgetting each one as I passed the guards into the next pointlessly demarcated zone. Village women in sky blue *burqas*, some Swedish girl with hepatitis. Her friend was on a smuggling charge in Delhi. Could I help her out? I walked up a thousand steps to a shrine. I attended a dog-fight. Truck headlights jogged up and down in the dust. In Kabul someone stole most of my money as I lay unconscious on a pavement outside a mosque. I converted the rest into gemstones, which I sewed into the hem of my shirt. Someone stole the gemstones.

I had no further thought of sustaining myself. I was happy not to feel at home. It would be misleading to say those years were blank. Many things happened to me. I lived on beaches, in the ruins of an ancient city crawling with snakes and scorpions. Up in the hills, I shared a bungalow with a Frenchman who called himself Ram Das. We did nothing but inject. We rarely went outside. He kept telling me that we were in Paradise. I was ill, feverish on pallets and mattresses. I squatted in a shit-encrusted hole while a man killed chickens outside, his feet just visible, caked with blood and feathers. I passed out in the waiting room of a doctor's clinic; it was comforting to lay my head on the cool tiled floor. Once I was paid to fly something across a border. It was in the lining of a suitcase. I carried the suitcase. I stood at the Customs table. I gave it to the man by the baggage claim. The second time I just took the case and travelled on. I was rich again, for a time.

With a sort of impersonal curiosity I noticed the horror I inspired in people. Perhaps, I began to think, I wasn't inspiring their horror at all. Perhaps I *was* their horror. I forgot what had happened before. The world was an illusion. Death teemed in the cities and over the empty land. The more I struggled, the more death I produced. Suffering rippled out of me as I thrashed about in the water.

At last I got what I wanted. There is a period of two years, between 1974 and 1976, of which I remember nothing at all.

One day I returned to Bangkok. I knew I'd been there before because the route to the red-light district was familiar. I arrived on foot. I'd been with a woman up in the north, but she'd died or left me. There was a weeping abscess on my arm and I was missing a tooth. For two or three nights I slept on the street in Patpong, curled up in an alleyway behind a go-go bar. 'Kee nok', the touts hissed at me, aiming punches and kicks to keep me away from their customers. Birdshit *farang*. The war in Vietnam was over, but the city was still full of Americans, uniformed soldiers and sailors, ex-GIs who couldn't face going home. I told them hard-luck stories as they tumbled out of the bars with their girls. I'd make them laugh by imitating fractured Thai English. Pussy smoke cigarette, pussy open bottle. There was a dealer who sat on a chair outside one of the prostitutes' short-time hotels, an old man festooned with protective amulets. If you bought his gear he'd let you shoot it upstairs, in a low-lit room with a record-player. That room was my Shangri-La, my El Dorado. I offered to sell him my passport.

I didn't recognize the *farang* shaking my hand in front of Yom's noodle stall. He kept saying his name, but I couldn't understand him. 'You see show?' I asked, trying to flip into my comic Thai-tout routine. 'You want see love show?' He bought me food and watched me fix up in his hotel room. I think he must have paid for the heroin too. I nodded off for a while and woke up and looked at him looking tearfully back at me and it really was Saul Kleeman, prosperous and tanned, wearing a loud batik shirt, trying to talk to me about Anna.

'Chris,' he said, for the tenth or twentieth time.

'No, man,' I told him. 'All that's in the past.'

'Anna,' he said. 'Anna's dead.' He told me what had happened and let me sleep in his room and took me to the doctor and gave me fresh clothes and some time later, a day or two days, he took me downstairs and put me in a taxi. I stared blankly out of the window at paddy-fields, my forehead pressed against the glass.

I never knew exactly what Saul was doing in Bangkok, or how to get in touch with him afterwards. He saved my life, and I've always been grateful to him, even if I sometimes wish he'd minded his own business. He looked well, I remember. I'd like to think things went all right for him. I retained very little of what he told me about Anna. What I know now I've gleaned in fragments, over the years. Some of it I only found out from sifting through God's unsorted stock of books.

Anna successfully fled Britain, with help from the PFLP. She disappeared from view for a time, living in the Middle East or North Africa, possibly in Libya, and next surfaced in 1974 as part of a team of terrorists who hijacked an airliner *en route* from Frankfurt to Tel Aviv, in an attempt to force the West German authorities to free prisoners of the RAF and Rote Zelle. They were partially successful. The prisoners weren't released but they were allowed to land in Algiers and fly out again on another plane, with a substantial sum of money. *Gun Girl*, the trashy biography illustrated with her ex-husband's photos – the Chelsea fashion shots and a couple of salacious nudes – dates from this time, when she was an object of almost hysterical media interest in Britain.

Class warfare is life process, wrote Anna and her comrades, who came from Japan and Germany and the refugee camps of Lebanon. *For us, production and destruction are identical.* Three months after the Algiers hijack, eight of them entered the West German embassy in Copenhagen, an imposing neo-classical building on the waterfront. They killed a security guard and a junior diplomat and took twenty hostages in an upper room. Once the Danish police had surrounded the building, they issued a series of demands, including the release of prisoners in Israeli and West German jails and the provision of an aircraft to fly them to the destination of their choice. After the first twelve-hour deadline expired, they took the economic attaché on to the balcony and shot him in the head. It is possible that Anna herself was the executioner. There is a photograph said to be of her, taken earlier that day, leaning out of a second-floor window, raising a fist.

The siege lasted almost eighty hours. Bonn and Tel Aviv refused to negotiate. On the third night, Danish special forces moved in and retook the building. During the assault, all the terrorists, seven hostages and three soldiers were killed. Anna's body, or the body that was identified as hers, was found in the conference room, badly burned: a booby-trap rigged by the terrorists had been detonated during the assault. The oddest aspect of the siege was the terrorists' reported use of a technique that in earlier communiqués they termed the ARC effect. Surviving hostages testified that they'd been herded into the conference room, where projectors and audio equipment were set up. For more than twenty-four hours they were subjected to some kind of audiovisual display, incorporating taped speeches and images of American atrocities in Vietnam. The purpose, it seems, was experimental – to induce ARC, an acceleration of revolutionary consciousness, to alter their politics with *son et lumière*.

The Anna of the embassy siege is someone I never knew, who'd travelled to a psychological place I could never follow. My Anna was a woman who consciously suppressed her own desires in the name of a greater good. Always, in some part of myself, I'd refused to connect the two, so it felt like a revelation, a coup, when I realized in France that it was possible she hadn't been in Copenhagen after all. When we were lovers, I would always pester her about the future. I wanted to know what she imagined, what sort of society she hoped to create. I think, covertly, I wanted her to describe how things would be for us, for me and her. I never understood why she always rebuffed my questions, until the day she angrily insisted I stop asking them. 'Can't you see,' she told me, 'that the future's not for us?' I didn't follow. 'Look at how we live,' she said. 'We're damaged people. There would be no place for us in the world we're trying to build.'

When I arrived at Wat Tham Nok I was in a state of agitated withdrawal. For the last hour of the journey, I'd been hassling the driver to let me out, but he only waved a hand and tapped his fingers against his pursed lips, indicating that he spoke no English. When I saw the golden spire of the *stupa* I realized my destination was a temple but nothing prepared me for what was to come, the prison conditions of the addicts' compound, the formation exercises in front of a huge portrait of the king. The abbot of Wat Tham Nok had been curing alcoholics and drug addicts for years using his own patented herbal emetic, a vile potion containing more than a hundred ingredients. Saul had paid for me to take the cure, giving instructions that I couldn't be trusted to look after myself and should be restrained if I tried to leave. This was how I came to spend my first twenty-four hours at Wat Tham Nok chained to a pillar.

I was barely aware of where I was. I thought Saul was present in the room, and screamed at him that he was a bastard pig traitor. I thought he'd sold me into slavery. They'd dressed me in a set of faded pink-cotton pyjamas. A novice monk had been left to monitor my progress. He must have been about twelve years old. He sat in the corner of the hall, silently watching me, flanked by a pair of plastic buckets.

When I'd calmed down, I was told where I was and asked whether I'd like help easing the withdrawal pains. That help turned out not to be methadone, as I'd hoped, but the name of the Buddha, written on a small piece of paper, which I was told to memorize and swallow, like a coded message. Over my head, the abbot intoned a cheery blessing. 'Repeat the sacred name when you feel craving,' he told me, through an interpreter. For a week I was rousted up at dawn from my pallet in the addicts' barracks and taken through the ritual of purging, vomiting into a trough while monks chanted and clanged hand-cymbals. There were more than twenty of us, Thai and foreigners; we muttered and swore our way through the sleepless nights in a dozen languages.

Round and round. The days and nights, turning circles. The brown jets of vomit. Clear running water, splashed over my face. I lived off fruit and bowls of rice broth and after a week it grew easier, the spasms in my gut more manageable and the world somehow crisper and more stable around me. I did small tasks about the compound, sweeping and mopping, folding laundry into piles. I repeated the name of the Buddha, usually abusively. One of the monks gave lectures in English. I listened to him describe the Four Noble Truths, the eightfold path that leads to the cessation of suffering. *Forsake anger, give up pride. Sorrow cannot touch the man who is not in thrall to anything, who owns nothing.*

But how to do that? Without heroin there was nothing to distract me from my self-disgust. I spoke about it in veiled terms to Phra Anan and he told me to take refuge in the Buddha. Officially I was 'cured'; it was time for me to leave. The trouble was that I didn't have anywhere to go. I couldn't see any way forward and though I still wasn't sure if I deserved to live, let alone live free of sorrow, I knew I wanted nothing more to do with death, my own or anyone else's. I asked if I could stay. Phra Anan spoke to the abbot, who agreed, on condition I worked hard and adopted the same rules as the novice monks. I was given a little hut in the monastery grounds and for the next four years Wat Tham Nok became my home. I shaved my head and wore the robes of a novice. I ate my last meal at midday. During that time I didn't sing or dance, take intoxicants or have sex. I didn't wear a watch. I wrote letters to people seeking treatment for their addictions. I counselled the foreigners, always careful to ensure they only knew me as Monk Saul or Monk Andrew, names I alternated with each new intake. I followed the real monks on their morning alms round and sometimes I handled money, which they were forbidden to do. I'd often walk behind them, carrying donations, the overflow from the metal bowls that the townspeople filled with rice and curry, with other monkish necessities, soap and candles, toothpaste, socks.

Wat Tham Nok and the little nearby town became the limits of my world, a body whose third eye was the fissure in the rock on the hillside where thousands of swallows nested, the 'bird cave' that gave the monastery its name. It was pleasant to sit in the assembly hall, with its giant reclining Buddha, too vast to contemplate at once, and attempt mindfulness in front of a segmented hand or toe or single passive eye, which seemed to look out on the world with infinite resignation. When my thoughts wandered, the statue's great eyes sometimes looked as dull as those of an opium-smoker. I'd try to observe my thought, see that it was fleeting, and relinquish it. I tried, in all things, to relinquish control. Then I tried to stop trying. *The greatest transcendence is not the greatest transcendence. Therefore it is called the greatest transcendence.*

Though I was lonely I found my work comforting, and as I followed the simple, menial routine through months and years, I gradually began to feel less connected to what I'd thought and done before. The monks taught that to escape suffering one must reject the impulse to act on the world. The desire for change, they insisted, is just another form of craving. I felt I'd no right to act at all, so it seemed all the easier to turn inward and imagine that in renouncing my politics I'd given up nothing important, just a source

270

of pain. As the world of the armed struggle faded, it came to seem like a dream. The liberation I'd fought for was surely impossible, illusory. *For now*, whispered Chris Carver. *For ever*, murmured the voice I heard in the tiny sounds of Wat Tham Nok, the beating of swallows' wings, the flick-flick of a monk's plastic sandals on a path. The *Dhammapada* begins, *Mind is the forerunner of all processes: it is chief and they are mind-made. If one talks or acts with an impure mind then suffering follows as the wheel follows the ox's tread*. So I tried to purify my mind, to accept that the only possible sphere of liberation was the self. I thought I had a chance to achieve peace. I might as well have been doing press-ups.

Two things happened. There was the blessing for Mr Boonmee's taxis, the last in a long line of last straws, and there was the postcard an ex-addict sent to the monastery office. She was a Canadian who'd found herself on holiday in southern England and decided to send us greetings from the cathedral town of Chichester. I picked it up out of the wire tray on my desk and in the face of its acid blues and greens, its little curlicued banners titling a selection of bland views, the room I sat in, with its stone floor and piles of dusty papers, seemed forlorn and somehow ridiculous, part of a childish game I was playing with myself. I was sick of the birds rustling in the trees, sick of the very air, which lately had been heavy with threats and corruption. It was one thing to renounce the world and contemplate the liberation of the self. It was another to sustain this while watching the monks greet military officers and local politicians arriving for the ceremonials on the king's birthday.

It took me a long time to put a name to my disillusionment. I wanted to go home. After so long living in an institution, the prospect of formlessness was frightening, but Wat Tham Nok had come to seem as oppressive to me as any Jesuit seminary, the monks no different from the guardians of established religion anywhere else in the world. When I went to the abbot to tell him I intended to leave, he made me a present of a protective charm and expressed the wish that I would soon find a wife and start a family. Then he returned to his papers, exuding an air of benevolent, unshakeable unconcern. Phra Anan was the same. I left Wat Tham Nok feeling I'd made no more impression on the place than a pebble thrown into a pool of water.

I landed at Heathrow airport in the summer of 1981, armed with the Canadian addict's postcard, a new passport, which had been issued without fuss by the British embassy in Bangkok, a tent and enough sterling to buy me a train ticket to the south coast. I expected to be arrested and I think, had it happened, I'd have accepted it with equanimity. But the immigration official barely glanced in my direction as he waved me through.

In Chichester I sat under the Market Cross and watched middle England go about its business, supremely oblivious to the wider world. It was the place depicted on the postcard, no more and no less. It gave me pleasure and a kind of relief. For the first couple of months I lived on a campsite, picking and boxing fruit to accumulate the deposit to rent a flat. By the following year I was living in a bedsit near the railway station, working for crazy Olla, trying to keep my head down and tread lightly, to live a humble life. I accepted the faintly ridiculous role in which I found myself, the inoffensive little guy in the woollen waistcoat, the ex-hippie selling scented candles and doing his best to hide from the sharp-suited eighties.

Then one day Miranda stopped browsing the rack of greetings cards and asked whether I'd like to take her for a drink.

Olla's shop was an odd vantage-point from which to watch the new decade assemble itself. After my long absence the difference in mood was stark. If I watched the news or read a paper, both of which I tried to avoid, I found myself dragged back into questions I thought I'd buried. Miranda used to berate me for my lack of politics. She was always getting involved in causes: Amnesty, Free Tibet. She bought mugs and sweatshirts. Her concerns had the character of enthusiasms, fleeting, scattergun. Once in a while she'd wonder aloud about going on a march. As her cosmetics business grew, she benefited from all the things she vaguely disapproved of, deregulation and low taxation and the other strategies of the disciplinarian economics that had bafflingly become known as the 'free' market, and because she'd never really understood the reasons for her disapproval, she gradually stopped vocalizing it and then, eventually, it was as if she'd never held such views at all and was free to compete, to run and jump and jostle with all the rest. And meanwhile, in secret, it gradually came to seem important to me to make something unified from the broken threads of my life, not to lose touch altogether with Chris Carver and his dreams of revolution. Did anything connect me with who I'd once been? And if not, what had I lost, owning only half of a life?

'When did you find me?' I asked Miles, as we sat in the pub, whose mid-afternoon pall was only accentuated by the piped music, a speeded-up woman singing about getting higher to the accompaniment of some kind of synthetic drumbeat.

'Her Majesty's government would love to say you were never lost, but you were. I heard they picked up Michael Frame a couple of years ago. A passport check, most probably.'

'Why didn't they arrest me right away?'

'Oh, they were probably saving you for a rainy day.'

'And here you are.'

'Here I am. Pitter-patter.'

He walked me back to the house and told me to make my arrangements because someone would be picking me up in the morning to take me to London. After he left, I sat in the study, watching the workmen larking about on the lawn and thinking how thin life was, how easily the whole charade of Mike Frame and Miranda Martin could be torn down, like an old net curtain.

Here, under the tower, I'm frozen to the bone, but the line of hilltops is clear along the horizon, the sky's blacks opening up into purples and inky blues, bruise colours. The smashed-up sky persuades me to get up and walk around, forcing blood into my legs, into my feet, which feel like two clubs inside my beaten-up tennis shoes. Likewise blood filters slowly into the sky, until finally the sun spills over the ridge like metal over the lip of a crucible and a faint heat starts to warm my face.

I make my way down the hill to the Bar des Sports and when it opens, I buy a cup of coffee and an apple brandy, which I sip, eyed suspiciously by the woman behind the zinc, who thinks, rightly I suppose, that I am up to no good and should be kept under observation. When the alcohol has risen through my body and broken my solid chill into constituent bergs and floes, I pay my bill and walk back up the sloping street to Anna's house. The line of doors winds upwards, some shabby, others neat and bright, and there are early signs of life, open shutters, a man on a Mobylette, its engine rising in pitch as it labours over the cobbles.

It occurs to me that maybe she will kill me.

Here is the door. It's painted a dull ochre yellow. I recognize the house beside it, with its row of geraniums in terracotta pots, the one belonging to the old women who told me Anna was Swedish.

I knock.

I hear her come to answer it. The door opens. She is wearing a cotton kimono, printed with a design of woodblock bamboo. Her hair has fallen over her face; as she looks up at me, she sweeps it back with one hand and stares, fixing me with clear grey-blue eyes, which, like her mouth, are nested in a tracery of delicate lines.

'Anna.'

'*Excusez-moi*?'

'Anna, it's me. Chris.'

'Who?'

'Chris Carver. I'm alone. No one followed me here, Anna.'

She looks blank. 'I don't think I know you.'

In both French and English, she speaks with an accent. Scandinavian, it sounds like. I look at her and say my name again. And a third time.

'Chris Carver. You remember me, Anna Addison. I know you remember me.'

'I'm not Anna. I never heard of any Anna. Do you know what time it is? It's very early in the morning.'

I look at her face and suddenly I'm not sure. It seems softer, ill-defined, not much like Anna's tribal mask. But it's been such a long time. Anything could have happened. She could have had plastic surgery.

'Anna Addison,' I say, with more insistence. 'Don't pretend.'

'I don't know this person.'

'Please, don't pretend.'

'I tell you I don't know her.'

I realize I'm scaring her. I hear myself raising my voice and her telling me she'll call the police and all the time I look at her, staring hard into her eyes as if daring her to blink, and finally I'm forced to admit that I'm completely adrift, without reference or marker.

'I'm sorry to have bothered you,' I say.

She slams the door in my face and I realize Anna is dead. She has been dead all along, a charred corpse in a Copenhagen conference room, mute and fanatical, fixed in the past like amber.

I walk slowly down the hill and phone Miles from the Bar des Sports.

'Where are you?'

'I'm in France.'

'What are you doing there?'

'I just saw Anna Addison. How about that?'

'Don't be stupid. Anna's dead.'

'Is she? Yes, I suppose she is.'

'Chris, where are you? I'm worried about you.'

'Is Anna dead, Miles?'

'Of course she's dead. She's been dead for ever. Are you all right?'

'I thought I saw her.'

'Chris.'

'What do I tell Miranda? I want her kept out of it.'

'Chris, you should come home.'

'Talk to me about Miranda.'

'You don't have to tell her anything, not if you don't want to. We can come and get you. Stash you away somewhere. How about it? A nice country hotel.'

'Run away. Fuck off and hide. Good plan.'

'Look, how about this? Twenty grand and a head start. More cash than that, if I can swing it. Forget what I said about a trial. I was angry. You come back, you do the interview, you hang around long enough to give the press a taste – until the job's done, absolute minimum, no more. We'll help you. Give you somewhere to hide out. Someone to handle your calls. Then it's over and you disappear. By the time the police, or whoever else you're afraid of, arrive, you can be long gone. I'll help you, Chris. Come in and I'll help you.'

'Don't lie, Miles. I'm too old to start again.'

'No, you're not. Like I said, more if I can swing it. Probably more like thirty grand.'

'And you could get me a passport?'

'Yes. That too. A clean slate, if that's what you want. All your sins forgiven.'

'Have you got kids, Miles?'

'Yes, a son and a daughter. Twelve and fourteen.'

'You still with the mother?'

'No.'

'Why not?'

'You know how it is.'

'No I don't. That's the funny thing. I don't know how it is. Never have.'

Miles gives me a number and an address in London. He wants me to ditch the car and fly. If I tell him exactly where I am, he'll sort it out. Just go to Toulouse. Dump the car. There will be a ticket waiting for me at the BA desk. He'll meet the flight. He can't help enough. His voice is soothing and richly compassionate.

I get into the car and head towards the *autoroute*. Behind me, the tower rises up like an amputated limb.

Because legality is just the name for everything that's not

dangerous for the ruling order, because the poor starve while the rich play, because the flickering system of signs is enticing us to give up our precious interiority and join the dance and because just round the corner an insect world is waiting, so saying we must love one another or die isn't enough, not by a long way, because there'll come a time when any amount of love will be too late. But it's something, love, not nothing, and that's why I pull over and find a callbox in a lay-by and punch a number into the phone. Miranda picks up on the third ring.

'It's me.'

'Oh, God. Mike? Where are you?'

'Chris,' I tell her. 'My name's Chris.'

Acknowledgements

Certain things are always erased or distorted in a novel and this is no exception. It seems worth saying that it is not a representation of the politics or personalities of the Angry Brigade, which carried out a series of bomb attacks on targets including the Police National Computer and the Employment Secretary's house in the early seventies. Readers who want information about the Angry Brigade are directed to the papers of the Stoke Newington Eight Defence Group, and writing by Gordon Carr, Jean Weir, John Barker and Stuart Christie. I am grateful to the librarians at the London School of Economics for use of their archive. Thanks to Andy Davies for information about police procedure. Quotations from the *Dhammapadda* are adapted from translations by Joan Mascaró and Ninian Smart. Mistakes in the translation or interpretation of the Pali Canon are my own. I have drawn on Ron Bailey's account of actions by London Squatters, and Chris Faiers's of the occupation of 144 Piccadilly by the London Street Commune, among many other sources. Contemporary respect is due to Dr J.J. King and all former denizens of the Mitre and the Bart Wells.

The Post Office Tower was bombed on 31 October 1971. No claim of responsibility was made.

He just wanted a decent book to read ...

Not too much to ask, is it? It was in 1935 when Allen Lane, Managing
Director of Bodley Head Publishers, stood on a platform at Exeter railway
station looking for something good to read on his journey back to London.
His choice was limited to popular magazines and poor-quality paperbacks –
the same choice faced every day by the vast majority of readers, few of
whom could afford hardbacks. Lane's disappointment and subsequent anger
at the range of books generally available led him to found a company – and
change the world.

*'We believed in the existence in this country of a vast reading public for intelligent
books at a low price, and staked everything on it'*
Sir Allen Lane, 1902–1970, founder of Penguin Books

The quality paperback had arrived – and not just in bookshops. Lane was
adamant that his Penguins should appear in chain stores and tobacconists,
and should cost no more than a packet of cigarettes.

Reading habits (and cigarette prices) have changed since 1935, but
Penguin still believes in publishing the best books for everybody to
enjoy. We still believe that good design costs no more than bad design,
and we still believe that quality books published passionately and responsibly
make the world a better place.

So wherever you see the little bird – whether it's on a piece of
prize-winning literary fiction or a celebrity autobiography, political tour
de force or historical masterpiece, a serial-killer thriller, reference book,
world classic or a piece of pure escapism – you can bet that it represents
the very best that the genre has to offer.

Whatever you like to read – trust Penguin.